Two powerful hands with claws seized Clint . . .

Hurled into the next room, the Gunsmith crashed into the kitchen table and tumbled to the floor.

Clint had lost the grip on the Springfield. He rose up behind the table and reached for the Colt on his hip. His fingers clutched air . . . the revolver had fallen out of its holster.

He heard the terrible half-wolf, half-human cry of the *chindi* as the outline of a nightmare figure appeared at the doorway.

The Gunsmith saw the shaggy, fur-covered shape with the snarling wolf snout and pointed ears approach him.

The *chindi* had come back for the kill. . . .

**Don't miss any of the lusty, hard-riding action in the
Charter Western series, THE GUNSMITH**

And coming next month:
THE GUNSMITH #46: WILD BILL'S GHOST

THE GUNSMITH

45

NAVAHO DEVIL

J. R. ROBERTS

CHARTER BOOKS, NEW YORK

THE GUNSMITH #45: NAVAHO DEVIL

A Charter Book/published by arrangement with
the author

PRINTING HISTORY
Charter edition/October 1985

ISBN: 0-441-30949-6

Charter Books are published by The Berkley Publishing Group,
200 Madison Avenue, New York, New York 10016.
PRINTED IN THE UNITED STATES OF AMERICA

**To Jim Leeper,
"Let go and let 'em suffer."**

ONE

A small green lizard clung to the ceiling above the Gunsmith's bed. He gazed up at the little reptile as he lay on his back, stark naked. He hoped Wendy Simmons would not notice the lizard, or, if she did, she wouldn't let the tiny critter upset her. Right now, Wendy wasn't looking up at the ceiling. Her eyes were closed as her head moved up and down, her soft full lips caressing the length of his erect penis. His cares slipped away and he drifted into thought.

The Gunsmith had been born Clint Adams. He still preferred to be called by his real name, but the title had been given to Clint many years ago when he was still a young deputy sheriff. A newspaperman decided to write a feature about Deputy Adams. Clint had already acquired an unwanted reputation as a lightning-fast gunman, but the newspaper fellow needed something unique to make his story more colorful.

Then he discovered that Deputy Adams was an amateur gunsmith who repaired and modified firearms as a hobby. So the newsman labeled Clint Adams "the Gunsmith." The nickname and the newspaper story got a lot of attention and attracted gunhawks like flies to a dung heap.

Trigger-happy kids, each eager to be known as "the man who killed the Gunsmith," came gunning for Clint Adams. Most of them ended their quest at Boot Hill. The Gunsmith's legend as the fastest gun continued to grow and there was nothing Clint Adams could do to stop it.

Clint decided he could not maintain law and order with a reputation that attracted gunslingers and troublemakers into the county. After eighteen years as a lawman, the Gunsmith turned in his badge and began to drift across the West. Fate played an ironic practical joke because Clint was only qualified for one trade other than lawman. He became a real gunsmith, traveling from state to state and town to town, fixing and modifying guns for a living.

One might think this would be a nice, quiet profession, but Clint's reputation as the Gunsmith preceded him everywhere he went. Young gunhawks still wanted to challenge the Gunsmith. Folks who needed somebody good with a gun tried to hire Clint. Occasionally, he accepted a job if he needed extra cash or the task appealed to his sense of adventure. Although Clint may have been reluctant to admit it, his natural curiosity and thirst for action got him as much trouble as his reputation.

There were benefits to his chosen lifestyle. Clint saw a lot of the country and he could generally do pretty much as he pleased, traveling wherever he wanted and staying or leaving whenever it suited him. Clint also encountered many lovely ladies. The more he moved about, the more women he met.

The Gunsmith had driven his wagon into Largo Gap, an obscure little town in the Arizona Territory. Largo Gap didn't have a very large population and Clint couldn't make much of a profit in such a small community. A couple of fellows wanted modifications on their pistols and a farmer, who lived in the county, needed an old shotgun repaired. Not much reason for Clint to stay in Largo Gap—except there was Wendy Simmons.

Wendy worked as the desk clerk at the local hotel. She was about twenty-three years old with shoulder-length blond hair, the color of goldenrod in the morning sun. She had the strong, firm body of a young woman, an hourglass figure, and large round breasts. A petite nose and her large expressive blue eyes were very beautiful, and her mouth was wide and inviting. Clint sensed the young lady was interested in him. That was enough reason to remain in Largo Gap one more day.

He invited Wendy to have dinner with him and she accepted. One thing led to another and the couple wound up in Clint's room that night. He took her in his arms and kissed her mouth. Wendy responded with wonderful passion. Their lips pressed together as their tongues probed each other's mouths. Hands gradually explored from shoulder to torso. Soon they began to unfasten buttons and to touch bare flesh beneath clothing.

The couple stripped off their garments. Clint was not disappointed by the woman's nakedness. Her skin was as smooth and white as polished ivory. The pink nipples that capped her breasts were already rigid with desire, and moisture like morning dew glittered on the golden triangle of her womanhood.

Wendy was also pleased with Clint's body. The Gunsmith was tall and slender with lean muscles and a firm torso. Numerous scars marred his body, tattoos of a hundred violent encounters. Many a bullet, knife, and club had bitten his flesh, yet none had maimed a limb. However, the Gunsmith had long ago realized that violent death was natural for a man with a reputation like his.

The most obvious reminder of violence was the jagged scar on Clint's left cheek. This had been caused by a flying chip of stone chiseled loose by a bullet. It could just as easily have taken out an eye. Had his opponent been a better marksman, the bullet might have gouged into Clint's face. The scar stared back at him in the mirror whenever the Gunsmith shaved. It told him that he was human and bled like other men. The legend of the Gunsmith might claim he was indestructable, but Clint Adams knew better.

The couple tumbled into Clint's bed and stroked each other with tender desire as the twin fires of their passion burned hotter and hotter. Clint fondled her breasts, teasing the nipples with his lips and teeth before drawing deeply on her breasts. Wendy proved even bolder as she ran her tongue down his belly. The woman opened her delightful mouth and began to treat Clint to paradise.

Then the Gunsmith noticed that damn lizard on the ceiling.

Wendy continued to service him, making love to his manhood. Just as Clint began to approach the limit, Wendy climbed on top of him. She straddled the Gunsmith's loins, raking her fingernails across the hair on Clint's chest. He reached up and played with her breasts. Leaning forward, the Gunsmith again placed his lips on her nipples. He braced himself on one arm as his other hand slid along the length of her torso to the hip and traveled on to her thigh. His touch moved slowly toward her center of love, but Wendy didn't need any further encouragement.

She raised herself up on her knees and found Clint's swollen member. Wendy held his malehood in place as she slowly lowered herself into position. He sighed as he slipped into the warm fleshy sheath. Wendy moaned with pleasure and slowly began to rock to and fro, working him deeper inside her womb.

The Gunsmith was an experienced lover and a considerate one. He always did his best to realize his partner's satisfaction as well as his own. Wendy was making this task easier because she had chosen the dominant role. Some men might object to this, feeling this aggressive sexual behavior was improper for a lady. Clint regarded this attitude to be pure bullshit.

He liked women to be aggressive in bed. He enjoyed the sensual attention and wild pleasure he received from such a fiery female. Making love was an occasion to cast off restrictions of "proper" conduct. The Gunsmith wanted his lover to feel she could do whatever she wished to find sexual satisfaction with him. If Wendy wanted to assume the more aggressive role tonight, Clint was happy to oblige her.

The lovely blonde seemed delighted with her opportunity

to set the pace of their lovemaking. She slowly moved up and down, gradually pumping her body faster. Eventually, she moved harder and harder. Wendy cried out as she reached her first orgasm. She was pleased and a bit surprised to find Clint was still firm inside her.

"You're some kind of man, Clint Adams," Wendy cooed happily, running her hands over his chest and neck.

"A woman like you brings out the best in me," the Gunsmith replied, his fingers stroking her velvet skin.

"I'd sure like it if you could stay in Largo Gap a few more days," she sighed.

"I gotta make a living," Clint told her. "That means I have to have customers. There just isn't anybody left in Largo Gap who needs a gunsmith."

"I could sure make use of the Gunsmith if he stayed in town," Wendy assured him.

"Just call me Clint," he urged. "And let's make the most of what time we have together."

Wendy once again began rocking against the Gunsmith's crotch. He pumped his loins with her motion, pacing himself according to her tempo. Clint thrust again and again. Wendy cried out in erotic pleasure as she moved faster and faster, matching his energetic thrusts. Suddenly, she gasped as another orgasm rode through her like a wave. The Gunsmith moaned with satisfaction as he finally dissolved into liquid warmth within the woman.

"Oh, God," she whispered. "That was wonderful, Clint."

"Yeah," he replied softly. "For me too. Let's . . ."

At a slight sound, Clint suddenly turned his head toward the door. His keen senses, honed by years of surviving countless lethal encounters, had detected a possible threat. Someone was positioned in the hallway right outside his door. Clint instinctively reached for the wooden grips of his modified Colt revolver in the gunbelt he had placed at the headboard before climbing into bed with Wendy.

"Clint . . ." she began, trembling slightly.

"Just relax," he told her, drawing his pistol. "I'm gonna check the door. You just stay here on the bed and keep talking. Not too loud. Just talk at a loud whisper like you're still having a conversation with me, all right?"

"I'll try," she nodded.

"Good," Clint said, kissing her on the forehead. "If there's any shooting, you just roll off the bed and get down on the floor. Stay there and you'll be all right."

The Gunsmith climbed from the bed and padded barefoot to the door. Wendy followed instructions and continued to talk softly, saying gibberish about the weather and how she got her job as desk clerk in the hotel. She was doing fine, Clint realized. Her voice remained steady and she didn't sound scared. Good. The lady was holding up under the stress, and her voice inflection would not warn the person outside the door.

Clint heard the door creak. He stood clear of it in case whoever was on the opposite side decided to open fire. However, a folded piece of paper was all the mystery caller delivered. It slid through the crack in the door and drifted to the floor. The Gunsmith heard a man chuckle softly with amusement, then footfalls as the man headed down the hall away from Clint's room.

The Gunsmith gathered up the note and unfolded it. He moved to the lamp in order to read the hastily scrawled message written in pencil. Clint's eyes widened with surprise as he read:

When you ain't too busy, let's talk over a drink. Meet you in the saloon later.

The note was signed, Tom Shatner. "Well, I'll be damned," Clint said with a grin.

"What is it?" Wendy asked, relieved that the incident hadn't turned into a deadly encounter.

"An old friend of mine is in town," the Gunsmith

answered. "Tom Shatner. Haven't seen Tom since Santa Fe about . . . oh, eight years ago, I reckon."

"Oh," the woman sighed, "but there's nobody named Shatner staying at the hotel."

"He's gonna wait for me in the saloon," Clint stated as he headed back to the bed. "And if I know Tom, he won't mind waiting there for an hour or so."

"I'm so glad," Wendy said with a smile.

TWO

Tom Shatner was seated at a table in the saloon. A pitcher of beer, accompanied by two glass mugs, sat in the center of the table. Shatner was sipping brew from one of the mugs. Clint was surprised to see the pitcher was still more than half full. The Tom Shatner he remembered would be ready for a second pitcher after waiting almost an hour in a saloon. Maybe it *was* his second pitcher.

No, Clint decided. The Tom Shatner he remembered wasn't sitting at that table. Eight years ago, Tom had been a tough-as-nails deputy marshal in Santa Fe. Deputy Shatner was a hairy hulk with fists of stone and nerves of steel. Yet Tom had been a good-natured man, well-liked by the honest citizens of Santa Fe. Clint had liked Deputy Shatner, too, although he'd seen the mean lawman bust heads in a barroom brawl. Nobody in his right mind would want to mess with big Tom.

But the man seated at the table was eight years older, his grizzled beard streaked with gray. Tom's muscles were coated with a layer of fat and he no longer consumed beer as if the stuff were going to be illegal by midnight. However, Tom Shatner's good-natured grin remained the same, and he still had a twinkle in his eye when Clint Adams approached the table.

"Glad you found time to see me," Shatner remarked as he took Clint's hand and shook it hard. "Sounded like I interrupted you back in the hotel. Almost knocked, but I heard a gal moanin' away.''

"Yeah," Clint said flexing his fingers to make certain they'd all still work after shaking hands with Tom Shatner. "I noticed that, too. Good to see you, Tom."

"Been a long time since Santa Fe," Shatner mused, pouring beer into the second mug. "Remember Marshal Killian? He up and died two years ago. We're gettin' to be a dyin' species, Clint."

"I know," the Gunsmith replied with a nod.

"Yeah," Tom looked down at the table. "Heard 'bout what happened to Hickok. Sorry, Clint. I know you and Wild Bill was mighty close*."

"Don't have too many friends left," the Gunsmith said. "All the more reason I'm glad to see you again, Tom."

"Feelin' is purely mutual," Shatner said. "Except I can't figure out how come you and me is about the same age, but you look so much younger."

"Clean living, I reckon," the Gunsmith said with a grin. "What brings you to a fly speck of a town like Largo Gap?"

"Heard you was here," Shatner answered. "I'm livin' in Fox County myself. Got a little town there with a bunch of Navaho Indians. Town is called Waco. Reckon they named it after a place in Texas so maybe it'd get big."

"Is the idea working so far?" Clint asked, sipping his beer.

"Hell," Tom said, "bigger ain't always better. Look, Clint, I ain't gonna beat around the bush. Got a favor to ask."

"Have to hear what it is before I say yes or no to it," the Gunsmith replied.

"Fair enough," Shatner stated. "I'm gettin' married tomorrow morning."

"What?" Clint stared at him in astonishment. "Holy shit, I figured when I saw you that your wild self had mellowed out a bit, but I sure didn't expect you'd changed *that* much."

"Well, I need a best man," Shatner said sheepishly.

---

*GUNSMITH #14: DEAD MAN'S HAND

"I won't let the bride know I'm a better man than you," the Gunsmith chuckled.

"What you mean by that?" Shatner glared at him, some of the old wild Tom still lurking somewhere behind his eyes.

"Just a joke, Tom," Clint assured him. "Honest, just a joke."

"Ain't funny, Clint." Shatner pouted. "I'm right lucky to get a gal like Ellie. Hell, I ain't no youngster and I ain't exactly rich neither."

"Tom," Clint sighed. "I'm sorry. I didn't mean to offend you. I'd be happy to be best man at your wedding."

"Well," Shatner began, "you're the only real friend I got around these parts, so I'd appreciate it if you'd be there."

"Be an honor, Tom," the Gunsmith told him.

"Ain't never been married 'fore," Shatner remarked. "Kind of scares me, you know. You never been married either, have you?"

"No," Clint smiled. "I like women too much to ever pull a dirty trick like that on a lady."

"What do you mean by that?" Shatner frowned.

"I mean I'd be a pretty lousy candidate for marriage," Clint replied. "I've got a reputation as a gunfighter hanging over my head. It'll be there until the day I die. No getting rid of it. Well, I can live with that, but I couldn't expect a wife to do likewise. Besides, I like to move around too much to settle down."

"You ain't too old to change your ways, Clint," Shatner told him. "I plan to settle down. Got myself a farmhouse outside of Waco. Gonna raise sheep and goats and maybe chickens. Already planted some potatoes and turnips. Indians didn't like me moving in there, but it ain't their land. Plan to have myself a good life with a good woman, by God."

"I'm sure things will work out for you, Tom," Clint assured him. "And I'll be right proud to be your best man."

"Thanks, Clint," Shatner told him.

"Quit drinking beer, Tom," the Gunsmith told him. "I'm gonna see if they have anything in this saloon that's fit for a toast to a future husband."

The Gunsmith suddenly stood up and shouted at the other customers in the saloon. "Listen up, everybody," he declared. "My friend here is getting married tomorrow. Let's all have a drink to toast his happiness. I'm buying the first round!"

A great cheer filled the saloon.

THREE

"Christ, Clint," Tom Shatner complained as he rode a piebald gelding alongside the Gunsmith. "My head's killing me. We shouldn't have drunk so much last night."

"Just a little hangover," Clint Adams told him, patting the long, strong neck of Duke, his magnificent big black gelding. "Never bothered you much before."

"Damn it," Shatner complained, squinting as the sun bombarded his eyes. "I'm out of practice. I've been tryin' to keep away from the bottle. Figure it ain't right for a married man to carry on like I used to."

"Better keep away from the whorehouses too," Clint grinned. "Wouldn't want to make your new bride ill."

"You oughta tell jokes to Apaches," Shatner complained. "They think it's funny when they tie a feller to a wooden frame and set a fire in his crotch."

"Speaking of Apaches," Clint interrupted. "This is Chiricahua country, isn't it?"

"They've been pretty quiet lately," Shatner said with a shrug. "Closest Chiricahua tribe is a good sixty or seventy miles away. Don't worry about 'em."

"Apaches are basically nomadic," Clint remarked as he scanned the dry flat ground interrupted only by sparse clusters of sagebrush and occasional rock formations. "They might wander in any direction and cover a hundred miles in less than a week."

"You ever come up against Apaches, Clint?" Shatner asked.

"A couple times," the Gunsmith replied. "I was once on a train traveling through Texas when a band of Mescalaro attacked it. Some of them were on foot and most of them didn't even have guns, but damned if they didn't attack the train.

"You'll probably find some pretty hostile Apaches in other parts of the Arizona Territory, but around here most of the Indians are Navaho, and pretty much civilized Navaho at that."

"Civilized," Clint snorted. "You mean they live like white men figure they ought to."

"Well," Shatner began. "The Navaho haven't done so bad since they took up white customs and all. Used to be a warrior race, you know. Had a reputation at one time for being as fierce as Apaches, and Navaho still regard Apaches with contempt. We whites are lucky different tribes don't get along. Navaho and Comanches hate the Apache, the Sioux and the Cheyenne hate the Shoshone, and everybody hates the Paiutes. We'd have a hell of a problem if they all decided to forget about old grudges and just concentrate on fighting the white-eyes."

"Yeah," Clint muttered. "They might do something uncivilized like try to take their land back.

"Don't tell me you figure we should give the country back to the Indians," Shatner snorted. "Hell, Clint, don't you know why the tribes don't get along? It's because they used to war with each other. Why did they have the wars? To take each other's territory, that's why."

"So you reckon it's our turn now?" Clint said dryly. "Well, I guess none of us deserves a halo, but I sure wish we could have all learned to live with each other without so much killing all the time."

"Shit," Shatner remarked, "folks had wars before this country got settled. Accordin' to the Good Book, when there were only four people in the world one of 'em murdered his brother. I reckon folks will keep killing each other for some reason or other as long as there are still people around.''

"Funny how some traditions seem to last forever,'' the Gunsmith commented, still watching the rocks. "How much farther to Waco?''

"About seven more miles, I reckon,'' Shatner answered. "Sure hope my head feels better before I see Ellie. I feel like hammered metal.''

"Yeah,'' Clint grinned. "But you seemed to be enjoying yourself last night.''

"Sometimes I figure you're an evil influence, Clint,'' Tom growled sourly.

"Sometimes I am,'' the Gunsmith admitted.

Suddenly a long brass tube appeared around the edge of a boulder. Clint's right hand flashed to the pistol on his hip. A scrawny figure, naked except for a loincloth and antelope hide boots, hopped into view. The Chiricahua put the Henry carbine to a shoulder and aimed it at the two white men.

The Gunsmith's revolver roared as he triggered two rounds. The Colt had been modified by Clint Adams to fire double-action, which meant he didn't have to cock the pistol manually between shots. Two big bullets crashed into the Indian's bare chest. The Chiricahua screamed and dropped his carbine. He tumbled from the boulder and fell lifeless to the ground.

Clint swung his feet from the stirrups and leaped from Duke's back. He landed nimbly on his feet and immediately yanked his Springfield carbine from its boot on the saddle. He glanced about at the rocks, certain there were more Apaches lurking there. A savage war woop confirmed this assumption.

Another Chiricahua appeared from a cone-shaped rock formation, an old Navy Colt in his fist. The Indian fired a hasty shot at the Gunsmith. A lead ball hissed past Clint's ear. An icy bolt of fear danced along the Gunsmith's spine, but his hands remained steady as he aimed the modified Colt at his attacker. The Apache thumbed back the hammer of his pistol. Clint shot him in the heart with a single, well-placed round. The Indian's body was kicked backward, falling behind a stone pillar.

Three more Chiricahua emerged from rocky shelters. Clint whirled to face them, Colt revolver in his right hand and Springfield carbine in his left. Two Apaches held compact bows and short arrows and the third had a war lance in one fist and a crude tomahawk in the other. One of the bowmen was out of pistol range. The other notched an arrow and drew the string.

"Good-bye," the Gunsmith rasped as he raised his Colt and squeezed the trigger.

A .45 slug caught the brave under his jawbone. It split his tongue in half and drilled through the roof of his mouth to burn a lethal tunnel in his brain. The Chiricahua tumbled backward as he released the bowstring. The arrow hurtled into the sky as if trying to lance a cloud. The Indian's corpse twitched slightly and then accepted death's claim.

The second bowman launched an arrow, but he still was too far away to accurately use his short-range bow. The wooden missile landed less than a yard from Clint's feet. The flint arrowhead bit deeply into the ground. The Chiricahua with the lance charged forward and hurled his weapon at the Gunsmith.

Clint tried to sidestep the spear, but he didn't have enough time. Suddenly he lashed out with the Springfield. The steel barrel struck wood, deflecting the flying lance. The projectile fell harmlessly to the ground as the Apache gasped in astonishment. However, no Chiricahua was about to choke in combat. The brave passed his tomahawk from one hand to the other and prepared to throw it.

The Gunsmith's Colt snarled, pumping a .45 round into the center of his opponent's chest. The heavy lead slug shattered the Apache's breastbone, driving shrapnel into the Indian's heart and lungs. The Chiricahua wailed, attempting a brief death cry, although he did not have time to finish it.

Without warning, two more Apaches materialized from

the rocks less than ten feet from Clint's position. One Chiricahua wielded a tomahawk with a stone head, while the other held a knife in one fist and a Remington revolver in the other. His pistol had either jammed or he didn't have any ammo because he held it by the barrel. He probably intended to use it as a hammer in close quarters—on the Gunsmith's skull.

Clint quickly braced the butt of his carbine against his left hip and aimed both the Springfield and the Colt at his attackers. The guns roared in unison. A .45 projectile tore into the throat of the tomahawk man, punching through his trachea and blasting apart vertebrae before severing his spinal cord. The Indian was dead before his body hit the ground.

A round from the Springfield, also .45 caliber, slammed into the chest of the other brave. The bullet burned through his solar plexus and plowed upward into his heart. The Apache was thrown backward, as if yanked by an invisible rope, and crashed into a boulder, the back of his head splitting on impact.

Another shot exploded. Clint turned to see Tom Shatner lower a Winchester rifle. Smoke curled from the muzzle of the weapon as the Apache bowman at the rock formation thrashed about briefly with a slug in his upper torso. The Gunsmith holstered his Colt and shifted the Springfield to his right hand.

"Reckon that's the lot of 'em?" Shatner inquired.

The answer charged down on the two defenders with a vengeance. An Apache leaped from a boulder above the Gunsmith, while another Chiricahua launched himself at Shatner, the flint point of a war lance aimed at the big man's back. Tom heard the attacker and turned swiftly, slashing the barrel of his Winchester to block the spear thrust. Shatner slammed a fist into his assailant's face, knocking the Indian to the ground.

Tom kicked the brave's forearm, sending the war lance hurtling from his opponent's hand. However, the Chiricahua braves are rugged people and tougher than adobe brick. He suddenly grabbed Shatner's ankles and yanked the larger man's feet off the ground. Shatner fell on his back and the Apache dived on top of him, trying to wrestle the gun from the white man.

Clint jumped away from the tomahawk-wielding brave who pounced down from the boulder. The Gunsmith hastily pumped his Springfield to jack a fresh cartridge in the breech. The Apache raised his stone axe, determined to smash his skull. Clint thrust the Springfield forward, almost jamming the muzzle in the Indian's mouth as he pulled the trigger. A slug pulverized the Chiricahua's face and blasted out the back of his skull.

The dead Apache slumped to the ground as Clint turned to see if his friend was all right. Tom Shatner's superior size and strength were too much for the Indian who was trying to grapple with him. Shatner had pushed the brave on his back and straddled the Apache's chest to shove the barrel of his Winchester across the brave's throat. Tom shoved hard, crushing his opponent's windpipe.

"Son of a bitch pissed on me," Tom growled as he angrily kicked the dead Apache in the ribs.

"He won't do it again, Tom," Clint told him, "but I suggest you change your clothes before you get married."

"I just hope Ellie doesn't wind up a widow 'fore she gets to be a bride," Shatner muttered.

FOUR

The Gunsmith and Tom Shatner arrived at Waco in Fox County without further incident. The community was small with a collection of adobe buildings. The structures were remarkably alike, varying only in size. The church with its bell tower and the jailhouse with iron bars in its windows readily stood out from the drab gray buildings.

A few citizens were waiting in the street in front of the church. Most were dressed in denim and cotton, although Clint was surprised to see someone clad in a blue tunic with brass buttons and a cap. He looked like a policeman from San Francisco or New Orleans. The Gunsmith asked Shatner who the man was.

"That's Chief Constable Puma," Tom answered, "head of the Navaho Police here in Waco."

"There's a police force in this little town?" Clint asked with surprise.

Shatner shrugged. "If you call three constables a police force, that's what they've got."

"Looks like they've got at least two more than they need," the Gunsmith remarked.

"Puma is the only real full-time constable," Tom explained. "The other two are just part-time lawmen. Beats

18

hell out of me why they do things that way, but Indians seem to like that system. Maybe they've had it shoved down their throats so much they're used to it now. You know most reservations have an Indian Police force, which is really controlled by a representative of the Indian Agency or Department of Indian Affairs or whatever Washington is calling it this year."

"Yeah," Clint sighed, "seems like they change the name whenever it gets too bad a reputation for lying and cheating the Indians. Too bad they usually keep the same bastards no matter what they call the outfit."

"Aw," Shatner grunted, "they change them fellers from time to time."

"Washington transfers them from one Indian reservation to another," Clint muttered. "But this place isn't a reservation, right?"

"Just a town with a lot of Navaho in it," Shatner confirmed. "No goddamn Indian agents here. The priest is the only white man who lives in Waco. The blacksmith is a Mexican and I think the doctor is, too. All the rest are Navaho."

The Gunsmith saw that this was true. The people of Waco had the copper-brown skin and rather flat features of Navaho Indians. They also looked almost grim, as if a funeral were about to take place instead of a wedding. Constable Puma stepped forward and touched the brim of his service cap.

Tom acknowledged the greeting and introduced Clint whom Puma seemed to know from his reputation.

"Hello, Mister Adams," the constable began; then directing his voice as flat as the Arizona terrain to Tom, he asked, "I hope you are not too nervous about your wedding?"

"Well, Clint and I got jumped by nine Apaches on our way here," Shatner replied. "I reckon a wedding ceremony can't be any scarier than that."

"That all depends on what scares you," the Gunsmith remarked.

"Nine Apaches," the constable raised an eyebrow as he turned his attention to Clint Adams. "I see the stories about the Gunsmith have not been exaggerated."

"Don't believe everything you hear," Clint said. "And I'd be obliged if you'd just call me Clint."

"Are you going to be in town very long, Mister Adams?" Puma inquired stiffly.

"I just plan to attend the wedding and maybe stay for the reception," the Gunsmith answered. "Probably be out of your hair before dusk."

"Clint," Shatner began, "I'd feel better if you stayed until morning. Wouldn't want you to get caught out there after sundown. Not with the Apaches actin' up."

"Well," the Gunsmith said and looked around, "I don't see anything that looks like a hotel."

"You can get a room in the back of the cantina," Shatner explained. "That's where I've been stayin' the last couple days. The house is built, but I want to spend my first night there with Ellie."

"Sounds fine to me," Clint assured him.

"Mister Adams," Constable Puma began. "I know of you. I hope you will understand if I feel a bit uneasy about your presence in Waco."

"I came here for a friend's wedding, Constable," Clint replied. "I don't want any trouble either."

"I could enforce a restriction on your right to carry a gun while within the town of Waco," Puma told him.

"Aren't you familiar with the Constitution?" Clint inquired. "The second amendment protects every American citizen's right to keep and bear arms."

"The Constitution also states that any adult male over the age of twenty-one, who is not incarcerated, is entitled to the right to vote in a national election," Puma replied with a thin smile. "There is nothing denying this right to Indians, but I assure you, we cannot vote."

"So your rights are denied by Washington and this justifies denying my rights here in Waco?'' Clint asked with a shrug. ''Well, I suppose I could just camp outside of town after the wedding 'cause I'm not turning in my gun and I don't give a damn what you think of that.''

''Easy, Mister Adams,'' Puma said, still smiling. ''I simply said I *could* order such a restriction if I had just cause to consider you a danger to the well-being of the citizens of Waco. Of course, you have not violated any laws and I don't believe there are any wanted posters for you . . . at least not in the Arizona Territory.''

''Does that mean if I behave you'll stay off my back?'' the Gunsmith asked.

''I believe we understand each other, Mister Adams,'' Constable Puma nodded. ''Now, if you'll excuse me, I must get back to my rounds.''

''Don't let us stop you,'' Clint urged.

Puma strolled along the walk, hands folded at the small of his back, spine as straight as a steel rod. Shatner moved next to Clint.

''Ain't he a different kind of Indian?'' Tom whispered.

''Sure is,'' the Gunsmith agreed, watching the constable walk around the corner of a building. ''Sounds like he was educated back East. Probably a formal education at that.''

''That's right,'' Shatner confirmed. ''Went to a college in Boston or New York. One of those uppity places. Puma studied law. He planned to join the Indian Lobby for the Navaho. Somethin' sure soured him 'cause he showed up here instead. Sure has a chip on his shoulder, don't he?''

''About the size of a small mountain,'' the Gunsmith stated. ''To hell with him. Let's check out this cantina you were talking about. Reckon you should be getting ready for your wedding and you could probably use a glass of courage to keep your knees from wobbling during the ceremony.''

''There's a surprise waiting for you in there, too,'' Shatner commented with a grin.

"Oh?" Clint raised his eyebrows. "What sort of surprise?"

"If I told you about it," Shatner replied, "then it wouldn't be much of a surprise, would it?"

FIVE

When Clint Adams entered the cantina, he immediately saw what Tom Shatner had been talking about. The young woman behind the counter was stunning, her dusky skin was clear and smooth as a baby's backside. The woman's mouth was wide with full lips and brilliant white teeth. Her eyes were truly beautiful, large and dark brown.

The Gunsmith noticed that the woman's face was oval-shaped with a hawkish nose generally associated with Cherokee or Cheyenne. Clint suspected the woman was a half-breed of some sort. Whatever sort of ethnic blend was involved in the lady's heritage, Clint certainly approved of the results.

"Hello, Tom," she greeted cheerfully. "Ready for the big day?"

"Reckon I wouldn't have come back to Waco if'n I wasn't," he replied with a grin. "Allow me to introduce my best man for the wedding. I know he's eager for me to introduce him to you."

"Clint Adams, ma'am," the Gunsmith announced with a polite bow.

She smiled. "My name is Mary Spotted Fawn. Spare me the jokes about my name. I've heard them all before. Actually, the name isn't funny in Navaho."

"Believe me," Clint began, "I wasn't going to make any

jokes about your name. It's a lovely name and it suits you very well.''

"Reckon I'll go in my room and get ready," Shatner announced. "Pretty obvious you two don't need me around." The big man disappeared into the back room.

"Would you care for a drink, Mister Adams?" she inquired. "Sorry, no hard liquor. Coffee or beer?"

"Coffee will be fine," the Gunsmith answered. "Please call me Clint instead of Mister Adams. That makes me feel old.''

"You don't look too old to me, Clint," Mary said with a wink as she poured him a cup of fresh coffee.

"I hope not," the Gunsmith said. "Thanks for the coffee. How much do I owe you?"

"It's free," Mary replied. "Consider it a toast to Tom's wedding.''

"Much obliged," Clint replied, accepting a cup of coffee. "Speaking of weddings, are you married?"

Mary Spotted Fawn laughed. "You certainly believe in making your intentions obvious."

"When a fella doesn't have much time," the Gunsmith began, "he's got to be sort of obvious."

"When are you leaving?" Mary asked.

"I figure I'd better go tomorrow morning," Clint answered. "I left my wagon in Largo Gap along with all my gunsmith equipment and most of my other worldly possessions. Figured I'd only be gone for a day, so I just rode Duke out here.''

"Duke?" Mary raised an eyebrow. "That's your horse?"

"Not just a horse," the Gunsmith replied, almost defensive. "Duke is a thoroughbred. He's the strongest, fastest, and smartest critter I've ever owned. Sometimes I wonder who owns who. Duke and me are more like partners than animal and owner.''

"Have you had Duke long?" Mary asked.

"Since he was a colt," Clint confirmed. "We've been through a lot together. I've been offered as much as a thou-

sand dollars for Duke, but I could never sell him. Be like
selling my best friend. Anyway, regarding why I figure I'd
better leave in the morning, your head constable isn't too
thrilled about me being here. Figure there's no sense in
getting the law riled by hanging around where I'm not
wanted.''

"Charlie Puma can be a bit hostile toward strangers,"
Mary admitted, "especially white strangers. He's very protective of Waco and he doesn't trust whites. I think he had
some trouble from whites at the college he attended."

"How's he feel about Tom and his bride moving into a
house right outside of town?" the Gunsmith asked.

"Charlie's not happy about it," Mary said. "A lot of other
folks object to it, too."

"They think having one white family around is a threat?"
the Gunsmith asked. "Tom Shatner is basically a nice,
easygoing fella unless he feels threatened or sees somebody
else in danger. He'll make a great neighbor and he'll back up
your constables if they ever need it. Tom used to be a
lawman, you know. And he was a damn good one, too."

"The people of Waco don't have anything against Tom
personally," Mary insisted, "but they object to where he
built his house."

"Why?" Clint asked, puzzled.

"Well," Mary began. "There is a legend that the area
where Tom built his house was once a burial ground long
before the Navaho came here. Perhaps a hundred years ago or
even longer."

"I don't know much about Navaho beliefs and customs,"
Clint admitted, "but I know most Indians take a dim view of
folks messing around the resting place of the dead."

"That's right," Mary confirmed, "but the story is only a
legend and no one knows for certain that it's true. There isn't
even a single marker to indicate that any grave exists. Still,
our people have avoided the area ever since we founded the
town of Waco."

"Well, maybe after Tom's been living there for a while

folks will accept him and they'll realize that the old legend is just a legend.''

"Perhaps," Mary said, "unless, of course, it really *is* an ancient burial ground.''

"What do you mean?" the Gunsmith asked, confused by her remark.

"You might think me superstitious, Clint,'' Mary answered, "but I believe there is some truth to the beliefs of my people. The dead are meant to rest undisturbed and there are spirits of vengeance with terrible powers that will punish any who disregard the eternal sleep of the dead.''

"Punish in what manner?" Clint inquired.

"Perhaps the spirits will only create nightmares and illusions to respond to the unrest suffered by the dead,'' Mary explained. "Or perhaps . . . perhaps more drastic measures will be taken.''

"Such as?" the Gunsmith asked grimly.

"Things too horrible to think of,'' Mary replied.

SIX

"I now pronounce you man and wife," Father McCoy announced solemnly as he closed his Bible. "You may kiss the bride."

Tom Shatner turned to Ellie, cupped her face in his hands, and kissed her. The grizzled former lawman wore a black suit with a string tie and he'd even trimmed his beard for the occasion. His new wife was a rather plump, pleasant-looking lady in her late thirties. The couple seemed very happy as the Gunsmith stepped aside and made room for the newlyweds to depart. Tom turned to Clint and heartily shook his hand.

"Thanks for comin', Clint," Shatner said. "I really appreciate you bein' here, old friend."

"My pleasure, Tom," the Gunsmith assured him. "I hope you two will be very happy together, Tom."

"We plan to be," Shatner confirmed, wrapping an arm around Ellie's waist.

The wedding had been conducted outside of the church in order to enjoy the afternoon sunshine. The couple received congratulations from everyone who attended the wedding—the entire town of Waco. However, the entire population was less than forty. Clint later learned that some of the guests were from farms in Fox County. The wedding was a big event and virtually everyone showed up.

But, the Gunsmith noticed, not everyone appeared to regard the event as a cause for celebration. A number of Navaho faces seemed grim, their eyes betraying resentment and perhaps even a trace of fear. Since Tom Shatner had done nothing to merit such feelings, Clint assumed this was solely because the Shatners were moving into a house located on an alleged burial ground.

The crowd moved to a trio of long picnic tables. The newlyweds cut the first of three cakes. This signaled that everyone should partake of the assorted sandwiches, potato salad, turkey, bread, and drinks which included tea, coffee, and beer. There was no wine served. Probably because anything stronger than beer was denied to Navaho. He'd seen some pretty wild drunken Indians, but he didn't think they were any worse than a bunch of liquored up cowboys who just got into town from a cattle drive.

A very attractive woman with olive skin and a large man with a similar complexion approached the newlyweds. The woman had long black hair and hazel eyes. Her features were delicate, beautiful in the classic manner such as one might find on the face of a cameo brooch. She seemed to have an aura of pure sexual excitement. At least, she had that effect on Clint Adams.

The man with her was almost as big as Tom Shatner, but there didn't appear to be any fat on him. His chest was broad and thick with muscle. The deltoids at his shoulders and massive biceps of his upper arms strained the fabric of his shirt. His angular face was dark and ruggedly handsome with black eyebrows and a mustache which drooped at the corners of his mouth.

The woman spoke to Tom and Ellie Shatner. They smiled and nodded. The big fellow with the muscles solemnly shook hands with the groom and said something, but Clint was unable to hear any of the conversation. Mary Spotted Fawn appeared beside the Gunsmith.

"You seem to have taken an interest in Dr. Reyes," she said dryly.

"Oh?" Clint replied.

"She's Dr. Sofia Reyes," Mary said. "The man is her brother, Luis. He's the blacksmith."

"*She's* a doctor?" Clint asked with surprise. "That's pretty unusual."

"I don't think she is a real doctor," Mary said with a shrug. "But she showed up here about three months ago and opened an office. We needed a doctor in Waco, but everyone was reluctant to accept a woman doctor. A few people have gone to her to have bones fixed or children treated for fevers and such. None of her customers has died yet and they all seem pretty satisfied with her work."

"Impressive," Clint commented as he noticed the swell of Sofia's breasts against her linen dress.

"I suppose so," Mary admitted. "It is not easy for a woman to run her own business. I know—I own the cantina."

Clint smiled. "I guess that means you'll be my landlady tonight. Tom suggested I rent a room in the cantina for the night."

"That'll be Tom's old room," Mary confirmed. "He won't be needing it now."

"Well," the Gunsmith began. "Then why don't we have dinner first . . ."

Clint ended the sentence abruptly when he noticed three men on horseback at the end of a picnic table. The rest of the wedding reception also fell silent when they saw the strangers. They were covered with dust and their shabby clothes clung to them. The Gunsmith noticed the three horsemen showed considerably more respect for the clean and lightly oiled pistols they carried than they did for their clothing.

A tall, thin man leaned forward and pulled his weather-beaten Stetson from his tawny head. His long, lean face split into a wide smile, revealing ugly yellowed teeth.

"Howdy," he greeted. "Reckon we caught you folks at a bad time. Havin' some party or somethin'?"

"Them vittles sure look good," another horseman remarked. He was a fat toadlike character with tiny eyes and a broad, flat nose. He licked his thick lips as he gazed down at the food.

"Hold on, Elmer," the skinny man told him. "Ain't polite to barge in on folks and gobble up their fixins at a celebration."

"Hey, Luke," the third man, a filthy fellow with a dirty beard said. He pointed an unwashed finger at Tom and Ellie. "Look at that. They's havin' a weddin' here."

"That's a fact, Mel," the scrawny Luke agreed." Always nice to see folks gettin' hitched. Hell, I got a couple wives somewhere or other myself. Give you a word of advice, friend. If'n a woman gives you too much crap, don't beat up on her. She might put rat poison in your food to get even. Happened to a feller I knowed."

"I'm the Chief Constable," Charlie Puma announced, stepping forward. "May I ask what you fellows want?"

"Passin' through, Constable," Luke said with a shrug. "Figured we'd camp outside town for a spell. Won't cause you folks no harm. Just gotta be careful what with the Apaches actin' up and all."

"Yeah," Mel added. "Them redskins is purely a worry."

"Watch your mouth," Luke snapped. "Some o' these fine folk is Injuns and they might not like you usin' expressions like redskins. Mel don't mean no offense, folks. He's just plum ignorant at times."

"Someone should enlighten him about the use of soap and water," Constable Puma remarked, gazing at the filthy, bearded rider.

"You bad mouthin' me, boy?" Mel asked angrily, his hand resting on the grips of a Smith & Wesson .44 caliber revolver in his belt.

"You draw that gun," the Gunsmith declared. "And I'll blow your head off, Mel."

"Shee-it," the bearded man snorted, dragging his pistol from his belt.

"Stop 'im!" Luke ordered.

Elmer, the fat man with the pig eyes, leaned over in his saddle and suddenly slammed a fist into Mel's shaggy face. The bearded man started to fall from his saddle, but Elmer grabbed the other man's shirt front and held him back. Mel still clawed at his revolver, so Elmer chopped the edge of his hand across Mel's forearm and quickly swatted the back of his hand across the hairy man's face.

Mel weaved unsteadily in the saddle, dazed by the rapid combination of blows delivered by the obese Elmer. Clint made a mental note about the three men. Actually, he made a note about each man. Luke was in charge of the trio. Elmer was a lot faster and probably smarter than he looked. Mel was dumber than a cracked brick, but he was also ready to kill for damn little reason.

"I apologize for this, folks," Luke said. "Mel just does some stupid stuff from time to time. Reckon that's 'cause he's so ignorant and all."

"You fellas are just passing through," Clint reminded them, "so you'll be leaving in the morning?"

"Maybe," Luke answered. "Who are you and why do you care?"

"The name is Adams," the Gunsmith said. "Clint Adams. And I care because the people of Waco seem to be a peaceful lot and I reckon you fellas aren't."

"Clint Adams, eh?" Luke's smile extended from one ear to the other. "Now ain't that a wonderment. A livin' legend right here in front of us."

"Jesus, Elmer," Mel muttered, dabbing blood from a split lip with his palm. "You didn't have to hit me so hard . . ."

"Shut up, Mel," Luke told him. "Unless you want to thank Elmer for savin' your dumbass life. You damn near got yourself killed by the Gunsmith. Let's go boys."

The three horsemen pulled the reins of their mounts to aim their animals east. They galloped to the outskirts of town. The Gunsmith watched them as Constable Puma approached.

"I don't need your help to maintain law and order," Puma stated. "I can do my job without your assistance."

"Next time I'll let you handle it alone," Clint replied dryly.

"You almost caused a gun battle, Adams," the constable

declared. "With all these woman and children here that could have been a disaster."

"Mel was reaching for his gun before I stepped in," the Gunsmith reminded him. "But don't worry. I figure Luke will keep a tight rein on Mel. Those fellas didn't come here to get in a shooting match. I don't figure they're Sunday school teachers, but they aren't kill-crazy lunatics either."

"Why do you think they're in town, then?" Puma asked.

"I don't know," Clint admitted. "But if they don't ride on tomorrow, I reckon you can expect some trouble from those fellas."

"Just don't cause any trouble yourself, Adams," Puma warned.

"Don't intend to," Clint assured him.

The constable walked away and Clint turned to Mary Spotted Fawn. "Now," he began, "before we were interrupted, I was trying to ask you to have dinner with me."

"In other words," Mary said, "you want to go to bed with me, right?"

"Uh . . ." the Gunsmith was unable to reply. He didn't want to say no and he didn't dare say yes.

"Well, it sounds good to me," she told him.

"I . . . I've never been one to argue with a lady," Clint said with a nod.

SEVEN

By sundown, the Gunsmith and Mary Spotted Fawn had stepped into the woman's bedroom. The reception party continued until late afternoon, so they had eaten enough to skip supper. Since they both realized the other shared the same desire for sexual contact, they spent little time on conversation.

Mary moved to a kerosene lamp and turned down the flame. The Gunsmith unbuttoned his shirt and unbuckled the gunbelt from his lean waist. The woman began to strip off her gingham dress, revealing a beautiful, shapely body with smooth copper-brown skin. Mary's breasts were large and firm, capped with pert rigid nipples. Her flat belly extended to rounded hips which tapered into well-formed thighs and long legs.

Clint finished removing his clothing and the couple moved to the bed. They sprawled across the mattress, hands stroking naked flesh eagerly. Clint fondled her breasts gently and lowered his mouth to the stiff brown nipples. Mary sighed happily as Clint's hand moved along her thigh. His fingers found the center of her love and he slowly massaged her.

The Gunsmith didn't rush lovemaking. He savored the experience and tried to prolong each sexual experience as much as possible. He had also discovered that it was best to wait for his partner to decide when she was ready to make love.

But Mary was soon ready. She slid a hand between Clint's thighs and gripped his hard penis to help guide it. Clint sighed as his cock slithered inside her. He turned his hips gradually to ease himself deeper. The woman moaned with pleasure as Clint slowly rocked his loins, sliding his rigid penis to and fro.

Clint paced himself, careful not to thrust too quickly. He waited until Mary began to arch her back to meet his thrusts before he lunged faster. Then he drove in faster and harder. She raked her nails across his bare back and wrapped her legs around his lower torso as the Gunsmith continued.

Mary abruptly gasped and convulsed in a wild orgasm. Clint slowed down and began to kiss and stroke her again. He gradually rolled his hips to begin building up her desire as he had before. Mary rose to the zenith faster the second time, her body quivering with another orgasm. The Gunsmith rode to glory with her and exploded inside her tunnel of love. Both lovers sighed with mutual satisfaction.

"Oh, Clint," Mary whispered as she snuggled against his chest. "That was wonderful. You're certainly just what I needed."

"I've got no complaints either," the Gunsmith assured her, gently stroking the woman's hair.

"Figure if you rest up a bit you can manage another round?" she asked, nibbling on his ear lobe.

"Reckon it's worth a try," Clint replied with a smile.

The sky was still pink and gold when the Gunsmith strapped the saddle on Duke's back. He wanted to leave Waco early. Clint had no reason to stay in town and he had to get back to his gunsmith wagon. Besides, it was unlikely a band of bloodthirsty Apaches would be patroling the prairie at daybreak. He patted his horse's neck and prepared to swing up into the saddle.

"Mr. Adams," Constable Puma called as he hurried toward the Gunsmith, "I'd like to have a word or two with you before you leave."

"Must be pretty important for you to delay me," Clint sighed, "since you seemed in such an almighty hurry to get rid of me before."

"I see no one has told you what happened," Puma began awkwardly, "but then I just found out a few minutes ago myself."

"What happened, Constable?" Clint asked, almost afraid to hear the answer.

"Tom and Ellie Shatner were killed last night," the Navaho lawman answered.

"My God!" Clint exclaimed, stunned by the announcement. "What the hell happened? Did the Apaches hit his place last night?"

"We're not certain, Mr. Adams," Puma replied, "but it appears they were killed by some sort of wild animal."

"A wild animal?" Clint snorted. "Tom Shatner was strong as a grizzly bear and a dead shot with a rifle. What kind of animal could have killed him?"

"It was probably a mountain lion," the constable explained. "Dr. Reyes is checking out the bodies to try to determine the exact cause of death."

"Have you seen the bodies?" Clint inquired.

"Yes," Puma nodded. "Unfortunately, I have."

"What do you think happened?" Clint asked. "What do you figure was the cause of death?"

"Very simple, Mr. Adams," Puma said stiffly. "Tom and Ellie were torn to shreds. They were literally clawed to death."

EIGHT

Dr. Sofia Reyes was still beautiful, but the blood-splattered, long white apron she wore diverted the Gunsmith's attention. Sofia looked weary when Clint Adams and Constable Puma entered her small, neat office at the west end of town.

"Have you finished examining the bodies, Miss Reyes?" Puma asked. He seemed to make a point of not calling her Dr. Reyes.

"I don't think I'm going to find anything else about them by doing more on the autopsy," Sofia replied.

"What did you determine as cause of death?" the Gunsmith asked.

She looked at him hard and frowned. "Who are you?"

"Name's Clint Adams," he replied. "Tom was a friend of mine."

"Oh," she nodded, "the best man. I remember now. I'm sorry about your friend, Mr. Adams. This is a very terrible thing. Newlyweds killed on their wedding night. Terrible."

"Agreed," Clint said. "But *what* killed them?"

"Well," Sofia began. "Both bodies were severely torn and mutilated. Primary cause of death arose from their throats being torn out. Of course, they also suffered excessive loss of blood, which probably contributed to death."

"What sort of weapon was used?" Clint asked.

"I've seen knife wounds before," she explained, "but these wounds are different. The skin was torn, not cut. There

36

are no punctures or stab wounds. I'm not an expert on animal attacks, but I'd say the Shatners were killed by a large, powerful beast with claws.''

''Then you think they were killed by a mountain lion?'' Clint asked.

''That would seem the most likely animal,'' Sofia shrugged. ''I don't know if a bear or a large wolf could have done this, but I've never heard of anyone being attacked by either animal in the Arizona Territory. I'm not even sure those animals are found in this region. I know Harry Two-Ponies would disagree, but I think we can disregard his story.''

''What story?'' the Gunsmith demanded.

''Just foolishness,'' Constable Puma said. ''Harry is an old fool and he drinks too much.

''I'd still like to know what this is about,'' Clint said.

''Harry Two-Ponies has a little farm about five miles from Shatner's spread,'' Puma began wearily. ''He found the Shatners dead this morning. Headed over to their place at the crack of dawn because he claimed he was visited by a . . . well, a *chindi* last night.''

''A *chindi*,'' Clint said, ''what's that? Some sort of premonition in a dream or something?''

''A *chindi* is more like a monster,'' Sofia answered. ''It's an animal that walks upright and it hunts people down and kills them.''

''Is this *chindi* supposed to be part man and part beast?'' Clint asked urgently. ''Like the sasquatch in California and Canada?''

''You mean that nonsense about a hairy giant living in the forests?'' Puma said dryly.

''The sasquatch *isn't* just a legend,'' the Gunsmith told him. ''I know that for a fact*.''

''Well, the *chindi* is quite different,'' Puma explained. ''The *chindi* is a spirit. How can I explain this in terms that a non-Navaho would understand? Oh, it's rather like the old

_____
GUNSMITH #21: SASQUATCH HUNT

legends of a Guardian Angel or perhaps a witch's familiar, a spirit assistant in the form of an animal. It's a popular belief among the Navaho—who haven't had the benefit of a proper white man's education, of course—that a *chindi* or spirit being looks after every Navaho. Not just throughout his life, but after death as well.''

''But Dr. Reyes called it an animal that walks upright and stalks people,'' Clint said.

''Well, Miss Reyes isn't a Navaho and she doesn't know all our beliefs yet,'' Puma sighed. ''You see, if a *chindi* is angered, it will possess an animal and use the beast to seek revenge. This animal can be anything. A bear, a mountain lion, a dog, or a even a frog or a cricket. But the most popular choice for *chindi* possession is a wolf.''

''The *chindi* is sometimes referred to as a wolf witch,'' Sofia added. ''Strange how every culture seems to have a special fear of wolves.''

''A wolf witch,'' Clint mused. ''I've heard of a critter called a werewolf, which is supposed to be a man who can transform himself into a wolf through black magic or something like that. Some folks in Europe still believe such things exist.''

''That legend was probably started because there were epidemics of rabies in Europe,'' Sofia declared. ''A pack of mad wolves could seem like supernatural monsters to a poor, ignorant peasant. There were also cases of man-eating wolves that were not rabid.''

''I've heard that, too,'' Clint sighed, ''usually from somebody who's never seen a wolf in his life. Trappers and forest Indians tell me they've never known of a true case of a wolf or even a wolf pack attacking a man unless rabies was involved.''

''That's probably true,'' Sofia said, ''here in America. However, in Europe, say three hundred years ago, plagues killed thousands of people. Thousands more died on the battlefields. Human corpses littered the countryside. Apparently, wolf packs came across these remains and ate so much human flesh they came to regard people as just another form of prey. That's probably how the werewolf myth got started.''

"Well," Puma said, "the *chindi* isn't supposed to be a man-eating wolf or a werewolf. According to legend, it is a spirit which possesses an animal. Kill the animal and the *chindi* will simply possess another beast and come after you again.''

"Sounds like fun," Clint muttered. "And this fella Harry claims he saw a *chindi* last night?''

"Really, Adams," Puma sighed, "this is too silly to waste time discussing.''

"A friend of mine was torn to pieces by something with claws, right?" Clint replied. "Now, that's a fact. Anything that can help explain that or maybe shed a little light on what happened, isn't too silly to consider.''

"Very well," the exasperated constable agreed. "Harry claims he heard a strange wailing sound last night. A haunting voice which was neither man nor beast, according to Harry. Then he looked out his window and—no doubt to his quivering alcoholic horror—beheld the terrible shape of a *chindi*. Or at least he claimed to see a wolf which walked like a man. I'm certain this drove him straight back to the bottle and he probably dreamed up some more rubbish, which he'll tell us about later.''

"Don't you think it's a little odd that he heard and saw a *chindi* the same night Tom and Ellie were killed?" the Gunsmith inquired.

"Odd, yes," Puma admitted, "but it isn't that important because Harry has been seeing and hearing a *chindi* for almost a month now. He tried to warn Tom Shatner about it, but your friend laughed in his face and kept building his house. The fact a mountain lion killed Shatner and his wife is, no doubt, a bizarre and tragic coincidence.''

"Yeah," the Gunsmith said without conviction. "I hope you don't mind if I stay in Waco for a while, Constable.''

"Oh, God," Puma sighed. "Look, if you want to try to

hunt down a mountain lion, be my guest. If you plan to hunt down a *chindi*, then you'd better ask Harry to share some of his corn liquor with you. I assure you, that's the only way you'll ever see a *chindi*."

"Thanks for your advice," Clint told him. "As a matter of fact, I think I will talk to Harry Two-Ponies."

"I'd rather you didn't," Puma said grimly.

"Why not?" the Gunsmith asked.

"Because all you're going to do is cause trouble," Puma declared, "just as your friend Mr. Shatner caused trouble. We don't like whites, Mr. Adams. They're bad luck to my people. Always have been."

"Waco didn't prove to be real lucky for Tom and Ellie, either," Clint reminded him. "And I think they may have been murdered, but you don't even intend to investigate their death."

"If you want to investigate your friend's death, you go right ahead and do it," Puma invited, "but you're making a mistake. And if you make too many mistakes in this county, you may find yourself sitting in a jail cell waiting for the circuit judge to arrive. My people are already frightened. I won't stand you driving them to panic. I hope we understand each other, Mr. Adams."

"Like I said," the Gunsmith replied as he headed for the door, "thanks for the advice."

NINE

Clint Adams followed some rather muddled directions to Harry Two-Ponies's farm. He was surprised when he found the place without much trouble. The Navaho farmer owned a small spread, covering less than two hundred acres. The house was made of adobe with a flat roof and goat hide curtains in the windows. Apparently, Harry Two-Ponies raised chickens and goats. His crops were turnips, potatoes, and whatever else he could grow in the dry climate.

Clint rode Duke to the farmhouse. Before he could dismount, a short, heavyset man emerged from the house with a double-barrel shotgun in his hands. Clint raised his hands to show they were empty.

"What do you want, white man?" the Navaho demanded, staring across the twin barrels. The shotgun trembled in his grasp.

"I was a friend of Tom Shatner," the Gunsmith explained. "I just want to talk to you. You don't need that scatter gun. I'm not here to harm you."

"We moved here to be away from white men," Harry declared. "You are not welcome here."

"Yeah," Clint sighed. "That's already been pointed out to me. But I'm a bit disturbed about Tom's death and I'd like to know all the facts before I just accept what Puma tells me."

"And what did Charlie tell you?" Harry demanded.

41

"He said Tom and Ellie were killed by a wild animal," Clint answered, "probably a mountain lion. He also mentioned that you saw a *chindi* last night. That's what I'd like to talk to you about."

"You whites don't believe in Navaho spirits," Harry snorted. "Did you come here to laugh at me?"

"A friend of mine was killed," the Gunsmith said grimly. "I don't feel much like laughing. And I asked you to put down that shotgun."

"Very well," Harry began, lowering his gun. "I'll tell you what I saw. Then you must go."

"Fair enough," the Gunsmith replied, swinging down from Duke's back. "Tell me about this *chindi*."

"We Navaho do not like to talk about such things," Harry began. "The spirit world exists and it does not take kindly to mortals speaking about it. I have seen the *chindi* twice now and I have heard its unearthly cry. I must meet with the Old One so he can help me cleanse my spirit. Even seeing a *chindi* can endanger a man's soul."

"When did you first see this *chindi*?" Clint inquired.

"Perhaps a month ago, by your measure of time," the Navaho said. "It was late and my family and I had gone to sleep. Then the cry of the *chindi* awoke us from our slumber. I told my wife and daughter to stay in the house as I armed myself and ventured outside. Then I saw the *chindi*."

He pointed to a rocky ridge roughly two hundred yards from the house. "I saw it there," Harry stated. "The *chindi* stood on that ridge, its form set against the full moon. It was the most terrible vision I ever beheld. A terror not of this world."

"How did you know it was a *chindi*?" Clint asked. "What did it look like?"

"The *chindi* had possessed an animal," Two-Ponies stated. "You will not believe me, but it is true. I saw a wolf that walked like a man."

"A wolf?" Clint raised his eyebrows. "But there are no wolves native to this area. Why would the *chindi* possess an animal that isn't found here? Wouldn't it be more logical to choose a mountain lion or a coyote?''

"The *chindi* is a spirit," Two-Ponies answered. "Its ways and reasons are different from those of mortal men.''

"Are you sure this *chindi* was a wolf on its hind legs?'' the Gunsmith asked.

"It stood erect,'' Harry began, "like a man. I saw the profile of its head. I saw the long snout and pointed ears of a wolf.''

"What did you do then?'' Clint asked.

"I returned to my home,'' Harry answered. "I chanted to the spirits to understand that I did not mean to gaze upon one of their brothers who had taken form on earth. I asked them to forgive me my mortal weakness and to protect me from the *chindi*.''

"I admit I don't know too much about spirits and such,'' Clint stated, "but from what little I've been able gather about the *chindi*, it's not exactly an evil spirit. Why were you so frightened when you saw the wolf witch?''

"Because the actions of a *chindi* seeking vengeance are not meant to be witnessed by mortal men,'' Harry explained.

"But last night you heard the *chindi* again and you saw it a second time,'' the Gunsmith mused. "Why didn't you stay indoors to avoid seeing the creature a second time if it frightened you so?''

"I am a man,'' he sighed, "and like all men, I am curious about things I don't fully understand. It was stupid and dangerous. I am fortunate that the *chindi* was stalking a definite victim and ignored me.''

"So you think the *chindi* was stalking Tom Shatner and took revenge on him for disturbing the alleged graveyard where he built his house?'' the Gunsmith asked.

"This is so,'' Harry confirmed. "The *chindi* appeared when Shatner first arrived and started work on that house. It was a warning that the ground was not to be disturbed. But Shatner ignored this and built his house. He and the woman moved into it and disturbed the rest of the dead buried there.

So the *chindi* took revenge.''

''Tell me,'' Clint began, ''the second time you saw the *chindi*, where was the creature?''

''It stood on the ridge as before,'' Harry answered, ''set against the moon.''

''Interesting,'' Clint remarked. ''The *chindi* made it easy for you to see him, but he stayed well out of range in case you took a shot at him.''

''That is an assumption,'' Harry said angrily, ''and a blasphemous one at that.''

''I don't want to offend you,'' Clint began, ''but you assumed that what you saw was really a *chindi*. After all, a spirit wouldn't be afraid if you put a bullet in him. And if this *chindi* wanted to keep his actions secret, why did he let you see him?''

''No mortal understands the ways of spirits,'' Harry insisted. ''And it is unwise to question them.''

''Father,'' a female voice called softly, ''Mother is preparing dinner. Shall she fix a plate for our visitor as well?''

Harry's daughter had stepped from the house. She was an attractive young woman, about seventeen or eighteen. Her long black hair was parted in the middle and braided along both sides of her round face. She smiled at the Gunsmith.

''Get back in the house, Rachel!'' Harry snapped. ''You know better than to disturb me when I am talking to another man. If I wished to share this conversation with womenfolk, I would have brought Mr. Adams inside.''

''I just wanted to see about the meal, Father,'' Rachel said, gazing down at her bare feet. ''Mother said . . .''

''I'll deal with your mother later,'' Harry said angrily. ''You both need a taste of belt leather. As for Mr. Adams, he was not invited here and he will not be staying for dinner.''

''Yeah,'' Clint said. ''I'd better be going. Nice meeting you, ma'am.''

''Nice meeting you too,'' Rachel replied with a smile.

Harry glared at his daughter. Clint decided he'd better leave before Two-Ponies got more upset and took it out on his wife and daughter. Clint prepared to mount his horse when he saw a pair of horsemen galloping toward the Navaho's farm. He recognized Constable Puma and assumed the other rider was probably a Waco lawman, too.

"I thought I'd find you here, Mr. Adams," Puma said. He didn't sound very happy.

"I was just about to head back to town," the Gunsmith told him. "What do you want?"

"We've just been to Shatner's house," Puma said. "We were looking through his personal effects to find out if he had any family who would have to be told about his death. We found nothing of that sort, but we did come across a will."

"And you want me to verify that Tom's signature is genuine?" Clint guessed.

"No," Puma sighed, "we don't have any doubt about that. It seems Tom Shatner had a pretty high opinion of you, Mr. Adams."

"He mentioned me in his will?" the Gunsmith asked with surprise.

"Yes," Puma said grimly. "In the event that both he and his wife should die—which, of course, is exactly what happened—you, Clint Adams, inherit his property."

"Does that mean you're our new neighbor, Mr. Adams?" Rachel asked with a grin.

Harry Two-Ponies turned sharply and smacked the back of his hand across his daughter's face. Rachel yelped with pain as she fell to the ground.

"Son of a bitch," Clint growled as he instinctively charged and slammed a fist into Harry's jaw.

The surprised farmer hit the ground next to his daughter. He tried to raise and aim his shotgun, but Clint's boot lashed out and kicked it out of his hands. Harry snarled with anger and leaped up, hands aimed for the Gunsmith's throat. Clint stepped forward and swung hard at his opponent's jaw. Harry's head bounced from the punch. Clint closed in fast and hammered the farmer with two left jabs, hitting him in the chest and on the point of the chin.

Harry fell again, landing hard on his backside. Blood oozed from his mouth and his eyes had adopted a glassy quality. But the farmer still tried to get up. His hands seemed to slide out of control when he tried to brace them against the ground, trying to haul himself erect. Harry fell again and lay panting on his side.

"You don't do so good when you take on another man instead of a woman," Clint growled. "Do you, neighbor?"

"Father . . ." Rachel rushed to Harry's aid, but her father brushed her aside and once again tried to get to his feet.

"Come on, Adams," Constable Puma snapped, "let's get out of here."

Clint mounted Duke, watching Harry Two-Ponies carefully. However, the farmer did not reach for his shotgun. He hauled himself upright and pawed blood from his mouth with the back of his hand.

"Adams!" Harry snapped. "You ever set foot on my property again, I'll kill you!"

"Does that mean I can't borrow sugar if I run out?" the Gunsmith asked dryly.

"Charlie," Two-Ponies continued, "you better run Adams outta town. Shoot him if he refuses to go. Otherwise, we'll all feel the fury of the *chindi*. We'll all be doomed."

TEN

"I can't believe you beat up Harry just for slapping his daughter," Constable Puma remarked as he and the other constable escorted Clint Adams back to Waco. "A man has a right to discipline his own children, Adams."

"I can't stand to see a woman mistreated," the Gunsmith replied simply. "Guess I lost my temper. Lucky Harry told me just about everything he could about the *chindi* before we got in that fight."

"Will you forget about the *chindi?*" Puma asked. "I already told you that Harry gets drunk and dreams up all sorts of nonsense."

"I'm not so sure," the Gunsmith stated. "His description of a *chindi* sounded to me like it could be somebody wearing a wolf head mask. The *chindi* was a good two hundred yards away at night—with only moonlight to help Harry see. No way he could tell if the *chindi* was really a wolf standing upright or a man trying to throw a scare into him."

"Why would anybody want to do that, Adams?" Puma asked, clearly exasperated by the conversation.

"To frighten people away from the alleged burial ground," Clint replied. "To be exact, the *chindi* impersonator was trying to scare away Tom Shatner and Ellie."

"That's a nice theory," Puma sighed, "but it doesn't make sense."

"Sure it does," the Gunsmith insisted. "The *chindi* tried

47

to scare off Tom. He dismissed the warning, the same as you're doing now. Then the *chindi* killed Tom and his wife and made it look as if a wild animal had done it. The Navaho who believe in the *chindi* will assume a spirit killed them, while officially the deaths will be reported as the work of a mountain lion or whatever.''

"That's all very clever, Adams," Puma said, "but Harry first saw a *chindi* at least a week before Shatner came to Fox County.''

"Are you sure about that?" Clint asked.

"Positive," Puma sighed. "People were still talking about the *chindi* sighting and considered it an omen after Shatner showed up and announced his intentions to build a house in that area. I also remember how Shatner was accusing the townsfolk of trying to scare him off. Claimed he found evidence of vandalism . . . are you familiar with that word?''

"Derived from the behavior of the barbarian tribe called Vandals," Clint replied wearily. "I attended school, too.''

"I'm impressed," Puma snorted. "Anyway, Shatner thought the Navaho were sneaking onto his property at night while he was gone. Claimed they tore up the frame of one house and burned down the second one. Shatner was sure determined. He finally built the place out of adobe to make it too hard for anybody to wreck what he'd done.''

"Do you believe the townsfolk did that?''

"Somebody must have," Puma stated. "I suspected good old Harry at the time. Especially after he had his *chindi* vision.''

"You know," Clint mused, "Harry found the bodies. He also claims he saw the *chindi* again last night.''

"Right," Puma said. "He stated that he rode out to warn Shatner first thing in the morning and found the mutilated corpses.''

"Isn't it possible that Harry could be the *chindi?*" Clint inquired. "After all, nobody else saw it and Harry certainly objects to the idea of having anyone living on that land . . .

or maybe he objects only to having white neighbors.''

"Harry is a bit hotheaded," Puma remarked, "but I can't imagine him committing murder.

"A lot of unlikely people turn out to be murderers," Clint told him. "By the way, why are we going back to town? I thought I'd take a look at Tom's property. After all, I own it now."

"I'm going to suggest that the mayor call a meeting of the town council," the constable explained. "If he agrees, then I'd like you to attend. I trust you have no objections?"

"None at all," the Gunsmith assured him, "unless you plan to try to run me out of town. If you do, I'll just go to my new home instead."

"Let's talk to the council first," Puma urged.

The Gunsmith and the two constables arrived in Waco shortly after noon. Clint had to wait for Puma to arrange the town meeting, so he decided the best place to relax would be at the cantina. The Gunsmith entered the tavern. Mary Spotted Fawn was stationed behind the bar and three customers were seated at a table. Luke, Elmer, and Mel—the three strangers who had ridden into Waco the day before.

"Oh, Clint!" Mary exclaimed, clearly happy to see the Gunsmith. "I heard about Tom and Ellie. My God, it's terrible."

"Yeah," Clint agreed, "I know."

"Hear this feller Shatner was a friend of yours, Adams," Luke, the scrawny leader of the trio commented. "Feller got killed by a mountain lion, right?"

"That's a popular theory," the Gunsmith replied. "You fellas got a special interest in the matter or are you just making conversation?"

"No need to get surly," Luke smiled. "Come here and have some beer with us, Adams. We'd like to talk to you about a couple things."

"I'll buy my own beer," Clint said, turning to Mary. "I'll take a mug, please."

"Coming up," she answered quickly.

"You ain't bein' very social-like, feller," Mel, the dirty, bearded character snorted. "You reckon you're too good to sit with us, Mr. Gunsmith?"

"I'm just not sure I want to be associated with you boys since I don't know what you're planning to do while you're in Waco," Clint shrugged. "I figure you've got some reason for staying in Fox County."

"We already explained why we're here," Luke said with a sigh as he began to roll a cigarette. "We're just passin' through."

"How many days do you plan to spend in Waco while you're 'just passin' through' town?" the Gunsmith asked, accepting a mug of beer from Mary.

"We make you nervous, Adams?" Mel asked as he scratched at his dirt-matted beard.

"Should you make me nervous?" Clint replied, sipping his beer. "You fellas said you wanted to talk to me, so talk."

"It's personal," Luke explained, tilting his head toward the bar. "Not the sort of thing this gal should be listenin' in on."

"I've got to go in the back and check on the stock anyway," Mary announced as she headed for a side door.

The Gunsmith would have gladly avoided talking to the three strangers. Of course, he could still just walk out of the cantina and refuse to cooperate with the trio. However, Clint was also curious about what they wanted.

"Is this private enough?" Clint asked after Mary left the barroom.

"Reckon so," Luke said. "You come here to attend your friend's weddin', right?"

"That's right," Clint confirmed.

"Did he happen to say why he chose to build his house where he did?" Luke asked.

"Nothing special as I recall," the Gunsmith answered.

"Could be you forget a thing or two, Adams," Mel snorted.

Clint noticed Mel's hands were under the table. One of

Elmer's hands had also slipped from view. Clint lowered his right arm and let the fingers hover near the walnut grips of his holstered Colt revolver. All three strangers stiffened.

"Ain't no call for gunplay," Elmer said, sweat covering his fat face.

"I hope not," Clint replied, "but I'd sure feel better if you boys would keep your hands on the table where I can see them."

"Shit," Mel growled. "If I had a gun drawn under this table, I could drop you 'fore you could draw that fancy six-shooter of yours, Adams."

"Figure you can shoot accurately under the table or through the wooden top?" the Gunsmith inquired. "If you miss, you won't get another shot. The first bullet had better bring me down, too. Even a man with a bullet through the heart can generally manage to get off a shot or two. With this double-action revolver, I might be able to fire three or four rounds before I die. Want to bet your life that I can't kill all three of you before I fall?"

"Now, let's all calm down," Luke urged. "Mel, Elmer. You fellers keep your hands where Adams can see them so he doesn't get to wonderin' if'n we'll stay friendly-like."

Elmer placed his hands on the table. Mel reluctantly followed his example. Clint hooked his thumb in his belt buckle and relaxed a bit.

"All right, gents," he began, "why are you fellas so interested in Tom Shatner's property?"

"Just makin' conversation," Luke replied. "Hell, Adams, we're just resting up in Waco for a while until we're ready to move on. You're a drifter, too. How come you're stayin' here?"

"I've got a couple reasons," Clint answered. "Neither of them is any of your business, but I'll tell you anyway."

"I'm listenin', Adams," Luke assured him.

"First," the Gunsmith began, "I came to Waco to be best man at Tom's wedding. That means Tom Shatner was a friend of mine. I don't have too many friends, so when one of them gets killed, I don't like it."

"So you're gonna stay around to hunt the mountain lion?" Elmer asked. "Best watch yourself, Adams. A man-eatin' cat can be a devil with fangs and claws."

"I've hunted big cats from time to time," the Gunsmith answered. "Hunted down a jaguar once and a killer grizzly, too. Trouble is, I'm not convinced a mountain lion killed Tom and his wife. I think they might have been murdered."

"Why would anybody want to do that?" Luke asked.

"A lot of the Navaho here objected to Tom building a house in an area that they believe is an ancient burial ground."

"So you figure an Injun killed them and tried to make it look like a mountain lion done it?" Elmer inquired.

"That's possible," the Gunsmith replied. "It's also possible some white men might have done it because they want the land for themselves."

"Why would a white man want some goddamn Indian graveyard?" Mel demanded.

"You tell me, fella," Clint said. "You boys seem pretty interested in that property."

"Just asked you a simple question 'bout why Shatner built his house out there," Luke insisted. "Seems a bit odd for a white man to want to live with all these Navaho for neighbors. Ain't exactly normal."

"So you're stayin' to try to find out if the Shatners was murdered?" Elmer asked Clint.

"That's right," Clint confirmed. "If they were murdered, I plan to find out and watch the bastard or bastards stand trial. And I don't care if they turn out to be Indian or white, I'll make sure I get to see the varmints swinging at the end of a rope."

"Never cared much for hangings myself," Luke commented. "Makes me uncomfortable just thinkin' about 'em."

"I wonder why," Clint said dryly.

"But you said you had *two* reasons for stayin' in Waco," Luke reminded him.

"Could be that pretty little Navaho gal who tends the bar here," Elmer mused with a sly grin. "She seems to have a real yearnin' for Adams."

"I wouldn't never fuck no redskin," Mel stated, scratching his armpit. "Injuns is disgustin'."

"I'm sure they speak highly of you, too," Clint muttered.

"Is the woman the reason, Adams?" Luke asked.

"I'm not telling you any details about my personal life," the Gunsmith answered. "But I'll tell you why I've got a personal interest in Tom's house and property. You see, I own it now."

"What?" Elmer glared at Clint. "*You* own it?"

"That's right," Clint confirmed. "Tom left it to me in his will. How about that, boys? I'm a homeowner."

"Yeah," Luke said, slowly drawing on his cigarette. "Well, what do you plan to do with that place?"

"Reckon I'll live there," Clint shrugged. "What else would I do with a house?"

"Well, congratulations," Luke sighed. "Hope you got better luck than the former owner. Just take care, Adams. If'n you're right 'bout a killer bein' after that property, you could be next on his list."

"I'm not an easy target, fella," the Gunsmith declared. "And anytime the killer wants to try me, that'll be just fine with me."

ELEVEN

Luke, Elmer, and Mel finished their pitcher of beer and shuffled out of the cantina. Mary Spotted Fawn opened the door to the storage room and emerged with a big revolver in her fist. The Gunsmith smiled as he placed an empty mug on the bar.

"You don't have to threaten me with a gun," he said. "Don't worry, I'll pay for the beer."

"I had this ready in case those drifters started any trouble," Mary explained. "I don't like the way they look."

"Can't say as I care much for the way they smell," Clint added.

"I was listening at the keyhole," Mary admitted, placing the gun on a shelf under the counter. "Do you really own the Shatner house now?"

"That's what Constable Puma says," the Gunsmith replied. "He didn't seem too happy when he told me so I don't figure he was joking about it."

"You can't stay there, Clint," she told him. "Hasn't what happened to your friend been bad enough?"

"So you believe in the *chindi*, too?" the Gunsmith asked.

"You know about the sightings of a wolf witch," Mary remarked. "And I imagine you just dismiss it as nonsense?"

"Tom and his wife are dead," Clint said. "That isn't nonsense. Unless I'm wrong, it's murder. Before I leave Waco, I have to know for sure. Those three yahoos who just left might be responsible. Or it could be somebody else, but I want Tom's killer period.''

"If you evoke the anger of a *chindi*," Mary began, "no gun or knife can protect you. You can't kill a *chindi*, Clint. It is a spirit that protects the souls of the dead. You are challenging a force with powers you cannot begin to understand.''

"If there is a *chindi* running around Fox County," Clint began, "he's a feller with a clever bag of tricks and maybe a wolf costume. But he's just a man. He'll bleed and die just like any other if I pump a slug in his chest.''

"How can you be sure?'' the Navaho woman demanded. "You think because the *chindi* is not part of your white science this means it does not exist?''

"There are many suspicious things going on, Mary,'' Clint answered. "But I don't reckon any of them are supernatural.''

"You don't realize what you're pitting yourself against,'' Mary said, shaking her head sadly. "You are inviting death, Clint.''

Constable Puma appeared at the threshold. He looked as if he wished he hadn't found the Gunsmith. Puma sighed and jerked his head toward the street.

"The town council is ready to see you now,'' he announced.

"Let's go,'' Clint replied. He turned to Mary. "See you later.''

"I hope so,'' she told him. "And I hope you'll think about what I said, Clint.''

"I will,'' Clint assured her.

He followed Puma outside. The constable led him across the street to the church. The church was actually a logical place to meet since it had a large, quiet room with pews for seating. Naturally, Father McCoy was a member of the council. Clint recognized everyone inside the building from the wedding, but the priest was the only person he knew by name.

"Clint Adams," Puma began introductions, "this is Walter Sun Tree, the mayor of Waco, and George Standing Elk, our chairman."

"Good afternoon, gentlemen," Clint told them.

"Don't take our titles too seriously, Mr. Adams," Sun Tree urged. He was a short, portly man with long black hair streaked with gray. "Most of the time I just operate the general store and George owns the livery and a tannery. We're not politicians, just citizens with titles."

"Sounds fine to me," the Gunsmith assured them. "Now, what do you gentlemen want to talk to me about? I reckon it has something to do with Tom and Ellie's death and the way I've been poking around trying to determine how they got killed."

"Actually," the mayor began, "it concerns the Shatner house."

"Which is now my house," the Gunsmith reminded him.

"We're aware of that," Father McCoy said grimly.

"Mr. Adams," said George Standing Elk, a tall, painfully thin Navaho with weary eyes, which seemed ten years older than the rest of his body. "Let's not beat about the bush. The town treasury doesn't have much money. Waco isn't exactly San Francisco. However, we are prepared to pay you two hundred dollars for your new property."

"That's a pretty generous offer," Clint replied. "Why do you want the place so badly?"

"You're aware that most people in this county believe that land is an ancient burial ground," Sun Tree began. "They're distressed about Shatner's house being on top of an alleged graveyard."

"The Navaho believe 'rest in peace' is more than a motto for a headstone," Father McCoy said. "Disturbing the dead is a terrible sin to these people."

"And they believe there will be a terrible price to pay for this violation," Puma added. "Naturally, after what happened to Tom and Ellie, folks tend to believe this is evidence of spirits fighting back. Of course, you already know about this.''

"And the stories of the *chindi*," the Gunsmith nodded.

"That's part of our problem, Mr. Adams," the mayor admitted. "Rumors of a supernatural avenger have terrified our people. Frightened people can be dangerous. We're offering to buy your property for the sake of your safety as well as for the well-being of our citizens."

"I appreciate that," Clint replied. "But what about the deaths of Tom and Ellie? I don't believe a mountain lion killed them. I think the situation is suspicious enough to at least consider the possibility of murder."

"Really, Mr. Adams," the priest sighed. "It is true that many people objected to Tom Shatner living in that area, but I know these people. They're not killers. They're good, decent people."

"I'm sure they are," Clint agreed. "But the Navaho are people and people are pretty much the same regardless of the color of their skin or culture. There's bound to be a couple folks who would be willing to commit murder if they thought a situation justified their actions."

"I know these people," Father McCoy insisted.

"You don't know those three drifters who rode into town yesterday," the Gunsmith stated. "Maybe they did it."

"Shit, Adams," Puma snorted. "Beg your pardon, Father. Look, Adams, why would those drifters want to kill your friend and his wife?"

"I don't know," the Gunsmith confessed. "But they seemed mighty interested in Tom's property. Are you fellas sure the legend about an old burial ground wasn't started to keep folks away from that area for a different reason?"

"What do you mean?" the mayor asked.

"Well," Clint began, "maybe some outlaws robbed a train or a stagecoach or whatever. They were forced to run and for some reason or other buried their loot somewhere in this area. Could be they started that burial ground legend to keep folks away until they could get back for it.''

"Why *didn't* they come back for it?'' Puma asked.

"Maybe they have,'' Clint replied. "Those three drifters don't strike me as traveling preachers. I wouldn't be a bit surprised if they recently got outta jail after serving a few years for armed robbery.''

"What a vivid imagination you have, Adams,'' Puma sighed. "You oughta be writing dime novels.''

"Truth can be stranger than fiction,'' the Gunsmith insisted. "And don't tell me it's so far-fetched. I've known of stranger things happening for real.''

"You've got a fascinating theory,'' the mayor admitted. "But it doesn't hold up. You see, the Old One remembers the legend from long ago. It started before your people fought the Revolution against the British. It is a very old legend.''

"Who is the Old One?'' Clint asked.

"He's the last of the old Navaho who lived here before this town was built,'' George Standing Elk explained. "Some say he's a hundred years old, and he must really be close to that age.''

"Interesting,'' Clint mused. "And he confirms that this legend is more than a hundred years old?''

"That's right,'' George Standing Elk said. "We don't know if the legend is true or not, but we don't want to upset the population of Waco anymore than they already are.''

"Mr. Adams,'' Father McCoy began, "I understand you are a drifter, a traveling gunsmith of some sort. You have no need of Tom Shatner's house. I'm sure you don't intend to take up farming and settle down in Waco. Why not sell the house?''

"I'm sorry, gentlemen,'' the Gunsmith replied, "I'm going to keep the house . . . at least, for now.''

"I was afraid you'd say that,'' the mayor sighed. "And I assume you intend to live there as well?''

"Naturally,'' Clint nodded.

"Uh-huh,'' Puma grunted. "You figure somebody murdered your friend so you're going to move into that house and wait for him to come after you, right?''

''Something like that,'' the Gunsmith answered.

''All right,'' Puma began. ''Let's assume for a minute that you're right. Shatner wasn't killed by a mountain lion and somebody killed him because he was living on that property. Tom Shatner was a former lawman and, according to you, he knew how to take care of himself. How do you know this killer won't murder you, too?''

''Tom didn't have any reason to expect trouble,'' the Gunsmith explained, ''but I'll be ready for it. If the killer tries to take me on, I'll try to get him first.''

''If, indeed, the killer is human,'' George Standing Elk said dryly. ''If it isn't, then your guns will be useless against a real *chindi*, Mr. Adams.''

TWELVE

"Home, sweet home," the Gunsmith muttered as he approached the simple adobe house.

Tom Shatner hadn't wasted time or effort making the dwelling a thing of beauty. It was a story high with a tar-patched roof and a single wooden door. The window frames were also made of wood and held glass panes in place. Crude linen curtains hung in the windows. Duke hesitated slightly as Clint urged him forward.

"Come on, big fella," the Gunsmith said. "I've heard enough ghost stories for one day. Don't you start getting scared of spooks, too."

The horse seemed to snort with dismay, but he trotted on toward the house that now belonged to Clint Adams. The Gunsmith glanced down at the ground and noticed a hole. He pulled back the reins to bring Duke to a halt and swung down from the saddle.

"What the hell is this?" he wondered aloud, kneeling by the hole for a better look.

The hole had not been dug by a foraging animal. The interior had been smoothly cut by a shovel blade. The pit was about four feet deep. Judging from the lack of erosion around the rim, Clint figured the hole was pretty recent. Probably dug less than a week ago. Maybe only a day or two.

"Must be an irrigation ditch," Clint said. "But I always thought those were longer. Hell, what do I know about farming? Could be a hole for a fence post or maybe Tom was digging a well.''

The Gunsmith took Duke's reins and led the animal to the house. Like most people who become attached to animals, Clint talked to his horse as one might talk to a trusted friend.

''That hole's probably nothing,'' he told Duke. ''But how do I know if those fellas back in Waco told me the truth about the Indian legend and the burial ground?''

Duke snorted sourly.

''I know,'' Clint sighed. ''You weren't there, but I told you about it on our way over here, remember? Anyway, could be some bandits buried something valuable here. If that's true, who dug that hole? Tom or somebody else? After all, I knew Tom Shatner a long time ago. Didn't really know him that well either. How do I know if he turned hootowl or not?''

Duke shook his head and whinnied.

''No,'' Clint sighed, ''I don't believe it either. Tom wasn't that type. Never was very greedy or ambitious. Settling down on a farm was sort of predictable for him. Had to happen sooner or later. Too bad it happened here and somebody killed him. Somebody or *something*.''

Duke blew air through his lips as if uttering disgust.

''Hell, no,'' Clint said sharply, ''I'm not beginning to believe in a *chindi*. I mean, it's possible—not probable—that Tom was killed by a mountain lion. I'm not much of a tracker, but let's see if we can find any footprints, or pawprints. Indians are generally pretty good at reading sign, but I figure Harry Two-Ponies had already figured it was the work of a *chindi*, so he wouldn't hang around here long enough to check for tracks. Constable Puma has been raised as a white man or at least trained by their schools. Doubt that he's as good at reading sign as I am.''

Duke snorted again.

''Hey,'' Clint protested, ''I'm not *that* bad, damn it. Anyway, man or animal, it must have left some sort of tracks.

If we don't find anything, then I'll start to consider the
possibility a ghost killed Tom and Ellie.''

The sun was slowly descending toward the horizon. Soon
it would be twilight. Clint realized even a superb tracker has
great difficulty trying to read sign after dark. However,
tracking is a science which requires time and experience.
He'd have a better chance of success covering a small area
carefully rather than trying to cover a lot of ground in a hurry.

Clint found a number of bootprints. The wind hadn't
blown much sand in the tracks so Clint figured they must be
pretty recent. Two or three days. He remembered a trick
taught to him by an old tracker years ago. Clint examined one
of his own bootprints and compared it with the tracks. The
size of the track and the depth of the indentation, compared to
his own prints, would give the Gunsmith a general idea about
the size and weight of the person who made the old tracks.

''Got two sets of prints,'' the Gunsmith told Duke. ''One
appears to be made by a fella who had a bigger foot than mine
and probably weighed more than thirty pounds more than I
do. Figure Tom made those tracks. The other set appear to be
made by somebody smaller and lighter. Reckon that'd be
Constable Puma. No earth-shaking news so far. Let's keep
looking.''

Clint found a set of prints that appeared to have been made
by a heavy man with small feet clad in moccasins. Probably
Harry Two-Ponies. Then he encountered an odd set of tracks.
They were partly trampled on by other prints, but Clint could
make out a wide indentation and four round marks similar to
claw prints.

''Jesus,'' the Gunsmith whispered, ''if that's a cougar
track, then it must belong to the granddaddy of all mountain
lions.''

He moved farther from the house and looked for more
tracks. He found one of the odd clawlike prints. It was wide
and slightly rounded with four talon marks at one end and a
slight indentation at the other. Clint frowned. The track
looked similar to the pawprint of a large predatory animal,

such as a big cat or an enormous wolf. But it was unlike any animal track he'd seen before.

"They said the *chindi* possesses animals and makes them walk upright like men," Clint recalled, wishing he hadn't been told the legend. "Get a hold of yourself. There's got to be another explanation."

Twilight began to set. The Gunsmith would have to continue trying to read sign in the morning. He took Duke to the small barn behind the house. There was a buckboard inside, but all the stalls were empty. Apparently, Tom Shatner's horses had already been taken into Waco. That was fine with the Gunsmith. He made certain Duke was well fed and watered before covering the animal with a blanket and heading back to the house.

He was surprised to notice another hole between the house and the barn. It appeared to be identical to the one he found before. Two feet wide and about four feet deep. This was beginning to look like a pattern, but the Gunsmith had no idea what it might be.

Clint entered the house and struck a match. He located a kerosene lamp on the kitchen table and began to examine the house he had inherited. The interior of the adobe structure consisted of whitewashed walls and plank floors. The furniture was simple and sturdy. The kitchen included an oven and a small water pump. Clint moved to the next room. It was practically bare except for a large bed and a chest of drawers.

"So this was going to be your castle, Tom," Clint whispered. "But it turned out to be your tomb instead."

He hated to rummage through his dead friend's possessions, but he wanted to see if anything offered clues as to Tom's death. Perhaps someone had killed Shatner because of an old grudge and imitated the *chindi* simply because it was a good cover under the circumstances. Clint found some clothes, mostly Ellie's, and some china, which never got unpacked. He found a few personal letters and none that suggested anyone would have a reason to kill Tom Shatner.

What about Ellie? The Gunsmith wondered. He knew

absolutely nothing about Tom's bride. Maybe she had an old enemy for some reason. Clint couldn't ignore any possibility. He checked through the woman's personal belongings. To his surprise, Clint found a bundle of love letters Shatner had written to the woman. She had obviously kept these for sentimental reasons. Clint felt like an intruder as he read over these intimate messages. He was touched by Tom's tenderness in the letters and surprised by his late friend's flowery style.

The letters told Clint more about Ellie. They revealed a sensitive, gentle woman whom Tom Shatner had loved very dearly. They could have been very happy together, he thought. But someone murdered the couple and Clint still didn't know why. Instead of finding answers, it seemed every time he looked into something connected with the slayings, Clint only found more questions.

"You're getting rattled, Adams," the Gunsmith told himself. "There are really only two questions you have to answer. Why and Who. Probably won't be able to figure out the latter until you find out about the former."

The Gunsmith decided to start over in the morning. He hung his gunbelt over the headboard of the bed, pulled off his boots, and stretched out on the mattress. Soon Clint drifted into a shallow sleep. His body automatically prevented him from falling into a deep slumber. Years of living with threats and danger had honed his reflexes and trained his senses to operate according to his environment. When threatened with danger, he would sleep with his senses alert to any sounds, vibrations, or odors that might be suspicious.

He slept for perhaps three hours before something made his muscles twitch instinctively. The reaction wasn't enough to wake the Gunsmith, but his sleep reached a shallower level. The sound of something striking earth outside his windows made Clint's eyes pop open.

He lay on his back, body motionless, as he allowed his eyes to adjust to the shadows that filled the room. He listened intensely for any telltale sound that might betray an opponent lurking outside the house. The Gunsmith's heart began to race with anticipation and he breathed deeply to control his nerves. He slowly looked around until his eyes found the window.

A face stared back at him. Two dark eyes gazed down a long snout. The creature's ears were raised and pointed. Its jaws were open, revealing sharp white teeth. The Gunsmith gasped, and he instantly reached for his double-action gun as a terrible ghostly moan echoed from outside, followed by a howl.

Clint snatched his modified Colt from its holster and swung the muzzle toward the window. He triggered two shots, the reports tumbling together so rapidly they blended into a single roar. Glass exploded from the window and the leering face vanished.

The Gunsmith leaped from his bed, pistol held ready. The thunder of hooves came from somewhere outside. Clint rushed barefoot to the door. He opened it and cautiously moved outside. The Gunsmith moved along the side of the house toward the bedroom window. A long, dark object lay on the ground beneath the window. It was covered with gray fur. Whatever it was, it wasn't moving.

The sound of the hooves became more distant. Clint ventured beyond the house and carefully scanned the horizon, still watchful of possible opponents who might be lurking on his property.

In the distance, a circlet of yellow light bobbed in the night. Northwest, the Gunsmith realized, heading toward Waco. The light seemed like a ghostly blob, but the Gunsmith assumed it was a lantern carried by the horseman who had hastily galloped away. Whoever the caller was, he had already ridden at least a mile from Clint's property. Trying to follow the mysterious rider would be stupid. Clint couldn't saddle up Duke and easily pursue the visitor in the dark. The rider would certainly see Clint coming after him. Then he could simply lie in wait in the darkness while Clint rode straight into whatever sort of ambush the bastard set up.

"Maybe next time, asshole," the Gunsmith growled as he approached the object at the window.

It was a coyote pelt with the head still attached. The dead animal had been propped on a wood pole, the sharp end of which had been driven into the ground at Clint's bedroom window. The coyote's head was smashed to bits. Two .45 caliber bullets can have that effect on flesh and bone—alive or dead.

"A calling card," Clint mused as he gathered up the coyote pelt, "from the *chindi*."

THIRTEEN

Without further incident the Gunsmith slept until dawn. He awoke to the sound of someone timidly rapping on the door. Still fully dressed, Clint rolled out of bed and drew his Colt before padding barefoot to the door. He cautiously opened it, aware that a wily opponent might change tactics, hoping to catch him off guard in the daylight.

A pretty, round face with dark brown eyes smiled up at him. Rachel, Harry Two-Ponies's daughter, had decided to pay the new neighbor a visit. Clint opened the door wide and leaned against the jamb, his modified Colt still in his fist.

"What are you doing here?" he asked, obviously annoyed.

"I thought you'd be glad to see me," Rachel said.

"I've already gotten on bad terms with your father and I don't need more trouble from him," the Gunsmith told her. "And I'm sure he'd be mad as hell if he knew you were here."

"My father is a bastard," Rachel said with a shrug.

"You shouldn't talk that way about your father," Clint replied. "It's disrespectful.

"You don't respect him," Rachel stated. "You beat him up when he slapped me. That old bastard is always beatin' up on me and Ma. It felt good to see him get some lumps for a change."

"I lost my temper," Clint confessed. "I'm not sure

whether I did the right thing or not, but I didn't like the way he treated you.''

"Then how do you feel about this?'' she asked, brushing back one of her braids to reveal a purple bruise on her left cheek.

"Jesus,'' Clint rasped, "does he do that sort of thing very often?''

"It's his favorite pastime,'' Rachel said bitterly. "Look at this.''

She suddenly slipped her buckskin dress up over her head. The motion was so quick, Clint was startled to find the young woman suddenly naked before his eyes. Her body was beautiful, young and firm with the smooth skin of youth and the glow of life not yet marred by years. However, her lovely flesh had suffered other punishments. Numerous angry red and purple bruises diminished her beauty. Clint's guts knotted when he saw how strap and fists had been used violently on her breasts and abdomen.

Rachel turned slowly and showed Clint her back and buttocks. These were marked by angry welts, tattoos of pain inflicted by her cruel father. Clint didn't know how to handle this situation.

"I'm running away from home, Mr. Adams,'' she announced, still naked, her buckskin dress clenched in a fist. "I'm nineteen years old. I should've been married years ago, but I'm never gonna find a husband as long as that bastard father of mine keeps me on the farm and treats me like a slave.''

"Look, Rachel,'' Clint began. "I'm not going to advise you to run away from home or tell you to go back to a father who mistreats you. The decision is yours.''

"I've already made it, Mr. Adams.''

"Call me Clint,'' the Gunsmith told her. "And I think you'd better put your clothes on, Rachel.''

"Oh,'' she said sadly, "the scars disgust you.''

"That's not it,'' Clint smiled. "You're a beautiful young woman and I'm only human, a man with all the natural impulses toward pretty ladies. So I think you'd best get dressed."

"Impulses?" she smiled. "Does that mean you'd like to make love to me?"

"Hold on, Rachel," Clint began, "I know you're in a hurry to get married and move out of this county, but I'm not."

"I don't want to marry you," Rachel replied with amusement. "You're too old. You're at least thirty or thirty-five."

"Yeah," he said dryly. "Actually I'm an ancient wreck older than forty . . . and never mind how much older."

"Forty!" she stared at him as if he had just confessed to being a hundred and ten. "God, that is old. Why, you'd probably die before I reached thirty."

"Probably," the Gunsmith agreed with a sigh.

"Well, you certainly don't look *forty,*" Rachel assured him. "In fact, you're very nice looking."

"Thanks," Clint shrugged. "We old fellas appreciate a kind word from time to time."

"I've got a pony outside with some supplies wrapped in a bedroll," Rachel explained. "But before I ride on and leave Fox County, I want to make love to you."

"Huh?" he stared at her. "Aren't you afraid of getting cobwebs from my ancient body?"

"You're not that old yet," she laughed. "I figure you'd be a gentle, but passionate lover."

She stepped closer and stroked her fingertips over the bulge at his crotch. "And I'd do my best to satisfy your needs, Clint."

"I'm sure you'll do a right fine job, Rachel," the Gunsmith agreed.

He drew Rachel close, pressing his mouth to hers. The young woman kissed him with fierce desire, darting her tongue into his mouth. Clint savored the kiss, his hands gradually sliding across her bare flesh. He fondled her breasts, feeling the nipples harden under his skillful touch. His lips moved to her neck, kissing and licking her from the nerve under her jaw to the base of her throat.

The woman eagerly fumbled with the buttons to his trousers, hastily trying to open his pants to free his aroused organ, which strained the cloth at the crotch. Clint led her to the bedroom and slid the Colt revolver into the gunbelt, which still hung at the head of the bed.

"Do you have to have that thing hangin' there while we make love?" Rachel asked, staring at the gunbelt with dismay. "It makes me nervous, Clint."

"Sorry," the Gunsmith replied, "but I'd get too nervous to concentrate on what we were doing if I didn't have that pistol handy. After all, two people were killed here a couple nights ago and the killer is still at large."

"I was trying not to think about that," Rachel stated.

"No need for you to worry about it," Clint assured her. "So long as I've got my gun within easy reach while we're making love."

He stripped off his clothes. Rachel examined his body with frank admiration and smiled with approval. They moved to the bed and climbed onto the mattress. Their mouths and hands eagerly explored each other's bodies, kissing, stroking, and fondling. The young woman gently took Clint's penis in her hands and worked her fingers up and down the length of his taut organ. Clint cupped her breasts in his hands and tenderly kissed them, sucking the firm nipples, slowly nibbling the rigid tips.

Rachel spread her legs, inviting Clint's entry. He readily accepted and lowered himself into position. She eagerly gripped his member and steered it to the center of her womanhood. Her boldness suggested Rachel was not a virgin, but the Gunsmith was not bothered by this. Experience in anything hones one's natural talents.

The Gunsmith slid into the warmth of Rachel's womb. Clint gradually worked himself deeper, allowing Rachel to set the pace. The young woman responded immediately, pumping her loins rapidly. Clint thrust quickly, driving himself inside her again and again. His lunges increased in tempo, and he drove deeper and harder as he heard her gasp with joy.

At last she cried out and sank her teeth into his shoulder, biting with painful force. The Gunsmith grunted and kept thrusting until Rachel convulsed in a primitive spasm of utter pleasure. Clint eased his passionate lunges and slowly repeated what was his tender foreplay. His cock was strained to the limit as he thrust once more, but the Gunsmith restrained his desire for sexual release. His manhood drove faster and harder until Rachel cried out. A second orgasm sent her into a trembling fury. Only then did the Gunsmith allow himself release inside the young beauty's cavern of love.

"My God, Clint," Rachel gasped breathlessly.

"Not so bad for an old fella?" he chuckled.

"Not bad at all," she confirmed.

"You didn't do bad," he told her, "for a youngster."

"Let's do it again," Rachel invited. "And we'll see who tires first."

The contest eventually ended in a stalemate.

FOURTEEN

Rachel left, riding her pony to the north. The Gunsmith didn't know where she was going or what she intended to do when she got there, and he did not want to know. The young woman could look after herself and Clint didn't want to get involved with any decisions she made after leaving his house that morning. Rachel would remain a pleasant memory. For the Gunsmith, that was enough.

He gathered up the coyote pelt and rode to Waco. It took awhile to find the constable's office, but Clint finally located it among the adobe structures. He found Charlie Puma seated behind a large oak desk. The Navaho lawman looked up at the Gunsmith with surprise when Clint entered with an animal pelt draped over his shoulder.

"Is something wrong, Adams?" Puma inquired.

"I've got a broken window at home," Clint explained, tossing the skin on the floor. "Shot the glass out when I fired two rounds at this thing."

"I see," Puma remarked, examining the coyote's bullet-shattered skull. "Aren't two slugs through the head overkill—especially when the animal is already dead?"

"Funny," the Gunsmith said dryly, "but I wasn't very amused when I woke up last night and saw this thing staring through the window at me. I would have shot the son of a bitch who propped that coyote up by my window if I could have gotten a clear target."

"Shooting a trespasser would be legal, Adams," the constable shrugged. "Next time bring me the trespasser's pelt instead of this sort of thing."

"Well, excuse me for taking up your valuable time," Clint snorted. "Just thought you'd like to know that somebody tried to scare me off my property last night. So long as we're wasting time talking about this, you might like to know whoever did it rode away on horseback, carrying a lantern. 'Twasn't a supernatural spirit which possessed an animal. It was a man."

"I've made a mental note of that fact," Puma assured him. "But what do you want me to do about it? We tried to buy your property. You refused to sell. Of course, the offer is still available."

"Are you fellas really just concerned with not upsetting the citizens of Waco?" the Gunsmith inquired. "Or is there another reason you want that land?"

"What is that supposed to mean?" the constable demanded.

"Maybe you know more about that property than you're telling me," Clint replied. "Maybe you've told the townsfolk that the land is an ancient burial ground in order to scare them away from the area."

"Damn it, Adams!" Puma snapped, jumping up from behind his desk. "You've no right to come in here and make accusations. Who the hell asked you to come to Waco in the first place?"

"Tom Shatner," the Gunsmith replied.

"But who asked you to stay?" the constable asked, already aware of the answer. "I know, I know. Tom Shatner. He left you his damn property."

"Constable," Clint began, "I'm not accusing you or the town council of anything . . . not yet, anyway. But I have to consider every possibility. I'm convinced Tom and Ellie were murdered and this coyote pelt . . ."

"Is not evidence of murder, Adams," Puma said, pointing at the pelt. "It proves somebody wants you to leave. Next time they may not be so gentle. Maybe they'll shoot your horse or toss kerosene through a window."

"Then there'll be a dead . . . what did you call it? Vandal?"

"That's your right, Adams," Puma nodded. "But there's a pretty good chance you might not be killing the man who murdered Tom Shatner. Mind you, I'm not saying anyone *did* murder him. You might just wind up shooting some poor Navaho who is terrified of the *chindi.*"

"Oh," Clint raised his eyebrows, "a poor innocent soul who might kill my horse or try to burn me alive?"

"A frightened person, Adams," Puma stated, coming around from behind his desk. "Frightened people are dangerous, Adams. This *chindi* business isn't just a bullshit story to the Navaho. They take it very seriously. They don't have the benefit of a white man's school. They believe in ghosts and spirits, and to them, these supernatural threats are as real as yellow fever or black plague is to us. Of course, maybe you consider Indians less than human anyway."

"Don't accuse me of being a bigot," Clint insisted. "When somebody threatens your life or property, you don't give a damn what color he is. You kill the bastard whether he's white, black, Indian, or polka-dotted."

"So far the only threat you've received is this flea-bitten coyote hide," Puma declared, gathering up the pelt and tossing it back at the Gunsmith. "Now, ask yourself if this is enough reason to kill somebody."

"We'll have to talk again, Constable," Clint remarked. "This is the most fun I've had since I found a rattlesnake in my bedroll."

"Maybe you should check your bed carefully, Adams," Puma smiled. "According to legend, the *chindi* can possess reptiles as well as wolves and mountain lions."

"Yeah," Clint agreed, "and if I died accidentally from a sidewinder's bite or a scorpion sting, it would be another case of natural causes. The Navaho who believe in the *chindi* would assume I was killed by the avenging spirit, while you'd just write a report that I died from another unfriendly animal.''

''That would suit everybody,'' Puma said, ''now wouldn't it?''

''It sure as shit wouldn't make me very happy,'' the Gunsmith replied as he draped the coyote pelt over his shoulder and headed for the door.

FIFTEEN

Sofia Reyes frowned as she gazed down at the crushed head of the coyote pelt. The Gunsmith rolled up the animal hide, covering the bullet-wrecked cranium with the fur. The Mexican beauty leaned against the desk in her office and looked at Clint Adams as one might examine a two-headed calf.

"This is certainly a grim gift your night visitor left you, Mr. Adams," she remarked. "But I don't see how I can help you."

"This may or may not have been left by the man who murdered Tom and Ellie Shatner," Clint explained. "Maybe it's just a frightened Indian trying to scare me off the Shatner spread, but I'm going to assume it's the *chindi* until I know for sure."

"The *chindi?*" Sofia smiled. "That's an odd thing for a white man to say. You don't honestly believe in Navaho wolf witches, Mr. Adams?"

"What matters is the Navaho believe in them, Dr. Reyes," the Gunsmith answered. "And please, call me Clint."

"Of course." The doctor's smile broadened. "If you'll call me Sofia."

"A pleasure," he assured her.

"But I don't think I can help you," Sofia sighed. "Tom and Ellie were killed by a mountain lion . . . or a large beast very similar to one."

"How can you be sure?" Clint asked. "I realize the bodies had been clawed and mutilated, but were there any teeth marks?"

"Teeth marks?" Sofia frowned.

"Sure," Clint nodded. "Look, predators are carnivorous. They kill to eat meat. If a mountain lion or a large bear killed Tom and Ellie, there would be bite marks as well as claw marks. Wolf claws aren't used much as weapons. If a big, rabid wolf happened to wander into Tom's farm and killed them, there should be plenty of bites and only a few claw marks."

"Well," Sofia began, "there were bite marks, of course, but death was caused by ripping out arteries, veins, and trachea. The killer was almost certainly a big cat, Clint. Didn't Constable Puma tell you about the animal tracks he found around the Shatner house?"

"No," Clint muttered. "He failed to share that information with me, but he and I have butted heads lately. Doesn't matter, though, because I found the tracks myself."

"Then why do you question whether or not the killings were committed by an animal?"

"Because the prints don't look right," Clint explained. "They're distorted, too large for a mountain lion unless he's a giant monster of a cat or has deformed feet. At the same time, the prints are too perfect."

"Now, I really am confused," Sofia admitted.

"Every print I found had exactly four round claw marks," the Gunsmith answered. "But both cats and bears step into their own footprints. When their front paws move forward, their hind legs walk right into the tracks they just made. Most of the time they only make two prints instead of four."

"So?" she shrugged.

"So stepping into their own tracks means prints should have irregular patterns," Clint explained. "Besides, cats have retractable claws. They don't extend their nails unless they have a reason. In other words, those are *not* the tracks of a mountain lion."

"Fascinating theory, Clint," Sofia mused. "So you're saying the beast walked on its hind legs, like a man, and extended its claws so its tracks would be obvious. That sounds like you're talking about a *chindi*. Don't mention this to the Navaho or we'll have a real panic on our hands."

"Not a *chindi*," Clint corrected, "a man impersonating a *chindi*."

"But the bite marks?" she reminded him.

"Maybe he used some sort of contraption with pointed metal or real wolf teeth that snapped shut on victims after he killed them with false animal claws," Clint replied. "May I examine the bodies? I'd like to see if they were really bitten. I mean, a real cat or bear would have ripped out chunks of flesh and muscle and eaten it."

"And you *want* to see that?" Sofia frowned.

"Poor choice of words," Clint admitted. "Let's say I *have* to find out."

"The bodies were buried, Clint," Sofia answered. "And I don't advise you to dig them up. The Navaho would have a fit. They're already upset enough about you living on property they believe is a burial site."

"Well," the Gunsmith began, "you examined the bodies. Would you say they had been partly devoured?"

"No," she admitted. "It didn't appear that they had been eaten. Simply killed."

"Do you still think it's impossible that the killer might be a human murderer disguised as a *chindi?*" Clint inquired.

"I still think the killer was probably a big cat or some other sort of animal," Sofia insisted, "but I think you've got ample reason to doubt."

"Thank you for that much," the Gunsmith said. "And I

want to apologize for taking up so much of your time.''

''You can see how busy I am,'' Sofia laughed. ''I'm afraid the town of Waco is not terribly eager to give a tremendous amount of business to a woman doctor. Especially one who is not really a doctor.''

''How did you happen to get into this line of work?'' Clint inquired.

''My father was a doctor,'' Sofia sighed. ''He had a very lucrative business with wealthy clients. We lived very well in Mexico until the revolution. Then, when Juarez took power, we were forced to flee. My father had been part of the old regime and that was not good. So we moved to the United States. Fortunately, he taught us English. It was a second language for us.''

''I noticed that your English is flawless,'' Clint remarked. ''Tell me, did your father manage to get as lucrative a practice in America as he had in Mexico?''

''No,'' Sofia admitted, ''we lived rather poorly here. After he died, Luis and I had to fend for ourselves. He learned to make a living as a blacksmith and I . . . well, I'd read my father's textbooks since childhood. I had assisted him with countless patients and numerous operations. Medicine is what I know best. Ridiculous as it may seem, I wanted to be a doctor. Thus, my brother and I wound up here in Waco.''

''I'm surprised you haven't gotten married,'' the Gunsmith commented. ''You're a beautiful woman, charming and intelligent. Why haven't you married?''

''Why haven't you?'' she replied. ''Or perhaps you have.''

''No,'' the Gunsmith answered. ''Came close once, but it didn't work out.''

''Let's just say my story is much the same,'' Sofia said. ''Tell me, Clint, when you have conversation at dinner, you don't talk about murder and wild animals devouring dead victims, do you?''

"No," he smiled. "And I'd be delighted to have dinner with you, Sofia."

"I'm so glad," the woman replied. "I was afraid you'd never ask."

SIXTEEN

The Gunsmith rode Duke back to his newly acquired property. His trip to town had been largely a waste of time, but at least he'd informed the constable about the night caller and he'd confirmed enough information to convince him that Tom and Ellie Shatner had not been killed by an animal. However, he still didn't know who the *chindi* was or why the Shatners had been murdered.

"Well, big fella," Clint told Duke, "we're not much closer to answering those big questions, are we?"

Duke snorted a negative reply.

"Yeah," the Gunsmith sighed, "but I don't know what to do next. Maybe the best thing is just to stay at home and hope the *chindi* comes after us."

Duke suddenly stopped and raised his head, ears twitching like a hunting dog. He uttered a deep-throated sound of consternation. Clint had long ago learned to respect the big gelding's warnings. Duke sensed danger and was seldom wrong about such things.

"Easy, big fella," Clint assured his horse, patting Duke's glossy black coat. "We'll move in slow and easy. There isn't much cover between here and the house, so be ready to move if we have to."

The Gunsmith drew his carbine from its saddle boot and jacked a shell into the breech. He gently drummed his heels against Duke's ribs, urging the horse forward. They slowly approached the farmhouse. Clint clearly saw two horses tied to the rail at the front of the house and two men busy digging a hole nearby. One man, painfully thin, wielded a pick which had a shaft as big as his waist. The other man was fat and shoveled out dirt at a steady pace.

"I'll be a son of a bitch," Clint muttered, certain he recognized Luke and Elmer. That meant Mel was probably nearby as well.

The harsh report of a rifle confirmed this suspicion. Clint barely glimpsed the orange flash of a weapon fired from the rear of the house. He was too busy diving from Duke's back. The Gunsmith held onto the animal's neck and turned the head slightly. Duke responded as he'd been trained. The big gelding folded his legs and dropped to the ground, rolling on his side. Clint fell to his belly and aimed the carbine at the house.

Luke and Elmer, if indeed that's who they were, bolted to the horses tied at the front of the dwelling. They leaped into the saddles as another shot rang out from the back of the house. A bullet struck earth about a yard in front of the Gunsmith. Clint stayed down as clods of dirt spat into his face.

The Gunsmith glanced up to see three horsemen galloping away from his property. Clint aimed carefully, peering across the sights. The fat man was at the rear of the fleeing trio. Clint tried to aim for a limb. The front sight aligned with the fat man's right forearm as the Gunsmith began to squeeze the trigger.

The fat man moved his arm as Clint fired his weapon. The projectile narrowly missed the fat man and struck the flank of another rider's horse. The animal whinnied in pain and rose up on its hind legs. The rider cried out as he slipped from the back of his mount.

Clint couldn't see the man very well, but he did notice a long, unkempt beard. The wounded horse fell beside the man. Tugging on the reins of his mount, the fat man steered his animal in a full circle and fired a Winchester at the Gunsmith. The chubby fellow held the rifle in one hand and fired from a moving horse. Not surprisingly, the bullet he fired did not come close to Clint Adams. The Gunsmith heard the projectile as it cut through air and soared toward the clouds above.

The skinny horseman galloped toward the fallen fellow. He held a six-gun in his fist. For a moment, Clint thought the pistolman was going to shoot the bearded hootowl. From the way the shaggy man held up his arms in terror, he probably thought the same thing. However, the scrawny gunman's pistol popped two rounds, pumping both bullets into the head of the seriously disabled horse.

"A little mercy," Clint muttered, aiming his carbine at the fat man. "Reckon they're not all bad."

He triggered his rifle. The fat man convulsed in his saddle and dropped the Winchester. From a distance of nearly two hundred yards, Clint could see only a crimson dot form at the obese fellow's chest. He slumped against the neck of his horse and tumbled from the saddle to the ground.

The bearded man leaped onto the back of the fat man's horse. The wounded man cried out for help. His skinny companion showed him the same sort of mercy he displayed with the injured horse. He shot the fat man in the head.

"You're getting monotonous, Luke," Clint muttered, now certain of the identity of the trio.

He pumped the lever action of his weapon, ejecting the spent cartridge casing and jacking a fresh round into the breech. However, the scrawny gunman and his bearded partner had successfully galloped out of range before the Gunsmith could aim his carbine. Clint whistled at Duke. The gelding immediately climbed to his feet.

"Good work, big fella," Clint told his horse, swinging into the saddle. "Now, let's go see what those bastards were up to."

The Gunsmith galloped to the house and dismounted. He

ran to the hole which the two men had been digging. The shovel and pick had been abandoned. He peered into the pit, but saw nothing. Clint gathered up the shovel and poked it into the hole. He used the blade to feel the bottom, but there did not seem to be anything buried beneath.

"Nooo!" a voice screamed in horror. "Nooo!"

Clint raised his head and dropped the shovel, right hand automatically reaching for the modified Colt on his hip.

At the horizon, the Gunsmith saw a lone figure mounted on a stout pinto, which hardly seemed sturdy enough to support his bulk. Clint couldn't be sure, but he thought the rider might be Harry Two-Ponies. The Navaho farmer quickly yanked the reins to steer his horse away from Clint's property. Then he broke into a panicked gallop.

"Shit," the Gunsmith sighed. "Hell, I'll worry about him later."

Clint found two more fresh holes on his land. There was no evidence any of them led to anything hidden under the ground. The Gunsmith then mounted Duke and rode to the dead man and horse. He wasn't surprised to discover the corpse was Elmer. Part of his face was missing, but Clint still had little trouble recognizing the fat man.

He knelt beside the dead man and rummaged through Elmer's pockets. It was an unpleasant chore, but he hoped to find something to indicate why the trio had come to his property and started digging holes like a pack of prairie dogs. Clint found some coins, some spare .44 caliber ammunition and a couple of pieces of candy. However, there was nothing to tell Clint Elmer's last name, let alone why he and the others had come to his property.

The Gunsmith checked the saddlebags on the dead horse. These were loaded with the usual trail supplies. He found more ammunition, most of it shells for the rifle that was still in the saddle boot. But the bearded man, almost certainly Mel, hadn't left anything in the saddlebags to indicate the reason for their visit.

"This place is getting awful popular for some reason," the Gunsmith told Duke. "And I reckon we'd better find out why before we get ourselves killed."

The gelding snorted and bobbed his head as if in agreement.

SEVENTEEN

"I'm getting real tired of you, Adams," Constable Puma groaned when the Gunsmith entered his office.

"I'm getting pretty sick of riding back and forth from my house to Waco, Constable," Clint replied, "but I thought you might want to know I shot a fella on my property."

"What?" Puma glared at the Gunsmith. He bolted from his chair. "Was he a Navaho or a white man?"

"One of those three white drifters," Clint explained. "The fat man, Elmer. I put a bullet in his chest, but one of his friends shot him in the head to make certain he wouldn't talk."

"You mean all three were at your place?" Puma demanded.

"That's right," the Gunsmith confirmed. "And they were digging holes all over the place. Started shooting at me when I approached, so I had to shoot back. The other two got away. Don't know where they headed."

"I'll get my men and check their camp outside of town," Puma declared. "Maybe you'd better stay here. If they see you, they might panic. I don't want any gunplay if it can be avoided."

"I'd rather come along, Constable," Clint replied. "If there is any shooting, you might be glad to have me along."

"I think we can manage without you," Puma insisted, gathering up a double-barreled shotgun. "Why don't you go to the cantina and visit Mary. You and she seem to be pretty close. We'll come back and let you know how things turn out.''

''I doubt that they'll even come back to Waco,'' the Gunsmith sighed, ''but I reckon we'll find out.''

''*We'll* find out first,'' the constable snapped. ''I don't want you to come along with us, Adams. I don't want you shooting these men on sight or scaring them into going for their guns.''

''Look,'' Clint began, ''I want them alive, too. Damn it, Puma. I want some answers about what the hell is going on here.''

''Well,'' the constable began, ''for your sake, I hope we find those bastards.''

''What do you mean?'' Clint frowned.

''I mean Harry Two-Ponies rode into town and ran around here telling everybody who'd listen to him that you've been digging up the burial ground,'' Puma explained. ''He said he saw you shoveling dirt, disturbing the rest of the dead and all that crap.''

''Jesus,'' Clint groaned, ''that's not what happened.''

''I've got some bad news for you, white eyes,'' Puma said savagely. ''It's your word against his. He's a Navaho. Anywhere else that would mean folks would believe you and tell the damn redskin to go to hell, but not here.''

''Oh,'' Clint said, ''you've got a different form of bigotry here. You think it's any better?''

''Hell, Adams,'' Puma laughed, ''I'm a Navaho. Of course, I prefer it this way. That's another reason for you to head for the cantina. I want you off the street. If these folks see your face, they might just decide to lynch you, Adams.''

''All right,'' the Gunsmith agreed, ''we'll do it your way, for now.''

''You bet your white ass we'll do it my way,'' the constable told him.

''See you later,'' Clint said and shut up before he lost his temper and said something else.

Clint Adams left the constable's office and crossed the street to the cantina. He noticed a Navaho couple walking along the plankway. They stared at Clint and hurried away from him as if afraid he might be carrying the pox. The Gunsmith didn't try to reassure them. That would only make things worse. He kept going to the cantina and felt relieved when he opened the door and entered.

"Howdy, Adams," Luke declared, aiming a pistol at Clint as he stood behind the bar. "Hoped you'd show up."

Clint's hand reached for his gun, but a hard metal cylinder pressed into the base of his skull. The Gunsmith froze as the sinister click of a pistol hammer being cocked sang in his ear. Clint slowly moved his hands away from his sides.

"What did you do to Mary?" Clint demanded.

"She's right here, Adams," Luke announced as he reached under the bar and hauled up Mary Spotted Fawn by her hair. The woman's face contorted in pain. A ribbon of blood extended from her split lower lip to her chin.

"You bastards—" the Gunsmith snarled.

Luke rammed the muzzle of his pistol into the side of Mary's skull and thumbed back the hammer. "Take one more step and you both die."

A vicious blow to the back of Clint's head filled his skull with painful white-hot light. He fell to his knees as the room swirled around him. The door slammed, vibrations jarring Clint from toe to scalp. He shook his head to clear it. The hard muzzle of a revolver jabbed him painfully under the ear.

"Try somethin' and I'll blow your fuckin' head off!" a voice hissed through the throbbing thunder inside the Gunsmith's head.

He was aware of his Colt being pulled from its hip holster. Clint turned his head and stared up the trunk of Mel's unwashed body. The filthy hootowl smiled down at him and suddenly kicked the Gunsmith in the ribs. Clint tumbled over on his side, groaning in agony.

"Fuckin' bastard," Mel snorted, swinging a mud-caked

boot into Clint's stomach. He kicked Clint again as the Gunsmith jerked about on the floor, gasping in pain.

"That's enough, Mel," Luke ordered. "We want him to be able to talk."

Luke dragged Mary from behind the bar. Her hands were tied behind her back, and he pulled her by the hair to haul her forward. As the Gunsmith slowly got to his knees, Luke aimed his gun at Clint. His head still ached and his stomach felt as if he'd just survived a stampede. Gazing up at his tormentors, he tried to breathe.

"Okay, Adams," Luke began, "where is it?"

"What?" the Gunsmith replied, confused by the question.

Mel's boot lashed out, the heel slamming hard into Clint's cheek. He fell to the floor on his belly. Blackness swirled around him and he began to drift on the borderline of consciousness. He heard Luke's voice call through a tunnel of cotton far from his ear.

"You damn fool!" the outlaw leader snapped. "Don't knock him out, damn it. We gotta question this son of a bitch."

"Shit," Mel replied, "he ain't but dazed."

A sharp pain in his ribs told Clint that Mel was kicking him again. The Gunsmith grunted and slowly dragged himself to all fours. His face seemed to pulsate with pain and the right side of his face was numb. Luke sighed as he holstered his six-gun and drew a Bowie knife with a seven inch blade.

"I don't want to have to whittle on this gal, Adams," he announced. "But I'll cut her up like a Christmas turkey unless you start talking."

"Look," Clint began, speaking thickly as his face began to swell, "you want to know where *it* is, but I don't know what you mean."

"Lyin' bastard," Mel snarled.

His boot swung once more, but Clint suddenly grabbed the outlaw's ankle with both hands. He yanked hard, nearly throwing Mel off balance and spreading the man's legs wide apart. Clint delivered a hard uppercut to his tormentor's groin, driving his knuckles into Mel's testicles with all the strength he could muster. Mel cried out in agony, his eyes bulging from their sockets as if about to explode from his head. The pistol in his right hand roared. The bullet struck the floor in front of Clint, splintering wood without touching the Gunsmith.

Clint shoved Mel, sending the hootowl sprawling across the floor. He quickly ripped open his shirt and reached inside for the .22 caliber New Line Colt tucked inside his pants. Luke lunged forward, knife held ready.

"I'll kill you, Gunsmith!" he snarled.

He had forgotten about Mary, obviously considering her totally defenseless. Mary suddenly stomped on the back of his knee. Luke cried out as his leg buckled and he toppled forward to the floor. Clint rolled away from the outlaw and yanked his "belly gun" from its hiding place.

"Damn you, Adams!" Mel hissed, cocking his pistol and pulling the trigger.

Luke screamed when the slug smashed into his back. Mel's bullet struck between his partner's shoulder blades and snapped his spine like a dry twig. The outlaw convulsed in agony. Mel, horrified by his mistake, stared in dumbfounded awe.

"Oh, shit," Mel rasped.

"Drop it," Clint ordered, holding the Colt in both hands for a steady grip.

Mel looked at the diminutive pistol, snorted with contempt, and raised his .44 revolver. The Gunsmith fired , a slug drilled through the hollow of Mel's throat. The outlaw dropped his revolver and uttered an ugly choking sound as blood squirted across his matted beard.

The Gunsmith climbed to his feet and approached the wounded hootowl. Clint's eyes narrowed as he lowered his aim and pumped a round into Mel's lower intestines. Mel dropped on his side and shook in a wild fit of uncontrollable pain.

"Guess the sun don't shine on the same dog's ass all the time," Clint snorted.

He kicked Mel in the face, crushing the man's mouth. He kicked him again and broke his nose. mashing it flat. Clint reached down and retrieved his revolver and shoved Mel's gun out of reach. No need, he realized. The outlaw had gone into a state of shock and would be dead in a matter of minutes.

The Gunsmith walked to Luke and grabbed his hair. He pulled the bastard's head upward and shoved the barrel of his Colt into his mouth.

"Listen to me, you son of a bitch," Clint growled, "I'm going to—"

Luke's eyes stared back without seeing a damn thing. He was already dead. Clint pulled the Colt from the mouth of the corpse and slammed it against the floor hard. Then he turned his attention to Marry and untied her hands.

"God, I was terrified," she confessed. "Those two just charged in here and hit me. Next thing I knew—"

"Don't worry," Clint assured her. "It's over now."

The door burst open and Constable Puma entered, his shotgun held ready. Another constable broke through the storage door and appeared at the bar a second later. He also held a scattergun in his fists.

"You fellas are a little late," the Gunsmith commented dryly.

EIGHTEEN

Constable Puma stared down at Mel's crushed face, life-less, glassy eyes stared up at him. With his boot he flipped the dead man over. He sighed as he turned to the Gunsmith.

"Did you have to kill them both?" he asked.

"Yeah," Clint replied, "or would you have preferred it if they killed me instead? No . . . don't answer that."

"Did either of them tell you anything before dying?" the constable asked.

"They tried to question me," Clint answered, sitting in a chair and gingerly rubbing the welt on his cheek. "Wanted to know where 'it' is."

"What?" Puma frowned.

"That's what I said and that hairy bastard kicked me in the face," the Gunsmith shrugged. "Reckon that isn't the right answer."

"Do you have any idea what they were talking about?" Puma asked.

"I figure they wanted to know about whatever is buried on my property," Clint sighed, "and I don't imagine these fellas were interested in a bunch of dead Indians."

"So you're going to suggest there's a treasure of outlaw loot buried there?" The constable shook his head. "We already told you what the Old One said about the legend."

"Maybe the Old One is full of shit," Clint snapped. "Or

maybe there *isn't* an Old One and you people are blowing smoke up my ass!''

"Wait a minute, Adams," Puma snapped in return.

"Charlie," Mary Spotted Fawn interrupted, "can't you see Clint's been through a terrible ordeal? Look at him! Those awful brutes gave him a vicious beating and they probably would have killed us both if Clint hadn't managed to turn the tables on them."

"He's great, isn't he?" Puma snorted with disgust.

"You deserve as much credit as I do," Clint told Mary. "Old Luke would have cut me up for sure, but you tripped him before the bastard could use his knife on me."

"That wasn't much," she insisted.

"It saved my life," the Gunsmith stated. "That means a lot to me."

"It's right nice you two are forming a mutual admiration society," Puma commented dryly. "But I'd still like to know what it was those two trash barrels were looking for."

"Three trash barrels," Clint reminded him. "Don't forget Elmer. He's still lying dead out at my place."

"So you can bury him when you get back," Puma said. "The fat bastard isn't going anywhere."

"I hope not," Clint replied. "Question is, what were they looking for and did they kill Tom and Ellie or did somebody else?"

"That's two questions," Puma corrected.

"Got any answers?" the Gunsmith asked.

"Maybe," Puma nodded. "Could be those three figured there was some sort of treasure buried out on that land. Hard to say where they got that notion. Maybe some delirious town drunk got his facts wrong or told them about a buried treasure in order to get a bottle. Anyway, they head out here to dig up a chest of gold or whatever."

"Why the *chindi* impersonation?" Clint asked.

"Maybe they knew enough about Navaho to be familiar with the legend." Puma shrugged. "Could be they read up on us before coming here."

"I doubt if any one of them could read his own name with a magnifying glass," Clint muttered. "And if they knew the place was supposed to be an ancient Indian burial ground, they'd probably figure the story from this alleged town drunk was just a lot of wind."

"Not after they learned another white man had claimed that land," the constable answered. "Especially a white man who turned out to be a friend of the Gunsmith."

"They didn't know that until they arrived here during Tom's wedding," Clint declared.

"Maybe," Puma said. "Anyway, they headed down to Shatner's home, killed the newlyweds, and made it look like a wild animal did it. Congratulations, Adams. Your theory turned out to be right after all."

"Only one problem," Clint said. "There was only one set of *chindi* tracks left that night."

"So only one of the bastards actually killed Tom and Ellie," Puma explained.

"Come on," Clint groaned, "it took two of them to have enough guts to tangle with Mary. You think any one of those shitheads would have had enough to take on Tom Shatner, man to man, armed only with a set of fake claws?"

"Maybe the fat one."

"Tom would have broken him in half," Clint insisted.

"So maybe he held a gun on Shatner and made him get down on his knees and ripped out his throat from behind," Puma said, getting steadily more exasperated with the conversation. "Why aren't you willing to admit it's over? We've got the killers, Adams. *You* got them, all right? Send a telegram to the newspapers and tell them to add another chapter to the legend of the Gunsmith. I'll back up your story, if you want."

"I don't contact any newspapers for any reason," Clint replied, "especially to add anything to a reputation I never wanted in the first place. That reputation will probably get me killed one of these days."

"Look, Adams," Puma sighed, "I'm tired of arguing with you. What will it take to convince you this is finally over?"

"How about some proof?" the Gunsmith replied.

"What kind of proof?"

"Well, if they killed Tom and Ellie," Clint began, "then one of them must have the claws used to murder the couple. Now, I already checked the saddlebags back at the farm. Let's find the other two animals, go through the saddlebags, and see what we come up with."

"They entered from the rear," Mary explained. "I suppose they tied their horses up at the back of the building."

"Gary," Puma spoke to the other constable, "are there any horses around back?"

"Sure are, Charlie," Gary confirmed. "Reckon they probably belong to these two at that."

"Well, get off your ass, Adams," Puma sighed. "Let's find out if the goddamn claws are with their gear."

"I'm coming, Constable," Clint replied as he rose from his chair. Suddenly, he felt woozy and landed on the seat once more. "Well, I'm almost ready anyway."

"Charlie," Mary said, "Clint has suffered a bad beating from those beasts. They hit him with a gun and kicked him in the body and face. It's a wonder he's still conscious."

"Reckon you'd better see that woman who calls herself a doctor," Gary said. "Could have something wrong with your brain, Mr. Adams."

"Not so sure he didn't have a problem before those fellers beat up on him," Constable Puma muttered. "Gary, you go tell the crowd outside the cantina to go home now and take Adams over to Miss Reyes's office."

"I'll go *after* we check those saddlebags," the Gunsmith insisted.

He struggled to his feet. The room weaved before his eyes, but Clint still walked unsteadily across the room. Puma told Gary to take care of the folks out front. He accompanied the

Gunsmith to the back door. Clint opened it and slumped against the door when the world started spinning around him once more.

"You'd better let me handle this, Adams," Puma told him.

"I'm all right," Clint insisted, pushing himself away from the door frame.

"You don't trust me to go through those saddlebags," Puma said dryly. "That's's it, isn't it?"

"Something like that," the Gunsmith admitted as he staggered toward the two horses.

"Let me do it before you pass out," Puma complained.

He unbuckled the saddles and dumped them on the ground. The Gunsmith dropped to his knees beside the bags and yanked them open. He pulled out a bundle of smelly clothing from one container and started going through the pockets.

"We'll have to search the dead men, too," Clint told Puma.

"I know," the constable replied. "After we finish here, you can crawl inside and we'll . . ."

Puma unfolded a sheet of paper he had taken from a shirt pocket. "I think I found something, Adams."

"What is it?" the Gunsmith asked, leaning forward for a better look.

The paper was a crude map. The town of Waco was marked and a line extended to an area marked with a thick black X. Clint recognized it as directions to the Shatner farm, which was now his property.

"But what were they looking for?" the Gunsmith wondered aloud.

"Maybe there's something else here," Puma replied, searching through the pockets of a pair of pants.

He removed a gold disk, slightly larger than a silver dollar. Puma whistled softly as he examined the coin. Clint braced himself as his head seemed to swim through a fog of black mist.

"Look at this," Puma said, handing the disk to the Gunsmith.

Clint blinked hard, trying to clear his vision. The gold circle was an intricate piece of art. The outer edge ringed a sun-shaped object with a pair of circles at its center. The spheres were circles within circles. Some designs had been carved on the coin in patterns suggesting fish or leaves. In the very center was a square-shaped face with wide-set eyes, a flat nose, and a long tongue hanging from a fierce mouth.

"What the hell is it?" Puma asked.

"I don't know," the Gunsmith admitted, "but whatever this thing is, it's made of gold. Real gold."

Without warning, the Gunsmith plunged into a soft black pit of unconsciousness.

NINETEEN

"Take it easy, Clint," a soft voice whispered as the Gunsmith's senses gradually returned.

A shape formed in the blurred cloud that surrounded Clint Adams. He blinked to clear his vision and a beautiful face smiled down at him. Sofia Reyes took a cold cloth from his forehead and ran its soothing coolness along his jawline. Clint sighed with relief.

"How did I get here?" Clint asked, glancing about to find himself in the doctor's office.

"Charlie Puma carried you in," she explained. "He said you passed out while you were going through the belongings of the two drifters you had a fight with. Looks like you've had a rough day."

"I've felt better," the Gunsmith confessed.

"You're lucky," Sofia told him. "No concussion, as far as I can tell. None of your ribs is broken, but I suspect one is bruised. No internal bleeding that I can detect. There's a bit of swelling from the bruise on your face, but that's already begun to go down. Jawbone isn't broken and none of your teeth is loose."

"As beatings go," Clint muttered, slowly sitting up, "it wasn't so bad."

He suddenly realized he was naked. Clint instinctively covered his crotch with his hands. Sofia Reyes laughed and handed Clint a towel.

"Don't be embarrassed," she urged. "I had to examine you completely."

"Yeah," Clint replied, wrapping the towel around his loins, "reckon you did at that."

"You have a very nice body, Clint," she told him. "Although, it looks like you've put it through hell more than once. So many scars. You'd better start taking better care of yourself or you'll wind up in a wheelchair before you're forty."

"I'm already forty," the Gunsmith replied. "That birthday came and went awhile back."

"Then you *are* in good shape," Sofia remarked, cocking an eyebrow. "But as one grows older, the body loses some of its ability to recover from injuries. You'd better remember that and try to avoid incidents like the one that happened earlier today."

"Well, I didn't plan to get attacked when I walked into the cantina," Clint assured her.

"Unless the attacker was Mary Spotted Fawn?" Sofia commented dryly. "That woman is so starved for a man to be inside her, it is a wonder she didn't rip your clothes off the minute you entered the place."

"No female has ripped my clothes off lately," Clint said, "except you."

"That was for professional reasons," she replied simply. "But sometimes I like my job better than others."

"Is that a compliment?" the Gunsmith inquired.

"It isn't a complaint," Sofia assured him and changed the subject. "I understand you killed the two men who attacked you."

"I killed one of them," Clint answered, looking for his clothing—and his gunbelt. "The other fella caught a bullet meant for me."

"You *are* lucky," Sofia declared.

"He was *unlucky*," the Gunsmith stated, "and his partner was a lousy shot. Where'd you put my clothes?"

"They're close by," she answered. "But you won't need them until morning."

"What do you mean?" Clint asked.

"I mean it's ten o'clock at night and you're going to stay here until sunrise." Sofia smiled. "For observation, of course."

"That sounds like fun," Clint answered. "But I have to take care of Duke."

"My brother has already seen to your horse," Sofia told him. "He commented that it is a very beautiful animal. Luis took the horse to his livery. You can be sure he will treat it with the very best of care until you are ready to leave in the morning."

"Looks like you thought of everything," Clint remarked.

"I try," she nodded.

"What about my gunbelt?" Clint asked.

"I think Constable Puma has it." Sofia shrugged. "Surely you can get through the night without it."

"I'm not so sure," the Gunsmith said.

"Your enemies are dead, Clint," Sofia told him, moving to the cot. "No one is here except you and I. Certainly, you do not feel threatened by me."

"A beautiful woman can be dangerous," he replied, "especially an intelligent woman who tries to think of everything."

"I wouldn't think that would intimidate you," Sofia commented, reaching for the towel around Clint's waist.

"I'm not intimidated," he assured her. "Just a bit cautious is all."

"Caution is for the timid, Clint," Sofia declared, "and neither of us fits that description."

Sofia pulled aside the towel and promptly buried her face in Clint's crotch. She opened her mouth and clamped her lips around the head of his penis. Slowly, Sofia slid her mouth along the length of his throbbing cock. She licked his member and slipped a hand between his legs to gently cup his balls.

Her tongue rolled over his hard penis. She took him fully in her mouth. Slowly she moved her mouth up and down, holding him firmly in her warm, moist grasp. She rode him until he felt himself near the brink.

"Sofia," Clint whispered, trying to warn her that he would soon explode.

Sofia kept sucking, faster and harder. He moaned with pleasure and finally released his load. Clint poured himself into the woman's mouth. She kept sucking him, milking him until she'd drained him of every drop.

"Jesus," the Gunsmith sighed, "you've sure got one hell of a bedside manner."

"Only with special patients," Sofia replied happily. "Now, rest up. I'm not through with you yet."

"Lord give me strength," Clint whispered softly.

TWENTY

A few hours after daybreak, the Gunsmith dressed and left Dr. Reyes's office. He headed for the constable's station and found Charlie Puma seated behind his desk. The Navaho lawman opened a drawer, removed Clint's gunbelt, and placed it on the counter.

"Lookin' for this?" Puma inquired.

"Yeah," Clint confirmed, "thanks. And, thanks for hauling me over to Dr. Reyes, too. She told me you carried me up there."

"Didn't have much choice," the constable shrugged. "You passed out in the goddamn alley. Oh, I think this belongs to you, too."

Puma took the Colt from the desk drawer and placed it next to the gunbelt. Clint buckled the latter around his waist and checked the revolver. Satisfied it was still fully loaded and in perfect working condition, the Gunsmith returned it to its holster.

"Reckon you two missed each other," Puma remarked, noting the care Clint took with his weapons.

"You bet," the Gunsmith replied, inspecting his "belly gun." He removed the spent cartridge casings and fished two fresh shells from a pocket. "Did you find anything of interest in those saddlebags besides the map and that gold disk?"

"Not a thing," Constable Puma remarked, "except for this."

He unfolded a thick sheet of paper. It was a wanted poster for Melvin Peterson, complete with a drawing of a bearded man with a Stetson on his shaggy head. There was a five hundred dollar bounty for Mel in Kansas and Colorado, where he was wanted for several charges of armed robbery and two murders, including the slaying of a deputy sheriff. Mel had been part of a small outlaw gang, numbering five men, led by Lucas Fitzgerald Brandon.

"Want to go to Kansas and pick up five hundred dollars?" Puma inquired. "Probably wanted posters on the other two as well, but they weren't silly enough to keep the damn things. Reckon the bounty on Luke would be even bigger than this."

"I'm not a bounty hunter," the Gunsmith said. "Might send a telegraph to let them know they don't have to worry about these fellas any longer."

"Yeah," Puma sighed, "reckon those three would start smelling pretty bad by the time you delivered them anyway."

"Didn't smell too good when they were alive," Clint added. "Well, what can we guess about these fellas? This wanted poster is two years old. They probably left Kansas and the Colorado area a long time ago, which means they probably moved to the Southwest—probably New Mexico, the Arizona Territory, or maybe Texas."

"Reckon they came across this map one of those places?" Puma inquired.

"That's what I figure," Clint confirmed. "I just wonder if they got that gold disk from the same source."

"Probably doesn't have anything to do with the map," Puma said, taking the coin from his pocket. "I can't make a damn thing out of these symbols and such. If this is a language, I never saw it before. Sure as hell isn't Navaho."

"Mind if I see it again?" Clint asked.

"You killed the fella who owned it," Puma said, tossing it to the Gunsmith, "so I figure you can keep it."

"Thanks," Clint said, examining the piece. "I don't think this is just a piece of jewelry, Constable. These symbols must mean something. It's probably an amulet or charm of some sort. What do you think?''

"I think poor folks don't carry lucky charms made of gold," Puma answered simply. "And those outlaws weren't rich."

"So what have we got?" Clint began. "Three hootowls who thought there was something worth killing for buried on my property. Of course, we still don't know if they killed Tom and Ellie. You didn't find the claws, did you?"

"No," Puma confessed, his voice weary, "but they could have buried the claws somewhere. Speaking of burying, that fat man you left back at your place had better be put in the ground. I'll send Gary along with you to help."

"That's a rotten job," Clint replied. "I'll do it."

"Quit trying to prove how tough you are, Adams," Puma snapped. "You took a nasty beating yesterday. Shouldn't push yourself too hard too soon."

"Why, Constable," Clint said, "that's mighty considerate of you. I'm surprised you're so concerned about my well-being."

"Adams," Puma began, "I don't know if I could ever like you. That doesn't matter. I don't have to be friends with a fella to be concerned about him while he's in my territory. Looking after folks is my job. You used to be lawman, you know what I mean."

"Yes, I do," Clint confirmed, "and you do a good job, Constable. If I rub you the wrong way, it isn't because I don't respect you or your authority. It's just you and I don't quite agree on everything."

"Be funny if we did," Puma said. "By the way, that offer to buy your land is still open. Town council will pay you two hundred dollars for that property."

"I'm not ready to part with it," Clint answered. "Not yet."

"Damn it, Adams," Puma groaned, "what the hell do you want to keep it for? We know who killed Shatner and his wife. Sure, we haven't found those claws yet, but they could be hidden anywhere. Maybe we'll never find them.''

"Give me a couple more days, Constable," Clint urged.

"That's not for me to decide," Puma shrugged. "But this town still isn't very friendly toward you, Adams. Oh, Mary and Miss Reyes probably like you just fine, but the rest of this community would like to see you leave."

"Well," Clint sighed, "unless you've got a law against self-defense, I haven't committed any crimes."

"Nobody's accused you of any," Puma assured him, "but Harry Two-Ponies still claims he saw you trying to dig up graves out at your spread. He says you reached for a gun when you saw him."

"I'd just been in a shoot-out with three fellas," Clint sighed. "Of course, I reached for my gun when he suddenly appeared and started yelling at me."

"Harry also thinks you have something to do with his daughter's disappearance," Puma added.

"His daughter is missing?" Clint inquired.

"She left a couple nights ago." Puma nodded. "Of course, everybody knows Harry beat his daughter a lot. Maybe Rachel just ran off, maybe she's hiding somewhere."

"Hell," Clint groaned, "you're sending a constable to accompany me, right? Why don't you have him check my property and see for himself? Rachel isn't hiding there. I don't know where that young lady is, but I can't say as I'd blame her for not wanting to get beaten by her father all the time."

"Can't say that I blame her either," the Constable said, "if that's what it's all about. Anyway, this town is getting mighty hostile toward you, Adams. Wouldn't hang around here if I was you."

"Why do *you* hang around, Constable?" Clint inquired.

"What do you mean?" Puma demanded.

"Well, you're an educated man," Clint began. "Obviously you have a sense of duty to this place, but I don't think you really care much for living here. What the hell are you doing in Waco?''

"The Navaho once tried to fight you white eyes," Puma began. "We got are asses kicked. All the Indians who fought your people got beat. The Sioux haven't quite learned their lesson yet. Neither have the Apache and a few other tribes. But it's pretty clear that your people are going to keep taking our land and shoving us onto reservations for a long time. Well, I figure the only hope the Navaho have is to adapt to a white world. The more we can adjust and become like your people, the better our chances for survival.''

"And you hope to help your people make that adjustment?" Clint inquired.

"That's right," Puma confirmed. "I'm also going to teach them never to let your people fully gobble up our culture and turn us into a dark-skinned reproduction of your own society. The Navaho aren't corrupt enough to fit in. I'm going to tell them not to choose sides with any of your people during white conflicts. The Cherokee backed the Confederates during the War Between the States and look what happened? They wound up with even less land and rights than they had before.''

"Constable," Clint sighed, "I'm not exactly a sterling example of white man's rule. In case you didn't notice, I'm a shiftless drifter who hasn't even stayed in one area long enough to vote. Don't blame me for what Washington does.''

"How about blaming you for what it *doesn't* do?" Puma replied. "You have a government by the *white* people, for the *white* people. Maybe if more selfish bastards like you cared about the Indians, we'd have a better chance of getting humane treatment from the government.''

"Maybe if you weren't so damn abrasive folks would be more eager to support some of what you say," Clint answered.

"Abrasive?" Puma raised his eyebrows. "Another fancy word.''

"It means you're an asshole, Constable," Clint told him. "Try cooperating with people instead of always being ready to fight. Believe it or not, I'm really not your enemy."

"No," Puma admitted, "you're just abrasive."

"That's a fact," the Gunsmith agreed with a shrug.

TWENTY-ONE

Clint Adams walked to the livery stable to reclaim Duke. He entered the building and discovered Sofia Reyes arguing with her brother. Clint had only seen Luis Reyes one time, at the wedding of Tom and Ellie, but the ruggedly handsome Mexican could not be mistaken for anyone else. The Gunsmith didn't know what the argument was about. He understood only a handful of words in Spanish and he wasn't close enough to hear much of anything.

Suddenly Luis snaked out an arm and slapped his sister. The blow was openhanded, but the palm stroke spun Sofia around and she cried out with pain. Luis grabbed her arms and glared at her. His big biceps swelled as he tightened the grip.

"*Puta del diablo!*" he hissed angrily, shaking Sofia.

"Brother or not," Clint announced, "that's enough!"

Luis turned his head toward Clint, his face a dark mask of rage. He shoved his sister aside. She fell to the floor of the livery. Clint glared back at the young blacksmith. He had a lot of muscle and Clint wasn't eager to take him on with his hands.

"How I treat my sister is not your concern, *señor*," Luis snapped. "You are not her husband."

"No," Clint replied simply, "but I figure if a man hits a woman, he's asking somebody to send him to Hell, one way or the other."

"Would you be so bold without your gun?" Luis asked, folding his muscular arms across his barrel chest.

"Well," Clint said, "the fact is, I've got my gun, so I reckon you'll never know."

"Luis," Sofia said sharply. *"Por favor—"*

"Shut up, Sofia," Luis snapped. "Señor Adams is a customer and a gringo customer at that. I will get his horse so he will leave happy with the service of this lowly peon."

The blacksmith turned and stomped away. Clint turned to Sofia. She rubbed the angry red mark on her cheek and smiled weakly at the Gunsmith.

"My brother and I have had a difference of opinion," she explained. "It's nothing really."

"That doesn't give him the right to slap you around," Clint insisted.

"He knows that I spent last night with you, Clint," Sofia stated. "Believe me, it will be better if you do not get involved in our argument. Please, Clint."

"All right," the Gunsmith agreed reluctantly, "but if he hits you again, I might not be able to resist the urge to put a bullet through his kneecap."

Luis led Duke from a stall and handed the reins to Clint Adams. The Gunsmith took them with his left hand, his right resting close to the modified Colt revolver on his hip.

"Much obliged," Clint said dryly. "How much do I owe you?"

"How much did you pay my sister?" Luis sneered.

"Nothing," the Gunsmith shrugged "I still owe her for seeing to my bruises and such."

"I will not charge you," Sofia declared.

"I do not give away my services," Luis snapped. "A dollar for taking care of the horse, Señor Adams."

"Here you go," Clint replied, using his left hand to fish a silver dollar from his pocket. He tossed it at his feet. "Ooops. Must have slipped."

The blacksmith bent over and picked up the silver dollar.

He held it in his right hand, gripped between fingertip and thumb. His arm trembled slightly as he squeezed hard, slowly bending the coin at the middle. He smiled at Clint and slipped the bent coin into his pocket.

"Gracias, *señor*," Luis said dryly.

"Doesn't the bent coin make it tough to stack your money?" the Gunsmith inquired.

"I don't think we have more business to do," the blacksmith declared. "I would like you to leave, *por favor*."

Clint took Duke from the livery. Gary, the constable, was already saddled up and mounted on a roan Morgan. The Gunsmith swung onto the back of Duke and trotted to the lawman.

"Ready to go?" Gary inquired.

"Sure don't want to hang around this livery," the Gunsmith replied. "Luis Reyes sure isn't the most pleasant fella I've met so far."

"He is usually pretty quiet," Gary shrugged. "Doesn't seem to bother anybody, but he is mighty protective of his sister."

"I don't think slapping her around is protecting her," Clint muttered as they started for the edge of town.

"Mexicans are like that," Gary remarked. "Bad tempers. The men beat their women a lot. Sometimes it's all females seem to understand."

"Reckon I've got a different idea about how to treat women," the Gunsmith sighed. "Sorry about you getting this lousy job, Constable."

"Don't worry about it, Mr. Adams," Gary assured him, "I don't mind burying strangers. Only bothers me to bury somebody I knew personal."

They galloped to Clint's property. From a distance, everything seemed the same as when Clint had left the day before, but as they drew closer, he noticed at least three more holes had been dug in the ground.

"Son of a bitch," the Gunsmith muttered, "somebody's been here with a pick and shovel again."

"You mean besides those three drifters?" Gary asked with surprise.

"Those holes weren't here when I left yesterday," Clint explained.

"Maybe you just didn't notice them before," the constable suggested. "After all, you were probably upset after shootin' that feller and being shot at yourself."

"I've been shot at plenty of times before," Clint insisted. "And the bullets came closer on more than one occasion. It never rattled me so bad that I forgot how to count. Those holes were not here before."

"Are you sure, Mr. Adams?" Gary asked. "I mean, Harry Two-Ponies yelled at you and sort of distracted you, too."

"Of course, I'm sure," Clint insisted. "Somebody's been here, either last night or early this morning. They've been digging up this land like a pack of gophers."

"Sure looks like it." Gary frowned. "At least, it looks like *somebody* has been digging around here."

"You think I did this?" the Gunsmith glared at him.

"I didn't say that," the constable said. "But I reckon we'd best dig one more hole and bury that Elmer feller 'fore the sun gets hot enough to start makin' him stink."

"All right," the Gunsmith sighed, "let's go bury the fat bastard."

They rode to where Elmer's corpse lay. Both men yanked back with a start when they saw the body. Duke snorted with protest at this unaccustomed rough handling. Clint patted his neck.

"Sorry, big fella," Clint whispered. "Just sort of took me by surprise."

"Jesus, Mary, and Joseph," Gary gasped, "you didn't mention nothin' about this."

"I didn't know nothin' about this," the Gunsmith answered.

"Thought you said you shot this feller," the constable said woodenly, staring at the corpse.

"I did," Clint answered. "And Luke shot him in the head, but I didn't leave him like this."

Elmer's body had been ripped to shreds. Torn flesh hung from his carcass. Of course, the blood had already seeped from the dead man's inert form, yet the sight was still obscene and gruesome. Chunks of torn muscles dangled from rent skin and severed arteries jutted from the terrible claw wounds.

"Look, Mr. Adams," Gary said, pointing at tracks surrounding the body, "are those cougar prints? Jesus, looks like some sort of monster, don't it?"

"Yeah," the Gunsmith agreed. "The *chindi*. He's come back, Constable."

"What do you mean?" Gary demanded.

"I mean it's not over," Clint replied. "God help us, it's only begun."

TWENTY-TWO

"Oh, God," Constable Puma groaned, "I'm getting so sick of seeing you, Adams."

"You don't know what sick is, Charlie," Gary replied. "What happened to that fat man is *sick*, sir. Just about made me throw up, too."

The Gunsmith and Gary had returned to Waco, dragging a make-shift litter, carrying the corpse of Elmer. The body had been covered with a horse blanket, but a crowd had quickly formed in the street. Voices whispered *chindi* even before the Gunsmith and Gary went into the constable station to tell Puma what they found.

"Adams," Puma sighed, "what the hell did you bring that fat fella's body into town for? And you, Gary, what the hell did you do with your brains to agree to haul that corpse into Waco?"

"Uh . . ." Gary swallowed hard. "I, well, I listened to Adams. He explained why we oughta bring the body here and it seemed to make sense."

"Sense?" Puma snapped. "What the fuck do you know about sense? If you had any sense, you wouldn't have brought the body into Waco. If you had any sense, you wouldn't listen to Adams. You don't work for the Gunsmith, Gary. You work for me, damn it. Or, at least you *used* to!"

"Take it easy on Gary," Clint urged. "I convinced him that we should bring Elmer's corpse into town so Dr. Reyes could examine it."

"And show it to the whole damn town in the process."
Puma rolled his eyes with exasperation. "Jesus, Adams! I
already told you these people are upset. In the last three days
we've had five killings."

"Three of which were self-defense," the Gunsmith reminded him.

"And Harry's daughter disappeared," the Constable continued. "There've been rumors about disturbing an ancient
burial ground and a *chindi* stalking victims in the night. Just
when it appears we've solved these mysteries, you have to
haul that fat bastard into Waco and stir up the hornet's nest all
over again."

"Wait a minute, Puma," Clint said sharply, "doesn't it
matter to you that those three outlaws are dead, yet *somebody*
is still digging up my property? Yet *somebody* or *something*
ripped up Elmer's corpse?"

"Something?" Puma frowned. "Don't tell me you're
starting to believe in *chindi*, too, Adams."

"What I meant was Elmer's body may have been mauled
by an animal," the Gunsmith explained. "I examined it and
didn't see any bite marks on the corpse and it hadn't been
eaten to any degree, so I doubt if it was slashed by a roving
mountain lion or whatever. Still, I figure Dr. Reyes should
take a look at it, too."

"Why?" Puma snorted. "Figure she should have her
dinner ruined, too?"

"She examined Tom and Ellie," Clint answered. "I
reckon she can tell us if the claw marks look the same. It isn't
very likely, but it's possible this was done by an imitator.
Somebody who ripped up the corpse to try to scare me off."

"Seems like a long shot to me, Adams," Puma said.

"I know," Clint agreed. "Somebody was digging up my
property again and it damn sure wasn't an animal."

"Folks around here figure you've been digging up your
own property," Puma sighed. "They were ready to believe
the three drifters did it, but now—"

"Constable," Clint began, "we've got a whole mess of

facts to deal with. The fresh holes in my property are facts. That mutilated corpse is a fact. Like it or not—and neither one of us does—this matter is a long way from being solved.''

"Let me take a look at Elmer's corpse," Puma announced wearily. "I saw the bodies of Shatner and his wife. I'll tell you if it looks like the same thing tore him up.''

"I still want Sofia to examine it," Clint commented. "Can't hurt to get her opinion.''

"You want my opinion, Adams?'' the constable asked. "I think the sooner you get out of Fox County, the better I'll feel.''

"The feeling is mutual, Puma," the Gunsmith assured him. "But there's a little unsettled business that has to be taken care of first.''

Constable Puma examined Elmer's corpse and helped the Gunsmith haul the carcass to Sofia Reyes's office. She shook her head with dismay as she pulled aside the blanket to gaze down at the mangled remains of the outlaw known as Elmer.

"This sure looks the same as the Shatner couple we found a couple days ago," Puma commented. "What do you think, Miss Reyes?''

"This man has been shot," Sofia answered. "He was dead before the body was mutilated.''

"Yeah," Clint replied, "we know that, but otherwise, would you say it looks the same?''

"Very similar," she confirmed. "Claw marks appear to be the same width apart. Probably done by the same instrument.''

"What sort of instrument?'' Puma asked.

"Animal talons," Sofia said. "Mountain lion, bear, whatever. You found this man back at your property, Clint?''

"That's right," the Gunsmith confirmed.

"No chunks of flesh have been bitten from the corpse," Sofia remarked. "I doubt that an animal would tear the body like this and not eat any of it, especially since it was dead already.''

"There was also a dead horse near the corpse," Clint added. "Whatever ripped up Elmer, didn't touch the horse."

"I've heard that a big cat which has become a man-eater will ignore an animal corpse for the body of a person," Puma said, "but this body wasn't eaten."

"Gary and I found some tracks that looked the same as those odd prints I found earlier," Clint declared. "Not exactly animal footprints, but they didn't look human."

Puma groaned, "Don't say that around anybody else or they'll figure you're talking about a *chindi* for sure."

"Then they'll figure wrong," the Gunsmith told him. "Look, anybody who could use claws to kill with and try to make it look like a wild animal or a *chindi*, would certainly be smart enough to have some boots that would distort his tracks, too."

"Well," Sofia sighed, "there isn't much I can do with this man's body. May as well bury him."

"We've had more funerals in the last three days than we usually have in a year," Constable Puma sighed. "Sure hope this trend stops soon or we won't have much of a town left."

The Gunsmith opened the door and stepped from the office. He stopped abruptly when he found himself staring into the twin muzzles of a double-barreled shotgun. The big gun trembled in the unsteady grip of Harry Two-Ponies.

"Damn you, Adams," the Navaho farmer snarled, slurring his words with a tongue heavy from alcohol, "what did you do with my daughter?"

TWENTY-THREE

Clint Adams slowly raised his hands to shoulder level. Harry weaved unsteadily, but he still pointed the gun at Clint. The farmer was pretty drunk and probably couldn't hit the proverbial broad side of a barn with a pistol or rifle, but a shotgun belts out a wide pattern of buckshot. At close range, close enough is good enough.

"Take it easy," Clint said gently. "I don't know where your daughter is, Harry."

"Lyin' bastard," the Navaho growled. "You talk or I'm gonna kill you."

"I didn't take her, Harry," the Gunsmith assured him. "She must have just decided it was time to leave home. Ask the constables. They'll tell you."

"Harry!" Charlie Puma snapped as he emerged from the doctor's office. "Put that thing down."

"You keep out of this, Charlie," Harry warned.

"You fire that cannon and you'll kill me, too," Puma declared. "You ready to kill the chief constable of Fox County?"

"Step aside, Charlie," the farmer warned, "I ain't got no quarrel with you."

"Come on, Harry," Puma continued, his eyes barely glancing toward Gary. The junior constable was slowly creeping up behind Harry. "You're no killer."

"Adams stole my daughter," Harry insisted. "And he's

been digging around the burial ground. The *chindi* warned us not to disturb that land. We shouldn't have let those white troublemakers build a house there. We should have run 'em off. Then the *chindi* would have rested and no one would have died.''

"If you pull that trigger," Puma began, "it won't be the *chindi* who'll hang for murder, Harry. Just put the gun down.''

"We never should have forsaken the old ways," Harry sobbed. "We became more white in our customs and traditions. That's when we offended the spirits. The *chindi* is our punishment for allowing the whites to turn us from the true path.''

Harry began to chant in Navaho. The Gunsmith had no idea what the farmer was saying. He hoped it wasn't a death song. Many Indians will chant a final song to the gods when they are about to die. If Harry were prepared to die, he probably wouldn't mind taking somebody else with him to the grave.

"Don't be a fool, Harry," Puma warned. He added something in Navaho.

Suddenly Gary pounced. The constable grabbed Harry's shotgun and shoved both barrels toward the sky. Harry's finger yanked a trigger and a burst of buckshot exploded at the clouds above. Gary twisted hard, trying to wrench the gun from Harry's grasp.

The Gunsmith leaped forward, arms outstretched. He crashed into the struggling figures. All three men fell to the ground. Gary managed to pull the shotgun from Harry's fingers. Clint climbed on top of the farmer and slammed a fist to Harry's jaw.

Harry Two-Ponies bellowed in rage and pushed Clint off balance. The farmer suddenly threw Clint on his back and pinned him down, fingers clutching at the Gunsmith's throat. Clint pried at the farmer's wrists, trying to break the stranglehold.

Charlie Puma charged forward and rabbit-punched Harry, hitting the farmer across the nape of the neck. Harry started to sag, but shook his head fiercely and continued to throttle Clint.

"Let go of him," Puma rasped, grabbing Harry's hair.

He pulled back the farmer's head and whipped a bent knee under Harry's jaw. The blow sent Harry Two-Ponies sprawling across the ground. The Gunsmith sat up, grateful to have the choking fingers from his throat. Harry started to rise, but Puma kicked him in the stomach. The farmer groaned and jackknifed at the middle. He vomited remnants of cheap whiskey and homemade wine.

"Thanks, Constable," Clint said as he climbed to his feet, rubbing his sore neck.

"You want to press charges, Adams?" Puma asked gruffly as he and Gary pulled Harry Two-Ponies up from the ground. "Armed assault with intent to commit murder. That's reason enough for us to lock him up until the circuit judge gets here next month."

"I don't think Harry really meant to kill anyone," Clint replied. "And I figure the judge would go extra hard on him since he's an Indian and he's been drinking hard liquor."

"And he assaulted a white man," Puma added.

"Well, this is one white man who'll show the poor bastard a little pity," the Gunsmith stated. "Why don't you just lock him up until he can sleep off his drunk and then send him home?"

"Sure thing," the chief constable nodded.

Puma and Gary dragged Harry Two-Ponies to the jailhouse. Clint figured he'd better get back to his farmhouse before dark. He climbed on Duke's back and left Waco. The Gunsmith patted his horse's neck and spoke to Duke as he rode beyond the town limits.

"Looks like we're right back where we started," Clint remarked. "Well, the three drifters aren't suspects anymore, but everybody else is left."

Duke seemed to snort in agreement.

"Let's see," he began, "Charlie Puma is smart and tough. He also doesn't like white folks in general and me in particular. Could be he wants to get rid of me bad enough to play *chindi*. But I don't think he'd kill anyone unless he had a good reason. Would a fortune in buried treasure be reason enough?"

Duke snorted again.

"Yeah," Clint said, "I don't know him well enough to say for sure. I don't know any of them that well. The town council could be hiding the truth from me. Hell, they might all be part of a conspiracy. Sofia and her muscle-bound brother showed up about the same time Harry claimed he first saw the *chindi*. Maybe they were here a bit longer than that, which would have given them enough time to learn more about Navaho legends concerning *chindi* and such. But why would they kill Tom and Ellie? Why would anybody kill to get their hands on that property?"

Duke uttered a soft sound, which could have been a sigh.

"Maybe they don't want the property," Clint mused. "Maybe they just want to keep folks off the alleged burial ground. No, somebody is digging up the land. But what if it *isn't* the same people? The drifters were digging holes in the land, too, but apparently, they didn't kill Tom and Ellie. The *chindi* might be somebody who is trying to scare off anyone who gets on the property—or kill 'em if they won't scare. But somebody else might be digging around there. Of course, I still don't have any idea what the hell they're looking for."

Duke neighed wearily.

"Sorry if I'm boring you," the Gunsmith said dryly, "but I think I'm missing something. Thought talking about it might help. I can't just ride out of Fox County until I know who killed Tom and why. Of course, I've left my gunsmith wagon at Largo Gap. I'll have to get it pretty soon. You're lucky you're a horse, big fella. You don't have to worry about stuff like this."

Duke seemed to ignore him.

"I know," Clint sighed, "I'm always getting you into these messes. Well, nobody's perfect."

Duke bobbed his head in reply.

"Yeah," the Gunsmith muttered, "figured you'd agree with that."

TWENTY-FOUR

The Gunsmith reached his farmhouse about an hour after sunset. He was worried about riding Duke after dark. When he reached the property, Clint dismounted and led the gelding on foot. Duke might break a leg in one of the holes that peppered the ground. Clint was relieved when he finally escorted Duke into the barn.

Suddenly the gelding began to paw the earth and raised his head to snort a warning similar to the warning he'd uttered the day before when Luke, Elmer, and Mel were waiting at Clint's property.

"Oh, shit," the Gunsmith whispered, "are you sure?"

Duke still sounded distressed.

"All right," Clint urged, "let's take it nice and easy."

He slowly dragged his carbine from its saddle boot before advancing. Clint cautiously entered the barn, holding the Springfield with the butt stock braced against a hip. He carefully scanned the structure, swinging the carbine like the antenna of a curious insect.

Clint allowed his eyes to adjust to the darkness within the barn. He searched the shadows for any intruder who might be lurking in the blackness. The Gunsmith slowly moved farther into the barn, guiding Duke across the threshold. He had to use the barrel of his Springfield to probe among the shadows in order to locate the horse stall.

"Here you go, big fella," Clint whispered, "you'll be safe

enough in here. I'll go find our unwanted visitor . . . unless you've got your horse sense mixed up.''

Duke hissed through flared nostrils.

''All right,'' Clint muttered. ''I'll shut up.''

The Gunsmith moved to the door of the barn and carefully slipped outside. Then he noticed a lantern's pale light at the rear of the house. The flame was obviously low because he had not noticed it before. Clint slowly approached the light, holding his carbine ready.

A terrible howl echoed through the night. It was a combination of a wolf cry and a human wail, the same fearful sound he had heard the night before. The Gunsmith froze in place, trying to determine where the cry came from. It seemed to be everywhere. From the east, west, north and south. Yet, most of all, it seemed to come from above.

Clint turned sharply. He barely glimpsed the shaggy figure that leaped from the roof of the barn. The Gunsmith tried to raise his carbine, but the shape collided with him before he could squeeze off a shot. Clint fell to earth as a powerful tug yanked the Springfield from his grasp.

The Gunsmith stared up at his attacker. The vision forced a gasp from Clint. The shape that hovered above him was a product of a nightmare. The enormous figure, covered with dense gray fur, had massive shoulders and a great arched back. The head was wide with pointed ears and a long snout. White teeth shone from the creature's open jaws.

But there were clothes beneath the wolf-skin robe. Eyes peered from the mouth of the animal mask. That the *chindi* was, indeed, a human being in disguise did little to comfort the Gunsmith. The long curved claws strapped to the killer's hands made the *chindi* as dangerous as any supernatural avenger.

The sight startled Clint Adams, but he instinctively reached for his modified Colt revolver. The *chindi* slashed a talon-studded hand as Clint's pistol cleared leather. Claws struck the frame of Clint's Colt and sent it hurtling from his grasp.

''Shit,'' the Gunsmith gasped as he braced himself against the ground and kicked out with both feet.

His boots crashed into the *chindi's* chest, staggering the killer. The beast-man grunted angrily and prepared to attack again. Clint scrambled to his feet, scooping up a fistful of dirt. He hurled the dust at the *chindi's* face, although he couldn't quite tell where the opening to the mask was located. The *chindi* growled angrily and seemed to curse under his breath. Clint wasn't certain what language the killer uttered, but he didn't think it was English.

The *chindi* lunged. Clint sidestepped a slashing claw and hooked a kick to his opponent's belly. The *chindi* barely grunted from the kick and swung a cross body slash at the Gunsmith. Clint yelped with pain when sharp talons ripped his shirt and scraped flesh.

He leaped away from the *chindi*, but the creature charged once more, both claws aimed for the Gunsmith's throat. Clint's hands rose swiftly and caught his attacker's wrists. The Gunsmith didn't try to struggle with the powerful opponent. He folded a knee and dropped backward on his buttocks. Clint's right boot rose to meet the *chindi's* abdomen. He straightened his knee and sent the killer hurtling over head.

The *chindi* fell to earth hard. Clint sprang to his feet. A sharp pain in his chest told him the claw wound in his chest had begun to bleed. Worry about it later, the Gunsmith thought as the *chindi* rose to his feet and prepared to attack once more.

The Gunsmith waited for his opponent to make the next move. The killer feinted a right hand claw stroke and swung the left. Clint had expected something like this and watched the shoulders of his opponent. The shift of the *chindi's* body was difficult to see in the dark and the wolf robe covered his shoulders, making the task more difficult. However, the Gunsmith still managed to dodge the attack and swung a fist to the side of the *chindi's* head.

"Damn," Clint hissed when he felt too much give under his knuckles. The Gunsmith had punched part of the mask and missed his opponent's skull

The *chindi* swept a hard forearm into the Gunsmith's chest. The blow struck under Clint's heart. He came off his feet and fell to the ground. The *chindi* jumped into the air, both feet aimed for a murderous stomp that could smash Clint's ribs as if they were made of glass.

The Gunsmith rolled aside. The *chindi's* feet stamped the ground where Clint had been a second before. The Gunsmith glimpsed the killer's boots. They were wrapped in wolf hide, curved claws mounted at the toe.

Clint pivoted on the small of his spine and lashed out with both legs. He snapped a scissors hold on the *chindi's* ankles. The killer bellowed with surprise when Clint twisted hard and tripped the *chindi*. The creature fell, but slashed a claw at one of Clint's legs. The Gunsmith gasped when the talons ripped skin on his right calf.

The Gunsmith scrambled away from the *chindi* and started to rise. The killer followed and came up from the ground at the same instant. A powerful backhand stroke sent the Gunsmith reeling backward. He stumbled, but managed to keep his balance until the *chindi* kicked his feet out from under him.

Clint fell to earth once more. His right hand struck something hard and cool. Metal and tubelike. His fist closed around the object as the *chindi* charged. Clint swung the Springfield carbine, holding it by the barrel. The walnut butt stock connected with the *chindi's* head. Or perhaps only his mask. Clint heard something crunch and saw the pointed ears of the wolf head sag.

The *chindi* clamped both clawed hands to his head and bolted for the house. Clint sat up, swinging the carbine around to put the stock to his shoulder. He slipped an index finger onto the trigger and aimed the Springfield at the broad back of his retreating opponent.

Clint hesitated. Shooting a man in the back was repugnant to him. Still, he couldn't let the bastard get away. Clint squeezed the trigger.

Nothing happened.

"Oh, Jesus," he rasped, aware the carbine had jammed.

The hammer stuck, probably damaged when the weapon had been thrown aside by the *chindi*. Clint didn't have time to clear the carbine. He scanned the ground rapidly and located his Colt. Clint discarded the Springfield and scooped up his pistol.

The hammering of hooves told him the *chindi* had already mounted a beast to try to gallop from the area. Clint dashed forward, but a torn muscle in his ankle twitched in protest. Clint's foot slipped and he fell heavily on his side.

"Come on, Adams," he said breathlessly, dragging himself upright.

A figure on horseback galloped southwest. The horseman held a kerosense lantern in his fist. The Gunsmith aimed at the shape, but hesitated. The rider's head appeared to be that of a normal man. *Shit,* Clint thought, *the son of a bitch removed the mask!*

Clint triggered his Colt. Orange flame bolted from the muzzle and knifed through the shadows. The horseman kept going. The Gunsmith held the pistol with both hands and aimed carefully, but trying to get a clear shot at a figure in the dark was difficult, even when the target carried a lantern. The Gunsmith fired a second shot. He missed again.

"Damn it," Clint muttered, gasping for breath as he lowered the pistol. His opponent was out of range.

The Gunsmith returned the double-action Colt to its holster and picked up the Springfield. He used the carbine for an improvised cane as he limped to the house. Clint entered the adobe dwelling and found a lantern. Striking a match, he fired the wick and carried the lamp outside.

Exhausted, the Gunsmith still refused to rest until he checked the grounds. As he expected, Clint found at least one more hole had been dug. A pick and shovel lay beside the newest pit. The Gunsmith started to hobble back to the house to see to his wounds. An object on the ground caught his eye.

Clint leaned over and gathered up the discarded remnants of the *chindi's* mask. The bizarre headgear had been made from a real wolf's head. The skull had been removed, but the hide, ears, and muzzle were fitted around a pasteboard frame. Apparently, the jawbones and teeth were still intact. The wolf's head was cracked open just below the left ear. The split extended across the mask to the bridge of its snout. One artificial eye was missing and the other was loose.

"Well," the Gunsmith sighed, "at least now I've got some evidence."

TWENTY-FIVE

The following morning, the Gunsmith rode into Waco and marched into the constable's station. He placed the *chindi* mask on Charlie Puma's desk. The chief constable stared at the head as if he thought it might come to life and bite him.

"There's your *chindi*," Clint declared. "Nothing supernatural about the bastard, but he's still real. The *chindi* is a man, a flesh and blood human dressed in wolf skins and armed with claws. Take a good look, Constable."

"I see it, Adams," Puma said, nodding his head woodenly. "You mean the *chindi* actually appeared at your house last night and left this? I mean, you actually saw him?"

"Saw him, hell," Clint snorted as he unbuttoned his shirt, "the son of a bitch almost killed me."

He opened his shirt to show Puma his bandaged chest. Clint yanked the wraps aside to reveal three angry red marks on his chest. The bandages were stained with blood, but the wounds had stopped bleeding.

"Jesus, Mary, and Joseph," Puma whispered. "What the hell did he use on you?"

"Like I said," Clint replied. "He has claws. I couldn't see them very well in the dark, but I think they're made of metal and they're damn sharp."

"Did you kill him?" Puma asked.

"I tried," Clint sighed. "My carbine jammed. The

hammer spring was broken in a fight with the bastard. I'll tell you, I don't want to go hand-to-hand with him again.''

"So he got away?'' the constable wanted to know.

"If he hadn't,'' Clint replied, "I would have brought you his corpse as well as that mask.''

"Well, did you recognize him?'' Puma inquired. "Was it someone from Waco or a stranger?''

"I couldn't see his face,'' the Gunsmith explained. "He was wearing that damn wolf head.''

"The mask is right here, Adams,'' Puma insisted. "Didn't you get a look at him without it over his head?''

"No,'' Clint admitted. "See, I hit him with the butt stock of my Springfield. That's how the mask got cracked. I don't think it hurt him, but the mask must have drooped over his eyes. The *chindi* knew I was armed with something and he couldn't see so he ran. Probably held the mask up to see and then discarded it when he reached his horse.''

"Well,'' Puma thought for a moment, "how was he built? Tall, stocky, thin, or fat? You must have been able to tell something about the jasper.''

"It all happened pretty fast and it was close combat,'' the Gunsmith answered. "The wolf robe added a lot of bulk, so I can't be sure how he was built. His back was arched most of the time so I'm not sure how tall he was either. All I can tell you for sure is he's strong as a bull and fast. *Real* fast. I drew my Colt and he swatted it out of my hand before I could squeeze the trigger.''

"Lots of muscles?'' Puma inquired. "Like Luis Reyes, the local blacksmith?''

"Yeah,'' Clint nodded. "I met him the other day. Any reason his name comes to mind besides the fact he's strong?''

"He and his sister showed up just a couple months before Harry first claimed to have seen a *chindi*,'' the constable answered. "And those two Mexicans keep to themselves. Nobody in town really knows them very well.''

"I'll grant you Luis has a mean streak in him," Clint nodded, "but I don't know if he's the *chindi* or not. I said the bastard was strong and fast, but that description could fit a lot of men. Like *you,* for example."

"Me?" Puma stared at him. "Why me?"

"When I passed out after that fight the other day," Clint began, "you carried me to the doctor's office. I reckon I weight as much as you do. Maybe a few pounds more. You're no weakling, Constable. Yesterday you took care of Harry Two-Ponies without working up a sweat."

"I'm almost flattered," Puma remarked, "but Harry was pretty drunk. Besides, why would I want to impersonate a *chindi?*"

"The town council is pretty anxious to get my property," the Gunsmith replied.

"And you figure they'd be willing to kill to get it?" Puma shook his head. "Father McCoy is part of the council. You figure a priest would approve of murder?"

"Maybe he doesn't know what the others are up to." Clint shrugged.

"But you think they could hire me to be their killer?" Puma frowned.

"I don't know you well enough to say for certain," the Gunsmith confessed. "But I hope you wouldn't do anything like that. You helped me out a couple times and I'm grateful for that, but I've known other men who helped folks and still turned out to be killers."

"At least you're honest," the constable sighed. "Well, if I was the *chindi*, I think I'd leave my wolf costume at home and just shoot you."

"Then it wouldn't look like an animal killed me," Clint commented.

"If you think I might be the *chindi,*" Puma began, "isn't it sort of foolish to confront me like this? After all, I could probably dry gulch you and blame it on Harry Two-Ponies. A lot of witnesses saw him try to kill you."

"I don't think you're the type to shoot a fella in the

back, Constable," Clint mused. "I don't think the *chindi*
is either. Now, you mentioned Harry Two-Ponies. Did you
wait until morning to turn him loose?"

"Don't tell me you think that drunken idiot could be the
chindi," Puma laughed. "Hell, Adams, Harry isn't clever
enough to get away with something like that."

"But maybe he's crazy enough," the Gunsmith commented. "He is sort of fanatic on the subject of disturbing
that alleged burial ground. Sure, he doesn't seem very
quick and he isn't all that strong, but Harry might change
when he dresses up as a *chindi*. Lots of crazy people are
like that. An insane person's speed and strength can be
extraordinary under such circumstances."

"Nice theory," Puma sighed. "But we didn't let Harry
Two-Ponies out of his cell until after dawn. Of course, I
know I'm still a suspect, so maybe you figure Harry and I
are conspirators . . ."

Clint asked, "Do you know where Gary was all night?"

"Adams!" the constable snapped, "I happen to be the
chief law officer for this county. How do I know you're
not the *chindi*? Maybe you made up that wolf mask, and
those wounds could be self-inflicted."

"That's horseshit and you know it," the Gunsmith replied simply. "I'd never even heard of Waco, Arizona before Tom Shatner met me in Largo Gap and asked me to
be his best man."

"That's what you say, Adams," Puma declared.
"Maybe you and he were partners from the start. Could be
you killed Tom and Ellie in order to claim his property."

"And what would I want it for?" Clint demanded.

"You tell me, Adams," the constable said, pointing a
finger at the Gunsmith. "You refuse to sell that property.
You insist that there's something buried there worth killing
for."

"There must be," the Gunsmith stated, "because
somebody tried to kill me last night. Look, I didn't come
here to argue with you. Just wanted to show you I have

evidence that the *chindi* is a human killer.''

"Fine," Puma snorted. "Why don't you come back when you can tell me *who* it is?''

"Oh, I will," the Gunsmith assured him.

"Adams," the constable began, picking up the wolf mask for a better look, "what do you plan to do now? Set yourself up as bait to try to lure the *chindi* to come after you again?''

"Maybe," Clint replied, heading for the door. "But this time I'll be ready for him.''

"He'll probably be ready for you, too," Puma warned.

"Then whoever does a better job wins," the Gunsmith said with a shrug.''

"Pretty high odds," Puma commented. "If you lose, you'll forfeit your life.''

"Yeah," Clint answered as he prepared to leave, "but the *chindi* is playing the same odds. That's good enough for me.''

TWENTY-SIX

"Madre de Dios!" Sofia Reyes commented as she inspected the claw marks on Clint's chest. "You've got to stop playing these dangerous games with such rough people, Clint."

"It's been one of those weeks," the Gunsmith said.

"What did you use to disinfect these cuts?" Sofia inquired.

"Whiskey," Clint replied. "Burned like hot coals so I figured it must have been good for me."

"Probably wood alcohol," she commented. "I hope you don't drink that stuff."

"After what happened last night?" the Gunsmith raised his eyebrows. "I gulped down half a bottle."

"You'll ruin your liver," Sofia scolded.

"I'll worry about that later," Clint replied. "Is there any infection or torn muscle?"

"No," Sofia assured him, "it's just a nasty scratch."

"The ankle he clawed hurts more," the Gunsmith admitted. "Not as bad as it did last night, but it's still sore as hell."

"Take off your pants," Sofia instructed.

"Hell," Clint replied, "I could just take off my boot."

"You treat your patients your way," Sofia said, "and I'll treat mine my way. Take off your pants."

"Aren't you going to bandage up my chest first?" the Gunsmith asked.

"What for?" she replied. "The cuts aren't bleeding. Bandages might cut off circulation. It's better if you let those cuts breathe. You know your skin breathes through the pores? That's a medical fact. Just try to wear a clean shirt and try not to get kicked around for a few days."

"I'll try," Clint sighed, "but sometimes it isn't really my fault."

"Sure, sure," Sofia said, obviously unconvinced. "Now take off your pants."

"You're the doctor," the Gunsmith replied.

He stripped down to his longjohns. Sofia motioned for him to keep removing his clothes. Only when Clint was stark naked did the lady doctor kneel in front of the cot to inspect his ankle. She frowned.

"This is a little worse," Sofia announced. "There is some slight muscle damage. It should heal all right. No ligaments are torn, but it'll be stiff for a week or so."

"Does it need to breathe, too?" Clint asked dryly.

"No," she answered. "I'll wrap it. Try not to put too much weight on this foot for a while, all right?"

"I'll do my best," the Gunsmith assured her.

With that said Sofia stood and began to unbutton her dress. "You are the best, my dearest," Sofia stated as she began to remove it.

"Are you sure you want to do this?" Clint inquired. "Your brother was pretty hard on you for spending the night with me before."

"What my brother does not know will not bother him," she told Clint. "But I think I'd better make certain the door is locked and the window shades are drawn."

"Does Luis always get so upset when you sleep with a fella?" the Gunsmith asked. "Or is it just gringos that upset him?"

"I don't sleep with many men, Clint," Sofia said, casting a frosty stare at the Gunsmith, "despite what Luis said about me. I take it you understood when he called me the devil's whore?"

"I don't speak Spanish," Clint said, "and I didn't mean to suggest anything concerning your morality. All I meant was whether or not Luis tends to be jealous."

"He is protective," Sofia explained. "I told you this before, I think. Just relax and let me check the doors and windows."

Clint waited until she returned to the cot. The woman continued to remove clothing. She smiled at Clint as she stripped off the final garments. Her beautiful ripe breasts bobbed free, nipples jutting forward erotically.

"Are you afraid of him?" the Gunsmith asked.

"Afraid of whom?" Sofia replied with a frown.

"Luis," Clint answered.

"He is my brother," she shrugged. "He loves me. He might discipline me when he considers my conduct improper, but that is his right. He is my elder by three years. Yet, Luis would never truly harm me."

"Maybe he's jealous of you because you're obviously smarter than he is," the Gunsmith suggested. "You speak better English than he does, you're a doctor . . ."

"I am not a real doctor," Sofia reminded him.

"Close enough," Clint said. "And your brother doesn't have your style. He lacks the qualities of education and genteel culture you possess."

Sofia laughed. "Unfortunately, this is a man's world, Clint. No woman is considered the equal of a man."

"That's bullshit," the Gunsmith said. "I've met women who were newspaper reporters, business owners, farmers, and even a lady bounty hunter."

"This is a silly conversation," Sofia remarked as she bandaged the Gunsmith's injured ankle, "for a naked man to have with with a naked woman."

"Maybe you've got a point," Clint admitted.

Sofia's hands slowly slid along Clint's inner thighs. Her fingers found his organ and gently massaged it. She leaned forward and kissed the head of his penis, gradually slipping her warm, soft lips over the tip of his manhood. Clint sighed with pleasure as Sofia's mouth expertly caressed his throbbing member.

She kissed and licked and sucked him until his cock jutted straight as an oak tree. Then Sofia climbed on top of the Gunsmith. She spread her long legs to straddle him. The woman steered him into position and lowered herself until he impaled her. Clint felt himself sink into the center of her womanhood.

Sofia gripped him like a warm, damp fist. She wiggled against Clint, working him deeper inside her. The Gunsmith moved his mouth to her breasts and gently teased them with teeth and tongue. He sucked her nipples tenderly as Sofia rocked slowly.

The woman began to raise and lower herself along the length of his stiff member. She sighed happily and increased the motion. Clint arched his back, thrusting his hard cock again and again. Sofia gasped and rode him faster. She gripped his upper legs. The woman trembled as a passionate climax flowed through her body.

Clint shuddered and released himself at the same instant. He groaned softly as he erupted inside Sofia's chamber of love. The woman moaned with great pleasure, feeling him release quiveringly.

"Now," she whispered, "didn't that make more sense than wasting time talking?"

"It was just what the doctor ordered," the Gunsmith agreed.

TWENTY-SEVEN

The Gunsmith emerged from the doctor's office. His ankle seemed to hurt less than before. Maybe Sofia Reyes had a special kind of healing magic not included in medical books. Or maybe Clint had spent an hour and a half thinking about every part of human anatomy except his ankle.

Whatever the reason, the Gunsmith felt in better spirits as he walked to Duke and prepared to mount the big black gelding. He noticed four Navaho Indians standing along the walk. Their solemn faces were definitely unfriendly. So were the rifles, shotguns, and pick-handles each man carried.

"Good morning," Clint greeted. The townsfolk glared back at him, their eyes ablaze with anger and hate. "At least it was . . ."

Six more Navaho citizens marched into the street. Every one of them was armed with a gun or a cudgel. More men followed. Dark copper faces expressed grim determination, fear, and cold-blooded hatred. The Gunsmith had felt more comfortable when the Apaches had attacked him on his way to Waco.

"You folks want to talk to me about something?" Clint asked, his hand poised by his revolver.

"Ain't no time for talk now," Harry Two-Ponies announced, stomping forward with a rope coiled over his

137

shoulder. One end of the cord formed a loop with the traditional knot of a hangman's noose.

Funny how that same remark had sounded so much better when Sofia said it, the Gunsmith thought.

"Evil and violence entered this town when you arrived," a grim Navaho told the Gunsmith, "and we have waited too long to do anything about it."

"Murderin' son of a pale-skinned slut!" Harry snarled. "You're to blame for everything that's happened in this county! The actions of the *chindi* are on your head, Clint Adams!"

The Gunsmith's Colt appeared in his fist so fast no one even saw him reach for the weapon. Clint aimed the pistol at Harry's face and thumbed back the hammer. It wasn't necessary to cock the double-action revolver, but the ominous *click-click* warned the townsfolk he meant business.

"Hold it, right there," Clint told the group in general and Harry Two-Ponies in particular. "Anybody takes another step or moves a weapon like he plans to use it, and I'll start shooting."

Nobody seemed eager to accept the Gunsmith's challenge.

"Now," Clint began, "what's this about?"

"The *chindi* killed my wife!" Harry Two-Ponies snapped, his voice breaking into a sob. "I knew when I saw the *chindi* that the gods had cursed me. Then Rachel disappeared and now . . . now my Edna is gone as well!"

"Oh, shit," the Gunsmith muttered under his breath. "Hold on now. Did your wife vanish too or . . ."

"I went home this morning and found her body lyin' on the floor," Harry sobbed. "She'd been torn to pieces! The tracks of the *chindi* were everywhere. The tracks of a beast which walks like a man . . ."

"I'm sorry about your wife," Clint said, "but I'm not responsible. The *chindi* is a . . ."

"We know what a *chindi* is, Adams," a voice called out from the mob. "It is a spirit, a force of nature like the wind and the rain. The *chindi* is like fire, destructive and violent, yet cleansing and powerful. If fire burns down a man's house, one does not blame the fire, but the person who carelessly started the blaze."

"And that's you, Adams!" Harry cried. "You and those white friends of yours. So far only whites have been killed . . . until now."

"These unbelievers desecrated sacred ground!" another Navaho declared.

The mob mindlessly shouted their agreement, their unity. This crowd had assembled to carry out an act based upon fear. They were ready to believe anything that might help them deal with fear. They were prepared to *do* anything that seemed to be a way to escape the terror that had turned the people of Waco into a lynch mob.

"Everybody stop clucking like frightened hens and listen to me!" Constable Puma shouted.

"There is no more time to waste with talk," Harry replied. "The *chindi* has now claimed the life of a Navaho, my Edna! She was a good woman and a good wife. You all knew her. She never harmed a person in her life, yet the *chindi* killed her!"

"The *chindi* struck out at the whites," another voice added, "but they did not heed its warning. Thus, the life of an innocent was taken, so we would open our eyes and do what has to be done in order for the *chindi* and the souls of the dead to rest once more."

"Shut up and listen to me!" Puma insisted.

"You protected this white devil, Charlie!" Harry stated. "Why should we listen to you? You have been corrupted by the ways of the whites. You're no better than they are!"

"Maybe we should get us another rope!" someone suggested.

"Best make it *three* ropes," the constable named Gary told them as he shouldered through the crowd with a shotgun in his fists.

"And you'll have to hang me, too," Father McCoy added, slipping through the frightened mass of frenzied humanity to reach Clint Adams's side. "But that shouldn't bother any of you. After all, I'm white, too."

"This does not concern you, priest," someone declared. "Go back to your church and pray to your white god."

"My God is your God, too," McCoy said in a loud clear voice. "Surely the Great Spirit would not approve of this madness. You people are talking about committing murder!"

"We're fighting a force the only way we can," Harry told him. "You do not understand such things, Father."

"I understand that murder is wrong," McCoy replied simply. "What more do I need to know?"

"Don't listen to that priest!" a voice urged. "Hang the pale-skinned liar along with Adams and these turncoats!"

"You folks better bring along some extra coffins as well as more rope," Puma announced, "because a lot of you will be doing some dying today as well!"

"I'd sooner die from a bullet than be prey to the *chindi*," someone answered.

"Then come on, big mouth," Charlie Puma invited, raising his shotgun, "I'll make your wish come true."

"Christ," the Gunsmith rasped, "what a mess!"

"Listen to me!" someone urged. "Please, listen to me!"

Mayor Sun Tree and George Standing Elk shouldered their way through the crowd. The mob finally fell silent, waiting to hear the two top elected officials in Waco.

"You all know that we represent the town council," Sun Tree began, "and you know that we tried to get Mr. Adams to sell his property—"

"It is not *his* to sell," a voice cried. "That land belongs to the dead!"

"Legally," Sun Tree began, "the land *is* his. He has a right to live there and a right to keep that property."

"Does he also have a right to endanger the lives of everyone in Fox County?" Harry demanded.

"Who is endangering life at this moment?" George Standing Elk asked. "You are ready to hang a man without a trial and you claim to be concerned about life? I would say this behavior is more dangerous than that of Mr. Adams."

"You all have become boot-licking cowards," a voice said with contempt. "You grovel and protect this pale-skinned pig from the justice of our spirits."

"So you're going to kill us, too?" Mayor Sun Tree laughed. "Do you think killing us will get rid of your fears?"

"The *chindi* is not just superstition," Harry Two-Ponies declared. "We all know it is real. We've seen what it can do. We've seen how it kills!"

"The *chindi* is a man!" Clint Adams shouted. "I know it is. I fought with it last night. I even brought the wolf mask the *chindi* left behind as he fled. That's right, the *chindi* ran from me when I grabbed a gun. Would a spirit flee in fear of bullets?"

"I've got the mask in my office," Constable Puma stated. "I don't know if Adams is telling the truth or not, but at least he can show us some proof to back up what he says."

"I can show you the proof of my wife's bloodied corpse!" Harry Two-Ponies cried.

"That's proof that someone has been killing people in a brutal, inhuman manner," the Gunsmith declared. "We've seen this before, but it doesn't prove the *chindi* is a spirit. I tell you, it is a man of flesh and blood, a man who is using your fears to get away with murder."

"We must know the truth," a voice announced. "If Adams speaks the truth, we must give him an opportunity to prove it."

The crowd broke into jumbled chatter. Some agreed with the last speaker, while others argued. However, the group was no longer a mob. The citizens of Waco had regained the ability to reason. The discussion was brief and the people quickly came to a decision.

"Clint Adams," a spokesman announced, "we will give you a chance to prove what you claim. Two days and nights, Adams. On the third day, you will bring us the *chindi* impostor or you will leave Fox County."

"I can't promise I can unravel this mystery in just two days," Clint replied.

"If you are still here when the time limit has expired," the spokesman said grimly, "then you will expire as well."

"You sure know how to strike a deal," the Gunsmith sighed helplessly.

TWENTY-EIGHT

"Well, Adams," Charlie Puma began as he watched the crowd break up and wander in different directions, "if you have any brilliant ideas, now's the time to bring 'em out."

"Give me a minute to think," Clint replied. "And thanks for coming to my rescue, Constable."

"Law and order is what I get paid for," Puma said gruffly.

"Thank you too, Father," Clint told the priest.

"Daniel stepped into the lion's den with only his faith." Father McCoy smiled thinly. "I had company. Besides, I know these people. They don't want to harm anyone. They're just frightened."

"And I'm thankful to you, too, Mayor," Clint continued. "And you, Mr. Standing Elk. Especially since you fellas tried to get rid of me before."

"We tried to buy your property and convince you to leave," Mayor Sun Tree replied, "but lynching is against our principles."

"Well," Clint sighed, "you fellas might have just ruined your chances of getting re-elected."

"Better that than to have your death," Standing Elk assured him.

"It would still be nice if you could solve this problem," the mayor remarked. "Any suggestions, Mr. Adams?"

"He probably won't share any notions with us, sir," Puma remarked dryly. "Figures we might be behind this *chindi* business."

"What?" Father McCoy stared at the Gunsmith. "My son, suspicions are one thing, but wild fear is another. I don't know if you're Catholic or not, but believe me, wolf witches and avenging spirits are not part of our religion."

"He figures you don't know about the conspiracy, Father," Puma commented. "Just us heathen Navaho."

"I'm not accusing anyone of anything," Clint explained. "Right now I don't really trust anyone. But I will tell you one thing."

"Well, don't keep us in suspense," the chief constable urged.

The Gunsmith took the gold disk from his pocket. "I know where this came from now," Clint announced.

"That's that coin or amulet or whatever that we found in that outlaw's saddlebags," Puma said. "Hell, I found it, remember? I know where it came from, too."

"Yeah," Clint nodded, pocketing the disk, "but now I know where Luke found it."

"Do tell?" Puma said dryly.

"Is that coin important, Mr. Adams?" Mayor Sun Tree inquired, slightly frustrated by Clint's coyness.

"Maybe," the Gunsmith answered.

"Well," Puma sighed, "are you going to tell us about it?"

"Not yet," Clint answered. "First, I want to find out more about *chindi* and my property. Figure it's about time I spoke to somebody who might have some answers for me."

"Who would that be?" Sun Tree inquired. "Or is that a secret, too?"

"Nope," the Gunsmith said. "Now, where can I find the Old One?"

"The Old One?" Puma glared at Clint. "Look, Clint,

he's a weary, very old man. You shouldn't get him all upset with crazy notions and accusations.''

"I don't want to upset anyone," the Gunsmith insisted. "But the Old One is supposed to know more about the burial ground legend than anyone else. It's logical I should talk to him about it. He's the expert.''

"All right," George Standing Elk said, "I'll take you to him.''

The Old One lived in a small adobe dwelling about a mile from Waco. The house was located at the base of a small rock formation. A campfire had been built outside the structure. Smoke still curled from the ashes. The Gunsmith remained mounted as George Standing Elk swung down from the back of his horse.

"Wait here," George instructed. "I'll talk with the Old One and see if he'll agree to talk with you.''

"All right," the Gunsmith agreed. "Does this old fella speak English?''

"The Old One speaks many languages," George replied with admiration, "including tongues which are no longer used. He is very wise, but even the wisdom of a century of life cannot prevent the years from taking their toll. He is a very weary man, bent by age, and soon he will embrace the spirits of death.''

"I'm not going to interrogate the old man with a club," Clint promised. "I just want to ask him a few questions.''

"Very well," George Standing Elk nodded. "The first question will be whether or not he will speak with you at all. We'll know the answer in a moment or two.''

George walked to the goat hide cover of the adobe house. He said something in Navaho, probably announcing himself. If the Old One replied, the Gunsmith could not hear his voice. George entered the house, stooping low to get through the tiny entrance. Seconds later, the goat skin curtain parted and George emerged.

"The Old One will speak with you, Clint Adams," he announced.

"Fine," Clint replied, climbing down from Duke's back.

"Can you find your way back to Waco without my help?" George asked.

"I can manage," the Gunsmith assured him. "You need to get back to town, Mr. Standing Elk?"

"The Old One wishes to speak with you alone," George shrugged. "He asked me to leave."

"However he wants to handle this is fine with me," Clint said. "Thanks for taking me out here. See you later."

George nodded and climbed onto his horse. The Gunsmith watched Standing Elk ride from the area, heading back toward Waco. Clint slowly approached the tiny house. He stooped to get through the door. Clint's right hand hovered near his modified Colt.

"Come, Clint Adams," a reedy voice spoke from within the house, "you have nothing to fear from me."

The Gunsmith entered. The interior, carpeted with buffalo hide, consisted of a single room, empty except for a small leather pouch and the wrinkled old man who sat cross-legged on the floor. The shriveled figure was dressed in baggy buckskin. Beads and animal teeth hung from the old man's neck. His hair was snow white and extended beyond his shoulders. His craggy, ancient face resembled a sculpture in aged parchment. Dark eyes, dim from years of strain, peered up at the Gunsmith.

"It is a pleasure to meet you, Clint Adams," the old man declared. Only his lips moved. If the Old One had not spoken, Clint would have thought him dead already. "I heard about you many years ago from a mutual friend. William Hickock. He spoke quite well of you, Clint Adams."

"He was a very fine man," Clint replied, sitting on the

buffalo robe, emulating the position of his host. "I apologize for disturbing you, sir."

"No apology needed," the Old One assured him. "It is true I live out here because I am weary of the company of most people. A hundred years is a very long time to tolerate human beings. All my family died long ago. I even outlived my own sons. No one will hear my death song and I do not care to share it. I'm even tired of life. A hundred years is too long for anything without finding it boring."

"Reckon so," the Gunsmith agreed, wondering if the old man was really as old as he claimed to be.

"There are few men I wish to meet who still live," the Old One commented. "I had hoped to meet both Ulysses S. Grant and Robert E. Lee to ask them what the War Between the States was all about. It never made much sense to me, although I heard little about it. But Lee died a few years ago and I understand Grant is still President of the United States."

"Last time I heard," Clint confirmed.

"I knew Andrew Jackson when he was still a general," the Old One laughed quiveringly. "He was a fine man. Very bold and very brave. But he had a temper, that one. You know he was the first president someone tried to assassinate. That's the word they use when someone murders an important person, isn't it?"

"That's the word," the Gunsmith nodded.

"The would-be killer tried to shoot Jackson, but his gun jammed," the Old One said with amusement. "They say Jackson damn near beat the fool to death with a walking stick before they could pull him off. Jackson has been dead for a long time now. More than twenty years, I think. Must be, because it was over ten years ago President Lincoln was killed. Too bad that assassin's gun didn't jam, too."

The Old One slowly turned his head toward the

Gunsmith. "I'm rambling," he apologized. "And you came to ask me about the legends of this place."

"My friend, Tom Shatner, built a house on the land that is allegedly a burial ground," Clint began.

"I heard such," the ancient Indian nodded weakly. "It is said he was killed by a *chindi*."

"Do you believe that?" Clint asked.

"When I was a young man," the Old One began, "many, many years ago, I remember hearing rumors of a *chindi*. White men disturbed the burial ground of the Navaho. One by one, those intruders died violently, attacked by animals possessed by the *chindi*."

"Do you think that really happened?" Clint asked.

"Why not?" the old man answered. "When you get to be my age, you no longer believe anything is impossible."

"The *chindi* who killed Tom and Ellie Shatner is a man disguised as an animal," Clint explained. "I know this. I fought the *chindi* myself. It's no evil spirit, just an evil man."

"This, too, has happened before," the Old One stated. "There are always men who claim to be gods or demons. Why not a *chindi*? Tell me, Clint Adams, how may I help you?"

"According to the legend," Clint began, "the burial ground is supposed to be for an ancient Indian tribe, one that dates back before the Navaho settled here. Correct?"

"That is the legend," the Old One confirmed. "It was said that the ancient tribe had come to the land, which is now the Arizona Territory, before the Americans had the Revolutionary War. That is even longer ago than when I was born. The tribe had once been very powerful, but they trusted gods who were not gods. The gods were devils in disguise. They crushed the ancient tribe. The Indians who fled scattered in many directions. Some of them lived here. The area where Tom Shatner built his house was said to be their burial ground."

"Where did these Indians come from?" Clint inquired.

"From the south," the old man answered, "far to the south."

"Do you know anything else about them?" the Gunsmith asked.

"They were lost here," the Old One sighed. "They found themselves in a land they were never meant to exist in. This was too strange and different for them. They died one by one. Died of sorrow for their lost tribe and loneliness—for they were the last of their kind and could never rebuild what the devils had taken from them. And as they died, they were buried. The others mourned their dead and wept for they, too, would soon die in this strange and hostile land."

"Sad," the Gunsmith remarked.

"Yes," the Old One nodded, "it is a sad story. Yet, it is only a legend and we do not know if it is true or not."

"Were there any stories that amulets were buried with the dead to protect them from evil or help them cross over to the next world?" Clint asked.

"Of course," the old man confirmed, "and it is assumed that a medicine man sang over the ground."

"What does that mean?"

"He sang to the spirits," the Old One explained. "He conjured and asked the spirits to protect the dead. He asked that their sleep be undisturbed and that any who defiled this eternal sleep pay the proper price."

"And now we have a *chindi* running around," Clint frowned. "Tell me, how is one supposed to deal with a *chindi?*"

"Deal with it?" the Old One inquired. "The *chindi* will not harm a person who is pure of heart. But it is a spirit, not a living creature. You cannot kill such a being. One may only stop a *chindi* by getting the medicine man, who summoned it to guard the dead, to lift his curse."

"But this medicine man has been dead for over a hundred years."

"Then you would have to contact his spirit and ask him

to lift the curse from the other world,'' the old man explained. ''But this *chindi* is not a spirit. You say it is a man, yes?''

''Yeah,'' Clint sighed, ''but I've only got forty-eight hours to find out who the hell it is. I thought maybe if I knew how a *chindi* is supposed to behave and how folks are supposed to defend against one, I might be able to guess what the false *chindi* would do next.''

''Does this man know you have only two days to find him?'' the Old One asked.

''He does unless he isn't living in Waco,'' Clint stated. ''And that means all he has to do is sit on his ass and wait for me to run out of time. Then I have to leave town or the good people of Waco will hang me.''

''Leave town,'' the Old One advised. ''I've seen hangings. It looks like a bad way to die.''

''Yeah,'' Clint said, ''I know.''

''So what will you do, Clint Adams?''

''I've got to try to make the *chindi* come after me,'' Clint stated. ''I've got to make him think he can't afford to wait two days for me to leave. He's got to believe time is running out for him just as fast as it is for me.''

''Do you know how you can do this?'' the Old One inquired.

''I've got a plan,'' Clint replied. ''It might not work, but it's the only bet I've got. Could be I'm guessing wrong and the plan won't work. I've already started carrying it out. If my theory is right, the *chindi* will try to kill me. If I'm wrong, then I'll just have to leave Fox County before they put a noose around my neck and have me dancing in the air.''

''And what does this plan consist of?''

''Telling a few lies to a few people,'' the Gunsmith answered. ''And hoping I'm using the right lure to draw the *chindi* into action.''

''Lure?'' the Old One inquired.

"I've got it right here." The Gunsmith showed him the gold disk.

"What is it?" the old man asked, straining his eyes to examine the patterns and designs on the metal.

"It's what I'm going to tell lies about," Clint explained.

"You know," the Old One began, "this false *chindi* has already killed two people."

"Three," Clint corrected. "Apparently he murdered Harry Two-Ponies's wife last night. Probably to convince the Navaho they were threatened by my presence in Waco. If that was his plan, it worked."

"Your opponent must be very clever and totally ruthless to murder an innocent person," the Old One declared. "He'll kill you if he gets the chance."

"Don't plan to make that easy for him," the Gunsmith answered.

"I hope not," the old man sighed. "It would be a pity if you died before I do."

TWENTY-NINE

Sofia Reyes was surprised when the Gunsmith entered her office that afternoon. She smiled and gestured for him to close the door; he followed instructions. The woman quickly wrapped her arms around his neck and kissed him, thrusting her tongue deep inside his mouth. The Gunsmith started to respond, then forced himself to concentrate on the reason for his visit.

"Sorry," Clint said, gently breaking the embrace, "I'm pressed for time."

"So I heard," Sofia replied sadly. "Two days isn't much time."

"I may not need that long," Clint stated, taking the gold disk from his pocket. "Will you keep a secret, Sofia?"

"Who would I tell?" she shrugged.

"Look at what I found," he told her, opening his fist.

Sofia gazed down at the disk, her eyes expanding and her mouth dropping open. "It's—it's beautiful, Clint. What is it?"

"It's gold," Clint replied, pocketing it. "What else matters?"

"Well," she said, staring at his eyes, "where did you find it? On your property?"

"Where else?" Clint smiled. "One of those holes an intruder dug just barely uncovered this thing. Saw a little

152

sparkle and reached inside. Look at what I found. Gold, Sofia. Real gold.''

"You figure there's more of it buried there?'' she asked. "Clint, you don't intend to look for more gold?''

"There aren't any evil spirits there,'' Clint scoffed. "And the *chindi* is just a fella dressed as a wolf. This is what he's after. But he doesn't know I'm aware of the gold. He'll just wait a couple days for me to leave and then figure he can move in and take it. But it'll be all mine by then.''

"Clint, that's terrible,'' she shook her head and turned away from him. "People have been killed and all you can think about is personal profit. My God, I thought I knew you better than that.''

"What's wrong with making a profit?'' the Gunsmith demanded. "If I stay here and get hanged, it won't bring Tom and Ellie back. Why shouldn't—''

"Will you please leave, Mr. Adams,'' she snapped, her back still turned to the Gunsmith. "Just leave.''

"Well,'' Clint sighed, "if that's what you want . . .''

"That's what I want,'' she said firmly.

Clint Adams left the doctor's office. He felt like a real son of a bitch. That was probably good because that was the impression he was trying to make on Sofia. He headed to the cantina. Fortunately, there was no one present except Mary Spotted Fawn. The Navaho beauty was also delighted to see Clint, until he produced the gold and told her the same lie he had told Sofia.

Mary's response was a solid right cross to the Gunsmith's jaw. His head jerked from the unexpected punch. Mary glared at him, eyes filled with anger and loathing. Clint put the disk in his pocket and rubbed his jaw.

"That was uncalled for,'' the Gunsmith told her.

"Get out of my place you son of a bitch,'' Mary said through clenched teeth.

"Keep my family out of this.'' the Gunsmith smiled. "Come on, Mary. The *chindi* is just an old wives' tale.''

"Aren't you forgetting your good friend Tom Shatner and his poor wife?" Mary snapped. "Doesn't that mean anything to you?"

"Of course, it does," Clint insisted. "But I might be sitting on a treasure of gold over there. You don't expect me to just let it lie for that murdering *chindi* fella to dig up after I leave? What sense does that make, Mary?"

"Get out of my sight," Mary ordered. "You're making me sick to my stomach."

"Aren't you taking this a little too hard?" he asked.

"I'll show you hard!" Mary snapped as she threw another punch.

Clint caught her arm. "All right," he said. "I'm leaving."

Her left fist suddenly snapped out and tagged him on the chin. Clint's head bounced from the punch, but he kept his temper and didn't hit her back. After all, he was acting like a greedy bastard so he had to expect to be treated like one. Clint released Mary and hurried to the door before she started to knock his teeth out.

The Gunsmith didn't bother to repeat his performance anywhere else in town. He had told two women about the gold and, the Gunsmith knew from experience, that meant it would be all over Fox County before long. Unless one or both ladies had a personal reason to keep the story a secret. He felt bad about using the women, but he had also lied to the mayor, Father McCoy, George Standing Elk, and Constable Puma.

Of course, the lie had been a bit different with Puma because he knew about finding the disk. Naturally, Clint didn't know more about the gold trinket than he had when they found it among Luke's belongings, but nobody else knew that.

His bullshit stories sure wouldn't make him popular, but what the hell. The citizens of Waco were ready to lynch him earlier that day, so Clint realized there was a risk involved. His remarks to any of the people about the gold might spread across town too quickly and draw too much attention from too many people. The lynch mob might reorganize and come after him. However, they wouldn't come for him after dark.

Only the *chindi* would come in the night.

Clint rode Duke to his property and arrived before dusk. The Gunsmith took Duke to the barn and checked it carefully for hidden intruders. He eyed the roof suspiciously as he emerged from the barn with the Springfield carbine in his hand.

The Gunsmith headed for the house and inspected his weapons. He made certain the carbine, modified Colt, and "belly gun" were all in perfect working order. He loaded all three weapons and returned the Colt to its hiding place under his shirt. He slid the other revolver into the holster on his hip.

Clint prepared to defend his house. There was only one door, but an opponent could enter through one of three windows. Clint covered the windows with blankets to prevent an adversary from peering inside. Then he used fishing line to string empty cans along the sides of the blanket. If an intruder tried to push through, the rattle of the cans would alert Clint to danger.

He didn't want to barricade the door. He wanted to be able to look outside, and keep an eye on the horizon as well as the barn. The house was made of adobe. It was unlikely it would be a target for an arsonist's attack, but someone might set fire to the barn. Luring him into the open would be a tactic in character with what he already knew about the *chindi*.

The roof of the house could also be set afire. Flaming arrows could be launched at the roof. In fact, the *chindi* might even be able to claw through the patched dome with his metal talons. But he couldn't do the latter without making a lot of noise. At least Clint hoped the *chindi* would make noise. Underestimating the sinister wolf witch would be the biggest mistake Clint could make. Whoever the *chindi* was, Clint couldn't rule out any form of attack.

The Gunsmith had a suspicion as to the identity of the *chindi*. He'd just as soon be wrong, but he was pretty sure about the killer. Right or wrong, he'd find out when (and if) the *chindi* attacked.

His opponent may or may not use the *chindi* disguise. Perhaps he'd come armed only with claws. The killer might decide to use a gun this time. Trying to guess what the *chindi* would do could be a fatal mistake. If Clint were correct about his foe's identity, there might be *two* opponents to deal with.

Twilight claimed the sky. Clint crouched in the doorway with his carbine held ready. He did not light a lamp, wishing not to present a silhouette for his enemy—or enemies—as the case might be. The Gunsmith heard a coyote howl in the distance. A shiver ran up his spine. He had heard the cry of a coyote hundreds of times before, but this time he associated it with the *chindi*.

"Take it easy, Adams," Clint told himself. "Don't get rattled already. You've got to stay calm, damn it."

Night fell. Stars twinkled in the velvet sky above. The surroundings slowly became dark lumps and shadows, which contained unseen dangers. The Gunsmith chided himself for letting his imagination conjure up spooks. There was nothing supernatural about the *chindi*, but that didn't make it any less unnerving to have an extremely dangerous, possibly demented, opponent lurking somewhere in the night.

"Come on, Mr. *Chindi*," Clint whispered. "Let's get this over with—"

Then he saw a pale light in the distance. The light bobbed as it approached—a lantern held by a person on horseback. Clint didn't think the *chindi* would be bold enough to ride right up to the house carrying a lantern. The wolf witch might be a lot of things, but Clint didn't figure he was stupid. The tactic might be a diversion to draw Clint's attention from the real attack.

The Gunsmith scanned the area, searching for any indication of an opponent creeping up from the shadows. He saw nothing. Clint noticed the lantern light was getting closer and closer. He heard the hooves of the horse pounding against the ground. Clint watched the light approach, still glancing to and fro in case another shape was moving in more clandestinely.

The rider slowed down. Clint couldn't see the horseman's face. A hooded cape covered the visitor's features. However, the Gunsmith noticed a long-barreled pistol clutched in the rider's hand that also held the reins. The horseman held the lamp high, mindful of the numerous holes forming a treacherous series of potholes in the ground.

The rider did not appear to be large. Clint frowned. The visitor's horse was a piebald pony. It wasn't the same animal the *chindi* had ridden the night before. Not that that meant anything. Clint raised his rifle.

"Hold it!" the Gunsmith ordered. "Drop that pistol and raise your hands or I'll shoot you right out of the saddle."

The rider dropped the revolver and slowly raised both arms. The motion caused the hood to fall back and lamplight to strike the horseman's face. But the face did not belong to a man.

"Good evening, Clint," Mary Spotted Fawn smiled and said, "You sure know how to welcome folks."

THIRTY

Mary started to dismount. The Gunsmith stepped forward and trained his carbine on the pretty Navaho, his eyes still darting about in case another visitor was moving through the darkness. Mary gasped, startled to see the Springfield staring up at her.

"Clint!" the woman exclaimed.

"Keep your hands in view, Mary," the Gunsmith warned.

"Are you crazy?" she demanded. "I didn't come to shoot it out with you, for crying out loud!"

"Maybe you'd better tell me why you are here." Clint replied.

"I want some answers," she said, "and I'm not willing to wait until morning."

"Why'd you have the gun in your hand when you rode up?" Clint asked.

"Well, that sure proves one thing," Mary sighed.

"What's that?" Clint inquired.

"That there is such a thing as a stupid question," Mary snorted. "Apaches ambushed you and Tom Shatner on the trail. A *chindi* or at least a killer disguised as a *chindi* has been murdering people around here. Just two days ago a trio of outlaws broke into my cantina and damn near killed us both. And you actually asked me *why* I'm packing a gun."

"Reckon that's a logical answer," Clint stated. "Maybe you'll like this question better: Why are you here?"

"Nice to see you, too, Clint," she replied, climbing down from her horse.

"Sorry I'm not being warm and lovable tonight," the Gunsmith said, "but I figure the *chindi* might come a-calling tonight."

"And you think I'm the *chindi?*" Mary laughed.

"You throw a pretty good punch," Clint replied. "But the *chindi* is bigger and meaner than you. He and I went a couple rounds last night. It could be he's got a lady friend sent ahead to distract me."

"I really think you're going loco, Clint," the woman groaned.

"Then please explain why you're here?"

"To find out why you lied to me," Mary answered. "You said you found that gold doodad in one of these holes, but Charlie Puma told me you two found it in one outlaw's saddlebags. He also told me you implied to him that you'd found something here that explains where the hootowl got his hands on that thing. He said you gave the impression you knew the outlaws had dug it up here. Seems you *wanted* Charlie and the town council to believe that, just as you wanted me to believe you found the damn thing in a hole here."

"If Pinkerton ever hires lady detectives," Clint sighed, "you ought to apply for a job."

"What are you trying to do, Clint?" Mary asked. "Convince folks to come after you with a rope again?"

"I'm trying to flush out the *chindi*," Clint answered. He scooped up Mary's revolver and thrust it in his belt. "Get in the house and we'll talk about it."

"Let's put my horse in the barn first," Mary urged. "I don't want her standing out here all night."

"All right," Clint agreed. "But keep your hands where I can see them."

"You really think I might be in league with the *chindi*."
Mary shook her head with dismay. "Do you want to
search me for concealed weaons?"

"Mary," Clint answered, "I'd love to use any excuse to
run my hands all over your body again, but right now I
have other things on my mind. If I allow myself to be
distracted, it might get us both killed."

"Then you don't think I'm buddies with the *chindi?*"
Mary asked as she led the pony toward the barn. "That's a
relief."

"I'm not ruling out the possibility entirely," the
Gunsmith answered, "but I think it's pretty unlikely."

"Then you have some notion about who the *chindi* is?"
Mary asked, glancing over her shoulder at the Gunsmith as
he followed her to the barn.

"I've got a person in mind," Clint answered, "but I
don't have anyway to prove it unless he tries to kill me
again."

"You must have told other folks that you found that
gold coin here," Mary said. "Of course, you told Puma
and the council that other story so everybody will wonder
if you're out here digging up the land, searching for gold.
But, that's just a big lie."

"Two big lies," Clint corrected.

"*Two* lies," she agreed, "but you told them for the same
reason."

"That's right," Clint admitted. "I'm hoping the *chindi*
will get worried about me finding the treasure before he does
and riding out of here in the morning with it."

"But who is it?" Mary frowned. "Don't tell me it's
Charlie."

"Puma found the disk before I did," Clint answered. "He
didn't have to show it to me. It meant nothing to him. He even
gave it to me when he could have kept it. No, unless my
theory is wrong, Puma can't be the killer."

"And what's the theory?" she asked.

"That the disk is somehow connected with the reason the

three outlaws came treasure hunting here," Clint explained. "And the *chindi* is interested in the area for the same reason."

"Do you know that the coin is connected?"

"No," Clint confessed. "It's a long shot, but if I'm right, all the pieces will fall into place soon."

"Pieces?" Mary asked.

"Look," Clint said, "will you get that horse in the barn so we can get out of the open? I don't like being a clear target in case the *chindi* decides to use a rifle instead of his oversized fingernails."

"All right," the woman agreed reluctantly.

Mary put the piebald in a stall while Clint stayed outside, paying attention to everything and frequently glancing up at the roof. Finally, Mary emerged from the barn.

"Clint," she began, "how can you know for sure if those outlaws found that gold disk here?"

"I don't think they did," Clint answered, escorting Mary to the house. "I figure they got it from the same fellow who drew up the map for them."

"Huh?" she asked, totally confused.

"The fellow was probably a grave robber," the Gunsmith answered. "After all, this burial ground has been here for over a hundred years. Somebody has probably been here before."

"Then this site really is an ancient Indian burial ground?" Mary asked.

"I believe it is," Clint nodded. "The way I figure it, a grave robber who was here a long time ago fled for some reason or other. Probably afraid he'd get caught by the Navaho who had moved here. Anyway, the fella probably got down on his luck and stupidly tried to make a deal with Luke, Mel, and Elmer. They probably killed the old fool and took his map."

"But what's the disk?" Mary asked.

"It's an amulet of some sort, I guess," Clint explained. "What matters is it's gold and where there's one body buried with a gold charm, there might be others.''

"But who else would know about it except this alleged grave robber you dreamed up.'' Mary frowned. ''Even the Old One never mentioned anything about gold amulets and such.''

"Well, I figure nobody here would know or even guess,'' Clint explained. ''But somebody who came from where the Indian tribe originally lived would be familiar with their customs and . . .''

"They found out the Indians moved here,'' she mused, following Clint to the house. ''But where did they come from? How can you know where they came from, damn it.''

"According to the legend . . .'' Clint began as he entered the house.

Suddenly two powerful hands with metal claws strapped to them seized Clint's carbine and yanked hard. The force hurled the Gunsmith into the room. He crashed into the kitchen table and tumbled over the furniture to the floor.

Clint had lost his grip on the Springfield. He rose up behind the table and reached for the Colt on his hip. His fingers clutched air. The revolver had fallen out of its holster. He heard the terrible half-wolf, half-human cry of the *chindi* as the outline of a nightmare figure appeared at the doorway.

"Oh, shit,'' the Gunsmith rasped when he saw the shaggy, fur-covered shape with a wolf snout and pointed ears atop its head.

The *chindi* had come back for the kill.

THIRTY-ONE

Mary Spotted Fawn screamed as she stood in the doorway next to the monster. The *chindi* swatted the back of a hand across her face. Mary tumbled outside and fell unconscious.

The *chindi* turned his attention on the Gunsmith and charged with a murderous snarl. Clint suddenly remembered the pistol in his belt. The Gunsmith yanked it from his belt, aimed, and squeezed the trigger. Nothing happened. Clint was accustomed to his double-action Colt. In the heat of the moment, he failed to cock the single-action pistol.

The wolf-thing suddenly scooped up the table and slammed it into the Gunsmith. Clint groaned as the blow struck the pistol from his grasp. The Gunsmith fell back against a wall as the *chindi* swung a claw at his face.

Clint ducked. The metal talons raked adobe above his head. The Gunsmith jabbed his left fist to the *chindi's* shaggy chest and swung an uppercut. His fist struck the lower jaw of the mask.

"Fuck this," Clint growled, quickly clasping his hands together.

He swung a powerful, two-fisted haymaker to the side of the *chindi's* head. The brute grunted as his head spun from the blow. However, the killer slashed across Clint's body in response. Clint hissed through his teeth as metal talons ripped his abdomen.

The Gunsmith grabbed the closest end of the table and

swung it toward his opponent. The *chindi's* claw slammed into the wooden top, blades sinking deeply into the furniture. He roared with anger as Clint twisted the table and rammed a corner into his breastbone.

The *chindi's* arms flashed, smashing both hands against the table with tremendous force. The furniture shattered from the powerful twin blows. Clint Adams lashed out and kicked the *chindi* somewhere between the ribs and hip. He couldn't be certain of the target because of the darkness and his opponent's wolf robe, but Clint felt his foot connect with something soft and heard the moan of his opponent.

Clint quickly grabbed the *chindi's* left arm and twisted it, trying to lock the elbow joint. He felt as if he were trying to apply a hammerlock to an oak tree. He swiftly kicked the beast-man in the abdomen and followed through with a blow between the wolf witch's shoulder blades.

The *chindi* lashed out with a rock hard forearm that sent Clint staggering across the room. The *chindi* closed in fast, sweeping both hands in a distracting blur. Clint cried out when sharp metal lanced his thigh. The *chindi* had kicked him with a claw-laced boot. The beast swung a claw at Clint's throat, planning to rip it open with the next stroke.

Clint's hands rose swiftly and snared the attacker's arm. He pivoted under the limb and yanked down forcefully, locking the arm at the elbow and shoulder. Clint kept pulling the limb. The *chindi* started to rise. Clint swung a boot and kicked his opponent in the head. The killer rolled on his back and wildly thrashed his claws to discourage Clint from throwing another kick. The Gunsmith jumped back and the *chindi* leaped to his feet.

Clint ripped open his shirt and tried to reach for his gun, but the *chindi* was too fast and charged before Clint could draw the little gun. Claws lashed out at the Gunsmith's face. Clint dodged the attack and glimpsed a muscular leg, swinging for his groin. The Gunsmith chopped a fist across the *chindi's* shin to stop the claw-studded boot from castrating him.

The *chindi* slashed a claw at Clint. The Gunsmith side-stepped and moved behind his opponent. Clint hammered a fist to the *chindi's* right kidney and then rammed an elbow to a shoulder blade. The *chindi* staggered forward. Clint raised a boot and stomped into the back of the *chindi's* knee as hard as he could.

The killer bellowed as his leg buckled and he fell to all fours. Clint clamped his hands together and swung them overhead, putting all his weight behind the powerful blow to the nape of the *chindi's* neck. The blow would have killed a normal man—a man's whose neck was not protected by a thick wolf robe.

The *chindi* suddenly rose up from the floor and rammed a broad shoulder into Clint's gut. Claws tore into Clint as the brute lifted him up like a bag of grain. The *chindi* whirled fiercely and hurled the Gunsmith. Clint slammed into a wall and slumped to the floor in a dazed heap.

A cruel laugh echoed in Clint's head. His vision was blurred, but he saw the horrible creature lumber forward, claws outstretched for the kill. Clint's hand seemed to crawl to his shirt. He touched the grips of the Colt and tugged on the diminutive pistol as the wolf moved closer.

The little gun came out blasting. The *chindi* shrieked when a bullet hit. Clint didn't know where the shot had struck, but he knew he hit the son of a bitch. The *chindi* whirled and ran for the bedroom as the Gunsmith triggered another shot.

If the second bullet struck the *chindi*, it did not slow him down. He dashed into the next room. The Gunsmith pushed himself away from the wall and stumbled after his opponent. He reached the doorway of the bedroom as the *chindi* dived headlong through the window. The blanket nailed across the window popped loose and glass shattered. The string of cans tumbled to the floor with a metallic clatter.

Clint fired a third round at the *chindi* as he plunged through the shattered window. The beast-man tumbled out of view. Clint rushed to the window and saw the *chindi* running from the house. He aimed carefully. Too carefully. Clint spent a moment too long aiming his weapon. When he squeezed the trigger, the *chindi* was out of range for the short-barreled "belly gun."

"Damn it to hell," the Gunsmith rasped as he jogged into the other room.

Clint struck a match. He found the kerosene lantern. The globe had been shattered and coal oil leaked from its ruptured base. However, Clint also located his double-action Colt revolver. He scooped up the familiar pistol and thrust it into his hip holster as he dashed to the front door. Mary Spotted Fawn stood in the doorway, rubbing the side of her face.

"You going to be okay?" Clint asked, cradling her face in his hands.

"I think so," she said in a shaky voice. "My God, what was that thing?"

"Well," the Gunsmith said, "it wasn't a Mormon missionary. Look, the *chindi* is wounded. I'm going after him."

"You're not leaving me here alone!" she insisted.

"No," he assured her, "I know where he'll go now. My lantern was broken, so we'll have to use yours. Travel will be slow in the dark, but we'll probably reach Waco about the same time he does."

"But he's on foot," Mary said.

"Not for long," the Gunsmith explained. "The other times he came here, he had a horse handy, along with a lantern. He probably has the animal waiting somewhere close by, ground hobbled and saddled up."

"But where is he going?" Mary demanded. "Who the hell is he, Clint?"

"I'll explain on the way," Clint promised. "But we can't afford to waste any time."

"Well," Mary smiled weakly, "at least you trust me now."

"Was there ever any doubt?" the Gunsmith grinned.

"Oh, shut up or I'll punch you again," she told him.

"Please, don't," the Gunsmith sighed, escorting Mary to the barn.

"Oh, God!" she exclaimed, noticing the blood stains on his shirt. "You're hurt."

"I know." Clint nodded. "Son of a bitch ruined another shirt."

"You've got to bandage those up," Mary said. "My God, Clint, you might bleed to death."

"I don't have time," he told her. Besides, the *chindi* is wounded, too. At least I don't have a bullet in me."

"Clint," Mary began, "you need a doctor."

"Don't worry," the Gunsmith smiled. "That's where I'm heading anyway."

THIRTY-TWO

The Gunsmith and Mary Spotted Fawn arrived in Waco about midnight. Clint could only estimate the time because his watch had been broken during the fight with the *chindi*. They led the horses into town. The Gunsmith was breathing hard as he tied Duke's reins to a hitching post.

"Clint," Mary whispered, "you're in no shape to do—"

"You go get the constable," the Gunsmith told her. "Tell him what happened and where to meet me, all right?"

"All right," she agreed reluctantly.

Mary kissed Clint lightly on the mouth. He smiled at her and nodded. She turned and headed for the constable's station. Clint Adams stumbled into the alley and nearly fell on his face when his head started spinning. The Gunsmith leaned against a wall and waited for the multicolored spots to stop floating around in front of his eyes.

Blood trickled from his torn shirt. The claw wounds in his abdomen and sides were bleeding badly. Crimson also oozed from his wounded thigh. His ankle felt as if it were full of broken glass and the wound in his chest had also started to bleed again.

"Well," the Gunsmith muttered to himself, "the *chindi* must not feel any better than I do right about now."

Clint lumbered through the alley. He limped to the rear of the general store and moved to the next building. Clint staggered slightly as his ankle protested the strain he put on it.

However, the Gunsmith kept his balance and covertly slipped to the rear door.

He lowered himself to a kneeling position. This proved too painful so he sat on his rump and took out a small leather packet, which contained some fundamental gunsmithing tools. He opened the case and selected two tools, a narrow cartridge probe and a thin cut-down hacksaw blade. Some time ago, Clint had discovered these instruments could be used in more ways than one.

Slowly the Gunsmith slid the probe and the blade into the keyhole. He felt inside until the metal teeth caught on the latch in the lock. Pressing the probe upward, Clint turned the blade gently. The slight *click* announced that the door was unlocked. The Gunsmith put his tools away and stood up. Drawing the double-action Colt from its holster, Clint carefully turned the knob and eased the door open.

He entered a small, dark room. The pungent odor of disinfectant and alcohol assaulted his nostrils. Boxes were stacked in one corner and a cabinet with shelves of dark bottles was pressed against a wall. Clint saw a strip of light glowing through the bottom crack of a door opposite him.

The Gunsmith crept to the door and placed an ear to it. He heard voices on the other side, a man and a woman. Clint could not understand the words or even hear them well enough to know if the couple spoke English. He opened the door just a crack and stared through the narrow opening.

Sofia Reyes was taping a bandage across the massive, muscular chest of Luis Reyes. The man lay on his back on the same cot where Clint Adams had made love to Sofia. The Gunsmith swung open the door and entered the room.

"Keeping late hours, Doc," the Gunsmith remarked, pointing his revolver at the pair. "If you don't get your rest, it could be bad for your health. Look what working at night did to Luis."

"How did you get in here, Clint?" Sofia demanded, trembling at the sight of his gun. "You have no right—"

"So have me arrested for breaking and entering," Clint

said. "The constable is on his way here anyway."

Luis started to sit up. He grimaced with pain and lay back again. The blacksmith's shirt was gone. He still wore a pair of denim trousers and buckskin boots with metal claws strapped to the toes.

"Where'd you put the rest of your 'big, bad wolf' costume, Luis," the Gunsmith inquired.

"Look, Clint," Sofia began, "my brother was injured while working today. A horse kicked him—"

"Save your breath, lady," the Gunsmith told her.

"Adams is right," Luis said, hissing through clenched teeth as he hauled himself into a sitting position. "It's over, Sofia."

"No," Sofia insisted, "Clint just wants the gold. We'll become partners. A fifty-fifty split. You take half and Luis and I will take half. That is fair, no?"

"I thought you were horrified by grave robbing," Clint said.

"Don't be absurd," she snapped. "Why should gold lie in the ground with the rotting remains of some superstitious Indian savages? Do you know how long we've searched for that gold, Clint? Do you know how many miles we've traveled?"

"All the way from Mexico," Clint sighed. "So I reckon you've been hunting it for a while. The Indians who were here before the Navaho, they were Aztecs, right?"

"You don't even know what that gold disk is," Sofia stated. "Let me tell you, Clint. It is an Aztec calendar. Isn't that remarkable? The Aztecs had a great civilization in Mexico hundreds of years before the Spanish conquistadores came in the sixteenth century. The Aztecs had streets and great buildings. They had pyramids like those of ancient Egypt, and they had a written language, numbers, and their own methods of dates, measures, and weights."

"I don't know much about the Aztecs," Clint confessed. "But I remember Cortés was mistaken for a god by the Aztecs."

"Quetzlcoatl," Sofia stated. "They thought Cortés was Quetzlcoatl. They honored him as a god and brought the conquistadores mountains of gold. The Aztecs had tons of gold, Clint. They had no idea how valuable it was."

"The Old One said that the ancient tribe had been tricked by gods who were really devils in disguise," the Gunsmith recalled. "Reckon that's what it must have seemed like to the Aztecs, especially when Cortés started to blast their city to bits with cannons."

"The Aztecs were a remarkable civilization," Luis said, "but they didn't have gunpowder. The Spanish crushed the Aztecs, but some of them fled. One small group wound up here, in what is now the United States."

"And they buried their dead where your house stands," Sofia declared. "I believe your house must be directly on top of the burial ground."

"How did you find out about this?" the Gunsmith asked.

"What I told you about my father is true," Sofia declared. "We were part of the ruling class of Mexico before Juarez took office. Here, in this country, we lived like peons. I swore that one day I would have the wealth which is my birthright."

"And your husband agreed to help?" Clint inquired.

"Husband?" she stared at the Gunsmith.

"You are clever, Adams," Luis chuckled bitterly. "How did you know Sofia and I are not brother and sister?"

"The other day you behaved more like a jealous husband than an angry brother," the Gunsmith replied. "Besides, it seemed pretty unlikely that the son of a rich Mexican doctor would become a blacksmith. You really shouldn't have gotten so angry with her for sleeping with me, Luis. After all, that was the reason you played this sister-and-brother act to begin with. So Sofia could use her sexual prowess to get information. It was also a good way to keep me occupied while you sneaked out to my place and dug up the ground looking for treasure. You should have just waited, Luis. Constable Puma was ready to blame everything on the three dead outlaws. And tearing up that dead outlaw was not only unnecessary, it was foolish.''

"Clint," Sofia began, stepping toward the Gunsmith, "if you turn us over to the constable, these Navaho will know everything. They'll never let you dig for the rest of the gold—''

"Maybe you're not as bright as I think you are," Clint told her. "I don't care about the gold. I stayed to solve the murder of a friend of mine, remember?''

"But this afternoon—'' she said, confused.

"That was an act, Sofia," Clint told her. "You and Luis aren't the only folks who know how to lie. As for the gold, there's a pretty good chance there isn't any left anyway. I didn't find that disk in a hole on my land. Puma and I found it in the saddlebags of one of those outlaws. In other words, there were grave robbers before you two showed up. You may have killed three people for nothing.''

"I didn't kill anyone!" Sofia announced. "Luis did it, Clint. He was the *chindi*. He's got the wolf robe and mask bundled in a blanket. The claws are there, too.''

"Sofia!" Luis cried, glaring at her.

"Shut up, you idiot!" she snapped. "You've failed me time and time again!''

"Like when he failed to kill me?" the Gunsmith inquired dryly.

"Ah, Clint," she smiled, licking her beautiful lips, "you and I are better suited for each other. Luis is the killer, not I. If you shot him to death, we could tell the constable that my brother was acting on his own. He had gone insane and believed he was a *chindi*. You are clever, Clint. Surely, you could convince Puma—''

"You little bitch," the Gunsmith hissed.

He acted impulsively, swatting the back of his left hand across her face before he realized he'd done it. Clint was startled by his own actions. He had never struck a woman in anger before, but then he had never met one who deserved it as much as Sofia Reyes. The woman staggered away from Clint, more surprised than hurt by his unexpected slap.

Suddenly Luis leaped from the cot. His arms flashed as he quickly seized Sofia from behind. One hand grabbed her hair, while the other gripped the woman's jaw. His massive shoulders twisted hard. Clint heard the ugly crunch of vertebrae snapping as Luis wrenched Sofia's head violently.

"Jesus," Clint gasped, staring into Sofia's sightless, dead eyes.

With a bestial roar, Luis hurled his dead wife at the Gunsmith. Her body crashed into Clint, knocking him off balance. The Gunsmith fell against a wall and tried to swing his Colt at the rampaging Luis. The big man charged forward like an enraged bear and swiftly chopped his hand across Clint's wrist, knocking the gun from his grasp.

Luis whipped the back of his fist across Clint's face. The blow sent Clint sliding along the wall. Luis lunged for his opponent's neck, both hands aimed at the Gunsmith's throat.

Clint clapped his hands and thrust them between Luis's arms. The tent of his elbows struck the larger man's wrists, knocking Luis's hands farther away. Clint raised his hands over head and chopped them down hard, striking Luis at the bridge of the nose. The Mexican howled when his nose cracked and blood squirted.

The Gunsmith slammed a fist into his solar plexus. The big man didn't even grunt. He swung a left hook to the side of Clint's head, which sent the Gunsmith hurtling across the room. Clint bounced off a wall and narrowly avoided a claw-studded kick aimed for his lower belly. The talons raked the wall, tearing out chunks of plaster.

Christ, Clint thought. *The bastard could rip my guts out with those things!*

He lashed a left hook to Luis's jaw. The big man's head barely moved from the punch. Clint rammed a hard right to his larger opponent's chest, hammering his knuckles into the thickest part of the bandage. Luis gasped in agony as the blow caused blood to spread across the bandage. Clint hit him with another left. This time the punch spun Luis like a top.

However, he did not go down. The powerful Mexican suddenly ducked his head and charged. He rammed Clint with bull-like force. The Gunsmith toppled backward and tripped over the cot. He fell to the floor hard. Blood dripped from the claw wounds he had received in the previous fight with the *chindi*. Luis hurried around the end of the cot and swung a taloned foot at Clint's face.

Clint rolled away from the kick. Luis lashed out with his claw-foot again, but Clint scooped up an end of the cot and blocked the second kick. Cloth ripped under the sharp metal. The Gunsmith shoved the cot into Luis while his opponent was still standing on only one foot. The big Mexican cried out with alarm as he lost his balance and fell to the floor.

The Gunsmith reached inside his shirt for the Colt as Luis scrambled to a blanket-bound bundle in the nearest corner. Clint's fingers slipped on the blood-drenched grips of his gun. He fumbled desperately and managed a rather clumsy draw. Luis ripped open the blanket and hurled an object at the Gunsmith.

A head with open jaws hurled at Clint's face. He instinctively ducked to avoid the mask and pointed the little pistol at his opponent. Luis lashed a kick. His boot struck Clint's hand and sent the "belly gun" flying from numb fingers.

"Now," Luis smiled, holding a set of metal claws in his fist, "I'm going to finish you off once and for all!"

He didn't have time to strap the *chindi* claws onto his hands, but he clenched tightly as he swung the talons at the Gunsmith. Clint jumped and snapped a quick kick to his opponent's groin. Luis gasped when the toe of Clint's boot smashed into his crotch. The Gunsmith moved in fast and grabbed the arm holding the clawed fist.

Clint twisted Luis's wrist, trying to force him to release the deadly talons. The brute snarled angrily and hooked a punch with his other fist, hitting Clint in the ribs. The blow struck an area already bleeding from a claw wound. Shards of hot pain burned through the Gunsmith's ribs as his breath spewed from his lungs.

The Gunsmith took his right hand from Luis's wrist and adroitly clawed it across his opponent's face. Luis screamed as Clint's fingernails raked his eyes. The Gunsmith suddenly pivoted and bent his knees to haul Luis's arm across his shoulder. He lifted up with his legs and quickly bent his back to send Luis Reyes hurtling over head.

Luis crashed into a window. Glass shattered and the flimsy framework gave way. The Mexican killer plunged outside. Clint headed for the door, his ankle throbbing with pain. The Gunsmith tried to turn the knob and yank the door open, but it was locked. The key was still in the door. He turned it, unlocked the door, and opened it.

Metal claws slashed at his face before he could step outside. The Gunsmith recoiled from the talon-laced fist and kicked the door shut. Luis bellowed with pain when the door slammed on his wrist. Clint rammed a shoulder into the door, putting all his weight behind it. Luis screamed again as his fingers opened to release the claws.

The Gunsmith moved away from the door, guessing what his opponent would do next. Luis kicked the door hard, smashing it open. Clint threw a right, slamming his fist directly into Luis's broken nose. The big man groaned and staggered backward, blood flowing from his crushed snout.

Clint reached up to grab the top of the door with both hands. He swung himself through the opening and thrust both feet into his opponent's chest. The kick propelled Luis off the plankwalk. He fell into the street, blood stains dyeing his chest bandages deep scarlet.

"Holy shit!" Charlie Puma exclaimed as he and Gary approached the doctor's office.

Clint Adams staggered outside and leaned against a rail for support. Luis slowly started to rise, his powerful body moving like a half-crushed beetle. The Gunsmith gasped for breath, his limbs as heavy as lead. Luis kept struggling to rise, apparently unconcerned about the pool of blood forming at his upper torso.

"Fuckin' bastard," the Gunsmith growled.

He lunged forward and swung a wild right cross. His body stumbled with the motion. Clint felt his knuckles connect with something hard. The impact traveled up his arm to vibrate against his shoulder. Then he fell on his belly in the dust.

The black cloud that swarmed over his consciousness was almost welcome. The Gunsmith sighed as he drifted into oblivion.

THIRTY-THREE

Clint Adams regained consciousness to find himself sprawled on a bed. A kerosene lamp with a low flame illuminated a familiar room with gentle yellow light. Mary Spotted Fawn sat in a chair beside the bed. She offered Clint a glass of water. He gratefully accepted and drank greedily.

"About time you woke up, Adams," Charlie Puma remarked as he stared down at the Gunsmith from the foot of the bed.

"How long have I been out?" Clint asked as he tried to sit up. He glanced down at his body to discover he was naked except for a towel over his crotch and numerous bandages on his wounds.

"About five hours," the constable answered. "Don't feel too bad. We've got Luis Reyes in a cell and he was still out cold when I left him."

"Luis," Clint said, "he's the *chindi*, Constable."

"Yeah." Puma nodded. "We know—found his wolf robe and claws along with another wolf mask. Of course, he was still wearing those boots with claws built into them."

"Check those prints with the old *chindi* tracks," the Gunsmith invited. "You'll find they match."

"I'm sure they will," Puma said. "Miss Reyes was lying on the floor with a broken neck. Reckon you know about that."

"Luis killed her," Clint explained. "She tried to get me to join up with her and use her husband for a scapegoat."

"Husband?" Puma raised his eyebrows.

"Sofia and Luis weren't really sister and brother," the Gunsmith answered. "It's a long story, Constable."

"I'm not going anywhere," Puma assured him.

The Gunsmith told Puma all the details and explained how the Reyes couple had come to Waco to try to claim Aztec gold, which they believed to be buried near there.

"I said before that I thought Luis was the *chindi*," Puma reminded the Gunsmith.

"Yeah," Clint admitted, "but you didn't have any proof."

"Neither did you until tonight," the constable stated. "How did you figure it out anyway?"

"Well, I lied to everybody about the gold," Clint began. "It was just a hunch, but I figured the disk had to be connected with the burial ground. After I talked to the Old One and learned that the ancient tribe that settled here had come from the south, I figured they might be Aztecs. The story about the false gods fit what the Aztecs went through when Cortés and the Spaniards conquered their empire. Sofia and Luis seemed the most likely folks to know about Aztecs."

"But you weren't sure?" Puma asked.

"I wasn't sure until the *chindi* attacked me again when I entered the house," the Gunsmith explained. "I had already fought the jasper once before and it ended in more or less a draw. The *chindi* would know that I'd have guns ready and waiting for him, yet he attacked me again without using a firearm."

"But how'd you know Luis didn't own a gun?" Puma asked.

"I didn't," Clint answered. "But whoever the *chindi* was, he had to have more faith in trying to take me on with his metal claws and muscles than a gun. Luis was the most logical choice. Figured it had to be him."

"Well, I don't think he's strong enough to bust out of jail," Puma remarked. "We'll keep him locked up until the circuit judge arrives. Sure as hell have enough evidence to convict the bastard. Only thing is, I hope that won't open a can of worms.''

"What do you mean?'' Clint asked.

"I mean the trial will be public and probably take place beyond Fox County,'' Puma sighed. "That means more folks are going to learn about that burial ground. Could be we'll have more and more grave robbers stirring up trouble again.''

"I don't know what to suggest, Constable,'' the Gunsmith admitted. "Of course, he could be 'shot while trying to escape,' but I doubt that you'd agree to something like that. I know I wouldn't.''

"Pain in the ass having principles,'' Puma sighed. "By the way, I trust you'll be willing to sell that property to the town council now?''

"Hell,'' the Gunsmith replied, "I'll sign the property over to them. I sure as hell don't need it.''

"I don't reckon that would be right, Adams,'' Puma told him. "Wouldn't be fair to you after all you've gone through.''

"I didn't stay in Waco to make a profit,'' Clint said. "I stayed to make certain Tom's killer was brought to justice.''

"But Tom Shatner left you that property in his will,'' Puma insisted. "That meant he wanted you to have something from him after he died. If you don't want the property, you ought to accept the money for it.''

"Maybe you're right,'' Clint smiled. "I'm stubborn at times, but it's a little silly to turn down a profit. Still, I think two hundred dollars is too much. The town treasury shouldn't have to lose that much money for a chunk of land. Tell the council I'll sell it to them for one hundred bucks. No more, no less. Sound fair?''

"I think that'll make everybody happy, Adams,'' Puma nodded. "I'll let you rest up now and—''

The roar of a gunshot bellowed from somewhere outside.

Puma drew his pistol and headed for the door. Clint started to get out of bed, but Mary shoved his shoulders back to the bed.

"You stay put," she chided. "Let Charlie take care of whatever it is. You've done enough already, damn it."

"I don't suppose you know where my gun is?" Clint asked, watching Puma disappear from the room into the main barroom of the cantina.

"I know where it is," Mary replied. "But you're not getting out of that bed, Clint Adams."

"Shit," the Gunsmith muttered as he lay helpless on his back.

Minutes slowly crawled by, but Clint did not hear another gunshot. Almost ten minutes passed before Charlie Puma finally returned to the cantina and strolled into the Gunsmith's room.

"What happened, Constable?" Clint asked anxiously.

"Shot came from the jailhouse," the constable answered.

"God," Clint rasped, "Luis escaped?"

"No," Puma answered, "and he sure ain't going to now."

"You mean he tried to escape and Gary shot him?"

"Not that either," Puma explained. "Harry Two-Ponies didn't go back to his home. He was staying with a friend here in town. Fella heard about Luis. Harry knew we had the *chindi* and that meant we had the fella who murdered his wife. So Harry crept down to the jail, stuck his shotgun through the bars of the cell, and blew Luis Reyes's head off."

"Guess you don't have to worry about a trial now," Clint stated simply.

"What about Harry?" Puma frowned.

"He executed the man who murdered his wife," Clint shrugged. "I don't know if that's a crime or not. You folks decide if you want to arrest him."

"Kind of a waste of time," Puma shrugged. "No jury would find him guilty."

"However you want to handle it," Clint said. "Justice

doesn't always come from a courtroom. What do you reckon the town will do with Tom's old spread?''

"Probably tear down the house and use the land for the same thing the Aztecs used it for. Reckon we need a cemetery. God knows we got enough customers for one now. Be kind of glad when you leave, Adams.''

"Me too,'' the Gunsmith admitted. "By the way, where are my pants?''

"Over there,'' Mary answered, pointing to a chair. Clint's clothing was draped over the backrest.

"Do me a favor, Puma,'' the Gunsmith began. "Check in the pockets and get that damn Aztec calendar.''

"Calendar?'' the constable asked.

"The gold disk with the funny symbols on it,'' Clint explained. "The one you found in Luke's saddlebags.''

"What do you want me to do with it?'' Puma asked.

"Bury it at the new cemetery,'' Clint replied.

"What?'' Puma stared at him with surprise. "You want me to throw away a gold relic?''

"Keep it if you want,'' the Gunsmith told him. "Just get it out of my sight.''

"Don't tell me you're beginning to believe in old Indian curses, Adams.'' Puma smiled.

"Let's just say I'm not so sure they don't work sometimes,'' the Gunsmith answered. "After all, everybody who tried to rob that Aztec burial ground died violently for it. The three outlaws, Sofia, Luis. Even Tom and Ellie who just lived there. I'd say that curse worked pretty well, wouldn't you?''

"I think I'll bury this thing,'' Puma stated as he fished it out of Clint's trousers.

"The Aztecs will rest better for it,'' Mary said with a nod.

"I know I will,'' the Gunsmith admitted.

"Folks,'' Puma sighed, "reckon I'll go help Gary clean up that cell. Or maybe I'll have Harry do it. After all, he's the one who made the mess.''

"Well, you won't get very far trying to make Luis clean it up," the Gunsmith told him.

The constable, moving toward the door, turned to smile at the Gunsmith. "Adams," he said.

"Yeah?" Clint replied.

"You might not think much of this town," Puma began, "except for Mary here. You haven't gotten a very pleasant welcome. I know I was hard on you myself—"

"Don't worry about it, Constable," the Gunsmith assured him. "Besides, I remember you and the town council rescued me from a lynch mob. No hard feelings."

"Call me Charlie," Puma urged. "And I hope you'll stay around Waco for a couple days to get a chance to see our better side."

"Clint's going to have to stay until he recovers from these dreadful wounds," Mary stated.

"Can't stay long," the Gunsmith replied. "I've got to go back to Largo Gap to get my wagon and the rest of my gear."

"We'll talk about how long you'll stay," Mary said with a smile. "You might just find a reason or two to stay for a while."

"Now," the Gunsmith said with a grin, "that wouldn't really surprise me a bit."

THIRTY-FOUR

The Gunsmith spent three days in Waco. The citizens of the tiny town were very pleasant and Clint enjoyed spending time with Mary Spotted Fawn; however, he was not a man to stay anywhere for long. Clint said his good-byes and rode out of Waco on the morning of the fourth day.

However, before he returned to Largo Gap for his belongings, Clint had one more person to say farewell to. He rode Duke to a small adobe dwelling a mile from town. The Gunsmith dismounted and approached the goatskin curtain at the door.

"Old One," the Gunsmith called, "this is Clint Adams."

There was no answer.

"Old One?" Clint called again.

"Come, Clint Adams," a reedy voice replied weakly. "Come into my home, my friend."

The Gunsmith pushed aside the curtain and entered. The ancient, wrinkled figure sat motionless on his buffalo robe. The Old One's eyes were closed and his mouth clamped shut in a straight line. His back was straight and his hands folded in his lap.

"I came to say good-bye, Old One," Clint explained. "I wanted to thank you again for your help and—"

The old man did not move. Clint leaned closer and looked at the old man's face. His eyes and mouth did not move. He did not appear to be breathing.

"Old One?" Clint asked, slowly extending his hand.

He barely touched the old man's shoulder. The ancient Indian fell stiffly on his side. The Gunsmith rolled him on his back. The Old One's mouth dropped open, but no sound came from his parchment lips. Clint placed a hand to the old man's chest. He found no heartbeat.

"Oh, Jesus," Clint whispered, a cold knot forming in his stomach. "But I heard him call to me . . ."

The Gunsmith folded the old man's hands on his shriveled chest. "You must have called to me just before you died," he said to the corpse, "or maybe I just imagined it."

The body was stiff as if rigor mortis had already begun, yet the old man did not have the stench of death. Clint didn't know what to do with the body. Should he bury it or notify townsfolk in Waco?

Clint remembered the Old One had no family.

"I wonder how long he would have been here unburied if I hadn't come along?" Clint mused.

The Gunsmith shivered. He wrapped the dead form in the buffalo blanket and slowly hauled the corpse outside. Clint glanced about. There was a small grassy area near the old adobe house. He decided this would be an ideal place to bury the Old One.

"You said after a hundred years you were tired," the Gunsmith remarked as he rolled up his sleeves to begin digging the grave. "Reckon now you'll finally rest, old man."

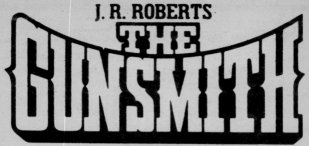

J. R. ROBERTS
THE GUNSMITH

SERIES

Prices may be slightly higher in Canada.

WISHING LAKE

REGINA HART

Kensington Publishing Corp.
http://www.kensingtonbooks.com

DAFINA BOOKS are published by

Kensington Publishing Corp.
119 West 40th Street
New York, NY 10018

All Kensington titles, imprints and distributed lines are available at special quantity discounts for bulk purchases for sales promotions, premiums, fund-raising, and educational or institutional use. Special book excerpts or customized printings can also be created to fit specific needs. For details, write or phone the office of the Kensington Special Sales Manager. Kensington Publishing Corp., 119 West 40th Street, New York, NY 10018. Attn: Special Sales Department. Phone: 1-800-221-2647.

Dafina and the Dafina logo Reg. U.S. Pat. & TM Off.

ISBN-13: 978-1-61773-564-6
ISBN-10: 1-61773-564-7
First Kensington Mass Market Edition: February 2015

eISBN-13: 978-1-61773-565-3
eISBN-10: 1-61773-565-5
First Kensington Electronic Edition: February 2015

10 9 8 7 6 5 4 3 2 1

Printed in the United States of America

To my dream team:

- *My sister, Bernadette, for giving me the dream*
- *My husband, Michael, for supporting the dream*
- *My brother, Richard, for believing in the dream*
- *My brother, Gideon, for encouraging the dream*
- *My friends, Marcia James and Linda H, for sharing the dream*

And to Mom and Dad always with love

ACKNOWLEDGMENTS

Special thanks to Elizabeth P. for information on the Day of the Dead celebration. Any inaccuracies are solely my misinterpretation.

CHAPTER 1

An explosive bang was Darius Knight's first clue of impending danger.

"We're trapped." The tension in Dr. Peyton Harris's voice sealed the deal.

Darius rose from his crouched position beside a box of old folders in Trinity Falls University's archive room. The cramped room measured approximately forty-five by thirty-five feet and was a claustrophobe's worst nightmare.

He navigated the space between two of the glorified bookcases stuffed with a hodgepodge of dented and dusty boxes of historical documents. Once he'd emerged into the main aisle, he crossed to Peyton. The university's history professor wrestled with the doorknob as though unwilling to believe the evidence in her hands.

"Let me try." Darius waited for Peyton to make room for him.

The top of her head just reached his shoulders. The powdery fragrance of her perfume was a blessed relief from the bitter stink of mold and age that blossomed around them.

Peyton stepped aside with obvious reluctance. Darius pressed down on the door's long, thin copper handle. It didn't budge, not even a little. His gaze dropped to the floor.

"Where's the door stopper?" Darius had watched Peyton kick the triangular block of blond wood into place beneath the door with the toe of her navy pumps. The wood should have kept the door open.

Peyton's caramel eyes widened in her honey-and-chocolate-cream face. "It must be on the other side of the door."

"Someone locked us in." And there was nothing they could do until that person chose to let them out.

Darius returned to the bookshelves to continue his documents search. His greatest concern was suffocating on the sour stench of his surroundings. Already his eyes were tearing.

"Why would someone do that?" Peyton's disbelief followed him into the stacks.

Hadn't she noticed the pointed comments and questions people made about them? Doreen Fever, manager of the café at Books & Bakery, had known him almost his entire life. Why was she now confusing his lunch orders with Peyton's whenever they were in the café at the same time? Was it to force them to interact with each other?

Darius stepped out of the book stacks and countered her question with one of his own. "How did you get assigned to take me to the archives?"

He watched the little professor smooth her hair. She'd pulled the rich copper mass into a tight bun at the nape of her slim neck. When he'd met her in July—four months ago—she'd worn her hair in a loose riot of curls that had framed her heart-shaped face. He preferred it that way.

"Foster asked me." Peyton referred to Foster Gooden, the university's vice president for academic affairs. "He said you needed information on Dr. Hartford's accomplishments at TFU for your article." She glanced around the room. "I hadn't realized the archives were such a mess."

Dr. Kenneth Hartford, chair of the history department, was retiring after thirty-five years with the university.

"You didn't have to agree." Darius leaned his shoulder against the side of the bookshelf and surveyed the archives.

This wasn't his first foray into the dingy room. He'd known it was a disaster. Foster insisted the university didn't have enough money to hire an archivist to maintain its historical files. Until they came into some sort of windfall—Foster's words—the room would remain as is.

On one side of the subterranean space, mismatched gray metal shelves and mahogany bookcases strained to hold archival records. On the other side, an explosion of papers buried scarred wooden desks and battered metal cabinets. They'd been left behind by people who were unaware or uncaring of the importance of recording the university's history. A maze of boxes formed an obstacle course in the space in between.

The archives' one salvation was a blue binder that struggled to maintain its position on top of an abused clerical desk. The binder cataloged the decades-old boxes that someone had labeled—unlike the newer arrivals, which were anyone's guess. Somewhere in one of those boxes was information on the honors program Dr. Hartford had revamped and the master's of political science program he'd created. Darius hoped he found the documents soon. He could use some fresh air. Or another whiff of Peyton's perfume.

Peyton crossed her arms over her chest. "Why wouldn't I take you to the archives?"

"Because you still don't trust me." Darius held her caramel eyes.

Peyton dropped her arms and her gaze. She checked her watch, letting the silence grow. "I wish I'd brought my cell phone."

She didn't deny not trusting him. Why did that bother him so much? "You wouldn't have gotten reception down here."

"Then how are we going to get out?"

Darius checked his silver Timex wristwatch, which displayed the image of Batman's bat-signal in the center. It was almost ten-thirty on this Friday morning in mid-October. "Give it twenty minutes or so. Someone will come." He returned to the files he'd been searching.

Peyton followed him. "How can you be so sure? And how do you know they'll come in twenty minutes?"

Was she oblivious to the matchmakers in Trinity Falls who were trying to push them together? Why did she think Foster had singled her out to take him to the archives? He knew it was against policy to have non-university personnel in the records room alone. However, the vice president could have accompanied Darius himself or asked his administrative assistant to escort him.

Darius sank into a crouch in front of the book-cases. "The people who locked us in here aren't malicious. They want to give us time alone together. They'd think twenty minutes was long enough."

Who had convinced Foster to trap him in here with Peyton? Was it Doreen? A better suspect would be Megan McCloud. The owner of Books & Bakery was the girlfriend of one of his childhood friends and a seasoned strategist. She'd shaped six inde-pendent, struggling town center enterprises into the Trinity Falls Town Center Business Association, a unified voice for their business community.

Or perhaps the responsible party was Ramona McCloud, Megan's cousin and mayor of Trinity Falls. Ramona was a meddler as well as the girlfriend of another of Darius's childhood friends, Dr. Quincy Spates.

Or maybe Quincy was involved. As a former Trin-ity Falls University professor, he and Foster knew each other well. Besides, the strategy was so lame, it had Quincy's fingerprints all over it.

"This is absurd." Peyton blew a disbelieving breath. "You're talking as though you know who these people are. If that's true, who are they and why do they want to trap us in here together?"

"They're trying to make a love connection be-tween us." Darius plucked from the archive box a folder labeled HONORS PROGRAM, 1981.

Success! It was always fifty-fifty whether he'd find what he was looking for among the decaying files. Triumph made him light-headed . . . or maybe it was the mold.

"A love connection?" Peyton seemed puzzled.

Darius left the box on the ground and stood with the folder. He turned to Peyton. She looked as though she was about to burst into laughter.

"Why is the idea of being set up with me funny?" He stepped around her and crossed to the clerical desk.

"They're trying to set *us* up? You and me?"

Darius eyed her over his shoulder. "Obviously, they don't realize you're uncomfortable around me."

"No, I'm not." Peyton rubbed her arms.

"Are you cold?" Darius plucked his coat from the chair behind the desk and offered it to her.

She lifted her right hand, palm out. "I'll be fine. Thank you, though."

Darius stepped forward, settling the garment on her shoulders. "My coat doesn't bite. Neither do I."

Peyton was drowning in Darius's midnight gaze. His lightweight winter coat surrounded her. She drew a deep, steadying breath and inhaled his scent—soap and cedar—clinging to his coat. His eyes searched hers.

Peyton looked away. "Thank you." Their voices echoed in the room . . . or was that her imagination?

"Don't mention it." Darius consulted the blue binder before crossing back to the bookcases to continue his search.

Peyton tracked the newspaper reporter's progress. He was a pleasure to look at: tall and slim with lean muscles his lightweight, bronze crewneck sweater and navy Dockers couldn't mask. When he hunkered down again to reach a box on a lower shelf, she swallowed hard, then asked for mercy. She let the silence soothe her for several long minutes.

"According to you, someone should be here in about ten minutes to let us out of this room." Peyton broke the silence, snuggling deeper into Darius's coat.

"Give or take." Darius appeared to have located the box he needed. He tugged it onto the floor and started sifting through its files.

"And you think this rescuer will be the same person who locked us in here in the first place, one of the matchmakers?"

"Probably." He seemed distracted.

"Don't you think that sounds just a little paranoid?"

Darius arched a brow. It was one of the sexiest expressions she'd ever seen. "Do you think Megan confuses other customers' purchases?"

Peyton was a little concerned that her last two hold requests from Books & Bakery had ended up with Darius. And Doreen was always trying to give her his food. Still . . .

"Why would Megan think *you* need help getting a date? She knows every woman in town is chasing after you."

"Every woman?" Darius straightened. In one fluid movement, he unfolded his long, lean body and turned to face her. He gripped an aged manila folder with his long fingers. "Including you?"

"*Me*?" Peyton rocked back on her heels. "Of course not."

"Pity." Darius held her gaze.

Peyton exhaled to ease the butterflies in her stomach. She checked her rose-gold Movado watch again. "Do you really think someone will rescue us in ten minutes?"

"Ten minutes or so." Darius crossed to the table. He collected the two worn-and-weathered folders he'd liberated from their boxes. Then he cleared a space on the corner of the table to sit.

"Did you get what you needed?" Peyton circled the desk to sit on its matching scarred chair.

She hadn't realized how close the seat would put her to the reporter. Was that his breath she felt across her hair? She could reach out and touch him. His scent teased her.

"Yes." Darius waved the folders. "I'll make copies once we get out of here, then return the original folders to their boxes."

Peyton was silent for several moments, surveying the row of bookcases in front of her and the framed photographs of campus scenes affixed to the once-white walls. She turned her attention anywhere and everywhere to avoid looking at the man in front of her. Everything about the reporter was distractingly sexy, from the shape of his head to the sound of his voice. Even the way he looked at her, as though no one else, nothing else, mattered. She adjusted Darius's coat to keep it from slipping off her shoulders. She didn't want to put her arms through his sleeves, though. That seemed too intimate.

She sighed with growing impatience. "What if no one comes?"

"When you first joined TFU's faculty four months ago, I promised not to write an article about you. I've kept that promise. I thought that proved you could trust me."

"What does my trusting you have to do with our being locked in here?"

"Why do I make you uncomfortable?" Darius shifted on the desk, giving her his full attention.

Peyton swallowed hard. "You're not my type."

"What type am I?" He gave her his arched-brow look again.

Why was he asking her these questions? "The type who has women throwing themselves at him."

Darius's intense, midnight gaze seemed to bore a hole into her mind. "You think I'm a player?"

"Aren't you?"

"You've been in town all of four months. What makes you think you know me well enough to judge me?"

"I'm not judging you. The people in this town seem to like and respect you—especially the women." Peyton couldn't resist that observation.

"And that makes *me* the player? Is that the reason you don't trust me?"

She took in the cool look in his eyes, the furrows across his forehead, the tightness around his lips. Had she hurt him?

"I—" Peyton's response was interrupted by loud knocking. A welcome relief.

"Is anyone in there?" Foster Gooden's voice was muffled behind the archive door.

"Yes. We're in here." Darius rose from the desk and walked toward the entrance. He glanced back at Peyton, lowering his voice. "As if he didn't know."

"We're locked in. Did you bring your key?" Peyton shouted at Foster as she hurried after Darius. She was fascinated as always by the fluid motion of his long, lean muscles. He must work out.

The clanging of keys on the other side of the locked door filled Peyton with joy. She was getting out of here. She stood beside Darius, waiting for Foster to unlock the door, offering them freedom and fresh air.

Foster pulled open the door, then kicked the triangular block of wood back into place beneath it. "You were locked in? How did that happen?"

Was it her imagination or did the university's vice president for academic affairs seem nervous? His smile was unsteady. His brown cheeks were flushed.

Darius inclined his head toward the door. "Someone removed that block of wood and let the door shut."

Foster's eyes widened. "Why would someone do that?"

"Why, indeed?" Peyton's eyes narrowed. Was there something to Darius' suspicions?

"Do you know the best thing about your mother's walking out on me?" Simon Knight's voice seemed to carry to every corner of the Books & Bakery café Saturday morning.

Seconds ago, Darius and his friends had been exchanging banter and laughter over breakfast at the café's counter. Now the group grew silent as Simon joined them. Darius cringed inwardly as his father dropped onto the bar stool beside him. Tension poured down his spine, stiffening his back like cement.

"This isn't the place." Darius lowered his voice and used his coffee mug to gesture toward the people around them.

Behind the counter, Megan stood with Ramona and Doreen. On the other side of the counter,

Darius sat beside Ean Fever, his childhood friend who was also Doreen's son and Megan's boyfriend. Jackson Sansbury, Darius's boss and a member of the town's founding family, sat with his girlfriend, songwriter Audra Lane.

Simon ignored Darius's perhaps-too-subtle request to change the subject. "I can do whatever I want, whenever I want, wherever I want. Last night, I ate dinner in bed."

Megan gave a slow blink of her cinnamon eyes. "Why would you want to eat an entire meal in bed?"

Ramona almost choked on her coffee. "What my cousin's trying to say in her overly diplomatic way is, unless you're sick, eating a meal in bed is one way to make sure you always sleep alone."

Simon settled back onto the bar stool. "Maybe I should tell Quincy to enjoy his final days of freedom before you join him in Philadelphia in January."

"Your wife walked out on you." Ramona shook her head. "I don't think Quincy would benefit from your relationship advice."

Doreen cut into the conversation. "What can I get for you, Simon?"

Darius gritted his teeth. It had been too much to hope his father would say whatever he had to say, then leave.

"I had breakfast at home." Simon pointed toward the pastry display. "I'll just take a slice of Boston cream pie and a coffee." He slapped Darius's back. "I'm really here to keep my boy company."

Darius had relived this nightmare every Saturday since his parents' separation in July. It was like a macabre version of the Bill Murray movie *Groundhog Day*.

"I have plenty of friends here." Darius took a calming breath and drew in the scent of coffee, bacon, confectioner's sugar, and cinnamon. He shoved his bacon and eggs around his plate. Maybe in time his appetite would return.

Simon accepted the mug of coffee Doreen gave him. "Yeah, but you're the only single one. Jackson's dating Audra. Ean's with Megan. Ramona's moving to Philadelphia to join Quincy. Even Doreen's dating again."

"Gee, thanks." Doreen offered Simon his slice of pie. It was served on a white porcelain plate that probably had more sense than he did.

"You give me hope, Doreen." Simon plunged his fork into the pie. "If you can reenter the dating scene so easily after being widowed after more than thirty years of marriage, the transition will be easy as pie for me." He chuckled at his own humor.

"Where's Alonzo?" Audra asked, referring to Alonzo Lopez, the town's sheriff and Doreen's boyfriend. "He usually joins us Saturday mornings."

In the songwriter's voice, Darius heard a desperate attempt to change the subject.

Simon chuckled. "Yeah, Doreen. You'd better check on your man. You don't want him running away with a younger woman."

Ramona crossed her arms. "You would know all about married men and younger women, wouldn't you?"

"Ramona." Jackson's low voice held a cautionary tone.

Darius appreciated his boss's concern for his feelings, but it wasn't necessary. He'd known for years the kind of man his father was.

He turned to Simon. "Why are you here?"

"You need someone in your corner." Simon jabbed Darius's upper arm with his elbow as he washed down more pie with a swig of coffee. "Don't let them pressure you, son. There's nothing wrong with being single."

Darius regarded Simon in disbelief. "You're not single. You and Mom are still married."

Simon scowled. "We're separated."

"Not legally." Darius searched his father's expression. If Simon was anxious to end his marriage, why didn't he file for divorce?

"Speaking as a lawyer, Darius is right." Ean lowered his coffee mug. "Your separation hasn't dissolved your marriage."

Ean shoved away his empty plate. In contrast, Darius's half-eaten breakfast cooled in front of him. Again. The only way he'd regain his appetite was if Simon left. Past experience demonstrated that wouldn't be happening any time soon.

"Are you and Ethel going to try to work things out?" Megan's question elicited a dry look from Darius.

His parents reconcile? Not likely. They'd been hurtling toward a divorce his entire life.

Simon grunted. "Why would I want to get back together with Ethel? I've never been as happy as I am now without her. In fact, I'm looking forward to getting back into the dating scene."

"I thought you'd never left it." Darius couldn't let Simon's hypocritical comment pass unchallenged.

His father glowered at him. "Now don't you start with me. A man makes one mistake—"

"Only one?" Darius interrupted.

Simon swallowed more pie. "I never said I was perfect. Still, your mother left me anyway."

"I don't understand that." Ramona rested her hands on the counter. "Don't get me wrong. I would have left you, too—after I knocked out all of your teeth."

"Ramona." Megan's voice carried a low, reproving note.

Audra set down her porcelain mug of coffee. It landed on the Formica counter with a decisive snap. "Let's get back to discussing the Halloween party. It's next week and I want to know what to expect from my first Trinity Falls Halloween."

Darius could have kissed Jackson's girlfriend for again trying to change the topic. She'd arrived in Trinity Falls from Los Angeles in July, just a few weeks before Peyton had arrived from New York. Audra had left briefly after Founders Day in August, but Jackson had wooed her back. The couple seemed more in love every day.

"Now that's a perfect example of what I'm talking about." Simon looked at Megan and Ramona. "Ethel never wanted to come to your Halloween celebration. Well, you can bet I'm coming this year."

Great. In addition to ruining Darius' Saturday morning breakfast routine, Simon was going to put a damper on the Books & Bakery Halloween celebration. He'd rather be locked in the smelly archives again—with Dr. Peyton Harris, of course.

Jackson leaned forward on his bar stool. "Simon, what are you going to do now that you're retired from the post office?"

"Oh, I've got plenty to do," Simon rushed to reassure him. "Plenty."

"Such as?" Darius prompted.

Simon laughed, tipping his head toward Doreen. "Oh, you think I pulled out of challenging Doreen for the mayor's job because I didn't think I could beat her?"

Ramona snorted. "No, we think you came to your senses."

Darius gripped his cup. "Your name never even made it to the election ballot. You didn't get enough signatures on your petition to enter the mayoral campaign."

Simon sulked. "That's another thing your mother ruined for me."

Darius's tension grew in his neck and shoulders. "You ruined that for yourself."

"Your mother's not an easy person to live with, you know." Simon finished his pie.

Darius clenched his teeth. "This isn't the time or place for this conversation."

Simon ignored his son's warning. "She's a bitter, angry woman. She's bitter and angry all the time."

Darius had had enough. He forced himself to move calmly as he rose to his feet. He pulled his wallet from his pocket and left more than enough money beside his plate to cover his breakfast.

"Thank you, Doreen." Darius turned to leave, ignoring his friends' concerned expressions. "I'll see you guys later."

But Simon wouldn't let up. "She wasn't even that good of a mother to you. Admit it."

Darius forced himself not to respond, not to

react. No, Ethel hadn't been a picture-perfect mother. But the whole town didn't need to know that. Although some probably suspected it.

Instead of replying, he hardened his heart and kept on moving. He'd had a lot of practice doing that over the years. So much practice, he'd begun to wonder whether he'd ever feel again.

CHAPTER 2

Peyton closed and locked her kitchen window. Her apartment still reeked of burned toast. It couldn't be helped now. She had a lot of errands to run and needed to get moving.

She was almost to her front door when the phone in her living room rang. Should she answer it? With a sigh, she turned around. It could be one of her students.

Peyton shrugged off her jacket. The low heels of her red Rockports were muffled on the gold carpet as she hurried back to her living room. She glanced at her phone, perched on the large, mahogany corner table. The caller ID mocked her. She should have ignored the summons.

She picked up the receiver. "Hello, Mom."

"Peyton, darling, what took you so long to answer the phone?" Irene Biery Harris was adept at masking her prying ways under a caring tone. She'd been that way all of Peyton's life. But by the age of five, Peyton had gotten wise to her pretenses.

"You caught me on my way out. How can I help you?"

"Where are you going?"

"I have a lot of errands to run." Peyton didn't want to go into the details of her last-minute shopping for her Halloween costume accessories. Besides, she still wasn't certain she was comfortable wearing the outfit Ramona had talked her into buying.

She settled onto her pale silver sofa. Apparently, this was going to take a while. She glanced at her wristwatch. It was just after ten o'clock Saturday morning. It was hard to believe that, almost twenty-four hours ago, she'd been locked in the archives with Darius Knight.

Plenty of women in Trinity Falls would have loved to have switched places with her. Instead, Peyton was more interested in the mystery still surrounding that event. Was Darius right? Were the town's match-makers set on pairing her with one of their most eligible bachelors? Why?

"Don't tire yourself out, darling." Irene adopted a nurturing croon. "It isn't good for your looks."

"Thank you, Mom." Peyton rubbed a hand over her face. "Why are you calling?"

"Your father and I have a wonderful idea to celebrate Christmas this year. We're planning a trip to Aruba!"

Her parents planned to travel for Christmas? The coward in her cheered their decision. "Aruba? That's wonderful. I hope you and Dad have a great time."

"We all will." Irene laughed. "You and Bruce are coming with us."

We are?

"Have you spoken with Bruce?" How could her soon-to-be-ex-fiancé, Bruce Grave, commit them to a Caribbean Christmas vacation without consulting her?

"Of course not!" Irene laughed again. "We wanted to share the surprise with you first."

This is a surprise all right.

"I had no idea you and Dad would ever consider celebrating Christmas anywhere other than New York. What brought this on?"

"You did! Your father and I love living in New York. We love everything about the city—the neighborhoods, the theaters, the museums. But after you decided to take a sabbatical from New York University to teach for a semester at that small college in Trident Forrest, Iowa—"

"Trinity Falls, Ohio."

"That's right. We decided to try something different, too. But we wanted to go someplace warm. And Aruba sounds so exciting, doesn't it? *Aruba.*"

"I don't think I can manage a Caribbean trip right now." Peyton rubbed her left temple.

"I know professors don't make any money. And I'm sure you're making even less now at that tiny college in Iowa—"

"It's a university, Mom. And it's in Ohio." Peyton held on to her patience with both fists.

"Yes. But I'm sure Bruce will pay for the trip. After all, you're practically married."

No, we aren't.

How was she going to get out of this? "It's not about money. This just isn't a good time."

"Why not? Isn't Christmas break the end of fall semester?"

Her mother couldn't remember Peyton was teaching at a university, not a college. Irene couldn't recall the name of the town or to which state Peyton had moved. But trust Irene Biery Harris to finally remember Christmas break was the end of fall semester when it benefited her.

"Yes, but I need to prepare for the start of NYU's spring semester." Peyton's lies were adding up. Why didn't she just tell her parents and Bruce the truth? *Because I'm a coward.*

"You can do that over the vacation." Irene's tone was dismissive. She'd made up her mind to have a family Christmas in Aruba.

"I'm sure that would be a lot of fun for me, pouring over syllabi in the hotel room while the rest of you frolic on the beach." Peyton smoothed her left hand over her hair. She'd left it free rather than wrestling it into the tight bun her mother insisted suited a college professor better. After all, Irene couldn't see her now.

Irene snorted. "It would be your decision to bring work on vacation."

Peyton's eyes slid over her glass-and-sterling silver entertainment center with the large, silver, flat-screen television, cable box, and DVD player. How could she end this nightmare?

"Why don't we talk about this when I come home for Thanksgiving?" Would Irene grant her this reprieve? It was still sooner than she'd planned to give her parents and Bruce her news.

"Thanksgiving is more than a month away." Irene was employing her whiny voice. "Your father and I want to make these arrangements sooner rather than later."

Peyton understood Irene's concern. Thanksgiving was November twenty-seventh. Today was October twenty-fifth. But she couldn't allow her mother to pressure her.

She glanced again at her watch. It was almost ten-fifteen. Books & Bakery's Halloween event would start at one this afternoon.

Peyton rose. "Mom, I need to get going. I'll call Bruce later to discuss the trip with him." More lies. How large would her web of deceit become?

"You do that, darling. You know, you're lucky to have a man like Bruce. Men like him—wealthy, attractive—can have any woman they want. He chose you."

"Yes, Mom." In fact, Peyton's parents had chosen Bruce. But what did Bruce really want—Peyton or a partnership in her father's investment firm? Peyton suspected she knew the answer to that.

"All right, darling. I hope to hear from you. Soon. I'll give your father your love."

"Thanks, Mom. Good-bye." Peyton recradled the phone.

Some of her enthusiasm for her day had waned. Her mother had just moved up her day of reckoning. Would she have enough time to prepare for it?

Darius tracked Megan McCloud's progress from her office to where he stood with their friends near the front of Books & Bakery. The bookstore owner looked like a very irritated Robin Hood. It was the last Saturday of October, the day Books & Bakery hosted its annual Halloween celebration and children's story time. For the event, Megan had chosen an archer's costume. Her tall, slender figure was wrapped in a formfitting, long brown vest; loose white shirt; black tights; and boot tops. The white feather tucked into her black felt hat vibrated with temper as she pushed past him, Ean, and Jackson.

Megan settled her hands on her slim hips before confronting her cousin and business partner. "Ramona, you hired *Stan* for our children's Halloween story time—*again?*"

Ramona looked toward the store's entrance. "Has he arrived?"

Not for the first time, Darius wondered whether Ramona had chosen her costume—*Star Wars'* Queen Amidala, complete with white jumpsuit and laser gun—as a tribute to her boyfriend, Quincy. Dr. Quincy Spates, who was now teaching at the University of Pennsylvania, couldn't make this year's Books & Bakery Halloween celebration. It was the first one he'd ever missed. But the *Star Wars* fanatic would have loved his girlfriend's costume.

"No, Stan hasn't arrived yet. Belinda told me you'd hired him." Megan referred to Belinda Curby, the owner of Skin Deep Beauty Salon. "Ramona, why did you hire the town *drunk* to read to children *again?* Don't you remember what happened the last time you did this?"

Ramona waved a dismissive hand. "That was last year. Stan's a changed man now."

"That's what you said last time." Megan's words were almost incoherent behind her clenched teeth.

Ramona seemed to consider the accusation. "No, I didn't."

Darius judged the risk of entering the fray and decided his odds were good. "Megan, I understand your concern, but maybe this time will be different. Let's give Stan a chance."

If it were possible, smoke would have billowed from Megan's ears. "Last year, he sang obscene bar songs to my customers—including the children."

"And Mom took care of that." Ean stepped closer to Megan, resting a hand on the small of her back.

Megan glanced at Ean. Her tense features eased just a bit. "That's true. Thank goodness for Doreen."

"Everyone deserves a second chance, wouldn't you agree?" Darius appealed to Megan's well-known sense of fairness.

"I'd agree." Ramona nodded.

Megan spun on her. "Of course you would. You're the one who hired him—*again*."

"If Stan's not sober, we'll take care of it," Jackson said. "But it's worth the risk to give Stan another chance."

Megan switched her glare from Ramona to Jackson. "How will you take care of it?"

Jackson shrugged. "I'll take him home."

"And I'll take his place reading to the kids." Ramona grinned. "They enjoyed my reading last year."

Megan looked from Jackson to Ramona, then back. "All right."

Darius's relief was short-lived as Megan zeroed in on him, Jackson, and Ean. They were on the precipice of another crisis.

Megan clenched her fists. "Oh, for heaven's sake! Where are your costumes?"

Ean rushed to reassure her. "We're wearing

costumes. I'm a corporate executive. I'm even wearing a power tie." He smoothed the red silk fabric.

"I'm a repairman." Jackson wore a brown flannel shirt tucked into faded blue jeans.

Megan narrowed her eyes at Darius. "Isn't that the same outfit you wore last year?"

Darius touched his gray stitch fedora. The name tag on his teal sweater read MEMBER OF THE PRESS. "I couldn't think of anything else."

"It barely passed for a costume last year." Megan scowled.

"Oh, here's Peyton." Ramona's voice was excited. "Doesn't she look *great?*"

Darius looked over his shoulder . . . and almost swallowed his tongue. *That* was Dr. Peyton Harris?

The pocket-sized siren striding toward him looked as though someone had painted her into an old-school Catwoman costume. She'd accessorized her black stretch polyester jumpsuit with matching gloves, a gold belt, and a long, gold coin necklace. Her headband with feline ears peeked over the top of her riot of copper curls. The university professor appeared to have stepped straight out of the campy 1960s *Batman* television series.

"You look *fantastic.*" Ramona greeted the shorter woman with a hug. Darius wanted to change places with the mayor.

Peyton returned Ramona's embrace. "Thank you. I've never worn anything this revealing before." She sounded nervous.

The professor stepped back and somehow ended up standing right beside him. How had Ramona managed that? Not that Darius was complaining.

"Thank you for wearing a costume." Megan sent a

scathing look toward him, Ean, and Jackson. "Not everyone got into the spirit of the event."

Ean protested. "Honey, we're wearing costumes. They're just very simple."

Peyton gave Darius a once-over. Her gaze lingered on his fedora. "What are you supposed to be?"

Darius tapped the white sticky label affixed to his sweater. "I'm the press."

"Are you serious?" Peyton laughed. The warm sound bubbled up from her chest to pour over him like spring water. "You could have put a little more effort into it."

"How?"

"I don't know." Peyton's caramel eyes danced with amusement. "Maybe you could have used a prop like an audio recorder or even a pen. But really, this is just sorry." Her voice broke on more laughter.

Darius gestured toward her jumpsuit. "You look great. I never would've guessed you were a Catwoman fan."

Peyton's laughter faded, but her smile remained. She had perfect teeth. "It was Ramona's idea."

He should have known. He'd bet his comic book collection that Ramona had encouraged Peyton to choose the Catwoman costume because the caped crusader was Darius's favorite superhero.

Darius stilled. He was thinking like his father. The realization turned his stomach. Not everything revolved around him. Maybe Ramona just knew the little professor would make a hot Catwoman.

"Great party, Megan." Simon's greeting came from right behind Darius.

So his father had been serious about attending the event this year. Darius forced himself to relax and face the older man. Simon wore a brown cowboy hat, navy shirt, faded blue jeans, black boots, and a brown duster. His red kerchief around his neck completed the Wild West look.

Megan gave Simon a beaming smile. "Thank you, Simon. Great costume." She sent another shaming look to the other men in the group.

"Thank you. I ordered it on the Internet." Simon squeezed his way between Darius and the university professor. "And who do we have here?"

Darius made the introductions against his better judgment. "Dr. Peyton Harris, this is my father, Simon Knight."

"It's nice to meet you, Mr. Knight." Peyton offered Simon a tentative smile.

"Call me Simon." Was his father flirting with the professor?

"I'm Peyton."

Tension built in Darius's neck and shoulders as he observed Simon's easy exchange with Peyton. *Am I actually jealous of my father?*

He considered Simon's costume again. "I didn't think you'd come."

"Your mother's the one who never wanted to come." Simon slid a glance toward Peyton. "Now that I'm a single man, I can go wherever I like."

Darius' stomach turned again. "You're not single."

Simon smiled. "Yet."

A movement in the corner of his eye drew Darius's attention. Stan Crockett hesitated just outside the group's circle. Darius waved him closer. "Hey, Stan."

"Hi, Darius." Stan nodded at him. He took a deep

breath and squared his shoulders before turning to the McCloud women. "Good afternoon, Ramona, Megan. Thank you for giving me another chance with the children's story time. I apologize for my behavior last year. I won't disappoint you today."

"Stan?" Megan blinked her wide cinnamon eyes. "You look great."

Stan's nervousness eased and a grin brightened his expression. "Thanks, I feel great. But I didn't know whether I should wear a costume."

Megan waved a hand. "A costume isn't necessary."

Darius shared a silent exchange with Ean and Jackson.

Megan's surprise was understandable. The Stan Crockett standing with them today bore very little resemblance to the town drunk who'd sang dirty ditties to schoolchildren last year. His green eyes were clear and direct against his healthy, though pale, skin. His dark blond hair had been washed and professionally trimmed away from his clean-cut, sharp features. Black Dockers and a brown sweater hung loose on his thin, six-foot frame. But the clothes were clean.

Megan continued to stare at Stan. "I don't mean to pry, but I've got to ask. What happened?"

Stan's chuckle broke in the middle. His gaze circled the other six people in the group. "I've joined an alcoholics recovery program, thanks to Darius."

All eyes turned to him. Darius kept his attention on Stan. "Stan's been sober for almost a year. His recovery is all thanks to his own hard work."

"No." Stan's reply was firm. "I wouldn't have been able to do it without your help and belief in me. You saved my life."

Their stares bore into him. Darius registered Peyton's attention more keenly than the others. But he was too self-conscious to return her gaze.

"Well, Darius, I guess you're not an asshole." Ramona's drawl broke his tension.

He looked into her smiling ebony eyes. "That's high praise from you."

There was a time when he and Ramona couldn't stand each other. Now that she was dating one of his best friends, they were both making an effort to get along.

Darius glanced toward the front of the store as three women entered dressed as flappers. He blinked, but the mirage didn't disappear. The new arrivals only drew closer.

"Mom?" Darius blinked again.

Beside him, his father tensed. "Ethel?" Simon sounded as though he were choking.

Darius's mother as well as Ean's mother, Doreen, and Jackson's girlfriend, Audra, wore similar flapper costumes: a black headband with a matching feather; sequined, tank-style dress with spaghetti straps and fringe hem; and black pumps. The only difference was the color of their dresses. Ethel's was silver, Doreen's copper, and Audra's gold.

Jackson crossed to Audra. He took her arm and spun her around, causing her hem to flare. "You're beautiful."

"Great costume, Mom." Ean's voice was warm with affection.

Darius's mother seemed like a different person. She looked ten years younger and ten times happier than he'd ever seen her. He didn't know what to say.

Simon didn't have that problem. "Ethel, what the hell're you wearing?"

"Who the *hell* wants to know?" Ethel shot back.

"You look great, Mom." Darius looked at the other two women. "You all do."

"I feel happier than I have in thirty-four years." Ethel slid her estranged husband a look before shimmying her hips so the fringe hem swirled around her.

"So do I." Simon's scowl contradicted his claim.

Darius rubbed his eyes with his left thumb and two fingers. Did either of his parents realize he'd been born thirty-four years ago? Did they care?

"Whose idea was the flapper costume?" Darius needed to change the subject. He was beyond tired of his parents' constant bickering.

Doreen gestured toward Audra. "Our resident songwriter."

Audra kept hold of Jackson's hand. "I thought it would be fun to dress up as a female singing group."

"What made you decide to come to the Halloween event this year?" Darius directed his question to Ethel. "You've never come before."

Ethel jerked her chin toward Simon. "*He* never wanted to come before, so we stayed home. Doing nothing. As usual."

Simon met Darius's eyes before confronting Ethel. "Me? *You're* the one who never wanted to come."

Ethel's glare was fierce. "What *bull*—"

"You can both do whatever you want, whenever you want. Why not stop arguing and enjoy that?" Darius' stomach muscles twisted into familiar knots. He didn't want his parents to argue, especially not in front of Peyton. She was new to Trinity Falls. Couldn't they give her more time before exposing her to their craziness?

Ethel looked toward her coconspirators. "I'm real grateful to Doreen and Audra for letting me be a part of their group."

Audra squeezed Ethel's shoulder. "It's our pleasure."

Ethel glowed from Audra's kind words. Why hadn't his approval meant as much?

Simon's scowl darkened. "You look ridiculous."

Ethel struck a pose, cocking her right hip and pressing her palms into the small of her back. "Jealous?"

Peyton's chuckle surprised Darius. She approached his mother, offering her hand. "Ms. Knight, I'm Peyton Harris, the new history professor with the university. It's nice to meet you."

Ethel shook her hand. "Yes, you arrived in the summer. Call me Ethel."

"Thank you. I'm Peyton."

"Darius!"

He turned at the sound of his name and saw his half brother, Noah Cale, striding toward him. Noah's mother, June Cale, followed in his wake. This is what he'd been afraid of when Simon and Ethel had turned up at Books & Bakery this afternoon. From the look in June's almond-shaped bright brown eyes, she had concerns about their reception as well.

Ethel's voice shook with fury. "Who the *hell* invited them?"

"I did," Darius answered quietly.

CHAPTER 3

This wasn't what Darius had wanted. He'd never meant to hurt his mother. But he hadn't expected Ethel or Simon to attend the costume party. They'd never come before.

"*You* invited them?" His mother's brown eyes were filled with betrayal. "Why?"

"Because they're my family." Darius willed his mother to understand.

She didn't.

Ethel turned her scorching glare on Simon, who flinched from its heat. She gave June and Noah a dismissive look before disappearing into the café.

Peyton felt the tension rolling over her shoulders and up her neck. And she'd thought there was drama in her family. What had just happened?

"I'm sorry." There was pain in Darius's voice as he apologized to his two guests. It broke Peyton's heart.

"It's not your fault." The woman put a protective hand on the young man's arm.

Darius embraced her. She hugged him back. A

sharp pain twisted in Peyton's gut. Envy? No way! But who was this pretty lady? There was no denying the resemblance between Darius and the young man. Was he Darius' son? Impossible! The newspaper reporter was too young to have a son who looked to be seventeen years old. What was going on?

"I'm glad you came." Darius stepped back but didn't release the woman's right hand. "Everyone, I'd like to introduce you to my brother, Noah Cale, and his mother, June. They're visiting from Sequoia."

His brother. Relief hit her like a tidal wave. Sequoia was one of the towns near Trinity Falls. Peyton remembered seeing signs for it as she'd driven into town.

She glanced at Simon. He was staring at the trio with wonder. Now she better understood the vitriol between Simon and Ethel. If Noah was his son—and there was no denying the family resemblance—he would have been born right in the middle of Simon and Ethel's thirty-four years of marriage. How long had Ethel known of Simon's betrayal with this much-younger woman? That kind of hurt cut deep. But Darius was right. Noah was his brother. He had a right to know him. In the reporter's position, Peyton would have done the same thing.

Darius continued the introductions, moving counterclockwise through the group. "Doreen Fever. Audra Lane. Stan Crockett. Megan McCloud. Our mayor, Ramona McCloud. Dr. Peyton Harris. Ean Fever. And my boss, Jackson Sansbury." He skipped Simon.

June looked a little overwhelmed. A blush pinkened her brown-sugar features. She dragged her fingers through the short, dark brown curls that exploded around her makeup-free oval face. "It's a pleasure to meet you all. Darius has told us so much about you."

Peyton added her greeting to the chorus of welcomes.

Ean gave Darius's brother a considering look. "I understand you play tight end for Sequoia High's football team."

"That's right." Noah's cocky grin was identical to Darius's. "And I understand you were Heritage High's star quarterback. Back in the day."

Laughter rolled through the group. Even Peyton enjoyed the exchange. Trash-talking must be another family trait.

Ean tossed his young target a calculating smile. "Trinity Falls was undefeated against Sequoia—back in my day."

"In mine, too." Jackson crossed his arms over his broad chest. "That would make it four straight years of Trinity Falls's dominance over Sequoia."

Noah threw back his head and laughed. "Well, if you old-timers have been reading the news, you'd know the tide has turned in the *decades* since you played high school ball. Sequoia has evened up the contest. In fact, we're going to beat you next month."

Peyton grinned at this form of male bonding. The laughter and comments coming from the rest of the group indicated she wasn't the only one enjoying the exchange.

Jackson looked at Ean before arching a brow at the high school athlete. "You think so?"

"It's inevitable." Darius clamped a hand on his

brother's shoulder. "Sequoia hasn't lost to Trinity Falls since Noah joined the team."

Simon's laughter boomed with pride. "Of course they haven't. Noah's a Knight."

"Actually, he's a Cale." June's voice was mild, but her brown eyes were steely.

Jackson tilted his head, meeting Darius's gaze. "Care to put a wager on that game?"

Ean's eyes widened. "D, you're going to bet against your alma mater?"

Darius shook his head. "I'm not betting against Heritage. I'm betting on my brother."

Peyton's heart melted at Darius's words. Noah's face darkened with a blush. The look he gave his older brother was near hero worship.

"I'll take your bet." Darius held his hand out to Jackson. "Loser buys the winner a beer."

Jackson shook Darius's hand. "Deal."

Noah frowned. "I can't drink."

"You can't gamble on the game, either, genius." Darius lightly smacked the back of his brother's head.

"Hey, careful with the hair," Noah protested, smoothing the close-cut style that also resembled Darius's.

Darius shook his head. "Was I ever that vain?"

"Yes." Five voices—Jackson, Ean, Megan, Ramona, and Doreen—assured him.

Peyton wiped tears of laughter from her eyes. She was glad she'd let Ramona talk her into coming to the celebration. These friends formed a family. They showed each other unconditional love and unwavering support, with few exceptions. It was a new experience for her, one she welcomed.

"I want in on this bet." Ean's comment drew her from her wistful thoughts.

Darius offered Ean his hand. "Absolutely. You can buy me an order of spicy buffalo wings."

"Now, wait a minute." June grabbed Darius's wrist, stopping the men from shaking hands. She offered Ean her hand instead. "You can buy *my* beer."

Laughter erupted again.

Darius patted June's shoulder. "That's the spirit, June. Anyone else want to stand with the champions?"

Megan smiled. "Darius, I love you, but you've lost your mind if you think Heritage is going down to Sequoia. You can buy my beer next month."

"And mine, too." Ramona set her hands on her trim hips. "The mayor's office will always support Heritage."

"You've got that right," Doreen agreed. "Especially after all the time and money I poured into that football program."

Audra chuckled. "Something tells me I won't have access to Doreen's Trinity Falls Fudge Walnut Brownies if I bet against Heritage."

"That's fine." Darius wrapped his arms around Noah and June again. "It'll just be the three of us against *all* of you."

"Not so fast." Stan stepped forward to stand beside June. "I'm putting my chips in with you. But someone can buy me a soda if Sequoia wins."

The group cheered again.

Simon squared his shoulders. "There's no way I'm betting against my sons."

Noah's eyes widened as though taken off guard by the older man's words.

Peyton was lost in the moment. Laughter and

friendship carried her away. Without stopping to think, she jumped sides. "I'm probably making a politically inadvisable move, considering I'm new to Trinity Falls and a professor with the local university. But for once, I don't want to play by the rules." Peyton pumped her fist in the air. "Go, Sequoia!"

Did the surprise in Darius's eyes mirror her own expression?

Boos and hisses mingled with cheers. But Peyton heard only Darius's laughter, warm, deep, and rumbling. She studied his close-cropped hair, angular features, smiling lips, then lost herself in his midnight eyes. This was the reason women in Trinity Falls were infatuated with Darius Knight. Yes, he was handsome—extremely attractive—and smart. But he also helped the town drunk get sober. He cheered for his school's rival because his brother was on Sequoia's team. He was a player with a heart of gold. She could see herself falling for him.

Peyton stiffened at the realization. She forced her attention away from Darius. She didn't need any more complications in her life. She had plenty to deal with as it was.

"Enough trash-talking, people." Megan raised her voice for attention. "We need to get ready for story time."

"Have you always been this bossy?" Ramona grumbled.

"Yes, you just chose not to notice." Megan's response was dry. "Stan, are you ready for your big moment?"

"Yes, ma'am." Stan sounded confident. But his movements seemed nervous as he smoothed his brown sweater. He followed Megan across the front of the store to the area set up for story time.

Megan seated Stan in an ornate, red velvet throne decorated for Halloween. Two large fake human skulls were staked to the seat's high back, and two smaller ones were driven onto the chair's arms. After Megan announced story time, Peyton watched as a stampede of children charged toward Stan.

Young children raced forward. Toddlers rocked on unsteady legs. Even teenagers managed to join the growing crowd without abdicating their cool. There were princesses and warriors, soldiers and other superheroes, astronauts and characters Peyton should have known—and would have if she watched more television.

Ean and Ramona joined Megan near the reading area. Audra tugged Jackson along behind her. The newspaper publisher looked as though he'd follow her anywhere.

"You coming?" Noah directed the question to his older brother.

Darius shook his head. "No, but you and June go ahead."

Noah and his mother joined the rest of the group at the perimeter of the entertainment. The young man grabbed a handful of wrapped chocolates from one of several candy bowls around the store. The crystal dishes were shaped like decaying hands.

Peyton surveyed the themed decorations hanging from the ceiling, affixed to the walls, and draped over the bookshelves. "Megan must love Halloween."

Darius eyed the decorations. "She loves all of the holidays."

Peyton nodded toward the story time area. "Stan looks amazed to have all those kids surrounding him."

Doreen hummed. "In the past, when they saw Stan, most people turned away." She looked at Darius. "You did a wonderful thing, helping him pull his life together."

"That was very caring of you." Peyton wondered at the blush rising up Darius's neck.

"Stan's a good guy." Darius's voice was tight. "He just needed a nudge in the right direction."

Doreen's eyes widened. "Look at him. You did more than nudge."

"OK, ladies, let's change the subject." Darius nodded toward the store's entrance. "Doreen, you've got company."

Doreen looked toward the front of the store. Her body warmed as she watched Sheriff Alonzo Lopez stride toward her. His was tall and lean in his sheriff's tan shirt, black tie, and spruce-green gabardine pants. He took off his brown felt campaign hat, revealing his still-dark, wavy brown hair. His coffee-brown gaze was intense; his chiseled café-au-lait features serious. As he drew closer, his gaze swept her from head to toe. The way he looked at her in her copper flapper's dress made her want to take it off.

Alonzo stopped in front of her. He greeted Simon, Peyton, and Darius before giving Doreen a quick kiss. It was a brief touch of lips that made her want more.

"You stop my heart, *mi amor*." His voice was low and rough.

"Now you know how I feel when I look at you."

Alonzo's eyes widened. How could her comment

possibly surprise him? Even now she was struggling not to swoon at the handsome lawman's feet. "I'm glad you stopped by."

"So am I." His gaze dropped again to her dress.

Doreen's cheeks heated. "I wish you could stay."

"So do I. But it means a lot for the deputies with young children to attend the celebration with their families."

He'd said the same thing last year. She admired him for putting others' needs before his own, but it would mean a lot to her to share this time with him, too. "Next year, maybe you could ask one of the other deputies without young children to mind the town while you attend our Halloween celebration."

Alonzo gave her a sexy smile. "That's my intention."

Doreen's lips parted in surprise. She hadn't expected him to agree so quickly. "Great. In the meantime, I'm looking forward to your Day of the Dead celebration."

Day of the Dead, a rather daunting name for a holiday that brings family and friends together to pray for and remember loved ones who've died. Doreen was excited to experience this Mexican holiday with him and their friends: Ean, Megan, Ramona, Jackson, Audra, Darius, and Ms. Helen.

"I'm glad you're coming." Alonzo took her hand. "It's important to remember our loved ones. Our memories keep them alive."

Doreen squeezed his hand. "It sounds like a very special celebration. I'll arrive a little early to help you get ready."

Alonzo was silent for several moments, holding her eyes. "Thank you. I'd better get back to work."

He gave her another kiss before straightening away from her.

She leaned into him, breathing his scent, soap and shaving cream. "I'll see you tonight."

Alonzo looked her over again. "Don't change your clothes." With a wink, he turned to leave, nodding good-bye to their friends.

Doreen's cheeks flushed. As she watched Alonzo cross the bookstore, she wondered whether her grin was as goofy as it felt. Alonzo held the door open for Nessa Linden, the Trinity Falls town council member and dental office manager, then he disappeared on the street.

Nessa made a beeline to the café entrance where Doreen stood with Simon, Peyton, and Darius.

Still glowing from Alonzo's flirtatious farewell, Doreen smiled as the smaller woman came to a stop in front of her. "Hello, Nessa. Nice costume."

"I wish I could say the same, Doreen." Nessa's smile was cool. "Do you really think it's appropriate for a Trinity Falls mayoral candidate to *ever* wear a flapper costume?"

It took Doreen a moment to register Nessa's attack. Although they'd grown up together in Trinity Falls, they'd never been close. But their relationship had chilled even more since the town's sesquicentennial celebration last August. Why?

Doreen sensed Darius's tension beside her. She didn't want to cause a scene during story time and risk ruining the children's enjoyment of the celebration. She kept her voice level. "What's wrong with my costume?"

Nessa raised her chin. "You need to represent

the office of Trinity Falls' mayor with dignity and decorum—always."

Was Nessa serious? "I'm not dressed as Lady Godiva."

Nessa's disdainful gaze took in Doreen's modest neckline and knee-length fringe hem. "You might as well be."

"I think she looks great." Darius came to her defense.

Nessa turned pitying eyes toward him. "As a young man, I wouldn't expect you to say anything else."

Darius crossed his arms over his chest. "Nessa, I don't know what's going on between you and Doreen, but please don't insult my intelligence."

Darius heard a small intake of breath from Peyton. In reflex, he rested what he'd meant as a comforting hand on her shoulder.

Nessa tracked his movement. She glanced at Peyton before returning her attention to Darius. "So close so fast, Darius? The rumors must be true."

"What rumors?" Darius had been about to remove his hand from Peyton's shoulder. But when he caught the taunting gleam in Nessa's eyes, he decided against it. With the feel of Peyton's skin warming his palm through her costume, the decision wasn't a hardship.

"That you're dating the university's new history professor." Nessa's expression was speculative. "Have you grown tired of the women of Trinity Falls?"

"W-we're not dating," Peyton stuttered.

"Yet." Nessa returned her attention to Doreen and the flapper costume. "The election is only ten days away. It's just a formality since you're running unopposed. However, try not to bring disgrace on the office. It'll reflect poorly on the town."

"What is this really about, Nessa?" Doreen stood straighter. "I can't believe you find this flapper costume so objectionable."

"I'm giving you a little friendly advice."

Doreen crossed her arms. "You walked into the bookstore loaded for bear and pointed your sights at me. Why?"

"Ladies, you may not want to continue this conversation here." Darius released Peyton's shoulder. He glanced around the store, scanning the curious glances directed their way. Trinity Falls was a small community whose residents' curiosity was close to insatiable.

Nessa ignored his warning. "The mayor's office is going to be handed to you just like everything else in your life. But don't expect me to let you continue to walk around this town like royalty."

Doreen's eyes widened in surprise, then narrowed with temper. Darius strained to hear her reply. "If you wanted to be mayor, Nessa, you should have run."

"Next time, I will."

Doreen inclined her head. "Until next time, then."

Nessa's glare shot sparks before she turned to leave Books & Bakery.

Peyton exhaled. "Who was that?"

"Nessa Linden." Darius observed Nessa's stiff gait as she left the store. "She's served two terms on the town council. I didn't think she wanted to be mayor, though."

"She didn't." Simon shoved his hands into the front pockets of his cowboy costume.

Darius faced his father, who stood on Peyton's other side. "How do you know?"

Simon's gaze drifted away. "She told me when I considered running for office."

Darius wasn't certain he bought that. Perhaps he'd press his father for more later. He turned to Doreen. "What happened between you and Nessa?"

"I don't know." Doreen's eyes remained on the front doors as though she could still see Nessa. "We've never been friends, but she's never been so confrontational toward me, either."

"She seemed to have it in for you." Simon shifted his stance.

Something in his father's voice put Darius on alert.

"And what did she mean that everything's always been handed to me?" Doreen sounded more curious than offended.

Peyton touched Doreen's forearm in a brief but sympathetic gesture. "Sometimes people make accusations that are unfounded and unjust."

"Like claiming someone's a player when he's not." Darius gave Peyton an innocent look, watching as a blush rose into her cheeks.

Peyton looked away from him and continued. "I wouldn't spend any time worrying about it."

Doreen shook her head. "I need to fix this. When I'm mayor, I'll have to work with Nessa and the other council members to get projects done."

"CeCe's council president." Darius straightened his fedora. "She'll keep Nessa from turning the council's work into Nessa's personal agenda."

Simon shrugged. "Nessa's off her rocker. I'd ignore her."

Darius faced his father, searching eyes that were so much like his own. "What do you know?"

Simon pressed a finger to his own chest. "Me? What do you mean?"

Darius gave Simon a hard look. "Either she told you something or you've heard something that would explain Nessa's behavior toward Doreen."

Doreen's wide-eyed gaze swung between Darius and his father. "Simon, is this true? Do you know something?"

Simon's expression grew haunted. "I don't know anything."

Darius set his jaw. "Yes, you do."

Simon raised his arms in surrender. "I agreed not to say anything."

Darius pressed harder. "Dad . . ."

Still Simon hesitated. His troubled gaze moved from Darius to Peyton, lingering on Doreen before returning to his son. "Nessa came to me last summer." He sighed. "It was her idea that I run for mayor against Doreen."

❧ CHAPTER 4 ❧

Simon Knight wasn't above lying. Darius knew that.
But as far-fetched as his father's claim sounded,
Darius believed he was telling the truth.

Still, Darius pinned Simon with a skeptical stare.
"Why would Nessa ask you to run for mayor of
Trinity Falls?"

"She thought I'd do a good job." Simon seemed
to believe his own words. "She said I was a strong
candidate to challenge Doreen in the election."

Darius shook his head. "Nessa may have told you
that, but those can't be the real reasons she wanted
you in the campaign." In his peripheral vision, he
caught Peyton's surprised expression. "What is it?"

Peyton's gaze slid from Simon back to Darius.
"I'm just surprised at how blunt you are."

Darius frowned. "What do you mean?"

"Never mind." Peyton shook her head. "Why else
would Nessa encourage your father to run for mayor
if she didn't think he was qualified?"

"That's what we're trying to understand." Doreen

studied Simon as though trying to determine what Nessa saw in him. "Simon doesn't get involved in civic issues. Everyone who knows him knows that. No offense, Simon, but it's the truth."

"None taken." Simon threw back his shoulders. "But, if everyone in town believes that, why did two hundred people sign my petition to have my name added to the ballot?"

"Two hundred people signed your petition, but there are fifteen hundred residents in town." Darius cocked his head. "What did Nessa say when you told her you were pulling out of the campaign?"

"Not much." Simon pinned him with a hard stare. "Just that I wasn't a viable candidate anymore because you'd introduced Noah." Simon said that as though it had been a bad thing.

"Maybe Nessa just wanted a competitive election." Peyton's comment claimed Darius's attention.

Darius snorted. "Then she would have chosen a stronger candidate than my father."

"I'm standing right here, Darius." Simon's tone was dry.

Peyton spread her arms. "Maybe people you'd have considered stronger candidates weren't interested in challenging Doreen for office."

"Then why propose a candidate at all?" Darius shoved his hands into the front pockets of his Dockers.

It took all of his concentration to have this debate with Peyton while she wore that smoking-hot Catwoman costume. The outfit was better suited to a completely different line of conversation.

Darius's gaze sought refuge at the front of the store. He found Noah and June standing with

Ean, Megan, Ramona, Audra, and Jackson on the perimeter of the story time crowd. According to his silver Timex Batman watch—and the smells of apple cider and fresh-baked cookies—story time was almost over. Judging by Stan's grin and the expressions on the children's faces, the reading was a huge success. Screams and shrill gasps periodically rent asunder the bookstore's usual quiet. Some of those sound effects came from the parents who'd brought their children.

Megan and Ramona were all but bouncing with joy. They didn't do their Halloween or Christmas events for the money. They did special celebrations for the children. Right now, both women seemed like big kids themselves.

Peyton continued. "Perhaps you should just ask Nessa what she's up to."

A look of horror settled on Simon's sepia features. "I wasn't supposed to let anyone know that she supported my campaign."

"Don't worry. I understand the need to protect a source." Darius looked around the group. "I'll find another way to learn what Nessa's up to."

"I appreciate your letting me join you for the town meeting." Peyton followed Vaughn Brooks, Trinity Falls University's concert director, into the town hall Tuesday evening.

They snaked their way through the crowd swelling the antechamber of the building's largest conference room. Vaughn's six-foot, broad-shouldered frame paved a path where Peyton was certain her five-foot-plus stature would not.

"You're a Trinity Falls resident now," Vaughn spoke over his shoulder. The hall's light shone on the smooth nutmeg-hued skin of his clean-shaven head. "You should witness firsthand how your new government works."

Peyton surveyed the crush of bodies around her as she unbuttoned her double-breasted burgundy wool coat. She'd thought Ohio would be colder in late October. She'd been wrong. "Are all of these people here for the council meeting?"

"Yep." Vaughn sounded pleased. "And even more will show up later."

Peyton stared in amazement. "I've seen crowds like this one lining up for Broadway shows."

Vaughn chuckled. "We're not quite ready for the stage. But our council meetings do get pretty entertaining."

Peyton smiled. Vaughn was such a nice person. He'd taken her under his wing, helping her navigate the university's campus and especially its administrative offices. Now he was helping her get acclimated to the town.

She stared at the band director's broad back as he led her into the assembly room. He was in great physical shape. A well-groomed goatee enhanced his ruggedly handsome features. But Trinity Falls was full of attractive men, a single woman's fantasy: Vaughn, Dr. Quincy Spates, Ean Fever, Jackson Sansbury, and Darius Knight.

Peyton was surprised to see even more people socializing in the assembly room before the council meeting. Doreen, Megan, Ean, Jackson, Audra, and Darius stood toward the front of the room.

Vaughn led her to them. "I thought it was time to

expose our newest resident to one of our greatest traditions, the Trinity Falls Town Council meeting."

"I thought the Books and Bakery Halloween celebration was the town's greatest tradition." Peyton struggled to keep her gaze from lingering on the reporter.

Several other women in the room didn't seem to have her willpower. In his gunmetal-gray sport coat, snow-white shirt, burgundy tie, and black pants, Darius looked as though he'd dressed for a men's clothing commercial.

"The Halloween celebration is just one of Trinity Falls many great traditions." Megan adopted a humble tone even as her wide chocolate eyes twinkled with mischief.

"I'm surprised to see you here, Vaughn." Darius's midnight eyes shone with challenge. "When did you start attending council meetings?"

Peyton frowned at the reporter's question. Why would Darius doubt Vaughn's interest in the meeting? Her colleague had been adamant that she attend at least one. Why would he be so insistent on her being here tonight if he'd never been to any?

"What do you mean, D?" Vaughn couldn't meet the reporter's eyes. "I've attended council meetings."

"Not in the six years since I've been covering them." Darius caught Peyton's gaze. "Don't look now, Doc, but I think we're back in the archives."

"What?" Was Darius referencing the supposed matchmaking scheme? Peyton turned to Vaughn. "Is that true?"

The band director's brow furrowed. "I don't know what he's talking about."

Peyton turned back to Darius, but he'd switched his attention to the other five members of their group: Megan, Ean, Doreen, Jackson, and Audra. His eyes twinkled with humor as he addressed them. "Which one of you geniuses put him up to this?"

Ean frowned. "Put who up to what?"

Darius pinched the bridge of his nose. "One of you, maybe more, has been playing matchmaker with Peyton and me ever since she came to town. It's been fun, I'm sure. But it needs to stop now."

Peyton confronted Vaughn. "Is that really the reason you suggested I attend this meeting?" This couldn't be happening. It was a mistake or misunderstanding.

Vaughn shook his head. "I don't know what he's talking about."

Jackson chuckled. "Meddling's more your style, D. You're always giving people your two cents on what they should do."

"My opinion is worth more than two cents." Darius gave Jackson and Audra a pointed look. "And I'm always right."

Jackson wrapped an arm around Audra's waist. "*Usually* right."

Peyton wondered at that pointed look. What had the reporter been right about, and how had it involved Audra and Jackson?

Audra touched Peyton's forearm. "Whatever reason brought you here, you won't regret it. I've attended a couple of these meetings and they're really interesting."

Peyton scanned the expectant expressions of the people surrounding her. "I'll stay. I don't have anything pressing to do tonight."

Against her will, her eyes sought Darius. He seemed to be silently laughing at her. Let him. She'd made the choice to stay because she wanted to be part of this community. No one was forcing her.

But she was curious. Peyton glanced around the assembly room. Any one of the dozen or so women undressing Darius with their eyes would be more than happy to go out with him. So why were his friends anxious to set him up with someone? And why had they chosen her?

Minutes later, Town Council President CeCe Roben called the meeting to order. The mayor, council president, and four council members sat behind a U-shaped walnut conference table at the front of the room. A four-foot walnut fence divided the audience from the working section of the assembly room.

Darius waited as their small group entered the third row of metal folding chairs. He gestured Vaughn and Peyton ahead of him. It wasn't because he wanted to sit beside the history professor. He told himself he preferred to sit at the end of the row.

He settled onto the chair. It took some adjusting to find a comfortable position. It was a wonder the rusted relic was still in use. Darius was certain it had seen more years than he had.

Then he froze. A fragrance as soft and sultry as a summer evening teased him. Talcum powder and lily of the valley wrapped around him and took hold of his mind. He was back in the university archives. He was with a petite and curvy Catwoman.

Peyton.

How would he get through this meeting when every breath he took shot straight to his lap? He should have sat between Jackson and Vaughn. Neither of them would have distracted him.

Against his will, Darius turned to Peyton. The little professor was struggling out of her burgundy wool coat. Darius held it so she could free her arms. Removing her bulky outerwear revealed her formfitting attire. Darius's gaze moved over her cream scoop-necked sweater, pausing on the curve of her breasts before continuing to her long, rose corduroy skirt.

"Thank you." Peyton's voice was low.

Darius raised his gaze to her caramel eyes. "Sure."

Mercifully, tonight's council agenda was short. The sheriff's office was investigating a series of Halloween pranks, including one in which the entrances to Heritage High School had been bolted shut from the outside, giving students an extra day off from school. The volunteer fire department requested additional funds for a computer upgrade.

Most of the agenda required just a few key phrases. Darius took detailed notes when necessary. Beside him, Peyton shifted in her seat. Often. Each time, her scent would float over him, causing the muscles in his lower abdomen to clench. Darius gritted his teeth and refocused on the council's discussion.

Revenue to date from Trinity Falls' sesquicentennial celebration had exceeded expectations. Orders for memorabilia were still coming through the Sesquicentennial Celebration Web site.

Ramona addressed the audience. "I want to thank Doreen Fever again for the wonderful job she did chairing the Sesquicentennial Celebration Committee."

The cheers swelled in the assembly room. Doreen was well known and well liked in the community. She acknowledged the recognition with a smile and wave. But her round, brown cheeks flushed with embarrassment. Darius laughed and clapped harder. Beside him, Peyton glowed with pride for Doreen.

Darius glanced back toward the council's U-shaped table. Nessa Linden appeared to be the only one in the room who begrudged Doreen her accolades. Why did the other woman dislike Doreen, and what had happened to escalate her resentment?

Applause died down, allowing Ramona to continue. "Council members, members of the community, I have less than two months remaining on my term. During that time, I'm going to address a critical need in Trinity Falls. Our Guiding Light Community Center turns forty years old in January. The center and its mostly volunteer staff provide a necessary service for our children and neighbors in need of assistance. But the center's renovations are long overdue. We must find a way to fund this capital investment."

Council member Christopher Ling spoke into his microphone. "I don't think anyone would disagree with you, Mayor. But from where do you propose to get these funds?"

Darius's hand flew across a page of his reporter's notebook as he made detailed notes of this announcement and Councilman Ling's question. In it, he heard the councilman's subtext: although the town's coffers were growing, Christopher wasn't going to approve a budget expenditure for the center's capital improvements.

Ramona folded her hands on the desk. "I'm going to task a committee with raising money for the center's renovations."

Nessa perked up at this revelation. "That's a wonderful idea, Mayor McCloud."

Christopher and the other two council members echoed their support.

Council President CeCe Roben spoke over them. "Mayor, what type of fund-raiser were you thinking of?"

Ramona shrugged a slim shoulder. "I'm going to leave that decision to the people in charge of the event."

CeCe ran her long, pale fingers through her auburn hair. "I'm concerned, Mayor, that after the Founders Day event, the town might be burned out on celebrations."

Ramona frowned. "I'm surprised to hear you say that, Madame President. After all, this is Trinity Falls. We love a good party."

The audience again erupted into applause. Darius smiled as he transcribed the exchange. Doreen was well regarded and would make an excellent mayor. But the town was going to miss their more flamboyant leader.

Nessa raised her voice as the cheers died down. "Well, I for one think it's an excellent idea, Mayor. You're leaving behind some very big shoes to fill. I hope our next mayor is as tireless, dedicated, and creative as you are."

Ramona smiled in response. But there was a chill in her voice as well as her expression. "Oh, I'm certain the woman the town will elect as my successor will be more than up to the task."

Darius took that as a direct quote for *The Trinity Falls Monitor* article.

Saturday morning, the first of November, Peyton indulged in breakfast at Books & Bakery. Her seat beside the café window was chilly, but the view was worth the discomfort. The trees lining the streets led her gaze into the nearby neighborhood and the profusion of vibrant autumn colors.

She opened her copy of *The Trinity Falls Monitor* before digging into her breakfast—spinach quiche, fruit, and coffee. Even this far from the café's kitchen, she could smell the fresh bread, confectioner's sugar, and homemade soups.

The sound of heels crossing the hardwood floor toward her made her look up. Ramona floated toward her like a runway model on the catwalk. Her tall, slender figure was clothed in a scarlet knee-length sweater dress. Black stiletto boots made her legs look even longer. Her glossy, shoulder-length raven tresses billowed with every step. With her wide ebony eyes and café-au-lait complexion, Ramona reminded Peyton of a young Dorothy Dandridge. She was the type of woman Irene Biery Harris could envision marrying Peyton's soon-to-be-ex-fiancé, Bruce Grave. Beside Ramona, Peyton must appear as a vertically challenged, mousy shadow.

"May I join you?" Ramona braced her left hand on the back of the chair opposite Peyton. Her right hand held a white porcelain cup of coffee.

Peyton glanced toward the front of the café where

Ramona usually shared breakfast with her friends. Jackson, Audra, Ean, Megan, Darius, and Doreen were at the counter.

"Please do." Peyton pulled her gaze from Darius's broad shoulders wrapped in an emerald-green sweater.

She was having breakfast with the mayor. At fifteen hundred residents, Trinity Falls wasn't in the same stratosphere as New York City. Still, she marveled the town's mayor knew who she was and sought her company.

"What did you think of our council meeting?" Ramona crossed her long dancer's legs and settled back on her chair.

"I enjoyed it." Peyton cut another slice of her spinach quiche with a fork.

"We're not as exciting as New York City." A slight smile curved Ramona's pink lips.

"I wouldn't know. I didn't attend city council meetings."

"I used to live in New York." Ramona sipped her coffee.

"You did?" Peyton almost choked on her quiche.

Although she knew Ramona planned to join her boyfriend, Dr. Quincy Spates, in Philadelphia in the new year, Peyton couldn't imagine the mayor living anywhere other than Trinity Falls, Ohio. This was her town.

"I used to think I wanted Trinity Falls to be more like New York—the shops, the culture, the sophistication." Ramona leaned forward, holding Peyton's gaze. "Now I realize my hometown has its own identity, and I never want it to lose that."

"I've only been here five months, but I agree

with you." Peyton ate more quiche. In the cozy neighborhood just outside the town center, she witnessed residents greeting each other on the street. "Trinity Falls is a very special place."

"Yes, it is." Ramona set her coffee on the table. "That's one of the reasons I brought up the fundraiser for the community center during the meeting."

"It sounds like a great idea. Community centers are vital for residents in need."

"I'm glad to hear you say that." Ramona rewarded Peyton with a smile. "I'd like you to cochair the fund-raising committee."

Peyton froze with a forkful of quiche in her mouth. Her gaze locked with Ramona's as she chewed, swallowed, and tried to speak. "You want *me* to cochair the committee?"

"Do you have any experience with fund-raisers?"

Peyton searched Ramona's serious expression. "I've volunteered on fund-raising committees in the past but—"

"Perfect." Ramona spread her arms.

"But I barely know the town."

"You'll bring fresh ideas to the project."

"I've never even *seen* the center much less used it."

"You won't have any preconceived notions of the facilities."

Peyton sighed. "Ramona, I'm very flattered that you thought of me. But I don't think I'm the right person for the job."

"Yes, you are." Ramona raised her hands to count off the reasons. "You're new. You're enthusiastic, and you're falling in love with my town."

"Your town?" Peyton gave the mayor a teasing look. "You're moving to Philadelphia in January."

"Trinity Falls will always be my town, and I want what's best for it. Will you help with the fund-raiser?"

"You need a chairperson who's been here longer. Their knowledge of the community would serve the town better." Peyton nudged aside a cantaloupe chunk with her fork.

"You wouldn't be leading the committee alone. There are a few people I've got in mind to cochair with you."

"Who?"

"I'd rather wait until I ask them." Ramona's smile didn't inspire trust. "So what do you say? Will you help the town?"

When she put it like that, how could Peyton refuse? "You don't waste any time, do you? You proposed the fund-raiser Tuesday night. It's only been five days."

Ramona leaned into the table, propping her chin on her palm. "You strike me as a decisive woman."

Peyton laughed her surprise. "This is a big decision."

"But it's for a very good cause." Ramona pinched a grape from Peyton's fruit bowl. "And it will be a good way for you to meet your neighbors and learn more about the community."

Peyton enjoyed fund-raising and she was good at it. She'd learned from the best—her mother. They'd worked together on several university as well as community fund-raisers. Ramona was right. She had the experience. Then why was she hesitating?

Because she was afraid she wouldn't be good enough. This would be her first fund-raiser without her mother's guidance. Could she handle the project without Irene Biery Harris's help? There was only one way to find out.

"All right." Peyton set aside her fruit. "I'll cochair the fund-raising committee on—"

"Wonderful." Ramona clapped her hands together. "You won't regret—"

"I do have one condition." Peyton held up both hands, palms out. "The other cochair has to be willing to partner with me. I don't want to be a part of a project with someone who isn't willing to work as a team."

"I'm sure he'll be happy to work with you." Ramona smiled.

"He?" Warning bells chimed in the back of Peyton's mind.

"Darius." Ramona looked toward the café counter. "I think this would be a great experience for him as well."

"Darius?" Peyton's eyes stretched wide as she, too, turned to look at the reporter. "I don't know if recruiting him would be such a great idea. He's going to think you're playing matchmaker again."

"I know." Ramona sighed. "He's so paranoid. I think it's the investigative reporter in him."

"Is he right?"

Ramona held Peyton's gaze. "What if he is?"

Peyton was both amused and incredulous. "Then I think you and your friends are going to be very frustrated. Darius isn't interested in me."

Why does that thought depress me?

Ramona gave her a secret smile. "What if you're wrong?"

CHAPTER 5

Alonzo's doorbell rang just before seven o'clock Sunday evening. The sound reverberated in his chest, causing his heart to skip a beat and his thoughts to scatter. *Doreen*. The time had finally come: November second, the Day of the Dead.

Hosting this celebration for Doreen and their friends was one of the most important things he'd ever done in his life. What if it backfired? Alonzo wiped his damp palms on the seams of his black denim pants, then crossed to his front door. He took a moment to gather himself before pulling it open. Doreen stood on the other side. She took his breath away. She always did. Her smile made his head spin and his body warm.

"I'm glad you came." Alonzo offered her his hand and helped her across the threshold.

"So am I." Her voice was warm but a little tentative, as though she wasn't completely confident of being here.

Alonzo drew her to him to greet her with a kiss.

Her coat was cool against his jersey and pants. He drew her closer to share his body heat, then lowered his head to hers. Her lips were soft and sweet, her body yielding in his embrace. Her mouth parted, allowing his tongue to steal inside. Her slender arms slipped over his chest to twine around his neck. Alonzo's body heated.

With a groan of regret, he stepped back. "You make me lose track of time."

Doreen opened her eyes and found his gaze. A sexy smile curved her lips. "You say that as though it's a bad thing."

"It could be awkward when our guests arrive." Alonzo took her hand and led her farther into his house.

His modest furnishings were a sharp contrast to her bright and cheerful home. Doreen had teased him repeatedly about his lack of decorating vision. He thought he'd been practical, but she was right. His living room's dark brown recliner, sofa, and area rug lacked the warmth of Doreen's pink-and-white furnishings.

"Is there anything I can do to help?" Doreen's attention settled on Alonzo's dining room table.

"That's the altar for our Day of the Dead ceremony." He studied his creation. How would she view it?

He'd spread a gold cloth over the mahogany table. On the center of the table, he'd stacked a purple box on top of a larger red box. He'd arranged glasses of water around the table and lit white votive candles in glass holders. He'd scattered gold, pink, and white marigold petals across the table and over the stacked boxes. A cross stood on one side. The scents of fresh flowers and incense filled the room.

"It's lovely." Doreen's voice was almost reverent.

"Thank you." He kissed the back of her hand before releasing her.

"Is there anything left to do?" She dragged her gaze from the altar.

"No, thanks. We can wait for the others to join us. I've got everything covered."

He hoped. He had a lot riding on the success of this event. What if Doreen didn't understand what he was trying to do? What if she misjudged him?

"I'm a little nervous." Doreen's laughter was self-conscious. "But I'm looking forward to this ceremony."

"There's no reason to be nervous, *mi amor*. This ritual is meant to invoke happy memories only. And to make the dead feel welcome and loved." Then why did he feel anxious?

Alonzo pulled together crackers from his cupboard, and cheese and a vegetable tray from his refrigerator. Doreen kept him company, asking about his day and telling him about hers. He set the refreshments on the silver Formica counter between his half-kitchen and the dining room. Their banter helped ease his tension and, he hoped, Doreen's nerves.

His doorbell rang three more times. The first time, it announced Ean, Megan, and Ramona. Minutes later, Jackson and Audra joined them. Finally, Darius escorted Ms. Helen to the event. Alonzo greeted the elderly town matriarch with a hug. Dr. Helen Gaston, or Ms. Helen as Trinity Falls' residents called her, was timeless.

Alonzo wrapped his left arm around Doreen's slim waist as he led his friends into his dining room. He didn't entertain much, which was the exact opposite of Doreen. During the past four months, he'd picked up a lot from her about entertaining. He incorporated that knowledge into the evening as he made his guests comfortable.

"Thank you for coming." Alonzo released Doreen and crossed to the altar. His gaze swept the small group. They each held a folder, bag, or envelope in which he suspected they carried their photos. "The Day of the Dead isn't a time for sadness. It's a time to celebrate and honor our loved ones who've died." He gestured toward the altar. "This is one way for us to remember someone we love who's passed on."

Darius indicated the altar. "Are those items symbolic?"

Ramona sighed. "I'm sure Alonzo's getting to that."

"It's all right, Ramona." Alonzo grinned. "I appreciate Darius's enthusiasm."

"Thanks, Sheriff." Darius gave Ramona a triumphant look.

Alonzo continued. "The glasses of water quench the thirst of our loved ones' spirits. The lit candles guide the spirits on their journey. The marigolds are synonymous with the Day of the Dead. And the incense removes negative energy."

Darius smiled. "Instead of using incense, we could just ask Ramona to leave."

"Darius, you're not helping." Under Doreen's firm tone, Alonzo heard a trace of amusement.

He held Doreen's warm brown eyes. "The most important thing to remember is that this is a celebration of the ones we've loved and lost. We're here to keep their memories alive so they're never forgotten. I'll go first."

Alonzo released Doreen's gaze and lifted a photo he'd placed on the table behind the altar. "Captain Cesar Vargas." He stared at the image of the slim, dignified older man in silence for a moment. His friend and former supervisor was in a sheriff's uniform, including a brown felt campaign hat. He then faced the picture outward so the others could see it. "As you can imagine, Jacksonville, Florida, where I used to work, is very different from Trinity Falls. Captain Vargas called me the son he wished he'd had. That usually meant he needed help with some household project. But he treated me like family and kept me from getting too homesick between trips back to Trinity Falls."

Alonzo put the photograph of his former mentor on the altar. "Who's next?"

"Me." Ms. Helen stepped forward, trading places with Alonzo. The tiny woman pinned the sheriff with a sharp look. "I'm going to get this picture back, right?"

Alonzo smiled from his place at Doreen's side. "I promise."

She nodded once in satisfaction, then held a framed black-and-white photo chest high. The picture's subject was a middle-aged woman. Her twinkling eyes belied her prim expression.

"This is my godmother, Mrs. Cora Mary Covington." Ms. Helen glanced again at the photo before continuing. "Covington was the family name of her fifth husband. She was my mother's best friend from childhood. Aunt Cora always used to tell me, 'Helen, be who God intended you to be and you will set the world on fire.' I thought she'd made up that saying. I was so impressed. It wasn't until I was in college that I realized she was quoting Saint Catherine of Siena."

Ms. Helen turned the picture to study it. "It doesn't matter, Aunt Cora. You still impressed me. And you inspired me to be the very best I could be." She placed the photograph lovingly on the altar before returning to stand in front of Darius.

"That's a great quote." Darius rested his hand on the tiny woman's shoulder.

Ms. Helen looked back at the reporter. She squeezed his large hand with her frail one. "It's advice we can all use."

Ramona walked to the altar. "I've got two."

"You always were an overachiever." Darius released Ms. Helen's shoulder. His teasing eased the growing solemnity.

Alonzo sent the reporter a grateful look. This was a celebration. He didn't want his guests becoming too serious.

"Thank you, Darius." Ramona's wry smile softened her sarcasm. She reached into her manila folder and pulled out a photo of an attractive older couple, laughing at the camera. She propped it on the altar. "My grandparents taught me the value of family and community."

Megan passed Ramona on her way to the altar. She set a picture of a beautiful young couple, gazing at each other beside the photo Ramona had offered. "I never knew my parents. They died when I was very young. But my grandfather said I inherited my father's business sense and my mother's determination."

"Determination? That's a polite way of calling you stubborn." Darius winked at Megan.

Megan's laughter cleared the cloud of regret from her elegant, cocoa features. "Determined or stubborn, as long as I get my way in the end."

Ean chuckled as he exchanged places with Megan. "My father encouraged me to set goals." He put the photo of Paul Fever on the altar. Even in the photo, the tall, good-looking man projected a powerful personality. "This picture was taken during my law school graduation. His grin was so big. I don't know whether that's because he was proud of my accomplishment or because he was done with my school bills."

Alonzo watched Doreen as Ean spoke of his father. A ghost of a smile curved her full lips. Her brown eyes were dreamy. She didn't seem distressed. What was she thinking? Had he done the right thing, hosting this celebration? He turned his attention back to the ceremony.

Audra placed a photo of a pretty young woman on the altar before facing the group. "My high school music teacher said talent would only get you so far. She challenged me to go even farther. I appreciated her encouragement. Eventually."

Audra returned to Jackson's side and nudged him forward.

"My daughter, Zoey." He placed a photo of a pretty, laughing little girl with long, brown hair beside the image of Audra's music teacher. "She died just before her ninth birthday."

"What would you like to tell us about her?" Audra's voice was encouraging.

Jackson kept his eyes on the image of his daughter. Slowly a smile stretched his lips and brightened his sienna features. He met Audra's eyes. "She gave me an appreciation for fairy tales."

Alonzo watched Jackson return to Audra. The two held hands, entwining their fingers. He glanced down at Doreen's hand. Would she welcome his touch now, or should he wait until the ceremony was over?

He raised his gaze, looking from Darius to Doreen. "Who wants to go next?"

Darius gestured toward Doreen. "Ladies first."

"You're always so chivalrous." Doreen gripped a plain white envelope on her way to the altar. She shot a worried glance at Alonzo, then looked away. "Tonight, I want to celebrate Paul Fever."

"He's a good choice," Alonzo spoke softly.

He hurt for Doreen—for both of them. He wished with all his heart he could convince her that he wasn't interested in replacing Paul. Even if he wanted to, he knew he never could.

Doreen drew Paul's photo from the envelope. She took a deep breath before displaying the picture. It was a color image of the tall, broad-shouldered man, wearing a pink-and-white apron as he displayed a tray of fresh-baked cookies.

"Paul taught me that true love is helping the other person to be the best she can be and supporting her goals." Doreen's throat muscles worked.

"In this photo, he's helping me bake cookies for a Heritage High School fund-raiser."

"I remember that fund-raiser." Darius continued in a deadpanned voice. "You would have raised more money if he'd just bought the cookies."

"You're probably right about that." Doreen's laughter joined her friends'. "But his heart was in the right place."

"Absolutely." Alonzo grinned.

Doreen left the altar but still wouldn't meet his gaze. Alonzo's stomach muscles tightened. Had the Day of the Dead celebration been a bad idea? She seemed to enjoy it, but did she understand why he'd wanted to share it with her? Paul had been his friend, too. He wanted to help her celebrate her late husband. He didn't want either of them to ever forget him.

"Your turn, Darius," Alonzo prompted the reporter.

Darius looked at the gift bag in his hand. "My contribution seemed like a good idea at the time. Now I think it's out of place."

Alonzo frowned. A quick glance around the room showed he wasn't the only one baffled by Darius's words. "We're celebrating loved ones who are deceased. No one is out of place, Darius."

The reporter expelled a heavy breath. He emerged from behind Ms. Helen and proceeded with weighted steps to the altar. The black-and-silver gift bag hung from his right hand.

"My deceased loved one isn't a person but still means a lot to me." Darius withdrew a photo from the bag and turned it to face his friends. "Most of you will remember Riddler, my black Labrador retriever."

Mystery solved, Alonzo grinned. He glanced down to find Doreen sharing her smile with him. He slipped his right arm around her waist and pulled her closer. She didn't resist him. Perhaps the event had been the right thing to do after all, for him and Doreen as well as for Darius.

"I remember that devil dog. He ate my favorite sandals." Ramona still held a grudge sixteen years later.

"Only the left one." Darius seemed compelled to defend his pet.

"And he polished off the ham I'd made for an Easter dinner. The entire ham." Doreen struggled to maintain her frown, even as a grin threatened.

Darius gave her an innocent look. "That was meant as a compliment."

"Was there anything Riddler wouldn't eat?" Megan asked.

"No." Ean shrugged. "He and Darius were alike that way."

"That dog followed you everywhere." Jackson grinned. "You should have named him Shadow."

Ms. Helen shook her head. "Riddler was the perfect name for Darius's dog. The Riddler is one of Batman's more interesting villains."

Alonzo nodded with agreement. "What did Riddler teach you, Darius?"

"Unconditional love." Darius placed Riddler's photo on the altar. In the image, Riddler was attempting to eat a football. "And how to evade the strong safety."

The former high school and college football player

returned to the group. Ms. Helen offered him a smile as she patted his arm.

Alonzo retrieved the bottle of red wine he'd saved for after the tributes. With Doreen's help, he filled and distributed the nine glasses. He asked his friends to bow their heads for a small prayer.

After the appeal, he lifted his glass. "A toast. To our loved ones who've passed on and the memories they've left behind."

He watched Doreen as he shared the toast. A cloud swept over her features. She averted her gaze from his and grew quiet again. If celebrating the Day of the Dead together didn't prove his feelings to her, what more did he have to do?

Darius sensed a trap. "You want me to chair a fund-raising committee?"

Had Jackson lost his mind?

Darius eyed his publisher warily from the cushioned gray guest chair opposite Jackson's polished oak desk. It was Monday morning, the day before the mayoral election. He had enough on his mind without puzzling the reason for this assignment.

In the almost four months since Jackson had resumed his responsibilities as publisher and editor-in-chief of *The Trinity Falls Monitor,* he'd settled into his office and routine as though he'd never left. That was thanks in large part to Audra. During the five months the couple had been together, she'd worked miracles on the former recluse who'd retreated from life after his young daughter's death. Darius was glad to have his friend and boss back at work. At least he had been—until Jackson sprang this morning's assignment on him.

Darius lowered his eyes while he tried to figure out his pal's plan. His gaze settled on Jackson's overloaded desk. On one corner was a stack of newspapers from neighboring towns as well as the nearby metropolitan paper, Cleveland's *The Plain Dealer*. Sitting on the opposite corner, closer to his computer, was a photo of Audra, laughing as she displayed the bass she'd caught during one of their many fishing trips. Next to that image was a framed picture of Jackson's daughter, Zoey, who'd died just before her ninth birthday, almost twenty months ago. The pain of her loss had overwhelmed Jackson. If it weren't for Audra's love and support, he wouldn't have been able to keep Zoey's photo on his desk. That would have been a shame.

Darius caught Jackson's dark eyes. "Why me?"

"You were at the town council meeting last week." Jackson propped his elbows on the arms of his black executive chair. "Before she leaves office, Ramona wants to establish a committee to raise funds for the community center's renovation. It needs a lot of upgrades."

Jackson's answer was evasive.

Darius tried again. "Why do you want me to cochair the committee? I cover the news. I'll write articles about the campaign and what the committee's doing. But I can't do a balanced job covering the news if I'm part of the story."

"You won't cover this story. Opal will."

Darius rubbed his eyes with his left thumb and two fingers. Opal Gutierrez was the *Monitor*'s rookie reporter. Darius questioned her training. He'd once accused her of being more like a Dictaphone than a newspaper reporter. Now she was assigned to cover a story in which he was involved. How would she approach it?

Darius gave a mental shrug. He didn't need to worry. He wasn't going to be part of the story. "I've never chaired a fundraiser."

"But you can convince people to do things you think are right, whether they want to do it or not." Jackson smiled. "You convinced Stan to get sober."

Darius shook his head. "That's not the same as talking them into giving me their money."

"Close enough."

"Come on, Jack." Darius gave his boss a skeptical look. "What's this really about?"

"The community center is very important to the town." Jackson crossed his arms. "I want the *Monitor* to be represented on the committee."

Jackson's words were sincere, but Darius didn't buy them. "Then why don't you chair it?"

"It would be overkill to have the publisher on the committee."

Darius wasn't buying that one, either. "Then Opal can sit on the committee and I'll cover the story."

Jackson shook his head. "I want you to represent the paper."

Is it possible he'd misjudged his friend's intention? "I'm flattered, Jack. But I'm not qualified for this assignment."

Jackson held up his hands, palms out. "You wouldn't be leading the committee by yourself. You'd be working with a cochair."

The muscles at the back of his neck tensed with suspicion. "Who?"

"Someone you know." Jackson didn't hesitate. "Dr. Peyton Harris."

Darius shook his head in disbelief. "So this is another attempt at matchmaking. Don't you have anything better to do?"

"No."

"I've heard that when people are in love, they want everyone to be in a relationship. But this is ridiculous."

"Why?"

Darius considered his boss and longtime friend. "Audra brought joy back into your life. Megan helped Ean reconsider his priorities. And Ramona is keeping Q from becoming an old maid. I'm happy for you guys. But don't try to fix me up. It's obnoxious."

Jackson sobered. "D, I'm saying this as a friend. You're becoming surly. You need someone to bring out your better side."

"Thanks for the tip." Darius stood.

"Just because your parents don't have a happy marriage doesn't mean you won't."

Someone had put Jackson up to this latest matchmaking ploy. Who was it? Doreen? Megan? Ramona? Quincy?

Darius frowned. "How did you jump from my dating Peyton to my marrying her?"

"She seems perfect for you."

"Why?"

"Because she frog-marched you out of her office the first time she met you." Jackson's expressionless tone and features masked his reaction to what Darius had thought was a little-known incident.

His skin warmed. "Quincy has a big mouth."

"He also has a point. Women usually try to hold on to you. Peyton literally threw you out." Jackson laughed at his own joke.

"I'm glad I can amuse you."

Jackson sobered. "Peyton is intelligent, attractive, kind, and employed. Why aren't you interested in her?"

"She's not interested in me, either, so you might was well stop trying to get us together."

Darius strode out of Jackson's office door and set a course for his cubicle. He was running away, this time from Jackson's comments and questions. What good would they do? He'd spent so much time running and hiding from his emotions, he didn't think he could feel anymore. He was like the Tin Man in *The Wizard of Oz*, searching for a heart.

∽⚬CHAPTER 6⚬∽

Peyton stared at her ringing cell phone Monday morning. It was Bruce. Again. He'd called twice today. Each time, he'd left the same message: *Peyton, it's Bruce. Call me.*

But she hadn't. She knew what he wanted. Undoubtedly, her mother had called him to invite him to spend Christmas in Aruba with the Harris family. In turn, Bruce wanted to know why Peyton hadn't extended the invitation to him first. Imagining their pending conversation was giving her a headache.

Her cell phone finally stopped ringing, but her relief was short-lived. Bruce didn't leave a message this time, which meant he'd run out of patience—and she'd run out of time.

Peyton checked her wristwatch. It was just after ten o'clock in the morning. Her next appointment wasn't for another four hours, when Darius would arrive to interview her for his article on Dr. Hartford's retirement.

No more excuses, Peyton. Return Bruce's call.

She took a deep breath, squared her shoulders, and touched the CALL button next to Bruce's number. He answered on the second ring.

"Where have you been? I've called you three times." He barked his greeting.

"I'm sorry. I've been in classes." Her initial impulse was to snap back at him. Why hadn't she?

"Never mind." He exhaled a short, irritated breath. In the background, Bruce's keyboard clacked in time with his hunt-and-peck rhythm. "Irene told me she and Carlson plan to spend Christmas in Aruba, and they want us to join them. Why did I have to hear this from Irene? *You* should have told me. I felt like a fool."

"I'm sorry." Again she bit her tongue even as she fantasized about wrapping his around his throat.

Peyton rotated her chair to face the window. In the distance, the little pond the university community called Wishing Lake reflected the late-morning sun. The kidney-shaped body of water lay near the edge of the campus. A wandering cement walkway framed the lake. In the center, a fountain kept the water in constant motion.

Wishing Lake . . . How many coins would it take to wish away my engagement?

"Don't do it again. You know I hate being caught off guard. Hold on." Bruce moved his telephone receiver away from his mouth. Still Peyton heard him tell his secretary, Leila, to make fifteen copies of the report he'd just approved. His voice was pleasant when he spoke to Leila. As pleasant as he'd been with Peyton before he'd proposed. Peyton glanced at her naked ring finger. Since leaving New York, she'd kept the four-carat, princess-cut diamond ring in its box in her suitcase.

Bruce returned to the line. "All right. Where were we? I told Irene we'd join them in Aruba."

Peyton grew cold, as though the autumn temperature had seeped into her skin. "I wish you hadn't done that."

"Hold on." Bruce called to Leila again, asking her to send a fax. His request was as sweet as sugar. "Of course we're going to Aruba with Irene and Carlson. It's what they want."

What about what I want? When was the last time someone had respected my wishes?

Her knitted brow cleared with realization. Five months ago. That was when Darius had agreed not to do an article about her for the *Monitor*. She'd been so afraid her parents and Bruce would come across the interview on the Internet and learn that Trinity Falls University wasn't a temporary aberration in her otherwise dutiful life. At first, the reporter had tried to pressure her into granting him an interview. But he'd eventually accepted her decision. He'd even bought her a dozen yellow roses to apologize for being a jerk. The memory made her smile.

"Did you hear me?" Bruce's sharp question burst Peyton's warm bubble.

"Excuse me?"

Another sigh. "I said we leave the morning of December thirteenth. Irene and I will give you the rest of the itinerary while you're in New York for Thanksgiving."

Peyton's beautiful view of vibrant autumn leaves and sunlight bouncing like diamonds on the surface of Wishing Lake darkened to a vision of a lifetime spent with other people ordering her around. "I can't leave December thirteenth. That's the day of the university's winter commencement."

"You'll have to miss it."

Oh, no, I won't. "I'd rather not. One of the joys of being a professor is watching your students walk during commencement."

"What about Irene and Carlson? After all they've done for you over the years, all they're asking in return is that you spend Christmas with them. Who in their right mind wouldn't want to spend Christmas in the Caribbean?"

Irene and Bruce seemed to work from the same playbook when it came to pressuring Peyton. If bullying didn't work, try guilt. Had Bruce picked that up on his own, or had Irene made the suggestion?

Peyton remained silent.

Bruce continued. "Don't tell me you'd rather spend Christmas in that boring little town."

That comment rubbed Peyton the wrong way. "You can't judge Trinity Falls when you've never even been here."

"Before you decided to spend a semester there, I'd never even heard of it."

"Well, you've heard of it now." Unconsciously, Peyton had clenched her free hand into a fist. She forced herself to relax.

"Don't tell me you're getting fond of that place. You've only been there a couple of months."

It had been five months. But it was good to know her fiancé wasn't missing her. "I enjoy it here. It's a lovely town with a welcoming community."

"Well, don't enjoy it too much. You're returning

to New York next month. Hold on." He moved the phone from his mouth again and called to Leila.

Peyton had had more than enough. "Listen, Bruce, it sounds as though you have a lot of work to do. I need to get ready for my next class. Let's wait until I come home before we confirm our Christmas arrangements."

"The arrangements can't wait, Peyton." Bruce seemed to have dismissed her as he directed Leila to move his next day's meetings around to accommodate a business luncheon.

"Why not?" Desperation sharpened Peyton's tone.

"Today's November third. Thanksgiving is another three weeks away. Irene's already confirmed the trip with her travel agent."

Peyton spun back to her desk. The muscles in her shoulders knotted. "Has she confirmed the dates and the number of tickets?"

"Yes." Bruce's keyboard clacked in the background. "Everything's set. All you have to do is show up."

Peyton swallowed a scream of frustration. "Bruce—"

"I've got to go, Peyton. When you get home, we'll set the wedding date."

Peyton listened to the dial tone in disbelief. Despite her objections, her mother and fiancé had booked her on a Christmas cruise to Aruba. They'd disregarded her wishes. Again.

And Bruce wanted to set a wedding date. Won't he be surprised when she returns his engagement ring instead?

"Thanks for agreeing to be interviewed." Darius's warm baritone strummed the muscles in Peyton's lower abdomen as the reporter followed her farther into her university office Monday afternoon.

"As long as the article's not about me, I'm glad to give the *Monitor* an interview." She was impressed by his manners as he waited for her to take her seat before folding his long, lean body into one of her two gray visitor's chairs.

"You still don't trust me."

Peyton tensed at his accusation. "I'm just verifying that the article you're interviewing me for is about Dr. Hartford's retirement."

"That's what I told you on the phone when we scheduled this interview." Darius propped his right ankle on his left knee. He spread open his reporter's notebook on his well-muscled right thigh. "What makes you think that's changed?"

Peyton considered opening the window behind her desk just a bit. Her office had become very warm.

She lifted her gaze to meet the challenge in Darius's eyes. His evasive answer didn't put her at ease. "So it's still your intent to write a tribute article on Dr. Hartford?"

"Very impressive." A taunting smile spread Darius's well-formed lips. "Instead of giving in to the impulse to punch me in the nose, you formulated that very proper and professional question. Did you develop your patience from teaching or did you go into teaching because you have patience?"

Peyton took her time studying the reporter's impossibly good-looking face: his classic sepia features; broad forehead; almond-shaped, midnight eyes; long nose; high cheekbones; full, well-shaped lips; and stubborn, squared chin. He was the most attractive man she'd ever met, and at this moment, she wanted to strike him.

"You're right." Peyton clung to the patience that so impressed the reporter. "I do want to punch you in the nose."

Darius threw back his handsome head and laughed. The sound—deep, full, and free—was infectious. Peyton struggled against her own smile.

His laughter quieted to a grin. Even his teeth were perfect. "What do I have to do to get you to trust me?"

"You can start by giving me a straight answer to my question."

"All right." Darius sat up on his chair and became very serious. "Dr. Harris, I'd like to interview you today for the article I'm writing on Dr. Hartford's retirement."

"Now, was that so hard?" Peyton folded her hands on her desk and leaned forward.

"No, it wasn't." Darius's penetrating stare caught and held Peyton's eyes.

She grew warm and flustered beneath his fixed regard. Her pulse beat too fast. She struggled with her breathing. Her thighs quivered. Peyton dropped her gaze. She never felt this way when Bruce looked at her. But everything about Darius—his looks, his voice, his scent—made her want to throw caution—as well as her underwear—to the wind.

Good heavens, why was she thinking about flinging her underwear at a virtual stranger? A blush scalded Peyton's cheeks. Her fiancé considered her cold. But if Darius could make her feel this way, the problem wasn't with her. No wonder most of the women in Trinity Falls were chasing after him.

"What questions do you want to ask me?" Was that husky voice hers?

"You've done a really great job with this office."

Darius looked around. "It's much nicer than when Quincy had it."

"Oh?" Peyton kept her eyes on the reporter. It wasn't a hardship.

"Quincy's a slob, at least at work." Darius's eyes roamed her office. "His house is clean. But when he had this office, it was cluttered, covered in dust, and reeked of burned coffee."

Peyton frowned. "He must have worked really hard on it before he left. It was very clean when I arrived."

"It even smells better in here." He caught her gaze again. "It smells like you."

Heat rose in Peyton's cheeks. "What do I smell like?"

"Talcum powder and lilies."

She swallowed hard. "It's important to me that students feel comfortable and welcome in my office. They won't feel that way if they have to climb over books to reach my desk or move stacks of papers before they sit."

"That didn't seem to bother Quincy." Darius gave her an admiring look.

Was he flirting with her? "What questions did you want to ask me about Dr. Hartford?"

Darius's lips curved in a slight smile. He pulled a mini audio recorder from his inside jacket pocket, pressed a button, then put the recorder on Peyton's desk.

Peyton eyed the technology suspiciously. "You're going to record the interview?"

"I thought you'd be happy about that. This way, you don't have to worry that I might misquote you."

She nodded toward his notebook. "Why are you taking notes if you have a recorder?"

"It's in case the recorder fails. I like to be prepared."

Peyton gave him a skeptical look. She wasn't comfortable with the recorder, but he did have a point. There was less of a chance he'd misquote her if he recorded their interview. "OK. I'm ready."

Darius sat back in his seat. "Dr. Hartford is an institution, not only at the university but also in Trinity Falls. As a new faculty member and a new resident to our town, what are your impressions of his many contributions to the university?"

Peyton's eyebrows rose. He'd impressed her with his first question. She felt challenged to give him an equally impressive answer. And that's how it went for the next thirty minutes. Darius tossed her thought-provoking questions for which she had to focus to provide intelligent answers. At the end of the half hour, she was ready for a nap. She'd settle for a beverage.

"Can I offer you a bottle of water?" Peyton rose and crossed to her mini-fridge on the other side of her desk.

"Thanks." Darius's pen raced across his notebook a moment longer.

Peyton circled his chair on her way to the refrigerator. She glanced over his shoulder, curious about the notes he was taking. His handwriting was illegible.

"It's a good thing you recorded my answers. Can *you* read that scribble?" Peyton surprised herself. She wasn't used to teasing people. The residents of Trinity Falls were changing her.

Darius looked at her over his shoulder. "It's shorthand."

"If you say so." She continued toward her mini-fridge. But with her next step, her heel caught on her office's small, multicolored area rug. She grabbed the back of Darius's chair to keep her balance.

Darius leaped to his feet, catching her waist to steady her. "Are you OK?"

In reflex, Peyton grabbed hold of his upper arms. She was more disconcerted by Darius's quick action than her near fall. She stared up at him, eyes wide and lips parted. "You have great reflexes."

His concerned expression softened. "It comes from playing ball."

"Oh." Her grip tightened on his biceps. The hard muscles beneath his navy jacket sleeves fascinated her. He must still work out. A lot.

"Are you sure you're all right?"

She tried to step back, but Darius held her fast. "Yes, I'm just embarrassed."

"Don't be." He released her.

Peyton's palms itched to feel his arms again. She turned from the reporter to cross to her refrigerator, and again her heel caught on the area rug. Her lips parted on a gasp as she felt herself falling. Once more, Darius grabbed her waist, stopping her from landing on her face. But this time, he hauled her flush against him.

Her breasts were crushed against his chest. Her hands gripped his broad shoulders. His warmth seeped into her skin. His scent—soap and cedar—clouded her mind.

Peyton tipped her head back. The heat of his gaze scalded her. Her fingers dug into his taut muscles as Darius lowered his head to hers.

~CHAPTER 7~

Peyton's body trembled as Darius's lips moved over hers. A bolt of electricity shot from her core to her heart. Or was it from her heart to her core? This must be what other women meant when they said someone "turned them on." She'd read about such reactions in romance novels. She'd heard about them in love songs and seen them in romantic movies. But she'd never experienced them herself, not once in her thirty years.

Peyton slid her arms up and over Darius's chest. She grew warm and wet as she absorbed his body's heat and strength. Darius shook under her touch. Peyton stilled.

Did I cause that?

Feminine power swelled inside her. Bruce had found her lacking. He didn't think she knew he found his pleasure elsewhere. But to have a man like Darius respond to her was her secret fantasy. Peyton gave in to the pull of Darius's hard, hot body. Lost herself in his intoxicating scent, his seductive touch, and his thrilling taste.

His tongue traced the seam of her mouth. He was asking her to let him in, requesting rather than demanding, giving her a choice. That consideration was far more erotic than the intimacy he sought. Peyton parted for him. Darius swept inside, caressing, stroking, planting in her mind an image of what their bodies could do. Peyton shivered. Her muscles went weak.

Darius's arms banded around her waist. He straightened, lifting her with him. Only her toes touched the floor. Peyton was losing control. Her head spun. Her body floated. She ached to wrap her trembling legs around Darius's hips and press her thighs to his sides. But even the thought was too scandalous.

I'm still engaged to Bruce.

She tore her mouth free. His name was all she could manage. "Darius."

Slowly he released her, letting her feet return to solid ground. But her legs were too shaky to stand on her own.

Darius caught her forearm to steady her. "Isn't this how we started?" His voice, husky and low, did wicked things to her still-throbbing muscles.

A blush heated Peyton's face as she realized Darius was referring to her tripping into his arms—twice. But her clumsiness had answered one question for her. Any doubts she had about ending her engagement to Bruce had gone up in flames beneath Darius's kiss.

Sex with Bruce had never been interesting. In contrast, the possibilities with Darius aroused so much more than her curiosity. But even as her body swayed toward him, her brain sent out warning alarms.

Darius Knight was the Derek Jeter of Trinity Falls. The Yankees shortstop was a confirmed bachelor with an inexhaustible supply of women willing to have their hearts broken. Did she want to be one of his casualties?

Peyton stepped back. "Do you have any other questions for me?"

Darius let his arm fall to his side. He hadn't been this confused by a woman since . . . He'd never been this confused. And why was she freezing him out after she'd kissed him back?

"You've answered all of my questions. Thanks." He should leave now. He needed to clear his head. "I'd like to call you if I have any follow-up questions."

"Of course." She sounded relieved.

Darius collected his recorder and notebook. He threw his coat over his arm. "Thanks for your time. I'll take a rain check on that water."

Maybe his parting shot had been unfair, but the blush that pinkened her honey-and-chocolate-cream complexion was worth it.

Peyton followed him to her office door. "I'm glad you're writing a tribute to Dr. Hartford. He's done a lot for the university."

Darius turned to her. Through her window, he could see Wishing Lake. The name of that particular body of water had always confused him. It was a pond, not a lake.

"Do you know how Wishing Lake got its name?" Where had that question come from? He was supposed to be leaving.

"Students throw pennies in the lake for good grades." She spared a quick glance at the window behind her.

Darius shook his head. "There are better ways to invest in their education."

"I take it that's not how the lake got its name?" Peyton's smile distracted him.

"According to Dr. Hartford, TFU's founder, Clara Butler, was desperate to start a school for the freed and escaped slaves who'd helped establish Trinity Falls." Darius nodded toward the window. "She stood by the pond and prayed for guidance and courage. And that night, she had a life-changing vision that told her what she needed to do to start the school."

"What did she need to do?"

"Build it."

Peyton's arched brows knitted. "That's it?"

"That's it." Darius met her gaze. "Wishing Lake isn't about coins. It's about faith and finding the courage to follow your dreams. But for some reason, students keep tossing pennies in the pond."

"That's poetic." Peyton looked at him as though she'd never seen him before.

Darius's eyes slid free of hers. "Dr. Hartford told me the story."

"I don't know Dr. Hartford well, but I'm almost positive he wouldn't have described the lake as you did."

She was right. No one would ever call Dr. Kenneth Hartford a poet.

The impish lights in Peyton's caramel eyes made him want to kiss her again. Darius pivoted toward the door. "Enjoy the rest of your day."

"You do the same. And thank you for the history lesson."

"You're welcome."

Darius made it out of her office and down the hall. He paused at the top of the staircase that led to the building's rear entrance. For too many years, he'd buried his emotions. It was an act of self-defense against his parents' frequent public displays of disaffection for each other. It also protected him from the many and varied ways their thoughtless words had hurt him. After a while, he thought he'd stopped feeling.

But kissing Peyton had proven him wrong. Darius started down the steps. He could still feel. His heart had punched him in the chest. His skin had burned beneath her touch—and his manhood had swelled uncomfortably in his shorts.

What was a former robot to do with these very human feelings?

"I'm stepping down as town council president."

CeCe Roben's declaration shouldn't have surprised Doreen. She'd suspected the council president had a major announcement. What else would bring her to Doreen's home on a Monday evening? CeCe wasn't in the habit of just dropping by. Still, Doreen was blindsided.

She cradled her cup of chai tea and stared wide-eyed at the other woman seated across from her at her mahogany dining table. "Why?"

The former council president released a deep sigh. Her pale blue gaze strayed across the cream-and-mahogany dining room, then back to Doreen. "I'm not ready to leave the council altogether. But I'm burned out. It's exhausting dealing with the posturing and obstruction. Sometimes I feel like the only responsible adult in the room."

"Is that really something you should be saying to

me the day before the election?" Doreen's question wasn't totally tongue in cheek.

CeCe's eyes twinkled with humor. "Perhaps not, but that's how I feel. I need to step back from the daily oversight of the council."

"For how long?" Doreen sipped her tea. The pearl gray clock mounted to the warm cream wall behind CeCe read almost six o'clock in the evening. Alonzo would be here soon. What would he think of CeCe's news?

"The rest of my term." CeCe stared into her cup of tea as though viewing her past. "This isn't what I'd planned on when I ran for council president. I want to serve the community, not negotiate with adults as though they were spoiled prepubescents."

"You need to do what's best for you." Doreen empathized with the former council president. She'd dealt with similar attitudes while serving on volunteer committees.

"The other council members were supportive." With her right hand, CeCe swept her shoulder-length auburn hair away from her oval face.

"You were a good council president. One of the best the town has ever had. You'll be hard to replace."

"Thank you, Doreen." A faint blush warmed CeCe's alabaster features.

"When will the council vote on your replacement?" Which of the members would want to take CeCe's place? As the soon-to-be-former council president had implied, it was a tough and thankless job.

"We've already voted." CeCe tucked her bone-straight hair behind an ear. "Nessa is the new council president."

"Nessa?" Unease snaked through Doreen, twisting

the muscles in her stomach. "Was the council's vote unanimous?"

CeCe gave her a strange look. "Yes. Actually, Nessa was the only council member who wanted to be president."

After two and a half terms as a council member, why would Nessa choose to become council president now, in the middle of her third term?

Doreen forced a casual tone. "Had Nessa ever indicated before that she wanted to be council president?"

"I don't think so." CeCe shrugged. "At least, she's never mentioned it to me."

Doreen's unease increased. "Whose idea was it for you to step down?"

CeCe's thin auburn eyebrows knitted. "Mine. I told the council I needed a break."

"In the middle of your third term?"

"I couldn't wait another two years, Doreen. I'm just burned out."

Doreen nodded, though she didn't understand. If CeCe was so disillusioned with the president's position, why had she run for reelection two years ago?

"Did you approach the council with your decision or did one of the members approach you first?"

CeCe frowned. "Why are you asking all of these questions?"

"I'm just curious." Doreen attempted a nonchalant shrug, but her grip was tight on her teacup. The pale blue porcelain was warm in her palm.

"Well, I wanted you to know I'd stepped down before you took office." CeCe sipped her tea.

"And that Nessa was now council president. I appreciate the warning." Doreen's tone was dry.

CeCe frowned again. "It's not a warning. I'm just letting you know."

"I'll be honest with you, CeCe." Doreen sat back on her chair. She set her feet in their fluffy, cool pink socks, flat on the hardwood flooring. "I think Nessa convinced you to step down so she could take your place as president."

"Why would she do that?" CeCe looked confused.

"Nessa doesn't want me to be mayor." Doreen recalled Nessa's attack during Books & Bakery's Halloween celebration.

"Why not? As much as you've done for this town, everyone knew it was just a matter of time before you became mayor."

"Apparently, Nessa doesn't see things that way."

"Has Nessa ever argued with you before?"

"No."

"Then why would she start now?"

"I'm not making this up, CeCe. So did you approach the council or did Nessa approach you?"

CeCe hesitated. "Well, actually, now that I think about it, Nessa brought it up to me."

Doreen sagged on her chair. "I was afraid of that."

"Are you glad the election's almost over?" At a vile hour the next morning, Darius stood poised to document Doreen's response into his reporter's notebook.

It was just after six-thirty the morning of November fourth, Election Day. The Heritage High School gymnasium served as one of the town's polling locations. He'd arrived early to cast his vote and cover the event for *The Trinity Falls Monitor.* Doreen had cast her vote already as well. Actually, she'd been the first in line.

Darius nodded at Lei Chang, one of the *Monitor*'s photojournalists, as she strode past him toward the parking lot. His coworker had arrived at the polls early to take the money shot of Doreen casting her ballot. Lei had taken several pictures of Doreen. She'd also photographed Jackson, Nessa, and other prominent Trinity Falls residents as they stood in line at the polls.

"I don't know why I'm so anxious. I'm running unopposed." Doreen's voice bounced with nervous energy. She folded her dark green winter coat over her left forearm. "Can you imagine how tense I'd be if someone was actually challenging me?"

"This is a big day. Your anxiety is understandable." Darius waited for a better quote.

Doreen's brown eyes widened. She slapped her hand to her mouth, then let it drop to her side. "I probably shouldn't have said that. I'm going to have to learn to be more careful of what I say around you."

"Only when I'm on the job." Darius gave her a reassuring smile. "What are your thoughts on the election?"

This time, Doreen took a moment to consider his question. "Right now, I can't think beyond how excited I am to get started. Ramona worked hard to get the town out of tremendous debt after years of mismanagement. I'd like to build on her successes and secure an even greater surplus."

"I look forward to hearing more about your ideas to do that."

The sound of the entrance door opening interrupted their conversation. A cold blast of air flew

down the corridor. Darius looked down the hall—
and lost his breath. The heels of Peyton's black
pumps snapped against the silver flooring. Her burgundy wool coat complemented the pink flush of
her cheeks.

"Good morning, Professor." Darius inclined his
head toward her. His body hardened with the memory
of their kiss.

"Good morning, Darius." Peyton's soft greeting
triggered a reaction in his gut. Her shaky smile
brightened as she stopped beside Doreen. "I imagine you had trouble sleeping last night."

"Your imagination is right." Doreen laughed self-
consciously.

"I'm excited to cast my vote for you."

"Thank you." Doreen's nervous expression relaxed.
Peyton nodded toward Darius before crossing
into the gym.

"I'm also anxious to implement Ramona's suggestion of a community center fund-raiser." Doreen's
comment brought Darius back to his interview.
"Have you given any more thought to cochairing
that committee?"

Darius stilled. "Was it your idea for me to be
cochair?"

"No, but I think it's a good one." Doreen shrugged
into her coat.

"I don't." Darius wrestled back his residual reaction
to kissing Peyton. "I don't need any help with my
personal life. I don't want help, either."

"We want you to be happy, Darius." Doreen
squeezed his forearm.

"I'm fine. I'll be even better when everyone respects my privacy."

Doreen released him. "All right."

Darius let the matter go, though he didn't believe for a second that Doreen and the others would stop meddling in his private life. He chatted a few minutes more with the soon-to-be-mayor before Doreen hustled off to Books & Bakery. Darius remained, hoping to get comments from other residents, not just Peyton.

Lei slammed back into the gym, bringing the cold front with her. Her petite form was bundled into a black winter coat that seemed three sizes too large for her. She shoved back her hood and shook her shoulder-length raven hair free. "It's colder than a witch's—"

"Yeah, it's pretty cold out there." Darius cut off the photojournalist's trademark vulgarity. "That's why I'm waiting in here."

"Lucky you with your cushy reporter's assignment." She marched toward him, pausing to deliver her scorn. "I had to get shots of the voters arriving, up close and personal. Do you expect me to shoot that shit through the glass doors?" She nodded toward the entrance behind her.

"No, I don't." Darius struggled to keep the laughter from his voice. He was used to the surly artist. "We're lucky to have your expertise."

"Damn right." Pleasantries exchanged, Lei stomped back into the gym.

Darius crossed the corridor to lean against the wall opposite the gym's entrance. He glanced toward the rear doors leading to the dark parking lot. During the May primary, he'd waited outside to interview voters. Not today, though. Lei was right. It was too cold.

But the cold clime didn't have a negative impact on voter turnout. The midterm ballot issues were enough to lure people to the polls. In addition to the mayoral election, there were several county, state, and federal considerations, including U.S. Senate and Congressional races.

Darius straightened from the wall as Jackson and Audra emerged from the gym. "A few words for the press?"

Jackson wrapped an arm around Audra's waist. "I don't think the newspaper's publisher should be quoted in one of its articles."

"Then don't speak as the publisher," Darius offered him a solution. "Speak as a member of the town's founding family."

"Nice try but we can't separate the two."

Darius shrugged. "I can. I'm sure other residents can, too."

"I don't want to influence anyone." Jackson glanced at Audra.

"Go on." The songwriter nudged Jackson in his ribs with her elbow. "You're not going to influence anyone. The article won't appear in the paper until tomorrow morning."

Jackson shook his head. "It'll appear online this afternoon—along with the hundreds of photos Lei seems determined to take."

"Just give Darius a quote." Audra smiled up at Jackson. "Don't make his job harder than it already is."

"Thank you, Audra." Darius gave Jackson a pointed look. "Listen to your better half."

Jackson sighed. "OK. As a member of the town's founding family, I'd like to say that Trinity Falls is fortunate the candidate who chose to run for mayor is as dedicated to the town as Doreen Fever has always been."

Darius's pen raced across his notebook. "Thanks, Jack. Anything you'd like to add, Audra?"

"Me? I wasn't expecting to be interviewed." Taken aback, Audra looked from Jackson to Darius in surprise.

"You've just moved from L.A. to Trinity Falls. From the perspective of a new resident, what do you think of our ballot issues?"

Audra considered the question. "Los Angeles has a much greater population, but the issues are similar—funding for education and other necessary community services."

Darius transcribed Audra's quote as she and Jackson left the high school.

It was a while before Nessa emerged from the room. Her expression was pensive. Darius approached her, pen and reporter's notebook at the ready. "Congratulations on being elected council president."

"Thanks." Nessa looked at him as though she was emerging from deep thought. What was on her mind?

"What are your plans for the second half of your term?"

"I'm going to continue the good work the council already has done to get the town back in shape, fiscally as well as physically."

Darius wrote down her response. It hadn't escaped his notice that Nessa had given the council credit for the town improvements Doreen had claimed Ramona had accomplished as mayor. He kept those thoughts to himself. "Do you have any comments on the ballot issues?"

"I wish the town had options." Nessa straightened as though preparing for battle—or a mayoral run. "The residents of Trinity Falls deserve to have a choice of mayoral candidates. For too many years, our candidates have run unopposed. That's not a democracy."

Nessa's words nudged Darius's memory. "That's almost the exact response my father gave me when he was considering challenging Doreen for mayor."

"Your father and I aren't the only people who feel this way. We're just two of many."

His eyes held Nessa's. "I've wondered who talked my father into running for mayor. Was it you?"

~~CHAPTER 8~~

Darius waited for Nessa's reaction. The new town council president needed to know she couldn't scheme in secrecy. Trinity Falls was a small town with very nosy neighbors.

Nessa didn't blink. "As I said, Simon and I aren't the only ones who feel this way. There are hundreds of people who could have planted that seed. I'm only sorry he dropped out of the campaign. If it weren't for the skeletons in his closet, he would've made a good mayor."

Darius doubted that. "Why didn't any of these hundreds of people run for office?"

"I'm sure there are as many reasons as there are people in Trinity Falls. But I'm hopeful things will be different in the future." Nessa straightened her shoulders as though once again preparing for the campaign trail. "Single-candidate mayoral races put an additional burden on the council. Now we have to ensure that the mayor doesn't abuse her position."

"Doesn't the council have to do that regardless of how the mayor gets into office?"

"Yes, but this is an added burden because . . ." Nessa's gaze swept the corridor as though seeking inspiration. "Well, if the candidate is uncontested, she may think she's entering office with a mandate."

Darius didn't buy that, but he recorded her words anyway. "What about you, Nessa? Will you run for office in 2018? Is that the reason you became council president?"

"I accepted the position of council president after CeCe Roben stepped down for personal reasons. My focus is on serving the town as council president and continuing the good work the council has accomplished to date." Nessa attempted to look down her nose at him. It was a difficult maneuver, considering Darius was half a foot taller than her.

"Thanks for your time, Nessa."

"Of course. You can call my office to schedule an interview about my becoming council president."

"Already done, Madame President. I'm just waiting for you to set the date."

Fleeting surprise replaced Nessa's arrogant expression. "I'll have my secretary call you after he's checked my calendar."

Long, jerky strides carried Nessa down the hall and into the parking lot. Was Nessa's secretary about to hear his boss's displeasure with his delay in scheduling media interviews? Hopefully not.

Darius looked at the notes from his exchange with the council president. Doreen was in for a challenging term. Despite Nessa's protestations, which were typical of politicians, Darius knew Trinity Falls would have a two-person mayoral race in 2018.

"The next four years are going to be interesting."
Peyton's lily-of-the-valley scent alerted Darius to her
presence just before her words.

He faced the professor. "You read my mind."

"Something tells me that's not often done."
Peyton's winged eyebrows took flight. Her caramel
eyes sparkled with humor. "Will I find my way back
out?"

Darius struggled against a smile. "What did you
think of your first experience voting in Trinity Falls?"

Peyton's expression told him she was claiming victory in this exchange of wits. Darius let her.

"It was definitely different." Peyton secured the
strap of her dark purple purse onto her shoulder.

"In what way?" Darius pulled his attention from her
full, moist lips, and readied his notebook and pen.

"I've only been here five months." Peyton shrugged
a slender shoulder. "I'm used to having at least a
year to consider the pros and cons of ballot issues
and candidates."

"Some people would consider that too much
time." Darius wrote quickly.

"I'm in academia." Her eyes twinkled again. "No
one makes quick decisions in academia."

"I've noticed."

"I'd rather be oversaturated with information than
feel as though I'm cramming for an exam."

"An exam is a good analogy to voting. What did
you think of the test?"

"It was a little strange having only one candidate
for mayor." Her eyes dropped to Darius's notebook,
then returned to his face. "But even if there'd been
ten or even twenty candidates on the ballot, I still

would've voted for Doreen. She's the right person for the job."

Her answer impressed him. It was a reporter's wet dream. He should return to his office and file his story. Now. But he couldn't bring himself to leave. He wanted more time with Peyton, more time to look at her, breathe her fragrance, remember their kiss.

Darius cleared his voice. "Why do you think she's the right person?"

"I've benefited from Doreen's warmth and generosity. She's made me feel like a part of the community since I moved here. And I've seen how much she cares for the town and its people. I can tell how much she cares about you."

Darius paused with his pen over the paper. "What do you mean?"

"I've seen the way she treats you, Quincy, and Ean. It's as though she has three sons, not just one."

"Quincy and I spent a lot of time at Ean's house." Darius smiled as those childhood images sped across his mind. "You're right. Doreen's a very generous person. Her house felt like my second home. It couldn't have been easy for her or her late husband, Paul. The three of us were loud, messy, and always looking for food." Ethel and Simon had never allowed that kind of unruly behavior in the Knight household.

"Those sound like great memories." Peyton's smile was wistful.

"They are." Darius stepped forward, pulled toward Peyton by an invisible thread. "We've been friends since elementary school, almost thirty years."

"That's amazing."

"Don't you have friendships that long?" Darius breathed in Peyton's soft scent.

"Over the years, my friends and I have drifted apart."

What would have happened to him if he, Ean, Quincy, and Jackson had lost contact over the years? He would have lost his anchors.

Darius shook off the thought. "Hopefully you'll make those kinds of friendships here."

"I'd like that." Her eyes were wistful. "I'd better get to work. Good luck with your article."

Darius blew out a breath. His reaction to Peyton wasn't going away. If anything, it was growing stronger. But could he risk acting on these feelings? He was his father's son, and Simon had made a mess of every relationship he ever had. Could Darius avoid making those same mistakes?

"Darius!"

The sound of his name being gasped in horror startled him. Darius spun away from his computer and was surprised again to find his mother standing in the entrance of his cubicle. Ethel looked as though he'd mortally wounded her.

"Mom? What are you doing here?" Darius's eyes dropped to the picnic basket in her fist. His confusion grew.

"I brought you *lunch*." Ethel hoisted the carrier. "Although that seems to have been a wasted effort."

Darius glanced at the paper bowl of chicken stew in his hands, and the still-wrapped turkey, bacon, and pepper jack cheese sandwich on his desk. "Why?"

"I thought you'd be *hungry*." Her eyes snapped with impatience. She lowered her arm. "Today's the election. I know how busy you are, covering it for the newspaper. I wanted to make sure you had something for lunch."

"I didn't know you were going to do that." How could he have known? In the seven years he'd worked for the *Monitor*, Ethel had never acknowledged his work nor had she ever visited his office. And she hadn't said anything to indicate her interest had changed.

"I wanted to surprise you. I guess the surprise is on *me*." Ethel took the few steps into his cubicle, setting the carrier on his desk with a thud. Her movements were a study in displeasure. "I didn't expect you to eat so early."

Darius checked his watch. "It's almost one o'clock."

Ethel's jaw clenched. "It takes *time* to put together a decent meal. I can't cook all of this at the drop of a hat."

"You didn't need to go to the trouble. I bought my lunch." Darius watched her pinched features warily.

"Where did you get *that*?" She made it sound as though he'd gone Dumpster diving. They both knew from where he'd purchased his soup and sandwich.

"The café at Books and Bakery."

"Doreen Fever has her own son to take care of. She doesn't need to feed *mine*." Jealousy bit into Ethel's words.

She began unpacking the basket. Darius swallowed a sigh. He spun his chair back to his monitor, then pressed a couple of keys to save his work.

Nothing less than his full attention would appease his mother now.

Plastic containers filled with salad and pasta covered Darius' story notes. Ethel placed a thermos beside the dishes and unwrapped bread.

She offered him an apple and a banana. "I couldn't remember *which* you preferred."

He'd never liked either fruit, but this wasn't a good time to remind his mother of that. "I'll take the apple. Thank you."

"For what?" She shoved the apple at him. "You've already *eaten.*"

The next few minutes were critical. His mother thought nothing of punishing innocent people for her disappointments. Her reaction to Noah was an example of this. Darius didn't want Ethel taking out her resentment about lunch on Doreen.

"The meal looks wonderful, Mom." He took the apple from her hand. He'd offer it to Jackson later. "You obviously went to a lot of trouble. Thank you. It's going to be a long day. I'd like to save your meal for dinner."

Instantly, Ethel's scowl disappeared. "That's a good idea." She wrinkled her nose at the soup and sandwich that comprised Darius's lunch. "You'll probably be hungry again in a couple of hours."

No, he wouldn't. Doreen's cooking seemed light but would stick to his ribs until this evening. After one of her lunches, he wouldn't need as big a dinner as Ethel had prepared. Again, not information he'd share with his mother—right now—if ever.

Darius considered Ethel's satisfied expression as she repacked the picnic basket for him. What was behind her unprecedented mothering? Darius glanced around his cubicle. It wasn't the ideal location for such a personal and personally dangerous mission. But this couldn't wait.

"How are you adjusting to being on your own now that Dad's moved out of the house?"

"He didn't move out." The storm clouds returned. "I *threw* that cheating snake out on his ass."

OK. Well, that was much more restrained than he'd anticipated. "Now you have more time to dedicate to things you've always wanted to do. You can put yourself first instead of tending to Dad. Or worrying about me."

"What does that mean?" Ethel's dark eyes narrowed. "You prefer Doreen's cooking to *mine*?"

How had she made that leap?

"What I mean is you can pursue your own interests. I can take care of myself, Mom." He'd been doing so for decades.

"Oh, *really*? Well, then, I won't go to the trouble of cooking meals for you, and you won't have to go to the trouble of eating them." She collected the picnic basket from his desk. You can just keep filling your face with Doreen Fever's cooking."

Darius stood, putting a detaining hand on Ethel's shoulder. He should have anticipated his mother's scorched-earth response. "I never said I preferred Doreen's cooking to yours. This isn't a competition. And I never said I wasn't going to eat the meal you cooked."

"Then *what* did you mean, Darius?" She raised her chin to a combative angle.

Her eyes demanded he beg her forgiveness. He just wanted this emotional torture to end, preferably without innocent victims.

"I meant exactly what I said." Darius rubbed his eyes. "If you're bored without Dad—"

"I'm not bored without Simon. What makes you think *that*?"

"The fact you packed my lunch." He gestured toward the picnic basket. "You haven't done that since I was five."

They locked gazes for several tense moments. Darius wasn't backing down. If she wanted to take out her anger and resentment for Simon on him, then fine. She'd been doing that even before he was old enough to understand it. But he didn't want her blaming Doreen for anything.

Ethel lowered her eyes. She placed the repacked picnic basket back on his desk. "If you want my dinner, you can have it. I'll try not to trouble you in the future."

"Thank you." Darius masked his relief.

"I'll leave you alone now." Ethel left his cubicle with her head held high.

Drained, Darius sank back onto his chair. He wheeled it around to brood with his computer monitor. He wasn't fooling himself. He may have won this skirmish, but the war wasn't over. What would boredom drive Ethel to do next?

Hours later, Jackson wandered into Darius's office. "Do you have a minute?"

"Sure." Darius saved his document, then swung his chair to face his boss. He gestured toward the fruit on his desk. "Do you want an apple?"

"Thanks." Jackson took the apple, examining it. "I'm making some management changes. Nothing will be announced until after the new year."

So why was he here now? "What kind of changes?"

"I've officially promoted Faye Liu to executive editor." Jackson settled onto Darius's guest chair. He'd left his navy suit jacket in his office. Newsprint marred the sleeves of his white dress shirt. "She kept the newspaper going while I was away."

Darius nodded. "Faye's promotion is very well deserved."

"She suggested you take over as managing editor."

Darius stared. "What?"

Jackson set his right ankle on his left knee. "Faye said you helped shoulder a lot of the responsibility without being asked and without asking for recognition. She appreciated that."

"I wasn't after a promotion. I was just trying to help." Darius was still surprised.

"I know and I appreciate what you did for me. But I need to make these changes." Jackson shrugged. "I can't perform all the tasks I had now that I'm renovating and managing Harmony Cabins."

"I understand, but I've always seen myself as a reporter."

"You can make your managing editor position whatever you want, as long as Faye's comfortable with it." Jackson stood. "Think it over. As I said, I'm not going to make an official announcement until after the new year."

"Thanks for thinking of me, Jack." Darius stood with his boss.

"There's no one better for the job." Jackson squeezed Darius' shoulder. "I hope you'll take it." He then left the cubicle.

Darius returned to his computer. Managing editor. He'd never considered the position before. But with Ean opening his solo law practice and

Quincy accepting a position with the University of Pennsylvania, perhaps it was time Darius made a change as well.

"Good morning, Mayor." Ean claimed a bar stool at the Books & Bakery café counter Wednesday morning.

Doreen felt a thrill—excitement, trepidation, both?—at her son's greeting. It was the morning after the election, and she was still walking on air.

"You're a little premature." She collected the coffee carafe before crossing to the counter. "I don't get sworn in until New Year's Day."

As she filled her son's coffee mug, Megan, her boss, joined her behind the counter. It was a few minutes after eight o'clock. Ean was her first guest of the morning. Darius, Ramona, Jackson, and Audra would be joining them soon. She missed Quincy. How was the professor settling in at the University of Pennsylvania?

Still, life was good in Trinity Falls. Her son had come home and was dating Megan. She'd won the mayoral election and was falling in love with the sheriff.

"I wanted to be the first to call you mayor." Ean's grin disappeared behind his coffee mug.

"Alonzo beat you to it." Doreen returned the carafe to the coffee station behind the counter. "We watched the election returns last night. It was silly, I know, since I didn't have a challenger. But I wanted to wait until all the precincts had given their counts before celebrating."

"That isn't silly." Megan filled two mugs with

coffee. "It shows you verify facts before making a final decision. That's one of the reasons I know you'll be a great mayor."

"You've always been so good for my self-esteem." Doreen accepted the coffee Megan offered her.

"On the other hand, *I'm* not as convinced you'll be an adequate mayor." Nessa's voice brought a chill to the camaraderie in the café.

Doreen swallowed her coffee before turning to their new arrival. "Good morning, Nessa. Can I get you anything?"

"I'm not staying." The other woman rested her hands on the empty bar stool beside Ean. "I understand CeCe told you I've replaced her as town council president."

"She told me she'd stepped down and that your bid for the position was unopposed." Doreen crossed back to the counter to stand opposite Nessa. "Similar to what occurred with my mayoral candidacy."

"Similar but not the same." Nessa's thin smile assured Doreen her message had been received. "I also want you to know I won't take into consideration what you may or may not have done for the town. Your past won't matter once you're sworn in."

Ean turned toward Trinity Falls' new council president. "Nessa, what's—"

Doreen clamped a warning hand on her son's shoulder. "I hadn't realized you were going to judge me from day one. If my past doesn't matter, what will you base your judgment on?"

"I'll consider only what you've accomplished since the election." Nessa's tone was both prim and condemning.

Doreen ignored the tension flowing from Ean's

shoulder into her palm, as well as the new arrivals she spotted in her peripheral vision. Her focus was on Nessa. "What would you expect me to accomplish between now and January first?"

"I'll expect you to get your personal matters in order. You're not morally ready to be mayor." Nessa's declaration was curt.

"Excuse me?" Doreen exerted pressure on Ean's shoulder to keep her son seated—and herself upright. Megan's presence beside her lent silent support.

"You're copulating with the sheriff." Nessa's nostrils flared with harsh judgment.

Doreen glanced at her new guests standing behind Nessa. "You're going to consider my private relationship with Alonzo when evaluating my performance as a public servant?"

"Yes, I am." Nessa drew her back even straighter.

"Will you judge my morality as well, Nessa?" Alonzo's quiet question came from behind the council president.

Nessa spun to face the sheriff. Standing with Alonzo were the dismayed and amazed Darius, Ramona, Jackson, and Audra.

The council president stuttered her response to the sheriff's question. "W-well, actually, Alonzo, I have no choice. But you won't be judged as harshly as Doreen, since, as mayor, she'll be held to a higher standard."

"You self-righteous—"

Alonzo cut off Ean's choked words. His coffee eyes were cold as he stared down at Nessa. "As much as I appreciate your interest in the state of Doreen's and my immortal souls, what we do in the privacy of our homes is none of your business."

Doreen shivered at Alonzo's coldness. He rarely spoke like that. Beneath her palm, the tension in Ean's shoulder eased a bit.

Nessa rallied. "Actually, Alonzo, as council president, the mayor's private life *is* my business. Her morality—or lack thereof—could have an adverse effect on her judgment."

Alonzo's voice grew even colder. "If it's all the same to you, Nessa, I won't have a politician judging my morality. I'll leave that to God. And I don't think Doreen would mind if I spoke for her."

"No, I don't mind." Doreen managed to respond to Alonzo even though Nessa's arrogance stole her breath.

Nessa's thin cheeks paled. She looked at Doreen, seeming to shut out the other people around her. "I've said what I came to say."

"Yes, you have." Doreen forced an even response.

Alonzo, Darius, and Jackson stepped aside to clear a path for the council president's exit.

Ramona slid onto the bar stool beside Ean. "What's gotten into Nessa? She used to be so rational."

Doreen collected coffee mugs for her friends. "She seems out for me personally."

"Are you all right?" Alonzo claimed her free hand once Doreen placed his mug within reach.

"Thank you for everything you said." Under Alonzo's touch, Doreen's hand stopped shaking.

"In Nessa, you've made a dangerous enemy." Audra took the stool next to Jackson.

"If she plans on giving you trouble while you're in office, you'll have to protect yourself." Megan walked along the counter, pouring coffee for the newcomers. "Keep a record of everything you do and every exchange you have with her."

"Megan's right." Ean nodded. "Don't let your guard down."

"I agree." Doreen sighed. "I wish I knew why she resents me . . . and what she's up to."

CHAPTER 9

"The bleachers are packed, and the game hasn't even started." Peyton followed Vaughn Brooks through the press of bodies in and around the Heritage High School football stadium Saturday afternoon. She was getting used to letting his broad shoulders clear a path for them through dense crowds.

"Fans arrive early for the marching band's pregame performance." The Trinity Falls University concert band director spoke over his shoulder as he led her to the visitors' side of the field.

It was the second Saturday of November, but the weather had turned unseasonably warm, allowing Peyton to leave her coat at home. Why had she thought Ohio would be so much colder than New York in the fall? She was comfortable in her newly purchased navy-blue-and-white Heritage High School Warriors hooded sweatshirt. She hadn't been able to resist the sales pitch. Besides, the purchase benefited the school. Granted, underneath the thick fleece material, she wore a jersey along with her blue jeans, thick tube socks, and black boots. If her mother saw her now, Irene "Fashionista" Biery Harris would go berserk.

"There are a lot of Sequoia High School fans here." Peyton stared in awe at the number of people crowded onto the bleachers. There were almost as many spectators on the visitors' side as the number of fans here to support the home team.

"It goes against everything in me to deliver you to Heritage's rivals." Vaughn stopped to gaze up at the Sequoia fans.

"I promised Darius I'd cheer his brother. You know Noah's a senior with the Sequoia Soldiers." Peyton grinned. This wasn't the first time the Heritage High School alumnus had groused about walking onto "enemy territory."

"Then he should have brought you to the stadium himself." Vaughn pointed toward the bleachers. "There's the traitor, third row from the top."

Peyton shaded her eyes with her right hand. She located Darius near the top of the stadium. June Cale, Noah's mother, was with him. Darius's midnight gaze locked with hers. Her heart did a plié, then pirouetted across her chest.

"I see him." Her voice sounded rusty. A cool breeze kept her cheeks from overheating.

"Good, because this is as far as I'm bringing you."

"I understand." Peyton offered her hand to her guide. She thanked him somewhat tongue in cheek. "I appreciate your assistance."

Vaughn shook her hand once before striding away, presumably to friendlier environs on the other side of the field. Peyton began her climb up the bleachers. Why had Darius and June chosen seats so high?

Darius stood as she approached. His beautiful sepia features were a study in surprise and confusion. It did things to her pulse to know that this handsome man was waiting for her. Peyton hoped her smile wasn't as dopey as it felt.

Darius stepped aside so she could enter the row. He leaned closer to whisper in her ear. "What are you doing here?"

Peyton shivered in response. "I told you I was going to cheer for your brother. Your seats are pretty high up."

"They give you the best view of the field." June shook Peyton's hand. "Thank you for joining us."

"Where's Simon?" Peyton sat. The right side of her body tingled where it came into contact with Darius. She shifted to give him more space.

"I don't know." Darius's voice was devoid of inflection. Tension surrounded him, communicating itself to Peyton.

"It doesn't matter, Darius," June assured him.

Darius didn't seem to hear her. "Stan was going to come, but he had to work."

Their exchange caught Peyton's curiosity. She understood why Darius was upset that Simon, Noah's father, wasn't at the game. But as Noah's mother, why was June certain Simon's absence didn't matter? There was more to the story here.

Peyton shrugged off her curiosity and turned her attention to the young men exercising on the field. "Which one of the teams is ours?"

"Our team's wearing the visitor's white. Heritage is the home team, so they're wearing their colors, navy blue and white." Darius eyed her with curiosity. "Have you watched many football games?"

He was doing that sexy thing again, arching his left eyebrow. Peyton exhaled. "This is my first."

Darius's eyes widened. "What made you come to this game?"

"I promised to root for Noah, remember?" Peyton frowned. Didn't he recall the bet from the Books & Bakery Halloween celebration?

His slow smile sped Peyton's pulse. "Thank you."

She found her breath. "You're welcome."

June patted Peyton's forearm. "You've chosen a great game. It's the last regular season game. Both Sequoia and Heritage are undefeated. The winner will go to the state championship."

As they waited for the pregame show to begin, Darius and June tried to prepare Peyton for her first football game. They explained the four fifteen-minute quarters, which were made longer by time-outs and fouls; the twenty-two young men on the field for each series, eleven each on offense and defense; the three phases of the game—offense, defense, and special teams; and the referees, whose calls were inevitably bad, unless those calls worked in Sequoia's favor. Even with her doctorate, Peyton wasn't convinced she'd be able to follow the game.

The Heritage High School marching band took the field for the pregame show. The skilled musicians performed an exciting medley of Michael Jackson songs, including "Beat It" and "Black or White." Dressed in their navy-blue-and-white caps and uniforms, the band members marched in time to the music, creating formations such as the Warrior logo.

Peyton couldn't sit still. Her rocking hips and wriggling shoulders drew Darius's attention.

"Perhaps you'd like to join the band?" His smile teased her. "I'm sure they could use you in the dance line."

Peyton gestured toward his tapping foot. "I don't want to meet the person who can sit still through a Michael Jackson song."

"Neither do I." Darius raised his hands in surrender.

When the performance ended, Peyton rose with the rest of the audience for a standing ovation. "They're exceptional."

"Yes, they are." There was pride in Darius's voice.

June leaned toward her. "If you think the Warriors' band is good, wait until you hear the Marching Soldiers."

Darius grunted. "Your football team will give Heritage a battle, but our marching band doesn't even have to step on the field to outperform yours."

June gasped. "Now wait—"

Standing between the rivals, Peyton took hold of their upper arms. "Get back to your corners. We're here to cheer on Noah. Stay focused."

She removed her hold from her companions as the band cleared the field. The announcer introduced first the visiting Sequoia Soldiers, then the home team Heritage Warriors.

Peyton craned her head, trying to spot Darius's brother. It was an impossible task, considering the identity-masking helmets and matching uniforms the forty-eight young athletes wore. "What's Noah's number?"

"Eighty-one." Darius pointed toward the Sequoia sideline. "He's near the bench."

Peyton spotted eighty-one standing with a coach and another player. The adult seemed to be giving the young men last-minute instructions or encouragement. She sensed the coach's intensity and his players' focus. It was contagious. Anticipation fueled her pulse.

The four quarters were a fierce battle of wills. The longtime rivals clashed in a well-matched competition. Peyton was swept up in the excitement as the stadium rocked with screams, shouts, foot stomps, and cheers.

Darius's company made the experience even more enjoyable. He stayed close to her, explaining each series—passing plays, running games, the value of a quarterback sneak at fourth and one. He seemed to enjoy introducing her to football, and she enjoyed his introduction. Peyton didn't feel stupid or annoying as he took his time answering her questions and making sure she understood what was happening and why. Handsome, intelligent, and kind. It wasn't any wonder Darius Knight was one of the most sought-after bachelors in Trinity Falls.

She also studied Darius's brother when the Sequoia offense went to the sideline. Noah spent the time urging on his teammates. He displayed passion and camaraderie, patting their helmets and hitting their shoulder pads. Had Darius played with the same drive and commitment? She gave the former high school athlete a sidelong look. She suspected he had.

More than three quarters later, Peyton's throat was raw from cheering on the Soldiers and blasting the referees. She tracked the Heritage kickoff. The Sequoia returner sprinted, weaved, and battled his way to the twenty-three-yard line. The clock drained to fifty-one seconds.

"We're down by three points. What do you think we should do?" Her eyes were glued to the Sequoia sidelines as she asked June and Darius for input.

June clenched her fists. "The score's twenty-three, twenty, Heritage. We need to get into field goal position, tie the game, and force an overtime."

Peyton shook her head. "Heritage will be expecting that."

Darius crossed his arms over his chest. "June's right. We won't be able to drive seventy-seven yards in fifty-one seconds. We should try for the OT."

The OT? Overtime. Peyton watched the sideline where Sequoia's head coach gestured emphatically to his young players. If only she could see his face, read his lips. *What was he telling them? What did he think?*

It didn't matter. Peyton's gut knew what Sequoia needed to do. "I say we go for it."

Her declaration was greeted with stunned silence.

"It's too risky." June's voice was a squeak of horror.

"Why do you think we should go for a touch-down?" Darius sounded curious. He would have made a good teacher.

"Our quarterback has a cannon for an arm." Peyton had borrowed that line from one of the many screaming fans around her.

"That's true." Darius's midnight eyes considered her. "But Heritage's defense is impenetrable."

Peyton smiled at the hint of pride in Darius's

comment. How hard was it for him to root against his alma mater?

"They can't cover every receiver, and Sequoia has a lot of weapons, including Noah." Using her new-found football terminology was almost as much fun as watching the game.

"We need the win." June sounded frantic.

"The championship's at stake." Darius nodded toward the field. "We need to go for the safe play."

"No guts, no glory." She'd plucked that quote from history.

Darius chuckled. "Are you sure this is your first football game?"

Peyton blushed at the subtle compliment. She hugged the words to her heart even as she shifted her attention to the field. The Sequoia offense lined up at the twenty-three-yard line. The quarterback was in what Darius had called the shotgun position. It was a good sign.

Peyton cupped her hands over her mouth and screamed, "Go for it!"

As though responding to her rally, the Sequoia quarterback shot a bomb down the far side of the field. It raced with Noah. His long legs ate up the yards, keeping up with the ball. Two defenders dogged him, covering him like peanut butter on jelly, butter on toast, white on rice. Peyton held her breath as Noah picked up speed. He leaped from the field, rising barely above his defenders as the ball dropped to him. With his body vulnerable in the air, he coaxed the ball to him with the tips of his fingers. He landed with his toes inbounds. His body went limp, then rolled off the field. Twenty-nine-yard reception. First down. Clock stopped. Ball on Heritage's forty-eight-yard line.

Sequoia fans went insane. Peyton exhaled.

The Sequoia Soldiers hustled to the line of scrimmage for their second play of the series. Forty-four seconds left to the game. The quarterback caught the snap from the center. The clock ticked. Forty-three, forty-two, forty-one, forty . . . A Heritage defender flushed the quarterback from the pocket. The ball handler scrambled to the right . . . thirty-nine, thirty-eight, thirty-seven . . . A short pass to the running back saved the broken play. Net gain of five yards. The Heritage defender creamed the Sequoia quarterback, planting him in the grass.

"Isn't that a foul?" Peyton shot off the bench. "Foul! Foul, ref! Can you hear me?"

"Zeus can hear you on Mount Olympus," Darius cracked drily. "There's the flag."

Peyton strained to hear the referee as he updated the crowd on the penalty. "Roughing the passer. Defense. Number thirty-eight. Fifteen yards. Ball on Warriors twenty-eight. First down."

"Yes!" June pumped a fist in the air. "Go for the field goal."

"We should go for the win." Peyton stared at the field.

"But there's only thirty-one seconds left." June gestured toward the field.

"June," Darius interrupted their exchange. "We can win this."

Peyton rewarded him with a smile. "Yes, we can."

She returned her attention to the field, pressing her fist against her lips. Peyton whispered into her hand, "I believe. I believe."

The quarterback took the snap. He danced back into the pocket. Noah waved for the ball from the fifteen-yard line. He was under double coverage, just as he'd been for most of the game. Other receivers were closer and more open.

"Throw it to Noah!" June was almost jumping up and down with impatience. "Throw it to eighty-one!"

The game clock counted down . . . thirty, twenty-nine, twenty-eight. The quarterback picked a more open target. The intended receiver bobbled the pass. The ball dropped to the field. Incomplete. The clock stopped at twenty-two seconds. Sequoia fans groaned their disappointment—all but one.

"I told you to throw it to eighty-one!" June screamed the frustration of a disappointed parent.

Sequoia called a time-out.

Peyton patted June's shoulder. "We still have twenty-two seconds and three downs."

June groaned. "We have to line up for the field goal."

Peyton pulled her gaze from Noah rallying his teammates. "Believe, June. Just believe."

"No guts, no glory." Darius muttered the quote with his eyes set on the field.

"You both are going to be the death of me." June swiped the sweat from her brow.

Sequoia returned to the field. Noah patted the quarterback's helmet as he jogged past his teammate. The ball handler took the shotgun position. Noah was farther down the line on the right. Two Heritage defenders stood away from the receiver. The center snapped the ball. The game clock drained: twenty-one, twenty, nineteen, eighteen . . .

The quarterback took four steps back. Linemen formed a protective pocket around him.

Peyton found Noah. He raced down the field desperately trying to shake his defenders. The quarterback bounced on his toes, buying time. Scanning left, scanning right, looking for an open man. Seventeen, sixteen, fifteen . . .

Throw the ball to eighty-one!

Noah's strides carried him ten, fifteen, twenty yards. Peyton willed him faster, stronger, farther than the backs chasing him.

Heritage defenders dogged the Sequoia linemen, crashing through the pocket. The quarterback pivoted free. Fourteen, thirteen, twelve . . . He sent the ball high. Silently, Peyton chanted, *I believe. I believe. I believe.*

A collective gasp rose above the stadium as the ball arced toward the end zone. Eleven seconds, ten, nine . . . Peyton's gaze scrambled to Noah. He jerked right, then cut left toward the goalpost. He sprinted toward the end zone, arms pumping, feet barely kissing the ground. He was flying.

But his back was to the ball. Peyton slowly rose to her feet. She wanted to scream, "Turn around!" But she couldn't form the words. She didn't have the breath. All she could do was watch . . . and hope . . .

I believe. I believe. I believe.

Noah crossed into the end zone, dogged by Heritage defenders in blue. Eight seconds, seven, six . . . He spun right, sighted the ball, then sprang to meet it. Defenders jumped with him. Noah reached higher, stretched farther, and pulled it into his chest. He fell back to the end zone, tucking the ball into his body, then rolled to his feet.

Touchdown!

Time ran out. Sequoia Soldiers 26, Heritage Warriors 23. With the extra point, the final score was 27, 23, Sequoia.

Sequoia faithful roared their victory. Peyton threw her arms wide and leaped into Darius's arms. She kissed him. Hard. He kissed her back. His arms tightened around her, pulling her into his body. Peyton froze. What was she doing?

She pushed against Darius's chest. "I'm so sorry."

"I'm not." He set her back on her feet, then pulled June into a bear hug.

"We're undefeated!" June released Darius to embrace Peyton. "We're undefeated!"

"Even better, we're going to the championship." Darius turned his cover model grin on Peyton. "How did you know?"

Peyton couldn't meet Darius's eyes. She'd literally thrown herself at him.

She nodded toward the field. The entire Sequoia team was celebrating on the fifty-yard line. "Noah's your brother. Determination runs in your family."

"They're both strong-willed men." June sounded giddy.

Darius' smile grew. "Well, ladies, I know some losers who owe us a drink."

"That's right. During the Books and Bakery Halloween event, your friends bet that Heritage would win." June threw her head back with a laugh. "Suddenly, I'm very thirsty. But I'd better take a rain check. I need to meet the team bus back at Sequoia High."

"I guess it's just you and me, then." Darius met Peyton's eyes. He stepped back to allow June and

Peyton to lead him down the stairs. "I'll drive us to the bar."

Peyton followed June from the bleachers. Why had she thrown herself into Darius's arms and kissed him? What had she been thinking? She hadn't been. Instead she'd given in to impulse. What had happened to the staid, dutiful Dr. Peyton Harris? Trinity Falls was changing her—or was it the sexy small-town newspaper reporter?

At the bar, Darius took a long drink of his soda, then gave Ean a smug smile. "Best I've ever tasted."

His childhood friend shook his head. "You've said that after every drink."

"And I've meant it each time." Darius sighed.

Despite Darius's taunts of bleeding his friends dry by ordering multiple rounds of beer, everyone knew he wasn't much of a drinker. Besides, he was still light-headed from the postgame kiss Peyton had given him almost an hour earlier. Jackson had bought him one beer. Since then, Darius had been tossing back soft drinks but of different brands. He didn't want free refills. What fun would that be? His friends had to come out of pocket.

Darius gulped more soda. "I told you not to bet against Noah. He caught Sequoia's winning touchdown."

Jackson drank his iced tea. "We saw it."

Darius gestured to his boss with his glass. "It was in the final seconds of the game."

"We were there when it happened, Darius." Ramona, who'd already bought Darius's and Peyton's sodas, dipped her celery stick into a bowl of ranch dressing. Spicy buffalo wings, loaded potato skins, and onion rings also crowded the table.

The sports bar's servers had pushed three tables together to accommodate Darius's party of ten: Jackson, Audra, Ean, Megan, Alonzo, Doreen, Vaughn, Ramona, Peyton, and him. He'd stuck to Peyton's side to ensure he, not Vaughn, got the seat next to her. How close had Peyton become with TFU's good-looking concert band director? She'd accompanied him to the town council meeting. He'd escorted her to the football game. Were they more than friends? Darius scowled. Was the attraction Vaughn's goatee?

"It was a great game." Peyton drank the soda Ean had paid for. "Watching those players' physical abilities was as thrilling as attending the BalletMet."

Ramona knitted her sculpted eyebrows. "You'd compare a football game to a ballet performance?"

"Yes, I would." Peyton shrugged her slender shoulders. "Both dancers and athletes are incredible to watch. They have strength, grace, and agility."

Alonzo swallowed more lemonade. "Good point."

"I don't see it." Ramona shook her head.

"I'm glad you enjoyed the game." Darius watched Peyton cut into a loaded potato skin appetizer with her knife and fork. Should he tell her that, at a sports bar, silverware was more like table ornaments?

In Peyton's company, he'd had an even better time than usual at the competition. He'd enjoyed introducing her to high school football. She was a quick study. And her strategic mind and competitive spirit had made her a great companion.

For the next hour, conversation moved on from the game to Thanksgiving, which was only three weeks away; Sequoia High School's appearance in the upcoming championship game; and the swearing in of the town's new mayor, Doreen Fever, on New Year's Day.

During a lull in their discussions, Peyton leaned backward to look down the table. "Vaughn, I hate to interrupt, but could you take me home?"

"No problem." The concert band director began making movements to leave. "I drove you to the game. I'll take you home."

No! Darius fought his panic. Vaughn wasn't going to take Peyton home. He was.

"I'm ready to leave now. Peyton, I'll take you home." He shoved back his seat and stood, pretending not to notice the knowing looks his friends exchanged.

Peyton's wide eyes were surprised. "Are you sure you don't mind?"

Darius offered his hand to help Peyton from her seat. "I'm sure." He also was sure he wasn't going to sit there while Vaughn and his goatee drove Peyton home.

∽CHAPTER 10∾

Peyton's seat belt connected with a *snick*. "I thought you didn't want your friends playing matchmakers with us."

"I don't." Darius backed out of the sports bar's parking space, doing his best to ignore the way his heart pounded in reaction to Peyton's proximity. Her warmth and scent filled the close confines of his nine-year-old black Nissan Maxima.

"Then why are you taking me home?"

Darius' mind scrambled for a response. "This isn't a date. I drove you to the bar and now I'm taking you home."

"I saw the way your friends looked at you when you made the offer."

So had I. "Ignore them." Darius made sure the traffic was clear before merging onto the street from the parking lot.

He didn't need directions to her apartment. When she'd first moved to Trinity Falls, his contacts had told him where the university professor lived.

"I'm not upset." Peyton shrugged her slender shoulders. "I'm just curious. Are you opposed to matchmaking in general or being set up with me in particular?"

His heart stuttered. Had he offended her? A quick glance in Peyton's direction found her caramel eyes mocking him. Darius's muscles went lax.

"Funny." His tone was dry. "I just don't like people . . ."

"Getting close to you?" Peyton attempted to finish Darius's thought.

Her question picked at a raw wound. "I have several good friends."

"But you're not dating."

"How do you know that?" He ignored his stirring irritation.

Peyton's throaty chuckle was like a daring caress across his lower abdomen. "If you were dating, your friends wouldn't be trying to fix you up with someone."

She had a point. "You said I was a player."

"I was wrong. I'm sorry."

Her words were simple, direct, and fed his soul. Someone who kept her promises and admitted when she was wrong. He was growing more and more attracted to the little professor. "What made you change your mind?"

"I realized women were flirting with you, but you weren't flirting back." Peyton shifted to face him. "During the game this afternoon, did you notice the women who were trying to get your attention?"

"No." He'd enjoyed Peyton's company too much to notice anyone else.

"I didn't think so."

Darius slid a look at her as he came to a four-way STOP sign. Was it his imagination or had she sounded smug?

"I'm surprised you noticed anything that happened off the field." He entered the intersection. "You seemed focused on the game."

"It was hard to ignore so many people glaring at me." She chuckled. "If looks could kill, I wouldn't have made it to halftime."

"I'm sorry."

"I kind of liked it."

Darius strained to hear her words. Startled, he looked her way. She was staring out the passenger side window, seemingly lost in thought. He didn't know how to respond to her comment, so he said nothing. The silence between them was comfortable.

The roads were quiet in Trinity Falls this evening. Barely a soul could be seen. The town was in mourning for its Heritage High School football team's loss to their rival Sequoia. He'd commiserate with his hometown and alma mater—except he was too darn happy for Noah. His little brother was going to the state championship. *Way to go!*

"Does this mean you've changed your mind about cochairing the community center fund-raising committee with me?"

Where had that question come from? "I haven't given the committee any thought."

"Could you think about it now?" She turned to him again. "Since you're willing to drive me home, I take it you no longer care that your friends are trying to fix us up."

Darius pulled into the parking lot of Peyton's

apartment building. It was a pretty, two-story building with eight units, black Spanish tile roofing and pale cream stonework. An ornate black metal staircase led residents and visitors to the second floor. The same metalwork framed the upper and lower balustrades.

"Which apartment is yours?"

"I'm surprised you don't know." Peyton gave him a cheeky grin. "I'm on the second floor."

Darius studied the four units on the top level. "I'll walk with you to your door." He turned off his engine and pulled the key from the ignition.

"Is Trinity Falls dangerous?" Her bright eyes dimmed with the question.

"We're not New York City, but you should never let your guard down wherever you are." He opened his door and rose from his seat. He started to circle his car to assist her, but Peyton was already standing and closing the passenger door.

"I know what you're doing." Peyton waited for him to join her.

"What?"

"You're trying to distract me from my original question."

The night was chilly but not too cold. He smelled firewood on the breeze. Wispy clouds slipped past the stars and over the moon.

Darius matched his steps to hers. "I really haven't thought about the fund-raiser."

Peyton tilted her head. "From what I understand, there's a real need to raise money for the community center."

"Yes, there is." The center's roof leaked, and the

heating, ventilation, and air-conditioning system needed repairs. It could also use new computers.

"Darius Knight! Is that you?"

Darius identified the female figure coming out of the shadows on the other side of the parking lot. "Evening, Ginny."

Virginia Carp stepped into a pool of light right in front of the apartment building. She slid a look Peyton's way. "Hello, Peyton." Her greeting cooled.

"Hi, Ginny." The professor sounded amused.

"Is she the reason you haven't called me?" Ginny jerked her head toward Peyton.

"The restraining order is the reason I haven't called you." Darius had known Ginny since junior high school. Three years ago, he'd filed a restraining order against her.

Ginny snorted. "That's in the past, Darius."

"It's a past I'd rather not repeat. Good night, Ginny." Darius allowed Peyton to climb the ornate metal staircase ahead of him.

Peyton led him to her apartment. "Why did Ginny file a restraining order against you?"

"She didn't. I filed one against her."

Peyton's wide caramel eyes met his as she closed and locked her door. "What happened?"

"Our relationship ended badly."

Ginny had agreed to a casual relationship with Darius. Then she'd changed her mind.

"That sounds like an understatement." Peyton leaned against her door and crossed her arms. "Who ended it?"

"I did." Darius rubbed his eyes with his fingers. "Ginny responded by keying the word 'jackass' on the hood of my car and spray-painting it on the front door of my apartment. She also sent a computer virus to my laptop."

Peyton gaped. "How do you know it was her?"

"She told me. Quincy convinced me to file the restraining order." He shrugged off his discomfort. "Could we change the subject?"

"Of course. Let's talk about the fund-raiser." Peyton held out her hand. "May I take your coat?"

Darius hesitated. "That wouldn't be a good idea, Professor." He watched a blush bloom across her cheeks.

Peyton dropped her arm to her side. "Oh, I didn't—"

He changed the subject for both their sakes. "I don't know anything about organizing a fund-raiser."

"I do."

"Then why do you need me?"

"I don't know Trinity Falls." Peyton straightened from the door. Her confidence had returned. "Who should I recruit to help with the committee? What type of event would interest the town? When and where should we have it? You could help me with those decisions."

Her enthusiasm was contagious. And the project was for a good cause. But he was becoming more and more attracted to her. If she was attracted to him, would she want more than a casual affair? That wasn't something he could promise her. And look at what had happened to his arrangement with Ginny.

Darius looked away. "Can I think about it?"

"Is there anything I can say to convince you now?"

He was tempted, very tempted. But he was also

scared, which was reason enough to retreat. "I need time to think."

"Fair enough." Peyton unlocked her door and pulled it open. "Thank you again for taking me home."

"My pleasure." Darius moved to the door. "Thanks for rooting for Noah."

She paused with her hand on the doorknob. "I hope he wins the state championship."

"I'll tell him." Though her message would raise additional questions. Noah had given him a teasing look when June, Peyton, and he had found his brother after the game. "Good night."

"Good night, Darius."

He watched her close her door and listened as she secured the locks. Only then did Darius return to his car.

How had his friends known Peyton would make him feel again? But more importantly, how could he be sure he wouldn't screw up this relationship? Peyton had asked whether he was afraid of getting close to people. Darius wasn't afraid; he was incapable. After all, he was Simon Knight's son. Simon had destroyed every relationship he'd ever had. The apple doesn't fall far from the tree.

The bell above the door to Ean's solo law practice chimed as Alonzo let himself into the suite Wednesday evening, Veterans Day. The building was near Books & Bakery in the Trinity Falls Town Center. The counselor recently had celebrated the practice's one-year anniversary.

At the sound of the bell, Ean appeared in the doorway of his office. "Hi, Alonzo."

Alonzo removed his sheriff's hat. "Do you have a few minutes?"

Ean's welcoming expression clouded. "Is everything all right with my mother?"

"As far as I know, she's fine."

Ean's relief was visible. He gestured Alonzo to precede him into the office. "Come in."

Alonzo crossed into the other room and lowered himself onto one of the two black leather guest chairs in front of the mahogany desk.

He rested his hat on his lap and glanced around the room. A lonely bamboo plant stood in its small, green ceramic pot on the bay windowsill. In a place of honor on the wall behind him, Ean displayed an oil painting of Freedom Park, created by Ms. Helen. The office also housed a laptop computer, ink-jet printer, two bookcases, and a couple of black metal filing cabinets.

Alonzo brought his attention back to Ean. "I've known your mother for a very long time."

"I know." Ean rested his elbows on the arms of his chair and linked his fingers together. The younger man studied Alonzo as though trying to read his mind. "You were friends in high school."

"I was friends with your father, too." Alonzo shifted in his seat. "Paul was a very good man, a very good friend."

"Yes, he was." Ean's tone was patient, belying the curiosity in his eyes.

"I've loved your mother since college." Alonzo's pulse was beating so hard he could barely hear himself. "But she was happy with your father. And her happiness was all that mattered."

"You're a good man, too, Alonzo, and a good friend."

Alonzo swallowed to ease his dry throat. He needed Ean to understand. "I'll always respect your father, and Doreen's and your memories of him."

"I appreciate that. I'm sure my mother does, too."

"I know I could never replace him. I wouldn't even try—"

"Alonzo, say what's on your mind."

He gripped the arms of the leather guest chair. His palms felt slippery against the wood. He drew a deep breath. Then another. He caught and held the younger man's olive eyes. "I want to ask your mother to marry me. But first, I'd like your blessing. You and your mother are very close. I don't want to cause any friction between you."

Ean's eyes widened. A myriad of expressions shifted across his features: surprise, curiosity, humor. "I should've known you were old-fashioned."

"What does that mean?" Tension knotted the muscles in Alonzo's shoulders. He'd imagined a variety of reactions. This wasn't one of them.

"It's not a bad thing." Ean held up one hand. "I just meant I shouldn't be surprised you asked for my blessing."

"I love your mother very much, Ean. She's intelligent, caring. She has a big heart."

"And she's beautiful."

"Yes, she is." Images of Doreen swept through his memories: her flapper costume from the Halloween celebration, the dress she'd worn to church Sunday, the sweats she wore around the house, her cream negligee . . .

Dammit, am I blushing? He shifted in his seat again. "I would be the happiest man on the planet if Doreen agreed to be my wife."

Ean sobered. "You've made my mother very happy, Alonzo. Like you said, that's all that matters. Of course you have my blessing."

"Thank you." Relief made Alonzo light-headed.

"When are you going to propose?"

"I'm not sure yet." One hurdle down, another to go. But the second was the biggest he'd ever faced. "I wanted to wait until after the election, when she'd have more time to relax and think about our future."

"Good idea." Ean nodded. "It's been a week since the election. That should be enough time."

"I never dreamed I'd have this chance. I want the proposal to be special." Alonzo rose. His legs were shaky with relief.

Ean stood, too. "You're setting the bar really high for Quincy, Jack, and me."

"Megan, Ramona, and Audra are special ladies."

"They are." Ean offered Alonzo his hand. "I'm sure you'll continue to make my mother very happy. But if you ever hurt her, I'll find you."

"You don't have anything to worry about."

Ean released Alonzo's hand and stepped back. "Good luck, although you won't need it."

"Thanks." Alonzo inclined his head, then turned to leave.

Actually, he could use all the luck he could get. What could he say or do to help Doreen realize he didn't want to replace Paul? He wanted them to build a future of their own.

"What are you doing here?" Darius had opened his front door to find his father outside his apartment Thursday night.

"Is that any way to greet your father?" Simon seemed surprised by the lack of welcome.

"Seriously, what are you doing here?" In the four years since he'd been living in the apartment, Darius's parents had never been to his home. He'd thought it was understood they never would. This was his Simon-and-Ethel-Free Zone.

"We should spend more time together."

So now he'd have to watch his Cleveland Browns NFL team continue its losing tradition during the Thursday night game while Simon competed for his attention? Was there no threshold to the pain a Browns fan had to endure? Darius stood back to let his father in.

Simon followed the beige wall-to-wall carpet into the living room. He glanced at the mahogany coffee table and matching end tables, the black leather sofa and matching recliner, and the black entertainment center and bookcase.

"What's for dinner?" Simon made himself comfortable in the recliner.

Darius squelched his resentment and locked the front door before joining his father in the living room. "I've already eaten."

"What?" The older man checked his watch. "It's only eight o'clock."

Darius settled on the far side of the sofa. "What's

with you and Mom? The other day she criticized me for eating lunch before one."

"You spoke with your mother?" Simon's expression brightened. "Did she ask about me?"

Was Simon delusional? "She kicked you out of the house, remember? Why would she ask about you?"

Simon gaped at him. "She didn't kick me out. It was my decision to leave."

Darius wasn't going to argue semantics. He returned his attention to his forty-eight-inch flat-screen television. "Listen, Dad, if you want to watch football with me, fine. But don't talk during the game. It's annoying."

Simon looked at the television. "Who are the Browns playing?"

"The Bills." Hadn't he just asked his father not to talk?

Silence lasted a few plays this time before his father once again spoke. "So how's your mother?"

"Why don't you ask her?" Darius grabbed the remote from his coffee table, pointed it toward the television, and pumped up the volume.

It was obvious Simon was bored and lonely, but Darius wasn't interested in playing twenty questions with his father while his team struggled for a winning season.

"I tried." Simon raised his voice to be heard above the game. "She won't return my calls."

"Can you blame her?" Darius's eyes were on the television, but his mind was in the past.

"What does that mean?"

Darius wasn't surprised his father was so clueless, but did he really want to get into this now while his team was fighting for football respect?

Why not?

Darius used the remote to mute the game, then shifted on the sofa to confront his father. "Put yourself in Mom's position. Three months ago, after thirty-four years of marriage, she discovered her husband has a seventeen-year-old son she's never heard of much less seen. This is after years of your denying you'd ever been unfaithful."

Simon shot from the recliner. His body was stiff as he pointed a finger at Darius. "I made one mistake. She's going to throw away *thirty-four years* of marriage over *one* mistake?"

"Which mistake are you admitting to?"

"The one I made." Simon lowered his arm. Tension still vibrated around him.

"You've made a hell of a lot more than one."

"What are you talking about?"

With his fingers, Darius counted off his father's transgressions. "You married a woman you didn't love—"

"I loved your mother when I married her."

"You lied to June when you told her you weren't married—"

"I never told her I was single."

"You had at least one extramarital affair—"

"June came on to me."

Darius unclenched his teeth. Simon was a piece of work. "You never took responsibility for Noah."

"June never told me she needed my help."

Darius stared at Simon. Was he serious? "That doesn't matter."

Simon raised his arm again. "None of this would have happened if you'd minded your damn business. What did you think you were doing?"

Darius wished Simon would stop pointing fingers at him, literally and figuratively. "I was thinking where there's smoke, there's fire. I was aware of the rumors. I'd heard the whispers for years, so I did some research."

"You mean you went digging into my personal business." Simon glowered at him. "I hope you're happy. You destroyed our family."

"No, Dad. You did, years ago." Darius stood and walked to him. "We've never been a family. Just three people who didn't have anyone else. But you destroyed even that with your lies."

"I'm telling you, I never lied." Simon's agitation increased. He was almost spitting his words.

"Why didn't you tell Mom about Noah?"

"It wasn't any of her business."

Darius's eyebrows jumped up his forehead. "She's your *wife*. You don't think she had a right to know another woman was giving birth to your son?"

"It had nothing to do with her." Simon spoke through his teeth.

"Apparently, she disagrees because she kicked you out." Darius returned to his seat at the opposite end of the sofa. "Oh, I forgot. She didn't kick you out. You left."

And who knew whether June Cale was the only woman Simon had had an affair with? She was the only affair they could prove.

"You'd better watch how you speak to me, Darius. I'm still your father."

"You're Noah's father, too." And how many other children? "When are you going to get to know him?"

"I came here to spend time with you, but all you

want to do is argue." Simon crossed his arms over his chest.

"You came here because you're lonely, but that's your fault. You never got to know us—or Noah. You were just a boarder in the house with me and Mom."

"I don't have to stay here and listen to this shit." Simon turned away from Darius. "You're just like your mother."

His father stomped across the living room. The threshold shook as he slammed the front door.

Accusing him of being like his mother didn't upset Darius. He would have been more upset to be compared to his father.

CHAPTER 11

"I do love Doreen's soups. Do you think she uses real dog meat?" Ms. Helen spooned up more chicken stew at the table she shared with Darius at Books & Bakery Tuesday afternoon, the ninth day of December.

"Probably." Darius stilled. His forehead creased in a frown. "Wait. What did you say?"

"What's on your mind, Darius? And don't bother to say nothing because I know it's something."

Of course Ms. Helen could tell something was troubling him. She knew him better than anyone. Wasn't that the reason he'd asked her to lunch?

Stalling for time, Darius lowered his soupspoon and glanced around the café. It was full but not as crowded as it typically was around lunchtime. He and Ms. Helen had been lucky to get a table. They'd arrived just after 11:00 a.m. Fortunately, Ms. Helen had been available for an early lunch.

He turned back to his soup. "My parents are driving me crazy."

"They've been doing that since you were old enough to realize they generally talked nonsense." Ms. Helen was right about that.

"I thought their separation would make it better, but it's gotten worse."

"That was bound to happen."

Darius was caught off guard. "Why?"

"I've told you before, your parents argue because they're insecure of each other's feelings." Ms. Helen stirred her stew. "And now that Ethel has met the proof of Simon's infidelity in Noah, she's increased the hostilities."

Darius arched a brow. "You think they're in love?"

"That's why your mother's furious and your father's still trying to impress her." The former university professor was in full oracle mode now. Past experience had taught Darius he'd need the patience of Job to wait on her answers.

"How is that possible?" Darius ignored his lunch. "My entire life, they've never had a kind word for each other."

Ms. Helen looked puzzled. "All this time, did you think your parents married because your mother was pregnant?"

"What was I supposed to think?"

"Your parents didn't have to get married, Darius. They wanted to get married. Then they realized they weren't ready for the commitment."

"I thought they hated each other." And him. Revelation after revelation. Ms. Helen was rewriting his past. "What are you saying? For my parents to stop arguing, they have to admit they're in love?"

"No, they have to forgive each other and let go of the past." Ms. Helen sipped her lemonade.

"That's easier said than done."

"I've been in love several times. Love isn't easy. Nothing worth having is."

"But how do you forget that your spouse lied to you much less had an affair? Could anyone's love survive that?"

"I don't know." Ms. Helen contemplated her soup as though she could see the past. "I remember how in love your parents seemed at first."

"And then I was born."

Ms. Helen's attention shot to Darius. She gave him a fierce look. "Their unhappy marriage is *not* your fault."

"But it was after I was born that everything went to hell." He pushed the words past the lump in his throat.

"You're not responsible for that. They are." Ms. Helen was adamant.

Darius reached past his untouched sandwich for his glass of iced tea. He drank it as he let his gaze circle the café again.

Outside, it was cold and dreary. But Books & Bakery was always welcoming. Or maybe he was projecting his feelings for his friends onto the shop. Ean, Jackson, Audra, Alonzo, and Ramona sat on bar stools, chatting with Doreen and Megan, who stood on the other side of the counter. When his friends had first arrived, they'd stopped at his table to say hello and to pay their respects to Ms. Helen, the queen holding court. His tension eased as he concentrated on his friends.

Darius set down his glass. "If my father loves my mother, why would he be unfaithful to her?"

"That's a conversation for you and your father. It's not my place to involve myself."

"*I'm* involving you." Darius was anxious to understand his father's motives. Could that help him understand his own? "Please, Ms. Helen, what do you think?"

Several beats of silence passed before she answered. "Your father isn't a courageous man. I think Simon's affairs were his way of trying to escape his situation even though he didn't want to leave Ethel."

"His way of having his cake and eating it, too." Darius nodded. That was a match for Simon's egotistical nature.

"If you want them to stop driving you nuts, you'll have to help them find a way to forgive each other."

Darius frowned at his sandwich and half-eaten soup. "How would I do that?"

"I haven't a clue. But you'll think of something. You've always had good insight about people." Ms. Helen pushed Darius's plate closer to him. "In the meantime, you'll need to keep your strength up."

Darius grunted. To accomplish a truce between his parents, he'd need more than insight. He'd need a miracle. Where would he find one in Trinity Falls?

The moment Peyton entered her apartment Thursday evening, she stripped off her heather pantsuit and matching pumps and exchanged them for her most comfortable pair of olive green jeans, magenta V-neck sweater, and her fuzzy orange slippers. It had been a long day, made even longer by the dread she'd wrestled with since she'd awakened.

Now wearing more comfortable clothing, Peyton

paced her living room, cordless phone in hand. She rehearsed one more time what she would say to Bruce before tapping in his cell phone number.

"This isn't a good time." Bruce sounded as though he was about to disconnect the call. What had she interrupted? It wasn't the first time she'd wondered.

"We need to talk."

Silence dropped on the other end of the line. Her stern tone must have surprised him. *Good.*

"Hold on." Muffled voices hissed in the background before he returned to the call. "What is it?" Bruce didn't sound like a man who'd been separated for five months from the woman he loved.

Peyton drew a breath, filling her lungs before plunging into the deep end. "I'd hoped to have this conversation during Thanksgiving break, but it can't wait."

"So I gathered." Bruce did sarcasm well.

She paced away from her overstuffed silver love seat, past her sterling-silver-and-glass coffee table to her ebony lacquered bookcase. "I can't marry you."

"Why not?"

It wasn't the tortured tone she could have hoped for, but boredom was better than the irritation she'd expected. She paced back to her coffee table. "Do you love me?"

"What does that matter?"

"It matters to me. A lot." She dropped onto the love seat. "Why would you marry someone if you didn't love her?"

"We're well suited." Finger tapping in the background punctuated Bruce's words. He had a tendency to keep rhythm to some internal beat with his fingers, a pen, a pencil, anything he could get his hands on. It was annoying.

"In what way?"

"In every way." The tapping stopped. Bruce's voice tensed. He was either losing patience or focus. A curious rustling sound came over the line.

"Except the most important one." Peyton stood to pace across the living room again. "We don't love each other."

"Your parents approve of me." His voice was breathless as he grasped at straws.

"I know they do." She leaned against her bookcase. "That's the real reason you want to marry me, isn't it?"

"Don't be paranoid, Peyton."

In the past, Bruce's belittling tone would trigger her change of topic. Not today. She was stronger, less willing to be brushed aside. Less confrontation averse. Had her time in Trinity Falls done that?

"Am I being paranoid, Bruce?" She returned to her seat on the sofa, crossing her legs. "My father's a partner in the investment firm in which you want to build your career. My mother's welcomed in the social circles in which you want to move. Marrying me would help your career and your social standing. What would I get?"

"That's your paranoia talking again." He knew all the buttons to push her temper. What he didn't realize was his tactics no longer worked.

"Paranoia would be my asking you about your relationship with your secretary."

"What?" Bruce's tone changed. He sounded almost

wary. "My relationship with Leila is strictly professional."

"Sure and fellatio isn't really sex." Peyton sensed his discomfort on the other end of the line. She'd hit a nerve. Being right wasn't always a good thing.

"We'll continue this conversation when you return to New York for Thanksgiving." Bruce's words carried a bite. "Maybe by then you'll have come to your senses."

"Is Leila getting impatient?"

"Peyton—" He choked off her name.

"The engagement is off, Bruce." Her tone was flat.

"What about Aruba? I've put down a deposit for the trip."

"I told you I wasn't going to Aruba for Christmas." Peyton sank onto the sofa planted between her bay windows and her coffee table. For once in her life, she had the upper hand. How empowering. "But your money doesn't have to be wasted. Why don't you take Leila?"

"This is ridiculous. Hold on."

Peyton pressed her phone tight against her ear. Rustling and mumbled voices carried to her. Someone was with him in his office, someone they didn't want her to hear.

Bruce returned to the call. "We've been engaged for months. You agreed to be my wife."

"That's right, your wife, not your ticket to the life you want. In return, you can't even give me your fidelity."

"You'd get a husband." Here was his snide tone again. "Men aren't beating down your door with marriage proposals, even with your family's connections. You're thirty years old, Peyton. I'm saving you from the shelf."

Who even says things like that anymore? "If you can't be faithful during our engagement, you're not going to be faithful after we're married." Bile rose in her throat. She swallowed it back.

Did her father know of Bruce's affair with Leila? If she could sense something was going on between her fiancé and his secretary, how could her father not? He worked twelve-hour days with them.

"Of course I'd be faithful to you."

Peyton's heart raced. She drew several steadying breaths. "Who's with you, Bruce?"

"What?" His voice was blank.

"It's Leila, isn't it?"

"What makes you think that?"

Peyton could barely breathe. "Is she giving you head while we're on the phone?"

"That's ridiculous! I resent—"

"Save it." A wall of fatigue fell on her. "She's welcome to you. I want a real marriage, one that's based on mutual respect and love."

Bruce barked a laugh. "Love is a fairy tale. You're too old to believe that myth."

Just thinking about Darius's kisses made her toes curl in the fuzzy slippers. Her thighs trembled; her core grew damp. If Bruce had never experienced what Darius's embrace had made her feel, she felt sorry for him.

"I want my pulse to race and my head to spin. I want fireworks. Most of all, I want to feel secure in the knowledge that my husband's penis will never know anyone else's mouth."

"There's nothing going on between Leila and

me." Bruce rushed his words as though he feared she would disconnect the call in seconds, which is exactly what she wanted to do. "We need to have this conversation in person. We can't end our engagement over the phone."

"I just did." She pressed the END button to disconnect the call.

Peyton had just taken her second step toward reclaiming her life from her well-meaning but misguided parents. Her first step had been moving to Trinity Falls.

What was next?

"Ms. Helen, why do you keep looking around like the government is spying on you?" Darius tucked the elderly lady's frail hand more securely into the crook of his arm.

He'd escorted his friend into the Heritage High School gymnasium Friday night. The gym had been converted into a banquet room in honor of Dr. Kenneth Hartford's retirement from Trinity Falls University after almost thirty-five years.

"I'm looking for someone, if you must know." Ms. Helen tipped her head back to frown up at him.

Her petite frame was draped in an oversized, thick scarlet sweater and slim black denim pants. Her black boots had modest heels and pointed toes. Sterling silver jewelry adorned her ears, neck, and wrists. Her snow-white hair was pinned back in a neat chignon.

"I'm your date." Darius pressed his hand to his chest. He wore a purple turtleneck sweater under his gray jacket. "It's not very flattering for you to look around for other men."

"It's definitely an ego boost to arrive on the arm of the handsomest man in the room. But you're far too young for me, Darius." She patted his forearm with her free hand.

"Ouch." He released her arm and faced her. "I still don't understand why we had to get to Ken's retirement dinner so early."

"I thought you wanted to give him your regards."

"I do."

"Well, if we'd arrived fashionably late, his throng of admirers would have made that nearly impossible." The former university professor adjusted the strap of her purse on her shoulder. "Now, let me mingle while you go find Ken."

"Fine." He kissed her forehead. "Try not to break too many hearts."

"Go find a single woman closer to your own age to spend the evening with." With that directive, Ms. Helen blended in with the neighbors who crowded the gym.

Darius went to pay his respects to the man of the hour. He navigated past the circular dining tables, which were covered in stiff white linen and set for eight people each, similar to the setup for Quincy's going-away party.

Darius found Kenneth's reserved table. Quincy, who'd traveled from Philadelphia for tonight's banquet, was already with the retiring professor. The two men sat at the table reserved for the guest of honor. Once the event officially started, Kenneth would share the reserved table with the university's president, vice presidents, division chair, and chair of the board of trustees.

The retiring TFU professor looked exactly like what he was: an older gentleman who'd spent his entire life in academia. Average height, thin, and bespectacled, Kenneth was wearing the requisite corduroy jacket with elbow patches, white shirt, and dark pants.

"Congratulations, Ken." Darius shook the professor's hand.

"Darius, thanks for coming." Kenneth's brown eyes twinkled with warmth and welcome.

"Thanks for the invitation."

"Of course. Of course." Kenneth released Darius's grip to spread his hands. "You've always done such a wonderful job, covering the university for the newspaper. How could I not invite you?"

Darius nodded at Quincy before returning his attention to the older professor. "Not much longer now before you're on the beach."

"No, it's not." Kenneth gestured toward the empty seat beside him. "Join us. Next week is Thanksgiving. Finals are the week after that; then I'm on my way to Florida, hopefully before the first real snowfall."

"Trinity Falls won't be the same without you." Darius lowered himself onto the red padded folding chair, placing the older gentleman between Quincy and him.

"Kind of you to say." Kenneth inclined his head.

Darius grinned at Quincy. "I'm surprised Ramona let you out of her sight."

"She went to find someone." Quincy smiled like a man in love.

Kenneth gestured toward Quincy with his water

glass. "I was just telling Quincy how good you made me look in the article you wrote for today's *Monitor*."

Darius shook his head. "You made yourself look good."

"Thank you." Kenneth folded his hands. "I'm looking forward to my retirement, but a part of me is worried about the future of the history department."

"Why?" Darius poured himself a glass of water from the pitcher in the center of the table. He offered the other two men a refill. Both declined.

"Most of my colleagues don't have the interest or drive to grow our department's programs." Kenneth sighed. "Although I do have some hope for our newest professor, Dr. Peyton Harris. She shows promise."

Kenneth was right. With that lady's drive and determination, she'd make the history department the envy of the university.

"Someone will step up to lead the department." Quincy stared into his glass of ice water.

Kenneth shifted in his seat to face the younger professor. "I'd hoped you'd be my successor, Quincy. But that was before you left TFU to teach at the University of Pennsylvania. Although I'm happy for you, to be completely candid, a part of me was disappointed."

Darius frowned as a shadow moved across Quincy's brown features. "Best-laid plans, Ken. But Quincy couldn't turn down an offer from Penn."

"Penn's a big adjustment." Quincy dragged his right hand over his clean-shaven head. "It's very different from TFU."

"Nothing worth having comes easily." Darius tossed back some water. "You'll make the transition."

"Didn't you sign a one-year contract?" Kenneth waved a dismissive hand. "That'll be over at the end of the spring semester. And I'm sure TFU will take you back."

Something more was bothering Quincy. His coal-black eyes were clouded. His sharp brown features were tense. Darius wanted to ask his childhood friend what was on his mind. But this wasn't the time or place.

Darius wiped condensation from his cool glass. "You've only been at Penn three months. You need time to adjust."

"I did my graduate studies there." Quincy shrugged his shoulders, clothed in a purple knit sweater Ramona must have bought for him. "I knew what to expect."

"But now you're a member of the faculty." Kenneth shook his head. "That's different."

Quincy stared across the room, appearing deep in thought. "I miss the flexibility of our academic department."

"TFU's a much smaller university, which allows it greater academic collaboration and creativity." Kenneth sipped his water.

Darius struggled in the role of devil's advocate. He didn't want to give Quincy reasoned arguments to remain in Philadelphia. Darius wanted his friend to come home. But was he being selfish?

He made himself focus on Quincy. "When you were deciding whether to leave, you said Philadelphia would give you access to historical research."

"Suppose Ramona doesn't like Philadelphia? She

thought she'd like New York, but she hated it there."
Quincy's gaze pinned Darius. "What if she hates
Philadelphia?"

Darius frowned. "You're borrowing trouble, Q."

Quincy dragged his hand over his bald head again.
"I'm wondering if I've made a mistake."

"Ramona will join you in January after Doreen is
sworn in as mayor." Darius leaned into the table.
"That will give you both five months before your
contract ends and you have to decide if you want to
stay at Penn or return to TFU."

Kenneth offered Quincy a persuasive smile. "At
TFU, you're the big fish in a smaller pond."

"You're my friend." Quincy eyed Darius. "I
thought you'd want me back in Trinity Falls."

Was Q joking? "Are you sure you have an advanced
degree?"

Quincy scowled at him. "Why are you always questioning that?"

Darius sighed. "It's because I'm your friend that
I'm asking you to give Penn a chance. I want you to
be happy, Q. Don't let fear hold you back."

"What about you, Darius?" Kenneth asked. "The
Monitor is a good paper, but have you reached your
potential there?"

Darius's lips curved in a half smile. "I've written
for a big metropolitan daily. This small-town newspaper is exactly where I want to be."

"Lucky us." Ramona's sarcasm came from behind
Darius as she circled the table toward Quincy.

Darius's gaze skipped over Jackson, Audra, and
Ms. Helen, who followed in Ramona's wake, to settle
on Peyton. The little professor wore a pink sweater

and a black ankle-length wool skirt. It wasn't her Catwoman costume, but she was just as captivating.

Darius tore his gaze from Peyton to give Ramona a dry look. "Thanks for the kind words."

"It was a weak moment." Ramona stood behind Quincy. She rested her hands on his shoulders.

Quincy reached up and took one of her hands in his.

Peyton shook Kenneth's hand. "Congratulations, Ken."

"Thank you." Kenneth took her hand in both of his. "I'm glad you could make it."

Jackson and Audra also offered their well wishes to the retiring professor.

The pleasantries appeared to be too much for Ramona. "Come on, Ken. Everyone's waiting for you to start the food line. I'm starving."

Kenneth chuckled as he pushed himself to his feet. "Then by all means, let me lead the charge to the buffet tables."

Minutes later, Quincy and Ramona led Jackson, Audra, Peyton, Darius, and Ms. Helen to an available table near the center of the gym-turned-banquet-hall.

Darius sat between Ms. Helen and Peyton. As it often did, the conversation among the seven friends hopped across different topics: Quincy's first semester at Penn, Peyton's first semester with Trinity Falls University, Ramona's final days in the mayor's office, Jackson's renovation of Harmony Cabins, Audra's latest songwriting contract, and Ms. Helen's progress on her memoirs.

"I still haven't found anyone to work on it with me." Ms. Helen sliced into the teriyaki chicken breast.

Darius forked up the seasoned rice. "I don't understand why you won't let me work with you on your memoirs. I wouldn't charge you."

"That's one of the reasons. I don't want this project to be a favor. I want to handle it professionally." Ms. Helen bit into the well-seasoned chicken.

Darius shrugged. "If you insist on paying me, I won't say no."

Ms. Helen slipped him a smile. "Let me think it over."

Ramona plucked a broccoli spear from her plate. "I think you don't want us to help because your memoirs are chock-full of steamy relationships. Am I right?"

Ms. Helen slid a look at Ramona. "You'll have to buy the book to find out."

Laughter rolled around the table before the conversation resumed.

"I'm looking forward to the end of my term." Ramona refilled her water glass. "Don't get me wrong. I've enjoyed being Trinity Falls' mayor. But I'll be glad when Quincy and I are once again living in the same city. Long-distance relationships suck."

Love softened the mayor's classic beauty. But Quincy's expression seemed strained. Was he still stressing over Ramona's reaction to living in Philadelphia? With a mental shake of his head, Darius returned to his meal.

The banquet's agenda included speeches from university administrators, praising the professor and thanking him for his decades of dedication to the institution and its students. Kenneth ended the evening with a brief but moving profession of his love for the university, its students, faculty, staff, and Trinity Falls.

"I believe in Trinity Falls and in Trinity Falls University." Kenneth cleared his throat and sipped some water before continuing. His voice was thick with emotion. "They were both founded on a simple principle: equality of opportunity makes a community strong. And as each community goes, so goes the nation."

Kenneth waited for the applause to end before continuing. "It's been my privilege to be a member of the university and of the town. I'm proud of my contributions to both and of the person into whom these experiences have molded me. God bless you all."

The retiring professor earned a standing ovation. Darius glanced at Peyton to find her wiping tears from her eyes. He was close to tears himself.

Moments after the banquet officially ended, Ms. Helen leaned past Darius to question Peyton. "Do you have a ride home, dear?"

"Yes, thank you." Peyton nodded across the table. "I came with Jackson and Audra."

"Oh no, dear." Ms. Helen's eyes widened. "Since it's so late, you should let Darius drive you home. Your apartment is a bit out of the way for Jackson and Audra. Darius is closer. I can ride back with Quincy and Ramona."

"Ms. Helen, you're not riding home with Quincy and Ramona. You're going to leave with the one you came with." Darius leveled the elderly woman a look. Had she joined the Darius-Needs-a-Girlfriend Bandwagon? He stood from the table and assisted Ms. Helen from her chair.

The older woman reached up and patted Darius's

upper arm. "It's too much trouble for you to drop off multiple people."

Why hadn't she considered that before she'd volunteered him to drive Peyton home—not that he minded. He'd considered making the offer himself.

"No, it's not. I'll take you home first." Darius pulled her small hand into the crook of his arm to escort her from the gym. "Then I'll drive Peyton home."

After wishing their friends a good evening and collecting their coats, Darius escorted Ms. Helen and Peyton to the parking lot. Ms. Helen insisted on sitting in the backseat of Darius's black Nissan Maxima, leaving Peyton with the front passenger seat. He closed and locked the car's doors, trapping Peyton's talcum powder and lily-of-the-valley fragrance inside.

The first stop was Ms. Helen's home, where Darius escorted her to her door and saw her safely inside. Then he climbed back into his car and pointed his Maxima in the direction of Peyton's apartment building.

Peyton shifted on her seat to face him as he pulled away from the curb. "You've had two weeks to think it over, Darius. Will you cochair the community center's fund-raising committee with me, or will I have to get tough with you?"

CHAPTER 12

Had she really said that? Peyton tensed in her seat. What had gotten into her? She opened her mouth to apologize, but Darius's response stopped her.

"That threat would be funny if the memory of you frog-marching me out of your office back in August wasn't still fresh on my mind."

"I'm really sorry about that." Peyton felt the burn of a blush rising from her neck.

"No harm done." Darius shrugged. "My shoulder was better in a day or two."

"What?" The interjection shot out on a breathless syllable. "I hadn't realized I'd hurt you."

"It was a minor injury. It wasn't even dislocated." Darius kept his eyes on the road. "And my back, well, that was just a twinge."

The silence lasted a beat or two before Peyton spoke. "I think you're making that up."

"I am."

She huffed a breath. "That's not even funny."

"Yes, it is." Darius slipped her a quick glance

before returning his attention to the road. "Quincy and Jackson got a good laugh from it."

"You told them?" Peyton was scandalized.

"I told Quincy. He told Jackson—and God knows who else." Darius braked at a four-way stop and looked at Peyton. "Quincy's got a big mouth."

Peyton covered her face with both palms. "Oh my word."

"Hey, don't worry about it." Darius moved through the intersection. "At most, Quincy told Ramona, Jackson, and Ean. And they probably told Audra, Doreen, Megan, and Alonzo. I think Vaughn knows, too."

Was that supposed to make her feel better? Peyton's hands muffled her groan of abject humiliation.

"It's not so bad." Darius checked his mirrors before switching lanes. "I know it sounds like a lot of people, but it's not even half of our acquaintances."

"You're enjoying this, aren't you?" Peyton scowled at him.

"Very much." He nodded solemnly.

Peyton crossed her arms. "Are you going to cochair the committee with me?"

"Yes." His response was that singular rough word.

In her mind, Peyton was screaming, and jumping up and down in triumph. She took a steadying breath. "Thank you. I couldn't do this without your help."

Darius pulled into her apartment parking lot and turned off the engine. He turned to face her. "The community center is important to Trinity Falls. But whatever we decide to do for the fund-raiser, it needs to be quick. The town gets bored fast."

With his engine off, the night was still and quiet.

They could be the only two people in the world. A nearby parking lot security lamp held the deepest shadows at bay.

With her eyes, Peyton traced the clean-cut, angular lines of Darius's face. "Anything else?"

"That's it for now." He pinned her to the passenger seat with his dark stare. "When do we start?"

Peyton was mesmerized by his midnight eyes. They were so beautiful and focused only on her as though she were the only thing that mattered in this time and place. "Let's wait until after Thanksgiving break."

"Thanksgiving break. Outside of the university, the rest of the world calls it Thanksgiving." His lips curved in a smile.

Peyton imagined herself tracing his full, well-formed lips with her tongue. She tore her gaze away. What had he said? Oh, right. "Are you going to correct everything I say during our project?"

"Only when you need correcting."

Peyton swallowed a laugh. She didn't want to encourage him. She unlocked the passenger car door. "Good night, Darius."

Darius stopped her with a hand on her shoulder. "Hold on."

The warmth and weight of his touch traveled through her coat to every muscle in her body. "What is it?"

"I'll walk with you to your door." He climbed out of the car and circled its hood.

When was the last time someone had helped her from a car?

Darius matched his pace to hers as they braved the lowering temperatures to cross the parking lot.

What was happening to her? She'd never been that interested in sex before. But now, every time she was around the reporter, she had an out-of-body experience. Her mind went blank and her tongue separated itself from her thoughts. She had to get herself together. She was a responsible adult, not a domesticated animal in heat.

Peyton fished her keys from her purse. "Thank you for driving me home." There, that sounded very civilized.

"You're welcome." He stood aside so she could precede him up the ornate black metal staircase.

"I'd planned to drive myself." Peyton led him up the steps. "I've been in Trinity Falls for five months now. It's time I learned my way around. But people have been very insistent on carpooling with me." Was she babbling?

"They want to make it easier for me to take you home." Darius's tone was wry.

She paused halfway up the stairs, frowning at him over her shoulder. "Why do you think this has anything to do with you?"

Darius arched a brow. "Vaughn brought you to the Sequoia game. But I brought you home."

"You insisted on driving me back."

"Jack and Audra brought you to Ken's retirement banquet, but I'm the one escorting you to your door."

Jackson and Audra hadn't seemed surprised to be relieved of chauffeur duty. "So you think this is all part of their plan to get us together?"

"I do."

Peyton continued up the steps. His body of evidence was growing. Perhaps he had a point. How did she feel about being the target of her new neighbors' elaborate matchmaking scheme with one of the most eligible, attractive, and sexy bachelors in town?

As her students would say, it was totally cool.

"Just because they're trying to get us together doesn't mean we have to fall in with their plans." Peyton unlocked her apartment door.

"I'm beginning to think their idea has merit."

Surprised, Peyton looked up at Darius and found herself captured by his kiss. His mouth settled on hers. He didn't touch her in any other way. His lips molded and caressed hers in a gentle invitation to a deeper intimacy. His tongue traced her shape in a vivid reminder of the pleasure they'd felt before—and that they could experience again, if it's what she wanted. It was.

Peyton twined her arms around his neck and pressed her body to his. The impediments of their coats frustrated her. Without breaking their kiss, Peyton lowered her arms to unbutton her coat. She stumbled a step or two as Darius walked her backward. Her apartment door slammed shut with an explosive bang.

Startled, Peyton jumped back. She stared at Darius, struggling for her bearings. His angular features were hard with desire. His midnight eyes burned with need.

"I'm sorry." His voice was rough and husky. "I kicked the door shut. I didn't want to put on a show for your neighbors."

Peyton's eyes shifted from Darius to the door and back. She crossed the room. Her hands hovered over the locks. *What am I doing? Is this what I want?* She'd ended her engagement. What was holding her back? Peyton turned the locks, then faced Darius again.

"Good call." She didn't recognize her voice. But gazing into the heat of Darius's dark eyes, she felt a familiar need.

Darius Knight was a dangerous man. With the sound of his voice, the look in his eyes, the touch of his hands, he could make her want things she'd never wanted before. Do things she'd never otherwise considered. What was it about him? What was it about her with him?

Holding her gaze, Darius raised his hands to unbutton his black wool topcoat and take it off. Peyton was distracted by the broad expanse of his muscled shoulders molded beneath his garnet turtleneck sweater. Navy corduroy pants clothed his lean hips and long legs. Darius turned to lay his coat on the back of her silver love seat. When he faced her again, there was a question in his eyes. Aware he was watching her every move, Peyton opened her coat. She let the weight of it fall from her shoulders and pool on the floor.

Darius's eyes glowed. His gaze roamed her pink sweater and ankle-length skirt as though he could see through them. Her body hummed with a strange, deepening desire.

Darius closed the distance between them. "You're so beautiful."

"You're the beautiful one." Peyton rose up on her toes.

Darius lowered his head to meet her. When their

lips touched, it was like an electric current arcing through her. Peyton's body shook. Darius tightened his arms around her. She dove into his kiss, exploring him, seeking him, teasing him with her tongue. She wanted to know him, his touch, his taste, his scent. She slid her hands up and over his sweater, feeling the hard muscles beneath. Peyton was drowning in sensation, on the verge of losing control.

Darius's head was spinning. Desire, raw and restless, swelled within him. Peyton was warm and responsive in his arms, feeding his need. He drank her gasps, swelled with her moans, and burned under her touch. Her taste, sweet and spicy, made him light-headed. Darius swayed on his feet.

Peyton pulled her mouth free. "My heart's racing. I can't catch my breath."

"I know the feeling." Darius pressed his face into the curve of her neck. He inhaled her scent and felt a tightening in his groin.

He kissed her neck, nibbling her skin. Darius traced his tongue along the shell of her ear. Peyton moaned. Her hips pressed into his. She claimed his lips again.

Darius tightened his embrace around her and drew her with him to the sofa. He walked backward, relying on memory to lead him where he wanted to go. The sofa came up against his legs. Darius fell onto it, taking Peyton with him. She gasped and he deepened their kiss.

Darius pressed his tongue inside her, groaning when she stretched out to meet him. He stroked her, caressed her, wrapped himself around her. His blood grew hotter and hotter as she responded to the ways he wanted to touch her.

Peyton lifted her head. "Darius." His name was a gasp on her lips. Her breasts burned into his chest.

"Yes?" His hands slipped under her sweater and moved up her back. Her skin was soft, smooth, warm. Arousing.

"I can't think." Her body moved against his.

"I don't think we're supposed to." Darius reached around to cup the side of her breast. The sensation was pleasure, pain.

"But I need to." Peyton struggled into a sitting position.

Darius let his hand drop. He sat beside her. "What do you need to think about?"

"This." Peyton's voice was tight. She waved a shaky hand. "I'm not ready. I thought I was." Her breath was light and fast. "I'm sorry."

"No, I'm sorry." Darius's body pulsed with unanswered desire. He clenched, then unclenched his teeth. "I didn't mean to push you."

"You didn't." Peyton's response was fast and firm.

"Just give me a minute." Darius was silent for several long moments, waiting for his heated muscles to cool. His body wanted to join with hers but his soul knew he needed to leave. Finally, he stood. Darius put on his coat, then turned for one last look at the little professor. "Good night, Peyton. Sleep well."

"You too." Peyton's voice was soft.

He again waited for her to lock her door before he started for the parking lot.

Darius had never felt so much so fast. But it was more than a strong physical attraction to Peyton. She made him feel more than anyone else ever had. Maybe this Tin Man really did have a heart.

CHAPTER 13

This was the worst Thanksgiving Darius had ever had. How was that possible? He and his mother were the only two people in the dining room of his family's house Thursday afternoon. Then why did it feel so crowded? The beige walls were closing in on him.

From her seat at the head of the walnut dining table, Ethel gave the impression of serenity, but there were telltale signs of tension: tight jaw, thinned lips, and narrowed eyes. She'd barely said ten words since he'd arrived. Was she giving him the silent treatment because he'd asked to have Thanksgiving lunch with her so he could see Simon later this afternoon? These holiday dinners were miserable enough when he'd had to spend it with Ethel and Simon together. Sharing a meal with each of them separately on the same day was an experience Darius was anxious to put behind him.

The silence dragged on. Darius had to say something before it drove him crazy.

"The turkey tastes good." He sawed another slice from the chunk of meat Ethel had tossed him.

"Thanks." Ethel allowed the conversation to lapse again.

Yes, she was definitely punishing him for having the early meal with her. But if he'd seen his father first, she'd have punished him for that.

Uncomfortable silences hadn't been as uncomfortable when there'd been the three of them. What made this worse was that he couldn't escape into his own mind. It would be too obvious.

Darius put down his knife and fork. Enough was enough. He couldn't continue this way. "Mom, why did you invite me to share Thanksgiving with you if you're not going to speak with me?"

Ethel forked up more stuffing. "I'm speaking."

"Two-word responses to my questions don't qualify as holding up your end of a conversation."

"What do you want me to say?" She still wouldn't look at him.

What was going on? Darius strained to read her thoughts. "I'm your son. I shouldn't have to coach you through a conversation with me."

"What do you want me to say?" She repeated the words with an edge of desperation.

"Tell me what you're thinking."

"You look just like him." She still wouldn't look at him.

Simon. He looked just like his father. He knew that. "That bothers you?"

"Yes."

He flinched. "Why?"

Ethel's hand shook as she dropped her fork onto

her white china plate. The sharp *clang* was a slap across his face.

"He lied to me. He treated me like a fool." Ethel clenched her fists, staring off into the middle distance.

"Yes, he did." Darius took a deep breath and forced an even tone. "But you knew he was lying— or at least suspected it. Why didn't you push him harder for the truth?"

"It didn't matter how many times I asked him. He just kept denying it, over and over and over again."

They'd never discussed this. As a child, he hadn't known the reason for the tension in their house. He only knew he much preferred his friends' homes because everyone was so much more relaxed there.

Darius studied the soggy stuffing. "I'd often wondered why you didn't leave him."

"Why should I leave?" Ethel stabbed a broccoli spear from her plate. "I paid half the deposit on this house. I pay half the mortgage. I told him to get out years ago, but he wouldn't."

They'd stayed in their tension-filled marriage because they were both too pigheaded to leave. He should have known. He'd thought—hoped—they'd tried to make their marriage work because of him. Instead, they'd stayed together because of a house.

"So instead of leaving, you stayed." Darius caught and held his mother's resentful gaze. "Instead of punishing him, you punished me."

"What are you talking about?" Ethel's frown darkened.

"You weren't at any of my football games."

"I fed you."

"You didn't attend my graduations."

"I clothed you."

"You never helped me move into the dorms at college."

"I was there for you."

"No, you weren't." Darius stood. What was the point of this? Thanksgiving? He'd be thankful when it was over. "Instead of snubbing Dad, you ignored me. Instead of giving *him* the silent treatment, you were cold to me. Is it because I look like him? Were you afraid I'd become like him?"

"I don't know what you're talking about." Ethel grabbed the napkin from her lap and threw it onto the table.

"Yes, you do." Darius's muscles shook with cold, though the dining room was way too warm.

Ethel stood as well. "You're talking nonsense."

"Will you ever stop punishing me for what you did to each other?" Darius pinned her with his stare.

"Get out." Ethel swung a stiff finger in the direction of the front door. "Get out of my house."

Darius folded his napkin and laid it on the table. "You won, Mom. You got the house."

Darius circled the long, walnut wood dining table and crossed to the closet to collect his topcoat. He yanked open the front door and left, never looking back.

"Did you know there are NFL games on television throughout the day?" Peyton met her parents' blank stares as they sat around the kitchen table Thanksgiving afternoon.

The big, bright kitchen had always been her favorite room in the house. It was the most welcoming.

And it was always painfully neat, from its black-and-white flooring and marbled countertops to the sterling silver appliances.

"When did you start watching football?" Her father, Carlson Harris, paused in the act of spooning up his chicken noodle soup.

The Harris family was enjoying a late breakfast/early lunch of soup, cheese, and crackers before their traditional turkey dinner fresh from the caterers.

"Ever since I attended a football game at one of the local high schools." Peyton attempted a casual shrug. Had she pulled it off?

"You sound as though you're putting down roots in that little town." Irene, her mother, laughed a little, but her dark eyes were concerned. "Don't get too comfortable there, dear. You're coming back to New York next month."

"Actually, Mom, that's something I wanted to speak with both of you about." Peyton stared at her plate of wheat crackers and Brie. This was as good a time as any to break the news to them. She took a deep breath. "I'm not coming home at the end of the semester."

"Excuse me?" Irene gave her a blank look.

"When are you coming home?" Her father picked up his glass of lemonade. His eyes were steady on hers.

"New York isn't home anymore." Peyton wasn't convinced it ever truly had been. "Trinity Falls is."

The silence was dense with confusion, denial, and disbelief. Her parents looked at each other, then back at her. Peyton's eyes found the coffee carafe on the counter behind her father. Her knees were too shaky to carry her that far.

"When did you make that decision?" Irene sounded lost.

"Before I left in July." Peyton held her mother's gaze with difficulty.

"When were you going to tell us?" Carlson's voice was unrecognizable.

"This weekend." Although, she hadn't intended on ruining the weekend this early.

"*Why* have you left New York? This is where you were born. You grew up here." Her mother's voice shook with emotion. "You started your career here. This is where *we* live. Why would you leave? And without even discussing it with us first."

Peyton's heart galloped in her chest. This was worse than she'd imagined. "I wasn't happy here, Mom. I needed a change."

"Why didn't you tell us this?" There was concern in her father's words. "You just snuck away like a thief in the night."

Peyton steeled herself against the imagery. It was true but no less hurtful. "I knew you'd try to change my mind."

"Damn right we'd try to change your mind." Irene's eyes welled with tears—of anger or sorrow? "It's ridiculous. It's dishonest." Her mother's words cut deep.

"I'm sorry, Mom."

"I don't want your apology." Irene stood. "I want you to keep your word and return to New York in December at the end of the semester. We even changed the date of our Aruba cruise to accommodate you."

"Your mother's right." Carlson's calm words were a

jarring contrast to her mother's emotional outburst. "That's the commitment you made to us."

"But I can't. I signed a contract with the university. Besides, I'm happy in Trinity Falls." Peyton tried willing her mother to understand.

"How can you possibly know that?" Irene threw up her arms. "You've only been there five months."

"What about Bruce?" Carlson asked.

Peyton drew a bracing breath, taking in the sharp scent of Brie. "I told you before I came home that Bruce and I ended the engagement."

"*He* doesn't consider the engagement off." Irene's tone and posture threw out a challenge.

"What is he going to do, knock me over the head and drag me to the altar?" Peyton was almost amused.

"Peyton!" Irene gaped at her. Small wonder. Her mother wasn't used to such open subversion. "We'd hoped you'd reconsidered your impulsive decision. You're never going to find another man who's as good a catch as Bruce. He's a rising star at your father's brokerage."

Darius' smile flashed across her mind. Her mother had never been more wrong. Irene Biery Harris wouldn't be impressed by Darius's reporter's salary. But he was a good person and a loyal friend. He made her heart pound and her body burn. That was more important to Peyton. "I don't love Bruce, Mom. And he doesn't love me."

"You'll grow to love each other." Irene tossed a dismissive hand.

"I want to be in love *before* I marry." Peyton sipped her lemon water. "And I want to be confident the man I marry loves me—"

"Love doesn't always last, Peyton. Your mother and I are lucky," her father interrupted. She heard his strained patience. "It's more important to us that you're well taken care of."

"I can take care of myself." Away from her parents' influence, she'd never been more confident of her capabilities.

Carlson shook his head. "You haven't given us any reason to believe that. Look at your most recent behavior. You assured us you'd return to New York in December and start planning your wedding to Bruce. Now we've learned you've moved to Trinity Falls and ended your engagement. You're reckless and impulsive."

"What were you hoping to accomplish?" Irene asked.

"You've both been telling me what to do, when to do it, and with whom." Peyton looked from her mother to her father. "That was fine when I was four. I'm thirty. It's past time I made my own decisions."

Her father regarded her with stern dark eyes. "We're trying to guide you so you don't make mistakes like moving to some town no one's ever heard of and breaking your engagement to a man who can take care of you in the manner to which we've made you accustomed."

"Dad, I have a career." Peyton carried her dishes to the dishwasher. "I'm accustomed to the manner in which *I've* been caring for myself."

"You're making a mistake, Peyton." Irene turned to follow Peyton's movements.

"Even if I am, it's my life. It'll be my mistake." Peyton tossed the remnants of her soup into the garbage disposal. She rinsed her bowl, then loaded it into the dishwasher.

"I invited Bruce to join us for Thanksgiving dessert." Carlson's announcement made Peyton's blood run cold.

She straightened from the dishwasher, closing the appliance's door before facing her parents. "It's your home. You can invite whomever you'd like."

Peyton left the kitchen, ignoring her parents' stunned expressions. Her back was straight, her shoulders squared. Inside, she was seething. They'd invited Bruce for Thanksgiving dessert. Obviously her parents weren't done trying to run her life. But they were mistaken if they thought she'd continue to let them. Paraphrasing Janet Jackson, she was in control now. She owed a great debt to Trinity Falls— and to one sexy, sensitive, small-town reporter.

In the end, Darius kept his commitment to share an early Thanksgiving dinner with his father. Just because things hadn't worked out with Ethel didn't mean he and Simon couldn't enjoy the holiday . . . he hoped.

Simon opened his apartment door in response to Darius's knock. The older man's eyes were wide and wild with stress and frustration. "I've burned the turkey. We're having sandwiches."

Darius nodded, taking in Simon's sweats and bathrobe. "May I come in?"

"Oh. Sure, sure." Simon pulled the door wide as he stepped back.

"Anything I can do to help?" Darius crossed the threshold and waited for his father.

"You can help me make the sandwiches." The response was grumbled over Simon's shoulder as Darius followed him through the apartment.

What a pigsty!

The living room looked like a spillover, walk-in closet. Discarded shoes marked a trail leading into the kitchen. The remnants of several days' worth of fast-food meals covered the coffee table and half of the sofa. Simon had been living in the apartment for only four months. But it looked as though he'd been collecting trash for years.

How had his mother kept a spotless home when she'd lived with a man who elevated making messes to an art form?

And what was that smell?

"Dad, how can you live like this?" Darius gritted his teeth. *Am I going to be sick?*

"Don't judge me, Darius. I'm doing the best I can."

That was hard to believe. The stench grew stronger the farther into the apartment they came. Darius crossed into the kitchen and froze. A pile of dirty dishes stood in a sink full of filthy water. He'd found the source of the stench.

Darius stepped back. "Get dressed. We're going out to eat."

"What? Why?" Simon frowned his confusion.

"Can't you smell that?" Darius gestured toward the sink. "Look around, Dad. Can't you see this?"

"I just need to straighten up."

"You need a hazmat team." Although a hazardous materials team probably would condemn the place. Darius rubbed his eyes. "Get dressed. I'm not eating here."

Simon looked around as though waking from a

deep sleep. "It's Thanksgiving. No place will be open."

"We'll find something."

"Fine," Simon muttered as he shuffled into his bedroom.

Minutes later, Darius sat at a booth in Trinity Falls Cuisine with a hastily dressed Simon. There were a few other patrons, mostly men, some alone, some with friends; a couple of students from TFU; and one or two couples.

The server had just brought their Thanksgiving plate specials: sliced turkey, stuffing, and broccoli. Simon attacked his plate as though he hadn't eaten real food in months. Darius enjoyed the silence for as long as he could.

"Have you seen your mother?" Simon came up for air.

"I had lunch with her." Such as it was.

"How is she?"

"Fine." Darius cut into the soft sliced turkey. "You, apparently, are not."

His father gave him a sharp look. "Yes, I am."

Darius forked up stuffing. "Your apartment is a cry for help. It looks like you're having some sort of emotional breakdown."

"I've been busy starting a new life. I haven't had time to fix the place up." Simon went back to his early dinner.

"Mom's starting a new life as well. The house has never looked better." Was that a low blow?

"Your mother is still living in the house I half paid for." Simon's voice was tight with anger. "Meanwhile, I have to furnish an apartment and get to know a new neighborhood. I never thought I'd be paying rent in my retirement."

"You said it was your decision to leave." Darius sipped his iced tea. "You've made your bed. Now you get to sleep in it."

"Your mother pushed me out."

"What would you have done if you were her?"

"I wouldn't kick someone out of his own home." Simon gulped his soda, then slammed his glass onto the polished wood tabletop. "I'd have tried to work things out."

"To do that, you'd have to take responsibility for the mistakes you've made."

"What about the mistakes *she* made?" Simon pointed his fork at Darius.

"What mistakes?" Darius frowned.

"She never understood me." Sighing, Simon stared morosely at his meal.

"Grow up." The words burst from Darius without conscious thought.

"What?" Simon's jaw dropped.

"Grow. Up." Darius leaned in. "You're like a spoiled child. Everyone else is responsible for your mistakes but you."

"How dare you!"

"Mom never understood you, so she's the reason for your multiple affairs."

"I didn't have—"

"June never complained, so she's the reason you didn't take care of your son."

"I'd've—"

"Instead of blaming them for your failings, you

should be thanking them for carrying you all these years."

"*What?*"

Darius's face was hot. His muscles shook. Another Thanksgiving meal wasted. Why had he chosen today to confront his parents?

"It's obvious from the filth in your apartment that Mom's been cleaning up after you for the past thirty-four years."

Simon's eyes bulged from his head. "That's bullsh—"

"And despite your lack of attention—or maybe because of it—Noah's growing into a good man."

"Don't talk to me that way. You may be grown, but I'm still your father." Simon's voice was rough with anger.

"Then be a role model I can be proud of. Instead I have nightmares of following in your footsteps."

"You could do a lot worse."

Simon couldn't believe his own words, could he?

"I don't see how that's possible." Darius hailed their server for the check. The verdict was in; this was officially the worst Knight family Thanksgiving ever.

⬯⬯ CHAPTER 14 ⬯⬯

Almost twenty minutes after dinner, Irene escorted Bruce into the sitting room, where Peyton waited with her father for their Thanksgiving dessert.

Bruce Grave looked like everything he wanted to be: wealthy and well connected. His lightweight V-neck oatmeal sweater and skinny gold slacks draped his model-slender frame. His soft, ebony curls gleamed. His fair skin was still ruddy from the cold.

Peyton had settled onto one of the pale silver–cushioned armchairs. Her father, dressed in a simple black cashmere sweater and black pants, had taken the other. That left the settee for Bruce and Irene.

Darkness had fallen outside. Carlson had pulled the heavy cream drapes closed over the room's two windows. A standing floor lamp provided ample light. But the room still felt shrouded in secrets and shadows.

Carlson and Irene appeared watchful as Peyton came face-to-face with the man who was her ex-fiancé— and who would remain that way. Bruce's expression was guarded. Whose idea was it that he try to reconcile with her? Was Irene that determined to get a husband for Peyton? Did Carlson want his protégé to take care of her? She could almost feel sorry for Bruce. Neither Carlson nor Irene took failure well.

"Hello, Bruce." Peyton slipped her hand into the right front pocket of her cotton-blend pants and brushed it over the ring box.

His brown eyes took in her snow-white crewneck sweater and leaf-green, straight-leg pants "You look lovely."

Too little, too late.

Bruce waited for Irene to settle onto the spindly silver settee before taking the space beside her. He played the gentleman when it suited him. Pity it didn't suit him more often.

Images of Darius giving her his coat when they were trapped in the archives, escorting her to her door each time he brought her home, tucking Ms. Helen's hand into the crook of his arm to help her to the parking lot ran through Peyton's mind. He was chivalrous to his bones.

Peyton blinked. The images disappeared and she was back in her parents' salon. "Shouldn't you be spending Thanksgiving with your own family?"

"Peyton, don't be rude." Irene adjusted her sapphire skirt as she crossed her long legs.

"I'm sorry, Mom." Peyton stood, crossing to the glass-and-sterling-silver coffee table in the middle of the room. "I'm just wondering what Bruce hopes to accomplish with this visit."

It was clear whose side her parents had taken. Their lack of support depressed her. Peyton served the bowls of pumpkin pie and vanilla ice cream.

"I would have thought my motive was clear."
Bruce tried a debonair smile as he took the spoon
and bowl of pie and ice cream from her. "I'm here
to win you back."

He looked so sincere, gazing deeply into her
eyes. She would have fallen for his act—if she hadn't
known him.

Peyton gave him a wide-eyed look. "Is that all right
with Leila?"

Bruce's pretty face stiffened. "What does Leila
have to do with us, honey?"

"She was with you in your office the evening I
called to break off our engagement, remember?"
She served her mother the pumpkin pie à la mode.

"We were working." Bruce's dark brown eyes appeared confused.

Peyton laughed without humor. She was strong
and in control as she never had been before. "Don't
insult my intelligence."

"Why does it matter whether his secretary was in
his office?" Irene gestured toward Peyton with her
dessert bowl.

"Leila wasn't working *with* him. She was working
on him." Peyton gave her father one of the two remaining desserts, then returned to her armchair
with the last bowl.

"What does that mean?" Carlson added pie and
ice cream to his fork.

Peyton studied the suddenly speechless Bruce.
Was that fear she saw in his eyes? It should be. "His
devoted secretary was giving him oral sex while he
was speaking with me—"

Bruce's soft features darkened. His laughter was
forced. "That's absurd."

"That's disgusting!" Irene's sharp tone denounced her.

"That's ridiculous." Carlson's growl condemned her.

Peyton heard again the rustling sounds as Bruce squirmed in his chair. She recalled his breath panting and hitching into the phone.

"I heard the two of you whispering on the other end of the line." Peyton wasn't certain from where her words came; months of frustration boiled over. "You were moaning as she sucked you to completion."

"Peyton!" Irene's blush rivaled her ruby sweater.

"I don't have to listen to these accusations." Bruce's voice shook.

Peyton arched a brow. "If you stay here, you do."

"Peyton." Carlson tried a reasonable tone. "You don't have any reason to be suspicious of Bruce. I'm in the office with him sometimes six days a week. I've never noticed any romantic gestures between him and his secretary."

"Their affair isn't the kind of thing they'd publicize in front of you." Peyton glanced at her father.

"Is that the reason you ended our engagement? You think I'm having an affair? With Leila?" Bruce gave a scornful laugh.

"No." Peyton returned her dessert to the tray on the coffee table. "I broke our engagement because I don't love you. But one of the reasons I don't love you is that you're a cheating dog."

"Honey, how can you say that?" Bruce stood, spreading his arms. "Yes, Leila is a very beautiful woman, but I proposed to *you*. I love *you*."

"You see, Peyton?" Irene pressed her hand against her chest as though preparing to swoon. "How can you doubt his love?"

"Easily." Peyton turned away from her mother and back to Bruce.

"Do you have any evidence to back up your suspicions?" Carlson sounded impatient.

So was she. "Do you mean like videos, photos, or panties in his condo? No."

"Then what makes you think Bruce is a cheater?" Her mother sounded confused.

"Why don't you tell them, Bruce?" Peyton returned her ex-fiancé's stare.

"Tell them what?" His mendacious eyes were wide pools of innocence. "Honey, you're starting to sound crazy."

"I was crazy before. Now I'm thinking straight." Peyton pulled the ring box from her pocket and crossed to Bruce. Taking his hand, she placed the box in his palm and wrapped his fingers around it. "I'll decide who I'm going to marry. And I've decided it won't be you."

Peyton strode from the salon and made her way to her old bedroom. It had become her parents' guest room when she'd moved out years before. She'd never felt so empowered. She was in charge now. She would live where she wanted to live, be who she wanted to be, love who she wanted to love. She couldn't wait to return to Trinity Falls—and Darius.

Thanksgiving evening, Darius straightened his shoulders as the front door of Doreen Fever's country-style home opened.

"You look like shit." Ean stood on the other side of the door, concern in his olive eyes.

"Thanks." Darius crossed the threshold as Ean

stepped back, opening the door wider. In contrast to the brisk chill outside, the Fever home was comfortably warm.

Excited conversations and laughter almost drowned out the sound of the football game being played on television sets in various rooms around the house. Straight ahead, Darius recognized the neighbors gathered in Doreen's living room. They exchanged smiles and nods as he waited for Ean to close and lock his mother's front door. For years, the Fever family's open house was a popular way to spend Thanksgiving evening. It offered great company and even better desserts.

"It was that bad?" After putting away Darius's coat, Ean led him farther into the home Darius knew as well as his own. Their lifelong friendship allowed the men to converse in comfortable shorthand.

"I should have gone to Florida with Quincy and Ramona to spend Thanksgiving with Q's parents." Darius nodded at a few more people as he wound his way toward Doreen's kitchen. The air was rich with the scent of confectioners' sugar, chocolate, cinnamon, and other spices. "He sent me a text this afternoon."

"I got one, too." Ean spoke over his shoulder. "I wonder how he's adjusting to Philadelphia. He didn't seem that happy when he came home last week for Dr. Hartford's retirement banquet."

Darius followed Ean into the kitchen. "I'm concerned about him."

"Quincy will be just fine." Doreen stepped forward, offering Darius a plate with a healthy chunk of her famous Trinity Falls Fudge Walnut Brownie.

"Doreen, you're a saint." Darius took the plate

and fork his friend's mother handed him. Then he crossed to Ms. Helen seated at the kitchen table in a bulky green sweater and pale brown slacks. He kissed the elder's cheek. "Happy Thanksgiving, Ms. Helen."

"It's good you came, Darius." She squeezed his shoulder.

"It was bad?" Doreen's brow knitted with concern.

Darius looked from Doreen to Alonzo beside her. Ean stood with Megan. Like her son, Doreen was referring to Darius's first Thanksgiving with his separated parents. He had nothing to give them.

Darius sliced into the moist, soft pastry Doreen had served him. "Your brownie will make everything right again. You should offer the recipe to the U.S. State Department. It could bring about world peace."

"All right, all right. I'll let you change the subject." Doreen shook her head with indulgent amusement. "I'm just glad you're here. I was afraid you wouldn't make it."

"Wherever your desserts are, I won't be far behind." Darius swallowed a bite of brownie, letting the chocolate and sugar improve his mood.

Alonzo chuckled. "Thanks for the warning."

The front doorbell rang again. Doreen and Alonzo excused themselves to answer it.

Megan hooked her arm through Ean's and met Darius's eyes. "The open house wouldn't be the same without you."

Ean grunted. "Except there'd be more pastries for everyone else."

Darius gave Ean a grateful look for his attempt at humor, then addressed Megan. "How's your first Thanksgiving without Ramona?"

Megan's smile was warm. "It's a little strange. But she's happy and I'm thrilled for her. She keeps saying she can't wait to join Quincy in Philadelphia."

Ramona had sounded a little too enthusiastic when she'd made the comment during Dr. Hartford's banquet. Had she been trying to convince herself or everyone else?

Darius sliced into his brownie again. "Is she nervous? This is the first time she's visiting Quincy's family as his girlfriend."

"She'll be fine." Megan chuckled. "I gave her a pep talk."

Darius raised his eyebrows. "What did you—"

"Darius." Doreen interrupted them as she and Alonzo rejoined the group. "Look who's joined us."

At the last minute, Darius remembered to hold on to the paper plate that carried his brownie. His wide-eyed gaze locked with Ethel's. "Mom, what are you doing here?"

Ethel surveyed the dining room. "I've heard of Doreen's Thanksgiving open houses for years. I thought I'd come by and see what all the fuss was about." Her expression made it clear she still didn't understand why people made a big deal of the event.

Doreen's smile was gracious. "You're always welcome, Ethel."

"Could you excuse us for a moment?" Darius took Ethel's arm to escort his mother from the kitchen to the relatively empty dining room. "What are you doing?"

Ethel jerked her arm from his hold. "Why did you haul me out of the room like a sack of potatoes?"

"Doreen has hosted these dessert parties for decades. Why did you choose this year to come?"

"Everyone else in town is here." Ethel waved an arm to encompass the few people in the dining room. "Why shouldn't *I* be here, too?"

The doorbell rang again, underscoring Ethel's point about the number of guests who attend Doreen's get-together. It also reminded him that he was missing the football games.

"All right, Mom." Darius forced his shoulders to relax. "Just please don't disrespect Doreen in her own house."

Ethel raised her chin. "I would *never* do such a thing."

Darius gave her a dubious look. He started to respond when he sensed someone beside him.

"The whole family's here." Simon's voice boomed with good cheer.

Darius' shoulders dropped as he turned to face his father. Maybe his parents thought meeting here was a great idea, but he couldn't think of anything worse. In the past, he'd used Doreen's event to escape from his family. Tonight, there was no escape.

"*Family*? What family?" At least Ethel kept her reply to a low hiss.

"Do we have to do this here and now?" Darius felt the familiar heat of embarrassment rising in his face. He was afraid to look around to see who else in the dining room was aware of the latest Knight Family Flare-up.

"This isn't *my* doing." Ethel defended herself to Darius, even as her glare held Simon in place.

"I'm always the one at fault. Is that it?" Simon shot back.

"That's *right*." Ethel wouldn't give an inch.

The front doorbell rang again. The crowd was

large and growing larger. Who else would be exposed to the Knight Family Feud?

"Why don't the two of you separate?" Darius placed a hand on each parent's shoulder. "Doreen has opened plenty of other rooms to her guests."

"Why do I have to leave?" they asked in unison.

If they didn't have an audience before, they had one now. Darius dropped his hands, fisting them at his sides. If one of them didn't move to another room, he'd drag both of them from Doreen's home. He didn't care how much attention that spectacle would garner.

"I don't care which one of you goes to another room," Darius said through clenched teeth. "But you can't both stay here, not if you're going to snipe at each other all evening."

Tense seconds that felt like minutes ticked by as Ethel and Simon locked gazes.

Finally, Simon looked away. "I'll move to the family room. There's a TV in there anyway. I can watch the game."

Crisis averted. Darius was almost weak with relief. "I'll be there in a few minutes."

Ethel gasped. "You're going to leave me by *myself* and go off with your *father*? *Typical.*"

Darius frowned. "You came by yourself."

"That doesn't mean I want to *stay* by myself."

"Then mingle, Mom. I'm going to watch what's left of the game." Darius headed back to the kitchen and his friends.

"Everything OK?" Megan asked Darius.

"Yes. What did I miss?" Darius reclaimed his brownie.

Despite Megan, Ean, Ms. Helen, and Alonzo's

obvious concern, they once again allowed Darius to change the subject.

"You didn't miss much, although Doreen's been gone a little longer than usual." Alonzo frowned in the direction of the front door.

Darius finished his brownie and nudged Ean. "Let's go see what's taking your mother so long."

Alonzo led Darius, Megan, and Ean out of the kitchen and across the living room toward the front door. The heavy, cool breeze rushing down the hallway toward them indicated the entrance was still open. Darius's curiosity spiked. Muffled voices floated toward him.

"Nessa, you're welcome to come in and enjoy some refreshments. But I won't allow you to insult me in my own home." This was Doreen's voice.

Without speaking, the group picked up their pace.

"Is something wrong?" Alonzo stopped beside Doreen in the front doorway.

Nessa surveyed the sheriff. "Alonzo, are you hosting this get-together with Doreen?"

"Doreen doesn't need much help." Alonzo had his game face on, making his thoughts difficult to read.

"Just like a married couple." Nessa pursed her lips. "But without the benefit of the blessing. Are there plans to make this little setup official?"

Darius felt the sting of the councilwoman's words as though they were directed at him. "Why are you in such a rush to get them married, Nessa?"

"Who left the door open?" Ms. Helen's querulous question preceded the older woman's approach. She made a place for herself between Darius and Alonzo. "Nessa? What are you doing here?"

"I'd hoped to share some fellowship with my

neighbors." Nessa folded her hands over the brown purse hanging from her left shoulder.

"Fellowship?" Ms. Helen gave a soft chuckle. "I know what you're doing, Nessa."

"I beg your pardon?" Nessa gave the older woman a pious look.

Ms. Helen's expression hardened. "This is a friendly gathering. You're not welcome to bring your poison here."

"I don't know what you're talking about." Nessa gaped.

"No?" Ms. Helen nudged Doreen's hand from the doorknob. "Go home and pray on it. It'll come to you." Ms. Helen closed the door in Nessa's face, then secured the lock.

Darius ended the stunned silence. "Ms. Helen, why did you do that?"

Ms. Helen shrugged. "Somebody had to make a decision. Doreen was letting all the heat out."

Doreen gestured toward the closed door. "I was trying to handle Nessa diplomatically. I have to work with her when I take office in January."

"Blame it on me, dear." Ms. Helen patted Doreen's back. "But someone had to save you from yourself."

Darius offered Ms. Helen his left arm. "There's never a dull moment with you. Let's get you into the kitchen. It's warmer in there."

"This isn't funny." Doreen walked with them. "Slamming my door in Nessa's face isn't going to improve my relationship with her."

Darius swallowed an inappropriate laugh. To have seen the look on Nessa's face . . .

"Ms. Helen's right. Nessa wasn't here for fellowship." Darius escorted Ms. Helen to the kitchen table. "But we do need to know what she's up to."

Doreen crossed to the oven. "I've been racking my brain, but I can't think of a thing."

"We'll all have to keep thinking about it." Ms. Helen released Darius's arm as she sank onto one of the blond wood chairs at the matching kitchen table. "Meanwhile, when are you and Peyton going to stop wasting time and start working on the fund-raiser for the community center?"

"As soon as she returns from New York." Darius leaned his hip against the yellow-and-white marble kitchen counter.

Ms. Helen nodded her satisfaction. "Good. It took you two long enough."

Darius frowned. The twinkle in his elderly friend's eyes made him uneasy. "Ms. Helen, are you the one behind the town's matchmaking schemes?"

"Don't you think I have better things to do?" Which wasn't exactly an answer.

God save him from well-meaning friends. Judging by their self-satisfied expressions, you'd think working together on the fund-raiser put Peyton and him one step from the altar.

But it wasn't the fund-raising committee that scared him. It was the physical attraction that intensified each time he saw the little professor that had him questioning his decision to cochair the committee.

Would he be able to resist her? Did he really want to?

CHAPTER 15

Alonzo studied the shadows moving across his bedroom ceiling Friday night. He'd spent so many years dreaming of having Doreen in his bed, her naked body pressed to his. Even after five months, he still couldn't believe his dream had come true.

He tightened his embrace, drawing her even closer to his side. Her firm, slender limbs were sprawled across his in the aftermath of their love-making. Her breaths were soft against his chest. Alonzo turned his head and placed a kiss on her hair. It was like silk beneath his lips. She smelled like spring flowers.

"Am I dreaming?" His pulse had returned to normal as his body cooled. But now his heart was racing again. Nerves.

"Maybe we both are." She whispered back with a smile in her voice.

Why was he so anxious? In his law enforcement career, he'd confronted armed sociopaths without a qualm. But the idea of asking the love of his life to marry him filled him with panic. He feared her rejection more than a bullet.

"Doreen, I'm going to retire next December, at the end of my term." That had sounded more romantic in his mind.

Doreen untangled her limbs from his and leaned back to look up at him. "Are you sure that's what you want to do?"

"I can afford to retire now." He met her dark eyes in the shadows. "I'm not rich, but I have money saved and good investments. I can afford to take care of myself. And someone else."

"You don't think you'll get bored?"

"Not with you." He stroked her knitted eyebrows with the pads of his left fingers, coaxing her to relax. "Besides, this will give me more time to volunteer for community projects. And you can teach me how to run the cash register so I can help fill in for you when you need to take care of your mayoral duties."

Doreen smiled. "You'd do that for me?"

"Of course." Alonzo frowned at the surprise in her voice. "We're partners, remember? In my entire life, I've never been happier than when I'm with you."

"You make me happy, too." Doreen cupped the side of his face with her small, soft hand.

Alonzo pressed a kiss into her palm. "I want to spend the rest of my life with you."

Doreen tensed within his embrace. "Alonzo—"

"Marry me, please, Doreen. You'd make me the happiest man on the planet if you'd agree to be my wife." Alonzo remained still, returning her gaze as Doreen searched his face.

"Is this about what Nessa said yesterday during our Thanksgiving open house?"

Out of all the scenarios he'd prepared for, that response wasn't among them. "Of course not."

Doreen wiggled free, tugging the bedsheets and blanket with her. She sat back against his headboard. "I'm not going to allow Nessa or anyone to pressure me into getting married."

It was as though she hadn't heard him. "I'm not pressuring you. I'm proposing."

"Marriage isn't something to be taken lightly."

"So I've heard." Alonzo pushed himself up to sit beside her. He was suddenly aware of the chill in the room.

"As much as I loved Paul, marriage is a lot of work."

"I'm sure it is."

Doreen gave him a hard stare. "Are you mocking me?"

"No, Doreen. I'm telling you that I love you and want to spend the rest of my life with you."

"But we don't have to be married to do that." Doreen clutched the sheet to her chest with one fist. "Forget Nessa. She's not the morality police."

"This isn't about Nessa." The pain in his chest was sharp, hot and deep, making it difficult to speak. "It's about you and me, and the fact that I've wanted to marry you for more than forty years."

"Alonzo, I don't know."

"What don't you know? Whether you love me? Whether you want to spend the rest of your life with me or whether you want to marry me?"

She looked stricken. "I care about you."

Oh no. Not the I-care-about-you speech.

"You said that to me forty years ago." Alonzo threw back the covers and marched to his closet. He grabbed his robe from one of the hooks and tugged it on. "I care about you, too, Doreen. I care so much that I want to be your husband. I want you to be my wife. What is it that you want?"

"I need time to think."

Time to think.

Was he rushing her? Doreen's husband of more than thirty years had died less than two years ago. Maybe he was being impatient.

"You're right." Alonzo belted his robe. He turned toward the door. "I'm sorry I rushed you."

"Where are you going?"

Alonzo spoke over his shoulder. "I need a glass of water."

More than that, he needed time to handle his disappointment. Doreen hadn't rejected him. She'd just put him on hold. But how much more time would she need to realize they were each other's happily-ever-after? What more could he do or say to convince her?

"Are you free for lunch, son?" Simon's voice came from behind Darius.

Surprised, he turned to face his father, who stood in the entrance to his cubicle at the *Monitor*'s office Monday morning. Darius's mind had been a million miles away. Well, not a million. The Guiding Light Community Center was only seven miles away. That's where Darius was meeting Peyton at eleven-thirty. After a tour of the center, they were having lunch at Books & Bakery.

"I'm afraid not. I have other plans." Darius stood and shrugged into his coat.

"Are you having lunch with your mother?" Simon sounded hopeful.

Darius rubbed his eyes with his thumb and two fingers. His parents' relationship had gone from bad to almost intolerable. He'd thought things would get better if they weren't together. He couldn't have been more wrong.

"I'm meeting Peyton for lunch. We're cochairing the committee to raise money for the community center." Darius buttoned his black wool topcoat. It was the first of December. Temperatures had nose-dived over Thanksgiving weekend.

"I didn't know you were cochairing a fund-raiser. How long have you been working on it?"

"This is our first meeting." Darius was uncomfortable with Simon's sudden interest in his life after thirty-four years.

"Oh." Simon stepped farther into the cubicle. "Well, how many people are in the group?"

"We haven't asked for volunteers yet." Darius had a sense of foreboding.

"I'd be happy to help." Simon rocked on his heels as though he'd solved all of Darius's problems. His father didn't seem to realize he was one of them.

"You've never served on a committee before." In fact, his father had never volunteered for anything.

"There's a first time for everything, son."

"We need people who are willing to work hard. This fund-raiser needs to move fast. We want to raise a lot of money in a short amount of time."

"Then I'm your man."

Somehow Darius had a hard time believing that.

"This is strictly a volunteer assignment. No one's getting paid."

"I know."

Darius eyed the older man suspiciously. "Then why do you want to do this?"

Simon's gaze slid away from Darius and wandered around the office space. What was his father looking for? There wasn't anything of a personal nature in his cubicle: no certificates, awards, photos, or knick-knacks. Just a bunch of project folders, reference books, two coffee mugs, and a guest chair he'd pilfered from an empty cubicle. Darius didn't know why he'd made the decision to keep his cubicle impersonal. He just preferred it that way.

His father faced him again. "I'm bored."

"Then clean your apartment."

"I did."

"I'm glad." And very, very surprised.

"I got caught up with all my bills. I even went grocery shopping." Simon made a face. "I'm not looking forward to doing that again."

Darius paused. "Have you ever gone to the grocery store before?"

Simon shoved his hands into the front pockets of his gray winter coat. He jiggled the coins he kept in there. "About thirty-four years ago."

Darius shouldn't have been surprised. Growing up, he'd known who was in charge of the Knight family household, and it hadn't been his father. Ethel must have felt as though she were a single mother with two children instead of a married woman raising a son with the help of another responsible adult.

He checked his watch. "I'd better get going."

Simon held up a hand. "What about my helping with the fund-raiser?"

How could he get out of this? "Peyton and I need to put together a group of people with various skills. How much experience do you have working with a project team?"

"Are you kidding?" Simon raised his brows. "I had a lot of coworkers when I worked for the post office. I know how to work with other people."

How well had he worked with those people? Darius remembered his father coming home, complaining nonstop about everyone, from supervisors to customers.

"What skills would you bring to this fund-raiser?"

Simon cocked his head. "Are you interviewing me for a job? I'm your father. Put me on the committee."

"It doesn't work that way."

"It should."

Darius checked his Timex again. He was going to be late. "I'm sorry you're bored. But there are other things you can do." *Things that don't involve me.*

"Like what?"

"I don't know." Darius shrugged, spreading his arms wide. "Get a part-time job. Take up a hobby."

"I want to work on the fund-raiser."

"Why?"

"You said I never got to know my family, that I was just a boarder in the house with you and your mother. I spent a lot of time this weekend thinking over what you said. I want a chance to correct that. This would give me that opportunity."

Trapped by his own words. But was Simon sincere about making amends for past mistakes?

"All right." Darius took a leap of faith. "You can be on the committee."

With luck, he wouldn't regret this decision.

Darius found Peyton sitting with Ms. Helen in the Guiding Light Community Center lobby. Her expression was warm and relaxed as she laughed at something the older woman had said. His heart squeezed.

She looked cool and professional in an orange sweater and dark green slacks. Minimal makeup accented her high cheekbones and her caramel eyes. Her mass of bright copper curls framed her heart-shaped face.

Peyton smiled as he approached. "Hi."

"Sorry I'm late." Darius kissed Ms. Helen's cheek, then offered his arm to assist her to her feet.

He turned to Peyton. Should he kiss her, too? Perhaps not yet, not here. Their last night together came back in heated detail. Darius pushed his fists into the pockets of his black winter coat.

"I've only just arrived myself." Peyton stood.

"We've been getting to know each other better." Ms. Helen smiled at Peyton. "But in the interest of time, we should get started on the tour." She led them across the lobby. "The first thing you should know about the center is that it opened January tenth, 1975."

Darius and Peyton followed Ms. Helen into the activity room. Darius had been eighteen the last time he'd been in the center. Over the past sixteen years, the facilities had grown worn and much worse for wear. But otherwise the center was clean and cared for, and seemed more or less the same.

The large, rectangular activity room was the size of a ballroom but resembled a high school gym. Darius, Ean, Quincy, Jackson, and Vaughn used to play basketball here in the winter. The hardwood floor gleamed. The air was bloated with wood polish and antiseptic. At the front end of the room, four basketball hoops were suspended from the ceiling. Bins full of basketballs and volleyballs lined the near wall. Across the room were Ping-Pong and gaming tables as well as exercise equipment.

Peyton led them along the perimeter, pausing occasionally to skim the bulletin boards, check the locked supply cabinets, and test the water fountains. "What did the town do before the community center was built?"

Ms. Helen took them across the activity room to an exit door on the other side. "What most communities do—we relied on our churches and schools for our programs. But as Trinity Falls grew, the community had greater needs."

"Such as what?" Peyton smiled her thanks as Darius held the door open for her and Ms. Helen to precede him into the study hall.

"Reemployment training." Ms. Helen stopped in the middle of the study hall.

Darius stood beside Peyton. "The center allowed the town to provide technology training for adults and students. It also provides an opportunity for youth sports and senior programming."

"And health and wellness programs for all ages," Ms. Helen added.

Peyton adjusted her bag on her shoulder. "The

center is even more critical to the community than I originally thought."

Considering he'd directly benefited from the center, Darius regretted that he hadn't paid more attention to its needs. He'd rectify that in the future, starting with his participation in the fund-raiser.

Ms. Helen concluded the tour by introducing Peyton and Darius to the center's director and some of its volunteers. They were thrilled about the fund-raiser and anxious to help in any way they could.

Darius followed Peyton and Ms. Helen back to the lobby. He turned to Ms. Helen. "Are you sure you won't join us for lunch at Books and Bakery?"

Ms. Helen looked from him to Peyton and back. Her brown eyes twinkled. "I'm having lunch with some friends here at the center. You two go and enjoy yourselves."

Darius kissed the elderly lady's cheek. "I'll see you later."

About thirty minutes later, Darius and Peyton were seated at a table at Books & Bakery after ordering chicken soups and turkey with provolone sandwiches. Darius had ignored the knowing looks from Doreen, Ean, Megan, and Ramona.

"I had an idea for the fund-raiser while Ms. Helen was giving us a tour of the center." Peyton dug into her soup.

"What?" Darius drank his iced tea.

"A birthday party and dance." Peyton beamed at him. "January tenth, the day the center opened, is a Saturday in 2015, too. We should host the fund-raiser then."

Darius considered her announcement as he ate

his soup. "That's only five weeks away. Does it give us enough time?"

Her small body seemed to vibrate with enthusiasm. "We can make this work."

"We could ask the center's director to let us host the dance in their activity room. It's large enough. And that way people can see where their donations are going."

"That's brilliant." Peyton clapped her hands together. "We'll charge an entry fee, which would include dinner. All proceeds will go to the community center."

Discussions of what they would need, what it would cost, and potential event sponsors carried them through their meal.

Peyton pulled her electronic tablet from her purse. "We need to pick committee members."

Darius took a deep drink of iced tea. The cool bite of it helped with what he was about to say. "My father volunteered for the committee. I'm sorry. I should have talked with you first. But he asked me as I was on my way to meet you."

"I think it's great that your father's on the committee." Peyton reached across the table, covering his hand with one of hers. Her touch sent a jolt through Darius, making him lose his train of thought. "My mother and I have volunteered together on a lot of committees. Those are some of my favorite memories."

Somehow, Darius didn't think he'd have a similar experience with Simon. "How many other people should we get for the committee?"

Peyton gave that some thought. "Five. With you, me, and your father, that will give us eight members.

If we need additional volunteers, they could help outside of the formal committee."

"Good point." Darius wrote in his reporter's notebook. "I'll come up with some more names."

"I want to make sure the university is represented on the committee." Peyton typed into her tablet. "We're Trinity Falls residents, too. We should be involved in the center's fund-raiser. I'll ask two other professors to participate."

Her words put a damper on his mood. "Are you going to ask Vaughn?"

"That's a great idea." Peyton did more typing.

Darius's grip on his pen tightened. She'd misunderstood him. "Is there something going on between the two of you?"

Peyton blinked her surprise. "You and I had something before Thanksgiving break. How many 'somethings' do you think I could have at one time?"

"You've spent a lot of time with him."

"Are you jealous?" Peyton's eyes widened with disbelief.

"Yes."

Peyton's honey-and-chocolate-milk complexion took on a rosy hue. She blinked again, then a slow smile stretched her full lips.

"Wow." She returned her attention to her tablet. "Should we invite your mother to join the committee? She might feel left out if your father's on it and she's not."

Why was she changing the subject? "So there's nothing going on between you and Vaughn, right? I just need some clarification."

"No, there's not." Peyton put her elbow on the table and set her chin in her palm. She gave him a look that scorched him. "Is there something between us?"

"I'd like there to be."

"We'll see." She went back to her tablet. "What about your mother being on the committee?"

We'll see? Was she flirting with him or just messing with his mind?

"That wouldn't be a good idea." An understatement.

"Are you sure? It could give your family an opportunity to get closer."

"No, it wouldn't." Having his parents volunteer on the same committee he was cochairing wasn't a bonding opportunity. It was a recipe for disaster, one he didn't want Peyton to witness.

"Why did you ask your father to be on your committee and not *me*?" Ethel stood framed in Darius's cubicle in the *Monitor*'s offices later that afternoon. Her hands were fisted on her hips. Her eyes blazed betrayal.

His mother's short, sharp question jerked Darius from the news story he was trying to file before his deadline. He rose to his feet. How had she found out?

The lightbulb came on. "Dad told you."

"He came to the house, looking for a *meal*." Ethel's thick, brown, wool winter coat was buttoned to her neck and masked her figure. A black knit hat pulled low on her head covered her hair.

Darius frowned. "You two had lunch?"

"Don't change the subject. Why did you ask your father to help you, but you didn't come to *me*?"

"Let's find a meeting room." Darius maneuvered around his mother and started down the aisle. He ignored the curious stares of coworkers as he led his mother to a vacant meeting room. Now that his parents were separated, they spent almost as much time at the *Monitor* as he did. How could he make this stop?

The first room he came to was available. Darius opened the door and motioned for his mother to precede him. "Have a seat."

"*Why* should I sit down?"

"Because I'm going to sit and I won't speak with you standing over me." Ms. Helen had taught him better manners than that.

"Fine." Ethel pulled off her hat, fluffed her hair, then took off her coat before settling onto the chair.

"Dad asked to be on the committee." Darius took the seat across from her. His answer wouldn't be good enough for Ethel. He checked his watch. He could give her ten minutes before he had to get back to his article.

"You told *him* that you were cochairing a fund-raising committee but kept that information from *me?*"

"Why would I tell you?" The Knight family didn't have the kind of relationship in which they shared everything with each other. Ethel knew that as well as he did.

The meeting room was small and sparse: a honey wood circular conference table, matching corner stand with a black conference phone, four black-leather-and-silver metal chairs, and a whiteboard affixed to the far plaster wall. Through the room's remaining two glass walls, Darius saw several curious coworkers looking his way. Opal Gutierrez, the rookie reporter, walked by twice, slowing down to observe them each time.

"Men *always* stick together," Ethel sneered.

"What does that mean?" Darius returned his attention to his mother.

"You're taking your *father's* side." Ethel stabbed a finger at him. "You were always closer to him than you were to me."

What a load of nonsense. Darius checked the time. "What do you want, Mom?"

"*Why* do you keep looking at your watch?" Her tone was waspish.

"I need to get back to work. Just tell me what you want."

"Did you rush your *father* when he was here earlier?"

Were they really doing this? "Mom—"

"I bet you didn't. I bet you gave him *all* the time in the world." Ethel leaned back onto her seat, crossing her arms and legs. "That's what I want. I want you to give me the same time and attention you give Simon."

Darius stood. He kept his expression carefully blank so his coworkers wouldn't be aware of the temper building within him. "I don't have time to indulge you. As I explained, I'm on deadline." Without another word, Darius turned toward the door.

"*Wait.*" Ethel's response shot across the small room.

Darius didn't want to wait. He wanted to walk through the door, return to his cubicle, and lose himself in work. He was thirty-four years old. He didn't want to be the rope in his parents' tug-of-war anymore.

"What is it?" He spoke over his shoulder.

"I want to be on the committee, too."

Darius briefly closed his eyes, praying for patience. "Why?"

"Your father's on it. It's not fair to exclude *me*."

Darius faced her. "This committee is not the place for you and Dad to work out your marital problems."

"You care more about your *father* than you do about me. You're not even thinking about me."

Darius rubbed his eyes. "Guilt has never worked on me."

"Please, Darius. I need to do something. I'm going crazy in that house by myself."

Peyton had been right—and he'd never been more unhappy. "All right. But the first time you and Dad argue during a meeting, you're both out."

Ethel's features brightened. Her eyes shone. Darius blinked at her transformation. He wasn't used to seeing her happy.

"Just make sure you tell your father that." She rose from her chair and crossed to him. His mother put a hand on his shoulder. Beneath her palm, his muscles bunched.

Still surprised by her smile and her touch, Darius couldn't form a response. In silence, he followed his mother from the room. He once again ignored his coworkers' curiosity as he escorted Ethel down the hall.

"When is the committee meeting?" Ethel buttoned her coat and tugged on her hat.

"We haven't scheduled one yet. I'll contact you

when we have the information." Darius stopped in front of his cubicle.

"All right. Good luck with your deadline." Ethel patted his shoulder again, then disappeared.

What had just happened? Darius sat at his desk. Ms. Helen had advised him to help his parents find a way to forgive each other. Maybe having them serve on the committee was his Trinity Falls miracle. Was it possible this fund-raiser for the community center would help his family? But at what cost?

CHAPTER 16

Darius found himself knocking on Peyton's door Monday evening. It wasn't a conscious decision to come here. His car had just pointed itself in this direction and taken him to Peyton's apartment.

"What's wrong?" She opened the door, stepping back to let him in.

She'd freed her hair from its constricting bun. The thick, curly waves vibrated around her heart-shaped face. Her blue-and-white Heritage High School sweatshirt was baggy on her small frame in contrast to her navy yoga pants.

"Why do you think something's wrong?" Darius watched as Peyton closed and locked her front door.

"Well, first, you're here." Her eyes sparkled at him as she reached for his coat.

Darius stripped off his black topcoat and handed it to her. "Thank you."

"Make yourself comfortable." She gestured toward

her furniture as she disappeared through a door off the living room.

Darius's wandering gaze found a small Christmas tree on a circular table beside her entertainment center. He nodded toward it when she returned without his coat. "When did you put that up?"

"Sunday night."

"Why did you get it?"

Peyton looked up in surprise. "It's Christmas." She gestured for him to sit on the sofa.

"But it's so small. And it's not even real." Darius lowered himself onto the right corner of the couch.

"You don't have a tree, do you?"

"Why bother?" Darius was uncomfortable under her amused regard.

Peyton settled onto the other end of her silver couch. "Why don't you stop bashing my tree and tell me why you're here?"

Her apartment smelled of cinnamon. Her matching sofa, love seat, and armchair were a pale silver with soft overstuffed cushions. The coffee table was made of glass in a sterling-silver frame. The cool, modern effect contrasted with Peyton's warm, traditional personality. It was at odds with the woman who'd decorate her elegant home with a plastic, wannabe Christmas tree. Who was she trying to be?

"I told my mother she could be on the fund-raising committee." Darius studied the little tree. Its fake branches were full of pretend apples and a few real candy canes, tinsel, and lights.

"I'm glad."

"I'm not. With both of my parents on the committee, I've just made this project more difficult. I'm sorry."

"Just make it clear to them that we don't have time for personal conflicts on the committee."

"I wish it was that easy."

Peyton searched his features as though she could read his mind. "What's really bothering you about your parents working on the fund-raiser?"

Darius wanted to ignore Peyton's question, but her gaze insisted on a response. "They've never volunteered for anything. They don't have any fund-raising experience."

"That's my role."

"Their antagonism toward each other will disrupt our meetings."

"We won't let it." She was boxing him in, dismissing his reasons as though they weren't perfectly rational arguments.

"You don't understand. Some people like to read. My parents' hobby is arguing, especially with each other." He tried to say it as a joke. It didn't come out that way. Darius shot off of Peyton's sofa and strode to her toy tree. "I'm not my parents."

"I know."

"I don't want to be compared to them." Darius glared at the decorations.

"No one's doing that."

"I've seen it. Every time my parents argue, people look at them and then me. They're thinking the apple doesn't fall far from the tree." Darius touched one of the fake red apples hanging from a plastic branch.

"You're nothing like your parents, Darius."

"Aren't I?" Darius shoved his fists into the front pockets of his black Dockers.

"Everyone has a complex about their parents.

We're afraid we're like them. We're afraid we're nothing like them. We have to realize we're our own people."

Darius sensed there was something more in her words. "You sound like you've given this a lot of thought."

"You think you're the only one with difficult parents?" Peyton shifted on the sofa to face him.

Darius took in Peyton's abundance of brown curls, serious caramel eyes, full red lips and stubborn honey-and-chocolate chin. "Are you afraid you're like your parents or that you're not?"

"Neither of the above." Peyton's shoulders rose and fell on a deep breath. "I used to be afraid I wasn't good enough."

Darius frowned. "Good enough for what?"

"Not what." Peyton shrugged. "I didn't think I was good enough for them."

"That's crazy." Darius returned to sit beside her on the sofa. He raised his right hand to cup her cheek. Her skin was soft and warm against his palm. Her scent, talcum powder and lily of the valley, reached out to him. It stirred memories of being locked in the archives with her, of her Catwoman costume—of her.

"What's crazy?" Peyton's voice was hushed. Her eyes mesmerized him.

"You're more than good enough for anyone." An invisible force drew him nearer to her. Just a taste.

Darius touched his mouth to Peyton's. His muscles went lax at the feel of her soft, moist lips. Peyton sighed, parting her lips and letting him in. Darius's muscles shook at the sensation. Warm, wet, sweet. His tongue swept inside, seeking her secrets. Her tongue reached out to meet his in a suggestive dance. She stroked him. He caressed her. She teased and tasted him. He embraced her.

Peyton's arms rose, caressing the muscles of his torso through his bronze sweater. Darius's heartbeat was heavy beneath her eager touch. His hands slid up her back. He pressed her warm, soft curves into his body, heating the chilled spaces.

Darius drew his hand up the side of Peyton's torso until his palm tested the weight of her breast through her blue sweatshirt. Peyton gasped and groaned deep in her throat. He drank in the sound. It affected him like alcohol in his blood. The pressure in his groin grew heavier, his caresses more urgent. But it was more than a physical reaction to the woman in his arms. It was emotional. This time he felt more than he'd ever felt before. He ached and burned. He needed and wanted.

Darius slipped his hand under Peyton's sweatshirt. His breath caught in his throat. The little professor wasn't wearing a bra.

Peyton gasped, breaking their kiss. Her nipple beaded, branding his palm. She arched her back, pressing her breast deeper into his hand. Darius bore the weight gladly. He kneaded her. Traced her curves with the back of his hand. Pinched her nipple with his fingertips.

"Your skin. So smooth. Soft. Hot." He spoke against her neck. Peyton shivered against him.

Darius wanted her closer. He lifted her onto his lap. Peyton straddled him, pressing her knees against his hips. Her movements were as urgent as his as she rocked her body against him. He licked his way up her neck, trailing his tongue against her skin.

He kissed her jawline, her cheek, the corner of her mouth.

"So sweet." He husked the words into her ear, loving the way she shivered against him.

Peyton groaned. "You're driving me crazy." She leaned forward and sunk her teeth against his shoulder through his knit sweater.

Darius's hips lifted between her thighs. "You're making me lose my mind."

Peyton chuckled into the curve of Darius's neck. She sat back on his lap. Reaching beneath his sweater, Peyton shoved the garment up and over his head, tossing it behind her. She leaned in, tracing her tongue in the groove between his pectorals.

"I've never felt this way before." She breathed against his damp skin.

His passion swelled. Darius gritted his teeth. "Neither have I."

Peyton sat up and stripped off her sweatshirt. Darius swallowed. Hard. He leaned forward and took her breast into his mouth. Peyton moaned.

He cupped her hips and stood. "Bedroom."

Peyton jerked her head over her shoulder and wrapped her legs around his waist. Darius followed her nonverbal direction. He carried her across the living room, down a short hallway to her bedroom.

This large, square space was more in keeping with the Peyton he was beginning to know—warm, colorful, and welcoming. Most importantly, there was a neatly made king-sized bed in the center of the room.

"Condom?" Peyton's voice was a breathless plea.

Darius released her beside him at the foot of the bed. He reached into the front pocket of his slacks and pulled out his wallet. He took a condom from a side compartment and laid it on the bed. "I didn't plan this."

"I'm not complaining." Peyton smiled.

They made quick work of the rest of their clothing. Slacks, yoga pants, underwear, socks, and shoes were strewn across the floor.

Darius drank in Peyton's nudity. Her figure was petite but powerful: narrow shoulders and full, firm breasts. Tiny waist, trim hips, and long, well-shaped legs. "You are so beautiful."

Peyton's body hummed. Already her senses were more heightened than they'd ever been in the act of lovemaking. She was damp and throbbing. Her skin was sensitive. With Darius, she felt like she was the only thing on his mind, the only woman in the world. Special and significant. The hunger in his midnight eyes filled her with confidence and a sense of power she'd never felt before.

She stepped forward, trailing her index finger from his chest to his hips. "Your body is art."

And it was. He was a flesh-and-blood Adonis. His broad, sculpted shoulders; six-pack abdominals; lean hips; long legs with powerful muscles. She must be dreaming. Her palms itched to touch him all over. She laid them flat on his chest, then dragged her hands down his body. She sank to her knees, drawing her hands to his thighs.

"Peyton." Darius choked on her name.

"Let me." She licked the length of his erection, then drew it deep into her mouth.

Darius cupped her shoulders. His fingers shook on her skin as he tried to lift her away from him. His voice was rough. "I want to come inside of you."

She wanted that as well. Peyton stood, walking into Darius's embrace. He lowered his head and kissed her hard. His mouth was demanding, making her even more anxious to feel him inside her. The ground shifted beneath her feet. When Peyton opened her eyes, she was lying on top of Darius, who was lying on her bed.

His heated gaze burned her. "Ride me."

Oh my.

Peyton had never been on top before. She was suddenly self-conscious. He'd be able to watch her. But then she could see him, too. And she would be in control. The idea had appeal. She found the condom he'd dropped onto the quilt.

She sat up, straddling Darius's lean hips. She scooted down to his thighs. Peyton opened the packet, then rolled the protection down the length of his erection. She loved the way he responded to her touch. "Are you ready for me?"

Darius's voice was husky. "Very."

She smiled into his heated gaze. "Just making sure."

She crawled back up his body, allowing her breasts to rub against his torso. Peyton rose up on her knees and positioned Darius at the opening to her core. She lowered herself onto his erection as Darius lifted his hips to slide inside her. He stretched and pressed her until her whole body was awash in pleasure. Her nipples tightened. Her core flooded with desire.

"So good." Darius pressed his head into her mattress.

"Mercy. You too." She leaned forward to kiss him. Darius caught her breasts in his hands. He stroked and caressed them, rubbing the nipples until she groaned. Moisture pooled in her. Her body heated. Her pulse raced. She sat back, riding Darius faster, squeezing him inside her harder. She arched her back, bracing her hands behind her on the mattress.

"Take what you want." His voice was a spell on her. Darius touched her spot, rubbing, pinching, patting her until her body quaked. "There?"

"Yes. Yes." The muscles in Peyton's thighs trembled. Her lower abdomen tightened. She rocked her hips against his finger even as his erection pushed deeper inside her. The pleasure was as sharp as pain. Her breath hitched in her throat. Her blood roared in her ears. Her heart pounded in her chest.

Darius grabbed her hips, pressing her against him and rising higher in her. "Let go. Just let go. I'm here. I'll catch you."

Peyton threw back her head as her body exploded. Wave after wave of pleasure rode over her, tossing her body in Darius's arms. And then she felt him coming. His hips lifted from the mattress. His fingers tightened on her thighs. They were suspended in time and space for seconds. Then they came crashing down.

Much later, Darius kissed Peyton's forehead before rolling onto his back. A chilled breeze came between them.

"Stay." Peyton turned toward him. Her voice was a whisper in the dark, half command, half plea.

Darius fought the urge to give in. "I don't have a change of clothes. I didn't plan this."

Peyton gave a throaty laugh. "Impulsiveness is sexy only to a point." She shifted, snuggling closer to his side.

Darius's body stirred. "I don't want people whispering about us. I don't want the matchmakers to know they were right."

"Were they?"

Darius waited for the fear to creep in. It didn't. He turned to face her. "What do you think?"

"I think you'd be more persuasive if you'd remembered to bring a change of clothing."

Darius laughed. "I'm sorry to disappoint you." He climbed from the bed and swiped his clothes from her floor.

"You didn't disappoint me." Her words were husky, filling his body with heat.

Darius had to leave before his good intentions went up in flames and he climbed back into her bed. He made quick work of dressing, though he was distracted when Peyton slipped out of bed and wrapped her sexy little figure into a pink cotton robe. Once they were clothed, Peyton led him to her front door. Darius stopped to get his sweater.

She paused with her hand on the doorknob. "Sleep well."

He touched his mouth gently to her kiss-swollen lips, then held her gaze. "You too."

Darius walked into the cold night. He waited for Peyton to lock her door. His body protested each step that carried him closer to his car and farther from Peyton's bed.

So this is what it was like to feel. He wasn't sure he enjoyed it.

**

Peyton followed the music rising from the front of the Trinity Falls University auditorium Tuesday morning. Her footsteps whispered against the red cement floor. But Vaughn probably wouldn't have heard a stampede of cattle charging the room. His piano bench was mere yards from her, but he seemed so far away.

She settled onto one of the second-row seats to enjoy his private performance. The haunting melody Vaughn lifted from the piano keys mesmerized her. The piece was sad and hopeful at the same time, heartbreaking and defiant. His mastery of the music was captivating. He should be giving concerts for millions. Why was he hidden in this small university auditorium, gifting his music to an audience of one?

The music ended. Peyton sighed, then stood to give her unwitting entertainer a standing ovation. "Encore! Encore!"

Vaughn looked as stunned as if he'd found himself naked in front of a classroom. "How long have you been here?"

"Not long." Peyton stepped out of the audience and approached the band director. "I couldn't imagine who was playing the piano at seven in the morning."

"I didn't think anyone would be here." Vaughn checked his watch.

"You're a very talented pianist. And it's a beautiful piece. What's it called?" Peyton leaned against the piano, facing Vaughn.

"'Untitled Opus Number Five.'" Vaughn closed the piano and stood.

"*You* wrote it?" Peyton's eyes widened.

Vaughn grinned down at her. "I do have a doctorate in music."

"I'm sorry. I didn't mean to offend you. It's just . . . it's beautiful." Peyton stammered her way through a lame apology.

"You didn't offend me. And thank you." Vaughn escorted her away from the piano and back up the auditorium's aisle.

Although Peyton's office was down the hall, she hadn't had many occasions to enter the auditorium, perhaps only twice, including the university's convocation at the beginning of the school year. It was a large room. Roughly six hundred mahogany chairs were separated into three sections and bolted to the red cement floor. Long, narrow Gothic windows were carved into the walls just below the ceiling. In the front of the room, a concert pit stretched between the groupings of folding chairs and the mahogany stage.

"You've written five pieces?" Peyton walked with Vaughn, grateful that he'd adjusted the strides of his much longer legs so she wouldn't have to run beside him.

"I've written more than that, but I've come up with names for most of them." Vaughn pushed his hands into the front pockets of his coffee-brown pants.

He had more pieces like those? "Does your concert band perform them?"

"No, people want to hear popular songs."

"You're wrong. People would love your work."

"Thank you." Vaughn's face darkened with a blush.

"What do you do with your music if your bands don't perform them?"

Vaughn smiled. "You ask almost as many questions as Darius."

"I'm sorry." Peyton's face heated with embarrassment, but she still wanted an answer to her question. She stared Vaughn down.

"I'm working on something." His words were barely audible.

"What is it?"

Vaughn stopped just inside the doors to the auditorium and faced her. "It's a musical. But not many people know and I'd rather not talk about it."

Peyton smiled. "I'm glad you're working on the musical. Thank you for telling me. I can't wait to attend your opening."

Vaughn rubbed the back of his neck. "I don't know if there'll be an opening."

"Make it happen. You're too talented for those songs to sit in a drawer."

"Thanks." Vaughn looked away again.

Peyton didn't mean to make him uncomfortable. He'd been so kind to her since her arrival at the university. She changed the subject. "I'm glad I found you. I wanted to ask if you'd be willing to serve on the fund-raising committee for the community center."

"I'd be honored. Thank you." Vaughn seemed relieved at the new topic. "Who else is on the committee?"

"I'm going to ask Olivia Stark." Peyton named the university's biology professor. "Darius's parents have volunteered. We're also going to ask Stan Crockett and CeCe Roben."

"*Both* of his parents?" Vaughn's brows rose toward his shaved head. "That should be interesting. I'm glad Darius is cochairing the committee with you."

Had she imagined the smugness in the music professor's response? "Vaughn, is Darius right about a matchmaking group?"

"Maybe you and Darius shouldn't spend so much time together." Vaughn started walking toward her office. "You're starting to sound as paranoid as he is."

"That doesn't mean we're wrong." Peyton fell into step beside him. "Are you a part of this group?"

Vaughn glanced down at her. "First, tell me if you're enjoying his company."

"I am." She enjoyed talking, debating, confiding in him. And last night's lovemaking had been a revelation.

"Isn't that all that matters?" This time, there was no mistaking the smugness in Vaughn's tone.

"You have a point." But what will she do when the town's most eligible bachelor loses interest in her?

Darius bounced his pencil's eraser on his desk as he waited for Peyton to answer her office phone. It was just after ten o'clock Tuesday morning. He hadn't stopped thinking about her since he'd woken up. He was still second-guessing his decision to leave her last night. Darius stared blankly at the document on his computer screen, too distracted to review the story notes.

"This is Dr. Harris. May I help you?"

Darius relaxed at the sound of her voice. It was strange and wonderful the effect she had on him. He pictured her sitting at the overly organized desk in her office. Was her hair pinned up? "Dr. Harris, this is Darius Knight. Are you free for lunch?"

"Are you asking me out on a date, Mr. Knight?" Her voice teased him.

"Don't you think it's about time?" Darius lowered his voice. Although he doubted anyone could hear his conversation above the usual shouts, ringing telephones, and clacking computer keyboards in the *Monitor*'s office.

"Yes, I do. But unfortunately, I have a class." She sounded disappointed. "Why don't you come to my place tonight and I'll make you dinner?"

It was Darius's turn to be disappointed. He smothered a groan at the missed opportunity. "I wish I could. I'm covering the town council meeting tonight."

"How late will it end?"

Darius skimmed the agenda he'd collected from the Trinity Falls Town Hall office on his way to work. It was long. "Pretty late. Then I'll need to come back to the office to file my story."

"Is it like that every week?" She sounded concerned.

Darius enjoyed the hint of caring in Peyton's question. "It's not as bad as it sounds."

"Can we have dinner tomorrow?" Peyton paused as though checking her calendar.

"I'd like that." Although he'd rather have breakfast with her.

"Great. We can talk about the fund-raiser."

Had they gotten their signals crossed? "That's not what I had in mind."

She laughed at his sarcasm. "Vaughn and Olivia agreed to be on our committee."

"So did Stan and CeCe."

"Wonderful. We have our eight members, which is excellent since we have less than five weeks to pull this off."

"Do you think we'll make it?" He didn't want to fail his first community fund-raising assignment.

"Failure is not an option," Peyton deadpanned the tagline from *Apollo 13*.

Darius chuckled. He was falling hard for the little professor. "I'll see you tomorrow."

He rang off. Wednesday couldn't come fast enough.

CHAPTER 17

Trinity Falls Cuisine was slow on Wednesday nights. Darius escorted Peyton into the fancy restaurant, confident his friends wouldn't be there to spy on him or make him uncomfortable.

"Good evening. Two?" The young hostess was probably a Trinity Falls University student. She seemed uncomfortable in her skinny black pants, starched white shirt, and narrow black tie.

"Yes, please." Darius rested his hand lightly on the small of Peyton's back. Her burgundy wool coat was soft beneath his palm, but he'd have preferred the warmth of her skin.

They followed the hostess farther into the restaurant. The scent of tangy spices and rich sauces hung heavy in the air. Lighting was low, lending the establishment a romantic ambience. But it wasn't so dim that Darius couldn't make out the beige-and-gray stone walls and dark wood trim. In his peripheral vision, he noticed the attention of the other diners, a few he recognized. They nodded, returning his gaze with open curiosity.

The hostess stopped beside a booth, waiting while Darius and Peyton settled in. "Your server will be right with you. Enjoy your evening." She handed each of them a menu, then disappeared after he and Peyton thanked her.

Darius studied the menu. The offerings included roasted chicken, wood-fired steak, rosemary salmon, and baked lemon tilapia. Darius' stomach growled.

"Sounds as though we got here just in time." Peyton chuckled.

"I guess so." Darius's grin was sheepish. "Anything look good to you?"

"Everything does." Peyton returned her attention to her menu. But Darius couldn't look away from her.

Peyton's copper curls bounced free tonight. He wanted to bury his fingers in its mass. Her honey-and-chocolate-cream complexion glowed against the warm gold of her cashmere sweater. Darius had committed to memory the way her straight black skirt traced her firm hips and slim thighs.

"You're so beautiful." He hadn't realized he'd spoken the words out loud until Peyton looked at him in surprise. She seemed uncomfortable with his compliment.

She smoothed her hair in a nervous gesture. "Thank you. So are you."

Darius's eyes widened in surprise. "No one's ever called me that before."

Peyton leaned into the table, lowering her voice. "Why do you think people stare at you everywhere you go?"

Darius tensed. They stared at him because he was Simon and Ethel Knight's son. But if Peyton wanted to believe it was because of his looks, he wouldn't correct her.

"Hi, I'm Agnes. I'll be your server tonight." The tall, slender college student suddenly appeared beside their booth. They looked younger and younger every year. "What can I get you to drink?"

Peyton glanced at Darius before answering. "May I have a glass of water with lemon?"

"I'll take an iced tea with lemon, please."

Agnes went to get their drinks.

Darius caught Peyton's gaze. "You're beautiful, kind, and intelligent. Why aren't you married?"

Peyton's gaze wavered only slightly. "I can ask you the same thing."

Yes, she could, but that wasn't a conversation Darius was ready to have.

He arched a brow. "Are you calling me beautiful, kind, and intelligent? Thank you."

Darius scanned his menu, deciding on the roasted chicken before setting it down and looking around the restaurant. Not many people were staring at them this time.

"There's something I've been meaning to ask you, but I don't want to pry." Peyton's admission made him both curious and cautious.

"What is it?" He searched her expression for a clue to her topic.

"From the discussion during the Books and Bakery Halloween celebration, I had the impression that Simon didn't introduce you to Noah. You searched for him."

"That's right."

"Why?"

Darius was taken aback by Peyton's question. When he'd first told his friends about Noah, whom he'd been visiting practically every weekend for the past six years, they'd wanted to know all about his brother and June, and why he'd never mentioned them before. His parents wanted to know why he'd destroyed their family by bringing Noah into their lives. No one had asked why he'd searched for his brother.

"I don't have an answer." Darius shrugged off his discomfort. "The rumors were all over town."

"That your father had another son?"

"Yes." He took a sip of his iced tea. "When I first heard that I might have a sibling, I wanted to know what his life was like. Was he being well cared for? Was he a good student? Did he like sports? Was he like me?"

"It sounds like you cared about him even before you met him." The admiration in Peyton's eyes made Darius squirm. "You're a good man, Darius."

"I just wanted to know." He shrugged again. "My father was too busy denying Noah's existence. So I tracked them down and found out for myself. That was six years ago."

"I'm glad you did." Peyton smiled. "Noah and June seem like wonderful people."

"They are." Darius sat back on the booth bench. "But I don't want to talk about myself."

"What do you want to talk about?"

"You."

Peyton met Darius's gaze. The look in his eyes was like a deep caress. She felt it to her core.

"Your water." Agnes reappeared. Her blond curls

shivered around her head. She served Peyton a glass of water, then gave Darius his iced tea. "Are you ready to order or do you need a few minutes?"

They both ordered the roasted chicken. Agnes again disappeared, leaving Peyton alone once more with Darius.

"So?" he prompted.

"What would you like to know?" Peyton searched his chiseled features.

"Why were you so opposed to my interviewing you for the *Monitor*?"

Peyton hesitated. Now that she'd returned from New York, his question was easier to answer. But what would he think of her? Would he consider her a coward? Because that's what she was.

She drank her water. "When I moved to Trinity Falls in July, my parents didn't know I wasn't returning to New York. I'd told them I was only staying for the fall semester."

The look of surprise on Darius's face would have been comical if Peyton wasn't so anxious for his reaction. "Why did you lie?"

She winced. "My parents' ambition for me was to become a full, tenured professor at New York University. But I was weary of the competition."

"Why didn't you just tell them that?" He sounded genuinely confused.

"That's what you would've done." Peyton recalled the Books & Bakery Halloween celebration. "I'm stunned by some of the things you've said to your parents. I wish I had the courage to say things like that to my parents, but I don't."

"What did your parents say when you told them you'd moved here?"

"They weren't happy."

"Did they try to change your mind?"

"Of course." Peyton could still hear their accusations. "They're used to getting their own way."

"Will they change your mind?"

Peyton held Darius's watchful gaze. "No, they won't."

"If they're used to having their own way—and you're used to giving it to them—what makes this time different?"

"I'm different." A whisper of a smile curved her lips. "I'm more confident. And that's because of this town and the people. Here, I feel accepted for who I am and who I want to be."

Darius studied her for a long, silent moment. What was he looking for? What was he thinking?

He lifted his glass of iced tea. "A toast to your new home and to your always being happy here."

Peyton touched her glass to his. "I'm sure I will be."

A great job in a terrific town and wonderful new friends. What more could she hope for?

The next evening, Darius sat on Peyton's right at the large conference table in one of the Trinity Falls Town Hall meeting rooms. Since she was the one with the fund-raising experience, he'd left the seat at the head of the table for her. He didn't want anyone to think he could answer the critical questions. He couldn't.

The meeting would start in a few minutes, at 8:00 p.m. on this Thursday night. Most of the committee members already had arrived. Darius looked at the six other people seated around the table, which could comfortably fit ten. Vaughn and Dr. Olivia Stark had walked in with Peyton. They sat across the table from him. The three professors must have left the university together. Stan, CeCe, and Ethel had shown up just a few minutes apart. They'd chosen to sit beside him. The only volunteer not yet accounted for was his father. *Why am I not surprised?*

He touched the back of Peyton's hand to get her attention. "Let's get started."

She glanced at her watch. "We can wait a few minutes for your father."

"No, we can't." Darius's voice was low but firm.

"All right." Peyton tugged a sheet of paper from the manila folder in front of her and grasped her pen. Facing the group, she raised her voice to gain their attention. "Thank you all for coming. We appreciate your willingness to help make this fundraiser for the Guiding Light Community Center a great success. As Darius and I explained—"

"I'm sorry. I don't mean to interrupt." CeCe looked around the table. "But shouldn't we all introduce ourselves first?"

Darius winced. Round-robin introductions? No way. "That's not necessary. We all know each other."

"You may think so but . . . well, I'll just introduce myself." She shifted in her seat, extending her right hand to Stan, who sat between her and Darius. "I'm CeCe Roben. I'm a member of the Trinity Falls Town Council."

Stan's eyes widened in surprise. He took CeCe's proffered hand. "We've met, CeCe. I'm Stan Crockett, formerly Trinity Falls' town drunk."

CeCe's whole body shook with shock. "Stan? Oh my gosh! You look so different."

The recovering alcoholic grinned, releasing CeCe's hand. "I guess I must for you not to recognize me after all these years."

Darius resisted the urge to check his watch. He waited for CeCe and Stan to finish. "Does anyone else want introductions?"

Murmurings in the negative circled the room. Across the rectangular table, Vaughn's dark eyes gleamed as though he found Darius's impatience amusing. Darius opened his mouth to ask Peyton to continue the meeting. A booming voice forestalled his request.

"Evening, everyone." Simon surveyed the meeting room. "What have I missed?"

Darius took a calming breath, drawing in the room's chilly, moldy air. "Take a seat."

Ethel shifted on her chair beside CeCe. "Is that supposed to be your grand entrance?" She snorted. "You know you can't come into a meeting late, then ask what you missed."

Simon appeared to be feeding off her negative attention. He lowered himself onto the chair at the foot of the table. "I'm sorry I kept everyone waiting. I was delayed by some important business."

Ethel snorted. "*This* is important business. If you were serious about volunteering, you would have shown up on time."

Peyton raised her hands, palms out. "Let's stay on topic." She lowered her hands and glanced at her sheet of notes. "Thank you for coming. As I'd started to explain, we have a very aggressive schedule. Darius and I have decided to use the fund-raiser to celebrate the center's fortieth anniversary with a dance."

"That's a clever idea." Olivia's dark eyes sparkled in her brown face.

"I agree." Peyton grinned at her colleague before again addressing the group. "Darius suggested we hold the dance in the community center so people can see the cause their money is supporting."

"That's my son." Simon's raised voice drew all eyes to him. "He's got a good head on his shoulders."

"*Your* son?" Ethel's tone was scathing. "I was practically a single parent."

The tension in Darius' shoulders threatened to snap him in two. He faced a familiar dilemma: Should he ignore his parents' outbursts or drag them from the room?

"Forgive me." Peyton once again lifted her hands. "I should have explained the ground rules first. As part of our fund-raising efforts, each committee member will be charged five dollars whenever their outburst takes us off topic. That means, Simon, you would've owed us ten dollars—"

His father gaped. "What?"

Peyton ignored Simon's interruption. "And, Ethel, you would've owed us five."

Ethel's gloating expression turned to shock. "Why—"

Peyton continued. "But since I hadn't explained the rules before, I won't fine you. However, starting now, each outburst that doesn't directly advance our meeting agenda will cost the violating member five dollars. Does everyone understand?"

Simon and Ethel glared at each other, then answered in unison. "Yes."

The other committee members agreed.

The burden had been lifted from Darius's back. He smiled at Peyton, who nodded in response.

"We have a list of tasks for which we need two volunteers each." Peyton tapped her pen against her meeting notes, checking off the tasks as she read. "We need a team to handle the registration database, another for catering and room reservation, and a third for entertainment and to coordinate printing for the event program. Darius and I will handle the fund-raiser's promotion."

Darius touched the back of Peyton's hand again, this time to interrupt her. He also just enjoyed the feel of her skin beneath his touch. "Before we get to the assignments, are there any questions?"

CeCe raised her hand. "How are we going to pay for all of this?"

He could handle that question. "Peyton and I have already received donations from local businesses to help cover our expenses. And we're going to continue to ask for sponsorships. The *Monitor* and the local radio stations are giving us free advertising."

CeCe inclined her head in approval. "It sounds as though you've already done a lot of work to cover the costs."

"It's still important to keep our expenses down," Peyton cautioned. "We want as much money as possible going to the center."

"What you're doing . . ." Stan looked at the people seated around the table. "You have no idea how much it means to people who need the help the center provides."

Darius squeezed Stan's shoulder. "No problem."

"We're happy to do it." Warmth filled Peyton's voice.

A chorus of agreement circled the table.

"The community center is going to let us use their activity room for free." Darius returned to the planning agenda.

Simon interrupted. "Bet that was your idea, Darius. You see? I told you my son had a good head on his shoulders."

Peyton held out her hand toward the older man. "Simon, you owe us five dollars."

Simon's eyebrows jumped. "But—"

Ethel exhaled an impatient breath. "You agreed. Now pay the woman."

The meeting quieted while Simon pulled five crumpled one-dollar bills from his wallet. He handed them to Ethel. The money passed from her to CeCe, then Stan, then Darius before landing with Peyton.

The little professor smiled. "I'll log this as our first official donation. Now, if there are no other questions, we'd like two volunteers to handle the registration database."

Olivia raised her hand. "I'll build the database."

"I'll help." Vaughn lifted a hand also. "Since we're both on campus, it'll be easier for us to work together."

"Great." Peyton made a note on her meeting agenda. "Catering and location arrangements?"

Stan volunteered. "I know the people at the center."

"I'll help Stan." CeCe volunteered so quickly Darius wondered whether she wanted to work with Stan or whether she just didn't want to be stuck with either Ethel or Simon. If it was the latter, he couldn't blame her.

Peyton wrote that down. "That leaves the entertainment and program assignment to Ethel and Simon."

Ethel gasped. "I don't want to work with Simon."

Simon looked smug. "Don't worry, Ethel. I won't show you up too badly."

The group agreed to meet again the following Thursday, then they wished each other a good evening.

Within minutes, Darius found himself alone with Peyton. "You run a tight meeting."

She tucked her meeting notes into her project folder. "Thank you. It comes from being a teacher. If students sniff out any weakness, chaos will ensue."

"Your solution to keep my parents from arguing was brilliant. Thank you."

"Not bad for spur of the moment." She gathered her purse, then led him from the room.

Darius fell into step beside her as they walked down the hall toward the rear entrance. "I wanted to ask you something." He winced at his lame opening.

"What?"

"You enjoyed the Sequoia–Heritage football game."

"It was a lot of fun." Peyton's grin brought back fond memories for Darius.

He forged ahead. "Noah's championship play-off game is tomorrow night in Canton. Would you like to go? I think you'll enjoy this game even more. It pits the two best teams in each state division against each other. There's a lot on the line."

Peyton gave him a teasing smile. "Are you asking me out on another date?"

Darius slid her a look. "I guess I am."

Peyton stopped to face him. "You guess? You're not sure?"

"No, I'm sure. I'm asking you out on another date."

"So soon? We just had a date last night."

"Is it too soon?" Darius settled his right hand on her waist. Peyton always made him feel like a high school freshman.

"No, I guess it's not too soon."

"You guess? You're not sure?" Darius gave her a taunting look. "Maybe this will help you decide."

Darius lowered his head and covered her mouth with his. His lips moved on hers, caressing, tasting, drinking in her sweetness. Peyton's body melted into his—or maybe it was the other way around. He groaned deep in his throat and pulled her closer. His heart beat against his chest. His breathing grew ragged. Darius's hands moved from the small of Peyton's back to the curve of her hips. He pressed her against his fullness. Peyton gasped into his mouth. Darius's blood sang with the sound. His groin swelled . . . and that's when he remembered where he was. Darius stepped back, holding on to Peyton so they could both keep their balance.

Darius cleared his throat. "Are you sure now?"

Peyton's laughter wobbled. "I'd love to go with you to the state play-offs. Thank you."

"Great. I'll pick you up at four. The game starts at seven."

"I'll be waiting."

Darius escorted Peyton to her car. He held her

door as she settled behind the steering wheel. "Drive safely."

Her soft gaze lingered on him. "Good night."

He watched her drive from the parking lot. His heart had been missing for so long. Now Peyton was making him come to life.

CHAPTER 18

"I'm sorry your team didn't win the championship." Darius sat at a table with his half brother, Noah, at Books & Bakery late Saturday morning.

The Sequoia Soldiers had made it to the state championship play-offs but had lost their divisional competition the night before. Darius knew how much Noah had wanted that title—as much as Darius had wanted it when he'd been in high school.

"I appreciate your being there even though I didn't get the job done." Disappointment clouded Noah's midnight eyes, which were identical to Darius's and Simon's eyes.

"You played a great game." Darius cradled his cup of coffee. "I was really proud of you."

"I don't know what bothers me more, that I blew my last chance at a championship or that I don't have any titles and you have two." Noah frowned at his glass of water and plate of Trinity Falls Fudge Walnut Brownie.

"Football is a team sport." Darius defended Noah

to Noah. "I didn't win those titles by myself. As long as you can look yourself in the mirror and say you left everything on the field, you can't blame yourself."

Noah didn't seem convinced, but Darius knew the younger man would eventually get the message. "I'd still rather have the title."

"I know the feeling." Darius sliced into his brownie.

"Hi, Darius." Michelle Mosley stopped by their table. Her voice was breathless with obvious nerves. Her wide, tawny eyes flashed from Darius to Noah . . . and stayed there. "I just wanted to check on you to make sure you have everything you need."

Darius struggled against a smile. Michelle was a sweet girl on the cusp of womanhood. At one point, she'd had an obvious crush on him. It appeared she'd now transferred her interest to his more age-appropriate younger brother. But Noah was looking at Michelle with only a vague expression of polite interest. His mind was probably still on the state play-off loss. The dummy.

Darius smiled at the high school junior who had eyes only for Noah. "We're fine, Michelle. Thank you."

Michelle had dyed her hair evergreen for the holiday season. It had been Valentine's Day red in February, magenta for Easter, and royal blue to celebrate Independence Day in July.

She pulled her attention from Noah's enjoyment of the brownie and focused on Darius. "OK. Well, let me know if you need anything. I'll just be right over there at the counter." She jerked her right thumb over her shoulder toward the front of the bakery.

Darius looked around the café. Doreen was at the cash register. The line of customers was long but moved at a brisk pace. A few diners enjoyed drinks and pastries at the counter. A few more enjoyed each other's company at the circular, blond-wood tables.

"Thanks, Michelle." Darius sipped his coffee.

Noah still hadn't responded. His lights were on, but no one was home. Michelle gave the younger man one last lingering look before returning to the bakery counter. Noah didn't notice.

Darius considered his clueless younger brother. "So what's on your mind? You didn't drive here from Sequoia just to tell me how disappointed you are by your team's loss."

"I need some advice."

"I'll do my best."

"I'm trying to choose a college." Noah traced the condensation on his water glass. "I want to go away like you did, be on my own and experience life in a big city. But at the same time, I don't want to leave Sequoia. I don't want Mom to be alone."

Darius swallowed a forkful of his brownie. "Don't worry about June. She'll be fine. This decision is about your future."

"But who'll look out for her while I'm away?" Noah's thin, sepia features were stark with concern. "Her whole life has been work and me. She doesn't have many friends. She'll be lonely."

"She has me, Noah. I'm one of her friends." Darius caught and held his brother's troubled gaze. "I'll check on her while you're at college. You just need to worry about yourself so that later you can take care of your mother."

"I know you care about Mom. But you have your own life." Noah stabbed another chunk of brownie. "That history professor is hot. God knows what she sees in you, but you'd be an idiot not to spend some time with her."

"Um, hi again." A high-pitched voice interrupted their conversation. Michelle was back. This time she was wielding a carafe of coffee. "Would you like more coffee, Darius?"

"Sure." Not really. Usually, customers brought their mugs to the counter. But since she'd come all this way, Darius thought it would be rude to decline her offer. "Thanks, Michelle."

"You're welcome." Michelle shot another glance in Noah's direction.

Darius caught her wrist as his mug threatened to overflow. "Thank you, Michelle."

"Oh. Sorry." Michelle turned again to Noah. His head was bent, absorbed with the remains of his brownie. She raised her voice. "Hi, I'm Michelle."

Noah looked up. His throat worked as he swallowed a mouthful of pastry. He lowered his fork, rose to his feet, and offered his right hand. "I'm Noah."

June would be so proud.

Michelle moved the coffeepot so she could shake Noah's hand. "Would you like some more water?"

"Yes, please." Noah gave Michelle his half-full glass. Michelle blushed as she turned away. Noah resumed his seat.

Speaking of idiots . . . Darius kept that observation to himself. "Peyton and I are seeing each other." Thinking of her gave him a warm feeling. "But that doesn't mean I'm going to forget my friends. Why don't you talk with June? Let her know you're worried about her."

"Could you talk with her?" Noah's eyes brightened with the idea. "I want to know what she's thinking."

"This is a conversation *you* need to have with your mother. Not me."

"Please, D. She'll be straight with you."

"Noah—"

"Please."

Darius took a deep breath. The air was heavy with the scent of pastries and other baked goods and the tang of the spices and fresh vegetables Doreen was using in the afternoon's soup.

He scowled. "Fine. I'll speak with June. First. But you'll need to speak with her on your own after."

Noah grinned, offering Darius his hand. "Deal."

Michelle returned with Noah's water. "Here you are."

Still grinning, Noah accepted the glass from her. "Thank you."

Michelle blushed again, then left.

Darius watched her go. "You know, I'm not the only idiot in our family."

"What does that mean?"

Darius's answer was a smile.

"Noah's not here," June called to Darius Sunday afternoon.

Darius looked up and found her standing in the doorway of her little wood-and-stone cottage at the end of the short, curving path. He'd made this trip to Sequoia, Ohio, a small town neighboring Trinity Falls, at least once a week for almost six years.

"I know." In the cold air, his breath formed white puffs with his words.

"I thought he went to see you yesterday." She stepped back to let Darius into her home. The cozy little cottage was full of natural light, bright colors, and fat, fluffy furniture.

"He did. I came to see you." Darius stripped off his black topcoat and gave it to June with his thanks.

"Why?" June hung his coat in her front closet, then led him into her living room. "Can I get you something to drink?"

"No, thank you."

June gestured him toward her foam green armchair. She sank onto the matching sofa, leaving the love seat empty between them.

The room was full of Cale family memories. Photos of Noah crowded the maple wood fireplace mantel and dotted the pale yellow walls. The images were records of his life from birth to young adulthood—first steps, first bike, prekindergarten graduation, First Communion, Confirmation, football.

"Noah's worried about you." Darius put his right ankle on his left knee.

"Me? Why?" June's voice lifted in surprise.

Darius chose his words carefully. "He's afraid to go away to college because he doesn't want you to be alone."

"That's stupid. He's going to an out-of-state university."

So much for diplomacy. "That's what I told him."

"What did he say?"

"That you don't have any friends." Darius watched closely for her reaction. "All you do is work and take care of him."

She rolled her eyes, shifting in the armchair as though uncomfortable. "He makes me sound like a martyr."

"Saint June."

"Far from it." She frowned. "Why didn't he talk to me about this himself?"

"He asked me to speak with you." Darius spread his hands. "He didn't think you'd be honest with him."

"As if." June heaved a sigh, crossing her arms and legs. "He needs to stop worrying about me and pick a university already."

Darius shrugged. "You know Noah. When he forms an opinion, only divine intervention will change his mind."

"Divine intervention?" June rose from the armchair to pace her living room. "I've never been called *that* before."

Darius laughed his surprise. "What are you going to do?"

"I can't understand why he'd tell you he's considering a local university when most of the ones on his wish list are out of state." June's voice was pensive. Her pace slowed.

"But he included a few that are in state, which means they're more than safety nets. He's legitimately considering them."

"Where would he go?" She gave him a dubious look as she paced back to her armchair. "Sequoia Community College? Trinity Falls University?"

"Those are good schools. You went to TFU."

"He's going out of state." June turned to cross to the fireplace again. "I've never been out of Ohio. That's something I've always regretted. I want more for my son."

"It's ultimately his choice, June."

"Staying in Sequoia's not what he wants."

"What are you going to do to change his mind?"

"I'm going to tell him that he's not staying in Ohio." June resumed her seat.

Darius lowered his right foot to the ground. "What are you going to do once Noah leaves for college?"

"Remodel his room and have sex." June crossed her arms and settled back into her armchair. "Not necessarily in that order."

"All right." Darius tried to mask his surprise. He failed. "Maybe you can word that a little differently for Noah."

"Of course." June rolled her eyes again.

Darius studied her in silence for a while. June was a beautiful woman, tall, fit, intelligent, and charming. At thirty-nine, she looked ten years younger, at least. "Why haven't you ever married?"

She snorted. "You're one to talk."

He smiled. "I guess we've both neglected our personal lives."

"I've been raising Noah. What's your excuse?"

Darius couldn't think of one.

Monday morning, it took a few moments for Darius to realize the knocking sound was coming from his cubicle in the *Monitor*'s offices. He looked over his shoulder to find Alonzo standing in the doorway in his sheriff's uniform: tan shirt, black tie, and spruce-green gabardine pants.

"Sorry to interrupt." The sheriff seemed to be waiting for an invitation.

"You're not interrupting. Have a seat." Darius spun his office chair to face his guest. "I'm not used to that sound. Usually people just walk in."

"I know you're busy." Alonzo lowered himself onto the beige tweed guest chair.

"There's no rest for the wicked."

"But the righteous don't need rest." Alonzo completed the quote.

"That too." Darius studied the older man's body language. Alonzo was tense. His dark gaze landed everywhere but on Darius.

"Have you decided whether to take that promotion?"

Darius froze, then realized the other reporters couldn't hear Alonzo's soft question over the usual newsroom cacophony of shouts, telephones, and typing. "You're not here to ask about my career plans, Sheriff. What's on your mind?"

Alonzo hesitated. "I need advice."

"On what?" Darius had interviewed state politicians who'd been more forthcoming.

"I proposed to Doreen more than a week ago." Alonzo sounded like he'd lost his greatest treasure.

Darius braced for bad news. "And?"

"She said no."

Darius was as disappointed as though he'd been the one Doreen had turned down. "Why?"

"She's comfortable with our relationship as it is now."

That didn't sound like Doreen. She was still afraid. "What do you want?"

"I've wanted to marry Doreen for more than forty years." Alonzo's response was fast and frustrated. "I'm not settling for anything less."

"So what happens now?"

Alonzo rubbed the side of his face. "She asked me to give her more time."

"What can I do?"

"Tell me what to say to convince Doreen to marry me."

Darius's mind went blank. When had he become the Dear Abby of Trinity Falls? "Sheriff, I've never proposed to anyone. I've never even wanted to."

"You helped Ean get back together with Megan when they split up last year."

"I explained the situation to Ean from Megan's point of view."

"You convinced Jack to reconcile with Audra."

"I told Jack what his life would be like without her: crap."

"You're the one who convinced me to tell Doreen how I felt in the first place." Alonzo leaned forward, resting his elbows on his knees. His voice lowered to a barely audible murmur as he spoke to the faded gray carpet. "I guess Paul will always be the love of Doreen's life. She'll never let me into her heart."

"You're already in her heart. Everyone can see that."

"Then why won't she marry me?" Alonzo looked up, his eyes dark with pain.

"Because she's afraid."

"Of what?"

"Of letting go of who she was with Paul." Darius frowned. "I thought you knew that. Isn't that the reason you had that Day of the Dead ceremony?"

Alonzo shook his head. "I had the ceremony to show her I'm not asking her to forget Paul."

Darius drew a deep breath. The *Monitor*'s office smelled like old newsprint and stale coffee, at least his cubicle did.

"This isn't about Paul. It's about Doreen. Put yourself in her place. She's dating again." Darius gestured toward Alonzo. "In a few weeks, she'll be mayor of her hometown. She's happy and excited. But there's a part of her that's afraid of all these changes."

"I understand her life's changing." Alonzo shook his head. "I just want to be a part of her future."

"But she doesn't feel ready for her future." Darius leaned back in his swivel chair and studied his friend. "You're not going to like my recommendation."

"What is it?"

"Don't propose to Doreen again."

Alonzo straightened on his chair. "You're not making sense."

"Doreen knows you want to marry her. Proposing again will just add to the pressure she's already dealing with. You'll know when she's ready to discuss marriage."

Alonzo stood, dragging a hand over his wavy, still-dark hair. He circled the visitor's chair. "It sounds risky."

"Doreen's worth the risk."

"Yes, she is." Alonzo gripped the chair's back.

"You're not going to lose her."

Alonzo stared at the ground for long silent moments. "All right. I'll try it. Thanks for your time."

"Good luck." Darius stood and shook the sheriff's hand.

"I'm going to need it."

Darius watched Alonzo leave his cubicle. The sheriff had never married. He probably had never even proposed to anyone else because his heart always had belonged to Doreen. He'd loved her for more than half of his life.

Darius's father stood in stark contrast to the romantic sheriff. In his entire life, Simon had never been able to commit to one woman. Even marriage hadn't made his father monogamous. What made two men so very different?

And was Darius capable of making the commitment his father couldn't?

CHAPTER 19

"Hey, Peyton." The neighborly greeting sang out of the shadows that crept across Peyton's apartment complex's parking lot Tuesday evening.

Peyton hoisted her briefcase from the passenger seat of her candy white Volkswagen GTI with her gloved left hand. She pushed back the hood of her winter coat with her right as she scanned the lot. Virginia Carp stood beside a nearby lamppost.

Peyton closed her GTI's passenger side door, then activated the car alarm. She dropped her keys into her coat pocket, pulled up her hood, and adjusted her purse strap. "Hi, Ginny. Are you waiting for someone?"

"Yeah. You." Ginny straightened as Peyton approached her.

The ominous words were at odds with Ginny's friendly demeanor. Peyton ignored a shiver of unease. A cherry knit cap protected Ginny's hair from the elements. Peyton eyed her neighbor's scarlet, quilted calf-length coat and matching boots with envy.

"What can I do for you?" Peyton huddled into her burgundy coat. Chubby snowflakes fell on her in slow motion, then melted away. Hopefully, Ginny wouldn't take long.

"Stop chasing after Darius." The words puffed from Ginny's lips in small clouds of frigid air.

The cold and snow were forgotten. Usually other women just took her boyfriends from her, just as Leila had taken Bruce. They'd never bothered to warn her away. Was this an example of Midwestern manners?

"I'm not chasing him." Peyton tugged her purse farther onto her shoulder and adjusted the weight of her briefcase. "We're dating."

She, Dr. Peyton Lynn Harris, was dating one of the most eligible bachelors in town, a man other women felt a need to warn her away from. Very cool.

"You're just like all the other women in town." Ginny looked her over dismissively. "Chasing after Darius Knight like he's the last little piece of meat and you're a starving bitch."

Well, that got real ugly, real fast.

"Apparently, the cold has gotten to you. I suggest you get inside and warm up." Peyton stepped around the other woman and started past her. "Good night, Ginny."

"You should listen to me." Ginny fell into step beside Peyton. "I'm trying to do you a favor."

"I appreciate your concern, but I'll be fine." Peyton continued toward the apartment building.

Residents' assigned parking was in the back of the lot, which freed the front spaces for guests. The accumulated snow made the asphalt lot slippery. Peyton moved as quickly as possible under these conditions. She wanted to get inside before she turned into a Popsicle.

"Darius'll break your heart. That's what he does." Ginny matched her stride for stride. She spoke louder as though her increased volume would convince Peyton she was telling the truth.

"Is that what he did to you?" Peyton kept walking. The air even smelled cold. She was more interested in getting out of the snow than in Ginny's prime-time soap opera antics.

"He told you that we've slept together?" Ginny sounded pleased.

"He said you'd dated for a while."

"We've slept together. A lot. That's how I know him so well. Yeah, he's great in bed—*really* great in bed—but he's cold and emotionally distant."

No, he isn't. Temper, alien and unwilling, stirred. Peyton looked at the other woman. "Darius is far from cold or distant. He's kind and caring."

"That's what I thought at first, too." Ginny crossed her arms over her chest. "Then, after he got what he wanted from me, the real Darius showed himself."

"And who's the real Darius?" Peyton eyed the other woman dubiously. Anger was burning away the cold.

"Oh, right, you haven't met him yet. The real Darius is the uncaring one, the one who refuses to commit. The one who chases after and sleeps with every woman he sees."

"I thought you said women chase after Darius." Peyton adjusted the weight of her briefcase as she stopped to face her aggressor. "Now you're saying he's the one who does the chasing. Which one is he?"

Ginny hesitated. "Both."

In her mind's eye, Peyton envisioned all of Darius's friends, the people he helped like Stan Crockett, his loving manner with Ms. Helen, his chivalrous behavior toward her.

"You're delusional." Peyton turned away. *Keep walking; ignore her.*

"*You're* the one who's crazy." Ginny chased after her. "Do you really think you can have a relationship with someone like Darius Knight?"

Peyton paused on the sidewalk. She held on to her temper with both hands. "Ginny, if Christian charity is the reason you approached me with your warning about Darius, then I'll thank you again for your concern. But I don't have time to argue with you over something that is none of your business."

She mounted the stairs to the second floor of the eight-unit apartment building. Were those Ginny's footsteps behind her? *Why won't she give up and go home?*

Peyton glanced over her shoulder. "Stop following me."

"Stay away from Darius." Ginny's voice trembled with anger. That was fine. Peyton was angry, too.

She mounted the landing. The roof's soffit had protected the second-floor landing from most of the snow.

"Peyton, I'm talking to you." Ginny's voice was becoming shriller.

Peyton clenched her teeth. She slid a glance at her neighbors' windows as she hurried past them. Could they hear Ginny? They must. Peyton's stomach muscles knotted. Was this how Darius felt when his parents bickered in public? Her heart went out to him.

She pulled her keys from her coat pocket as she

approached her apartment. Peyton unlocked her door, then faced Ginny. "If Darius is the one with the problem, why does the sheriff have a restraining order on file against you?"

Ginny gaped. "He *told* you?"

"If you continue to malign Darius's character, I'll make sure *everyone* in Trinity Falls knows about that restraining order." Peyton shoved off the hood of her coat to stare down the other woman. A red haze clouded her vision. "I'll stand in the middle of the town center, holding a five-foot sign with your picture and the word *stalker* in big, red block letters across your forehead. Do you understand me?"

Ginny's lips thinned. "You'll be sorry you crossed me."

"Do you want to bet who'll be sorrier?" Peyton's body shook with fury. The cold was a distant memory.

Ginny held Peyton's glare a moment longer before stomping away. Peyton watched her nemesis disappear down the stairs, then entered her apartment. She slammed the door shut, dumped her briefcase on the floor, and tossed her purse onto her sofa. Still bundled in her coat, she walked into her kitchen. Peyton filled her kettle with water from the faucet and set it on the stove to boil. She grabbed a mug, tea bag, and sweetener from her cupboards.

No wonder Quincy had urged Darius to file a restraining order against Ginny. Virginia Carp was seriously unhinged. Darius may not be worried about his crazy ex, but Peyton had a feeling Ginny was more of a threat than Darius thought.

* * *

"Is everything OK, Doreen?" Megan's question barely penetrated the fog in Doreen's head.

She and Megan were chatting in Books & Bakery's modest kitchen in the early hours of Wednesday morning before the bookstore opened. It was a routine they'd developed when Doreen had first started working for Megan almost two years ago. The younger woman kept her company as she baked the day's first batches of pastries.

Outside, it was cold and dark, with Christmas only fifteen days away. Not that Doreen was counting. But inside, the industrial oven kept the kitchen warm and cozy. The pastries filled the room with the scents of sugar and spice.

The kitchen was Doreen's dream. It was bright and lined with modern, industrial equipment. Best of all, the cupboards were positioned within her reach. No need for stepladders.

"Yes, I'm fine." Doreen hustled around the room, crossing the white-tiled flooring to pull ingredients from the silver refrigerator and add them to the electric mixer. "Why do you ask?" She set the industrial-sized oven to warm.

Megan relaxed onto one of the two decorative honey wood chairs set in the corner of the cozy kitchen. Her cloud of dark, wavy hair swung around her shoulders as she rested her elbow on the matching circular table. "Well, for one thing, you just cracked a couple of eggs over the trash can and dumped their shells into that bowl of flour."

"Omigosh." Doreen dropped onto the marble counter the ingredients and cooking utensils she'd been gathering and returned to the baker's island in the center of the room.

"You're not OK, are you?" Megan's voice was soft concern. "What's on your mind?"

Doreen poured the flour, salt, cinnamon, and eggshells into the trash can and gave the bowl a thorough washing. She dried her hands on her chef's apron. "Alonzo proposed."

"Oh, Doreen! I'm so happy for you! That's wonderful." Megan hesitated. "Isn't it?"

"I told him I needed more time." Doreen pulled fresh ingredients from the cupboards and started over.

Megan sighed her disappointment. "What did Alonzo say?"

Doreen shrugged defensively. "He agreed to wait, but I could see he wasn't happy about it."

"I understand his disappointment." Megan crossed her legs. The emerald-green skirt suit made her honey brown skin glow. "But I also understand why you'd need more time."

"I'm glad someone does because I'm not sure I do." Doreen's eyes stung with unshed tears of frustration. She blinked rapidly. "I'm also not convinced it'll do any good."

"Doreen, you've had a very eventful couple of years." Megan recalled the most recent occurrences. "Paul died in February 2013. You started working for me in May of that same year. Then five months later, Ean came home. You ended 2013 by announcing your mayoral campaign. Then in January 2014, you managed the town's Sesquicentennial Celebration Committee."

"That's a lot." Doreen added cocoa, nutmeg, and butter into the electric mixer. She hand mixed the ingredients when she was home. But if she tried that at the bakery, she'd have developed carpal tunnel syndrome by now.

Megan joined her at the baker's island. "That's the reason I understand why you'd need time. Marriage is a life-changing event."

"I can hear the 'but' in your voice." Doreen had known Megan and her cousin, Ramona, since they were little girls. She liked to think she knew them almost as well as she knew Ean.

"I don't understand what you're afraid of." Megan's words brought Doreen up short.

"What makes you think I'm afraid of something?" Doreen cracked four fresh eggs into the bowl this time and tossed the shells in the trash where they belonged. She added sugar and vanilla.

"Come on, Doreen. Everyone can see how much you love Alonzo. And he loves you, too."

Doreen turned off the electric mixer, then combined the contents of the two bowls. She wrapped in a cup and a half of wheat flour and two cups of walnuts as she gathered her thoughts.

"All of my life, I defined myself by what I did, and Paul was a big part of that. I loved to bake. So when we were house hunting, Paul understood the kitchen was important to me." Doreen sprayed the baking pan with oil. "He supported my need to participate in community projects. I wouldn't be where I am today without him."

Doreen placed the baking pan with its Trinity Falls Fudge Walnut Brownie mixture in the industrial oven.

Megan broke the short silence. "Paul Fever was a wonderful husband and a loving father."

"I see so much of Paul in Ean." Doreen stood with her back to Megan.

"And he was a very good friend to my family," Megan continued. "But the question is, how do you want to face the future?"

"What do you mean?" Doreen frowned as she swept away the remnants of the brownie ingredients.

"You've entered a new phase in your life, Mayor-Elect Fever." Megan smiled, invoking Doreen's new title. "Do you want to experience it with Paul's memory or with Alonzo?"

Doreen considered Megan's question as she started the cinnamon rolls. Trust her friend's analytical business mind to identify the central issue. Alonzo's proposal wasn't about the past. It wasn't even about the present. It was about her future. What did she want that future to look like? Of course, God would have the final say. But given the choice, what did she want: the memories she'd made with Paul or the ones she could make with Alonzo?

"Lead the way." Darius followed Peyton as she weaved past tables in the crowded Books & Bakery café. It was Thursday afternoon, two weeks before Christmas. They were supposed to be discussing the community center fund-raiser. Still, Darius considered this a date and had insisted on buying Peyton's lunch. He was aware of the attention they'd drawn, but he didn't care. It was a liberating feeling.

The store was bursting with Christmas cheer: garlands and stars, wreaths and ribbons. Customers carried purchases away in the Christmas Books & Bakery bags. Red-and-green napkins had replaced the traditional white ones. Holiday music played softly through speakers strategically positioned throughout the store. Additional decorations would appear in time for the popular Christmas Reader Appreciation Celebration next Saturday, a week before Christmas. That's when they'd unveil their tree.

Peyton set her tray on a table in the far left corner of the dining area. She gestured toward the nearby window. "Look at this. It's like a Christmas card."

The window framed the shops at the northwest intersection. Trees were outlined with snow and dripping icicles. Oversized ribbons formed foot-long bows around the lamps on Main Street.

A smile tugged at Darius's lips. "Will you be warm enough?"

"I'll keep my coat on." Peyton peeled her gaze from the window. "I forgot you're probably used to this view."

"I like seeing it through your eyes." Darius shrugged off his topcoat.

They slipped into conversation easily: football games, both college and pro, their mornings and plans for the week. And then the discussion turned to the fund-raiser, what they'd accomplished and what remained on their task list.

Darius finished off his chicken noodle soup. "I think we should ask Ms. Helen to be our keynote speaker."

"I agree." Peyton sipped her lemon water. "Ms. Helen would be the perfect speaker for this event. She's been involved with the center since the beginning.

"Great." Darius gathered his sandwich. "I'll ask her tonight."

"I think we should go together." Peyton finished

her sandwich. "That would make it more of a formal invitation from the event cochairs."

"All right. I'll pick you up after work." Darius swallowed more iced tea. "And I'll let Ms. Helen know we're coming."

"Thank you."

A comfortable silence settled between them, until a few beats later when Darius spoke again. "Are you leaving for New York right after commencement Saturday?"

"I'm not leaving until next Saturday, December twentieth." Peyton lifted her chicken sandwich. "I'll return December twenty-sixth, the day my parents leave for their cruise."

"Why aren't you going with them?"

Peyton shrugged one sexy shoulder. "I don't want to."

Fair enough. "I'm glad you're only going to be gone for a week."

"So am I." Peyton smiled into his eyes. Minutes later, she was the one to break their companionable silence. "Ginny and I had a talk Tuesday night."

Dread crawled up Darius's back. "About what?"

"She warned me to stay away from you."

Darius stilled. "Did she threaten you?"

"No, she just annoyed me."

"What did she say?" Darius gritted his teeth as Peyton's cheeks turned pink. That couldn't be a good sign.

"It doesn't matter."

"It matters to me."

"The only reason I brought this up is that I thought you should know."

"Peyton. Tell me." Darius willed her to talk to him.

She hesitated a moment longer, then lowered her voice. "She said you'd break my heart."

It was worse than Darius had imagined. "Do you believe her?"

"Of course not." Peyton reached across the table and covered his fist with her small hand. "Stop comparing yourself to Simon."

"We should file a report with the sheriff."

Peyton shook her head, drawing her hand back. "We don't need to involve Alonzo. Besides, I think she's done with us."

"What makes you think that?"

Peyton's gaze slid away from Darius. "I told her I'd tell everyone in town she was a stalker and that you had to file a restraining order against her."

That couldn't have gone over well. Ginny had nearly lost her mind when he'd requested the order. "That would take care of the situation."

"She forced my hand." Peyton lowered her voice again. "I just pointed out that, if you were such a horrible person, why was *her* name the one on the restraining order?"

Darius arched a brow. "You said that?"

Peyton straightened in her chair as though offended. "It's a legitimate question. She has no right to talk about you like that. She's a hypocrite and a liar."

It was strange to have someone so passionately on his side. "Thank you, Peyton."

"For what?" She frowned.

"For handling Ginny for me."

For making me believe that happily-ever-after is possible for me. For helping me find my heart.

CHAPTER 20

An hour later, Darius was back in his cubicle in the *Monitor*'s newsroom, giving one of his news stories a final read when Opal Gutierrez interrupted him.

"Is it true that Jack Sansbury offered you the managing editor position?" From the threshold of his cubicle, Opal hurled the question at him like a blade.

Why can't everyone be like Alonzo, knocking politely, then patiently waiting to be invited into my cubicle?

Darius saved his computer file before turning to his unwelcomed guest. Opal's hands were on her hips above her slim purple pants. Her dark eyes shot sparks at him. Even her dark hair seemed to vibrate with outrage.

"What makes you think Jack offered me a promotion?" But Darius knew the answer. He'd asked a trusted colleague to spread the rumor a week ago. He'd wanted to know how his promotion would be received, who would be resentful and who couldn't care less. Several people were trying to work their way into his good graces. He hoped they soon realized he didn't have any good graces and would go back to treating him like a normal person.

In contrast, Lei Chang had e-mailed him a list of demands: She photographed only hard news; she did not photograph happy-face images, social events, or community celebrations. And she worked alone. Nothing would ever change Lei. Thank goodness.

Opal's eyes flared wider. "The rumors are all over the office. And they're bullshit."

Well, now he knew how Opal felt. She was the newest member of the newspaper's staff and the only one who was angry.

"Why is it bullshit?"

"How could he just hand you the position?" She threw up her hands in exasperation. "He should have posted it so that everyone who's interested could apply."

"Are you interested?" Darius stretched his legs and crossed them at his ankles.

"Why not?" Opal narrowed her eyes. "Do you think I'm not qualified because I'm a woman?"

Oh, well played. "That's a strange question, considering our executive editor and second-in-command happens to be a woman."

"I would have liked an opportunity to interview for the promotion." Opal took a step closer.

Between him, Opal, and Opal's temper, Darius's cubicle felt crowded. "You're only two years out of college. I have twelve years of experience." *Not to mention you're a sloppy reporter.*

"This is cronyism, pure and simple." Opal stabbed her right index finger toward Darius. "You and Jack went to high school together. That's why you get preferential treatment."

"I'm sorry you feel that way, especially since it's not true."

"I work just as hard as you do."

That isn't true, either. "It's not only about your work ethic. It's about experience."

Opal paced away from Darius, then back. She pulled the fingers of her right hand through her heavy, black hair. "This isn't fair and you know it. I'm going to complain to Jack."

Darius shrugged. "He has an open-door policy."

Opal's gaze wavered. Had she expected a different reaction?

"This isn't fair." Opal blew out a frustrated breath. "He's only been back at work four months and he's already turned everything upside down. All I want is a chance."

"You'll get your chance, Opal. You just have to be patient." Patience probably wasn't a concept with which she was familiar.

"I don't see that happening in this boys' club. I'm going to talk to Jack." She stormed out of his cubicle.

Darius's hand hovered over his telephone receiver. He should warn Jackson that Opal was going to bring her complaints to him.

On second thought, why ruin the surprise? Darius dropped his hand and returned to his news story.

Around six o'clock that evening, Peyton stood with Darius on Ms. Helen's porch. The covered landing provided some shelter from the biting wind.

Darius pressed the doorbell, then moved closer to her, placing a hand on the small of her back. His tall, lean body lent additional protection from the cold. The gesture itself warmed her.

Ms. Helen didn't keep them waiting long. A curtain moved in one of the front windows. Seconds later, the tiny lady appeared in the doorway wearing a pearl gray lounge suit and fuzzy pink slippers.

"You're a little late for your shift, aren't you?" She stepped aside to welcome them in.

Peyton glanced at Darius in confusion. It was only six-twenty in the evening. She thought they were early.

"Ms. Helen, I called to tell you I was going to be late." Darius gestured Peyton to precede him into the house, leaned down to kiss their hostess's wrinkled cheek.

"Yes, you did do that." Ms. Helen closed and locked the door.

Their hostess's home smelled like apple cinnamon and looked like Christmas. Seasonal lights and garlands traced the archway between the front room and the rest of the house. A six-foot-tall Christmas tree dominated the room. It drew Peyton like a spell with its twinkling lights and vivid colors.

"What a beautiful tree." Her voice was breathless with awe.

The tree was covered from top to bottom in elegant ornaments and tiny lights and crowned with an angel. The skirt swirling at its base sparkled with green, gold, blue, silver, and red glitter. The entire display was a tribute to the joy of the season.

"Thank you, dear." Ms. Helen sounded pleased.

"Peyton has a tiny Charlie Brown tree sitting on a table in her apartment." Darius's voice teased her.

"Shame on you, Darius. At least she has a tree." Ms. Helen shook her head. "One of my watchers helped me decorate it. I thought they could at least make themselves useful when they stop by."

"I wish you wouldn't call us that." Darius shrugged out of his coat.

Ms. Helen turned to Peyton. "When you get to be my age, people parade in and out of your house at all hours of the day to make sure you're still breathing. Darius has the last shift at six o'clock."

Ms. Helen's explanation only increased Peyton's confusion. "Why do people come to your home in shifts?" She tugged off her gloves and tucked them into her coat pockets.

"That's not what we're doing." Darius helped Peyton out of her coat, then hung it next to his on the ebony coat tree across the room. "She exaggerates the story more each time she tells it."

"I don't want you all thinking I'm some foolish old woman, falling for your I-was-in-the-neighborhood stories. I'm not." Ms. Helen turned to Peyton. "Megan McCloud and Ean Fever have the earliest shift. They stop by around six in the morning for a glass of water on their way home from their jog."

"That *is* early." Peyton glanced at Darius.

Darius inclined his head toward Ms. Helen. "What she doesn't tell you is that she's waiting for them with the water."

Ms. Helen continued. "Alonzo stops by around noon on his way to lunch at Books and Bakery. Doreen drops in around three o'clock after work. Then Darius arrives at six."

"She makes a good argument, Darius."

"We care about you, Ms. Helen." Darius spread his arms. "You can't blame us for that."

"That's the only thing keeping me from not letting the lot of you into my house." Ms. Helen led them into her kitchen. "Would you like some tea? Doreen has been pushing this chai stuff on me. It's not bad."

"I'd love a cup. Thank you." Peyton sank into the seat Darius held for her. She offered him a smile over her shoulder.

"Do you have regular tea?" Darius took the seat beside Peyton.

"Three cups of chai tea coming up." Ms. Helen filled her kettle with filtered water, then set it on the stove to boil.

"Thank you, Ms. Helen." Darius shook his head at the older woman's deliberate contrariness. "Peyton and I would like you to be the keynote speaker for the Guiding Light Community Center fund-raiser."

Ms. Helen pulled the mugs from her cupboards. "I thought you said the fund-raiser was going to be a dance."

Peyton nodded. "It is."

Ms. Helen added teabags to each of the three cups. "Why do you need a keynote speaker for a dance?"

Peyton folded her hands on the table. "We want someone to speak to the importance of the night's event and the value of the community center to Trinity Falls' residents."

"You were the impetus behind the community center being built in the first place," Darius added.

"Well, if you want me to speak, I'm sure I can

come up with something to say." Ms. Helen looked from Darius to Peyton. "What time do you want me there?"

Peyton felt a thrill of excitement. With Ms. Helen agreeing to be the speaker, everything was coming together. "We're hoping to reserve the community center for seven to ten p.m., Saturday, January tenth. We haven't confirmed the times yet, though."

Ms. Helen nodded. "Let me know when the times are confirmed and if there's anything in particular you want me to say."

"Terrific." Darius shot his cover model grin. "Thanks, Ms. Helen."

"You're welcome, dear." Ms. Helen searched Darius's features. "How are things going with your parents on the committee?"

"Peyton's keeping them in line." Darius covered Peyton's left hand where it rested on the kitchen table. "It must be her years of experience as a teacher."

"That ability to keep people in line does come in handy in a lot of situations." Ms. Helen's gaze dropped to Darius's and Peyton's hands before meeting Peyton's eyes. "Yes, everything's falling into place."

Peyton saw the approval in the older woman's dark eyes. Her cheeks heated with a blush. She hoped things were coming together. She was falling in love with the sexy and sensitive newspaper reporter. But did she have what it takes to hold on to the town's most eligible bachelor?

* * *

Darius glanced at his watch as Peyton began the second community center fund-raising committee meeting the Thursday before Christmas. They'd gathered in the same town hall conference room. Everyone had arrived on time and had taken their same seats. With a little more luck, they'd conclude the meeting within the hour. He was anxious to spend some time alone with Peyton before she left for New York on Saturday.

Peyton was speaking when Darius tuned back in to the meeting. "Vaughn and Olivia, I think the registration acknowledgment letter you drafted is perfect. Does anyone have any comments?"

"I do." Simon raised a hand. "I think everyone's name should appear on the letter, not just yours and Darius's."

"Typically, it's only the committee cochairs who sign the thank-you letters," CeCe pointed out.

"I don't care," Simon countered. "We're all doing work for this event. We should all get the credit."

"Usually, the committee members are listed on the event's program guide," Olivia explained. The biology professor was dressed in faded blue jeans and a Cleveland Browns NFL team sweatshirt. Her short, brown hair was pulled back with a clip.

The last time the committee had met, the university was still in session. All of the professors had arrived to the meeting in business-casual slacks and sweaters. Now TFU was on Christmas break. Vaughn looked as though he hadn't shaved since winter commencement almost a week ago.

However, Peyton didn't appear to understand the definition of dressing down. She looked ready for the classroom in a pale purple sweater, dark blue corduroy slacks, and low-heeled black boots. Her explosion of copper curls bounced around her face. Sapphire earrings hung inches above her narrow shoulders.

"Well, who's in charge of the program guide?" Simon frowned around the large conference table at the seven other members in attendance.

"That would be us, Simon." Ethel gave her project partner a sarcastic look.

"Us?" Simon's jaw dropped. "How do you know that?"

"Peyton sent an e-mail to everyone with detailed assignments two weeks ago." Darius struggled to keep his impatience in check. "Did you get it?"

Simon dropped his gaze. "I haven't read that e-mail yet."

"Well, that explains why you don't know what you're doing." Ethel gave her estranged husband a disgusted look.

Darius took a calming breath. "Do you have any updates for us?"

Simon shrugged. "I didn't know what I was supposed to do."

Ethel kissed her teeth. "Then you should have contacted Peyton." She turned a smug expression to Darius, seated on Peyton's right. "I've booked Wesley Hayes to be our disc jockey for the evening. I asked him to do it for free as a donation to the center, but he agreed to give us a discount instead."

"We can pay Wesley his usual rate as part of the cost for the event," Peyton rushed to reassure the other woman.

CeCe leaned forward on her chair. "Can you provide us with a budget update for the project? I'd like to make sure we're not exceeding the money we're bringing in from the business donations."

Darius made a note of CeCe's request. "We can do that."

"Thank you." The council member sat back on her seat.

Stan looked from CeCe to Darius. "CeCe and I met with the community center director. She put the fund-raiser on their calendar from seven to ten p.m., Saturday, January tenth."

"I'll tell Ms. Helen." Darius wrote down the times.

"Their volunteers are going to handle the cooking and the decorating, as long as we reimburse the center for the cost of the food and supplies." Stan closed the notebook from which he'd read his updates.

"We told them they'd have to stick to a budget, though," CeCe added.

Darius made another note on his writing tablet. "Peyton and I will verify an amount, then get that number to you."

He glanced at his watch again. Peyton gave him a questioning look. He shook his head, then looked away, embarrassed to have been caught checking the time.

Peyton addressed the group. "That's all of our committee updates. Are there any questions?" The room was mercifully silent. "Then let's adjourn. Merry Christmas, everyone."

The committee members returned her Christmas wishes. Darius stood but waited with Peyton as the others filed out of the room. His parents lingered.

"Are you two coming?" Simon asked from the doorway.

"We'll be a while." Darius rested a hand on the back of his chair. "Don't wait for us."

Ethel frowned. "We still haven't discussed what we're doing for Christmas."

Darius wasn't looking forward to a repeat of Thanksgiving. "We can talk about it later. It's still a week away."

Simon lifted his chin toward the little professor. "What are you doing for Christmas, Peyton?"

Peyton looked from Darius to Simon. "I'm going to New York."

Ethel's face relaxed into a smile. "That's nice. I hope you have a safe trip."

Simon nodded. "Me too."

"Thank you." Peyton watched his parents leave. "I don't think they like me."

"They don't like anyone." Darius took her hand and helped her to her feet. "Alone at last."

"Is that why you kept checking the time?" Peyton's laugh was low and sexy.

"I can think of better ways to spend my last two days with you." He circled her waist with his arms, looking down into her bright eyes.

She smiled up at him. "You make it sound as though I'm never coming back. I'll only be gone a week."

"It'll be the longest week of my life." Darius sighed. "I'll take you to the airport Saturday."

"Thank you." Peyton cupped the side of his face with her soft, small hand.

Darius kissed her palm. "And I'll be waiting for

you at the airport next Friday. So don't let your parents talk you into staying in New York."

"I won't. I promise."

"And don't look up any old boyfriends, either." Darius' smile faded. A cloud had moved across her pixie features, but it was gone so quickly. Had he imagined it? "What's wrong?"

"Nothing." Peyton's smile returned. She let her hand drop. "And you have nothing to worry about."

She turned away to collect her notes and her white three-ring project binder. She packed those items into her tote bag and hooked her bag and purse onto her left shoulder. Her movements seemed jerky and distracted.

Dread built in Darius's gut like a block of ice. He believed Peyton when she said she'd return to Trinity Falls after Christmas. However, he also sensed there was something she wasn't telling him.

"Are you ready?" Peyton's question startled Darius from his thoughts.

He grabbed his writing tablet. "Sure."

Darius placed a hand on the small of Peyton's back and escorted her from the room. She smiled up at him. Her caramel eyes were clear and bright. Had he imagined those earlier clouds? He was probably once again allowing the trouble in his parents' marriage to poison his relationship with Peyton.

After all, why would she need to keep secrets from him?

ᏋᏋ CHAPTER 21 ᏋᏋ

Darius's pulse jumped when he found Peyton waiting outside his apartment after work Friday evening. "I thought we were getting together later. Have you been waiting long?"

He crossed the upper-level landing with long, swift strides. Darius caught Peyton around her waist and lowered his head to hers. He'd intended to give her a quick kiss on her luscious mouth, but his lips wanted to linger. Peyton's eyes opened slowly.

"I finished packing sooner than I'd expected." She was breathless.

Darius waited a moment for his mind to clear. "I'm glad you came."

"I can tell." Her lips curved into a seductive smile that made his pulse jump again.

Darius unlocked his apartment door. As he stepped back to let Peyton enter first, he noticed the object on the ground beside her feet. "What's that?"

"It's my Christmas tree." Peyton lifted the sad, little thing from the ground. "It's my gift to you."

She waited for Darius to lock his front door before thrusting the fake plant at him.

"Um, thank you?" Darius gave her a dubious look.

Peyton chuckled. "Stop holding my tree like a baby with a dirty diaper." She took back the fake plant and looked around for a place to set it.

"Sorry." Darius removed his coat, hanging it in his coat closet and waiting for Peyton to give him hers. What was he supposed to do with a fake plant?

"I realize you aren't excited by the holiday season, which is a completely foreign concept to me." Peyton crossed into Darius's living room and positioned the plastic evergreen on his coffee table. "But my tree needs someone to watch it while I'm gone."

"What's to babysit?" Darius took her coat and hung it in the closet. "The tree's not real." Was this tree conversation a test or some sort of coded message? How do you care for a fake tree?

He watched as she smoothed the white cotton skirt across his table, then centered the plastic evergreen on top of the material.

"I don't want you to babysit my tree." Peyton straightened to observe her handiwork. "I want you to watch it so you can benefit from its Christmas spirit. I don't want it going to waste in an empty apartment while I'm in New York."

"I appreciate what you're doing, but I'm never going to be the kind of person who makes a big deal about the holiday season." Darius dragged a hand over his close-cropped hair. "I'll say 'Merry Christmas.' I'll exchange gifts. But beyond that, what's the point?"

"How can you say that?" She spread her arms. "That's like saying, 'I'm never going to fly to Paris.'"

"No, it's not." Darius arched a brow. "I can see myself going to Paris. It's more like my saying, 'I'm never going to the moon.'"

"Everyone enjoys the season, whatever holiday they observe." She gave him the stubborn look that signified the demise of any argument he tried to put forward.

Darius tried anyway. "Apparently, everyone doesn't."

"I understand Christmas isn't a joyous occasion with your family." She crossed to him, placing her small hands on his forearms. "You may not have happy memories from your childhood. But you can change that by making better ones now."

"How am I supposed to do that when you're leaving for New York in the morning?" His words were husky.

Peyton offered him a soft smile. She raised her arms to his shoulders. "I'm here tonight. Let's make a memory."

Darius lowered his head to Peyton's for a kiss that needed to satisfy them both for seven long days. He pressed his lips to hers, coaxing her to open for him. She did and his tongue swept inside. Her taste was as warm and sweet as hot chocolate on Christmas morning. Darius deepened the kiss, stroking her, caressing her, showing her what he wanted: him loving her and her loving him. Peyton drew his tongue deeper inside her mouth, giving him a taste of what she desired. Darius groaned.

He held her body closer to his. It was as though he'd waited forever just to hold her in his arms. He wanted her closer to him. Her soft curves pressing into his body filled the emptiness inside him with her warmth and light.

Darius slid his hands beneath Peyton's pale purple sweater. Her supple skin was warm and inviting beneath his palms. He broke their kiss, pushing the garment up and over her head. Her copper curls bounced free as he pulled the sweater away from her and tossed it onto his sofa. His gaze dropped to her flesh-colored, silk demi-bra.

Darius swallowed, tracing the curve of her right breast. "I think I had a dream that started with you wearing that."

Peyton's full, pink lips curved in a seductive smile that made his knees shake. "Show me how it ends."

He helped her strip off his dark brown sweater, tossing it on top of hers. Her eyes darkened as she stared at his torso. Her touch was gentle as she explored his pecs and abdomen.

Darius swept her off her feet and cradled her against his chest. "I'll show you, but it may take a while."

He strode into his bedroom and lowered her to the carpet at the foot of his bed. Together they discarded the remainder of their clothes. With Peyton naked in front of him, he was almost overcome with the desire to study her curves, lines, muscles, and secrets. He needed to wrap her in his arms and sink deep inside her. Darius lay next to Peyton on his king-sized mattress. He leaned over her and kissed her, losing himself in her scent, her touch, her taste. He drew his right hand from her shoulder over her left breast, pausing to mold, shape, and caress the firm mound. He rubbed his hand against her nipple. The sensation of her pebbled tip against his palm heated his blood.

Peyton shifted restlessly beneath his touch. Darius

swallowed her moans, emboldened to move lower, explore farther. His right hand moved past her tight waist, over her flat stomach, and between her quivering thighs. He cupped her nest of curls, feeling Peyton tremble against him. Her breath grew fast and shallow, quickening his desire. He released her lips and sought her breast, ringing her puckering nipple with his tongue. He drew her tip into his mouth as he parted her curls with his middle finger.

She opened her mouth on a gasp, pressing her head back into his pillow and lifting her hips to meet his caress. He rubbed her spot as he suckled her breast. Her body grew warmer, her breath shorter. Darius released her breast and shifted down her body, inserting himself between her long legs.

Peyton almost cried out when he released her breast. Her body was on fire. She could hear her blood rushing in her head, feel her pulse beat between her legs. The sweet sensation of Darius's mouth, tongue, and hands on her body was an experience she never wanted to end. She felt his breath above her curls. He separated her, spreading her folds.

Peyton's eyes flew open. Was he going to . . . "Darius!"

Darius's tongue stroked her deep. Peyton's body was under his control. He licked her; she rose to meet him. He kissed her; she moved against his mouth. He nibbled her spot, and she spread her legs wider.

Peyton squeezed her eyes shut as her muscles screamed. "Darius, I can't . . ."

"Yes, you can."

She shivered as his words whispered against her. Peyton strained toward her highest pleasure point.

She ached for her release even as she never wanted these feelings to end. Her muscles stiffened, the pressure building higher and higher, tighter and tighter. Her pulse thundered and roared in her ears . . . Then her body exploded, rocking in Darius's hands, her hips twisting and turning. Peyton muffled her screams behind her forearm as her head pressed into the pillow.

Darius rolled away from her. Peyton opened her eyes to find him reaching into his nightstand. He pulled out a condom, then quickly sheathed his erection. Darius returned to her. Peyton looked up at him as he balanced his weight on his forearms above her. His angular sepia features were hard with desire. His muscles were bunched and shaking from self-restraint. Peyton lifted her legs and wrapped them around his hips, pulling him closer to her.

"Show me how it ends," she repeated her earlier invitation.

Darius found a smile for her. "With pleasure."

He lowered his hips, joining their bodies. His growl deepened her desire. Peyton gasped as he stretched her. She closed her eyes, loving the feel of him inside her. She rocked her hips, squeezing him. Darius lowered his lips to her for a kiss. Peyton opened her mouth, taking his tongue, sucking it the same way she worked his length. Darius pressed against her. Peyton rose to meet him, finding a pace and rhythm that made her body burn. Darius grabbed her hips with his hands, rubbing her against him. Peyton panted and gasped as her muscles tightened all over again. Her body stiffened, then shattered in his embrace. Darius's hips moved faster, deeper, harder as he joined her. He pressed her hard against him, arched his back in his release. Peyton held on tight as they flew apart, then came back together.

"What are you doing here?" Darius blinked twice before he believed what he saw. Both of his parents were standing together outside his apartment door Saturday afternoon.

"What kind of welcome is that for the woman who birthed you?" Ethel crowded Darius, giving him no choice but to let his parents into his home.

"Or for the man whose DNA is in your blood." Simon followed Ethel into the apartment.

"I wasn't expecting you." Darius locked his front door, then trailed his parents into his living room. His gaze dropped to the manila folder in his father's right hand. Its presence stirred only mild curiosity.

Darius had just returned from taking Peyton to the airport. He missed her already. Facing his parents without the little professor's presence depressed him even more.

Why were his parents at the same place at the same time? And why had they chosen his apartment? They'd never visited him before their separation. He'd always gone to their house. That's the way he preferred it. More and more, it seemed as though this separation, which he'd been expecting for decades, had been a mistake for the entire family.

"Can I get you something to drink?" Darius shrugged on the coat of civility. It was a tight fit.

"No, thank you." His mother handed him her coat.

"I'm fine." Simon followed Darius to the closet.

Darius put away his parents' coats, then returned to his living room. Ethel had settled onto the left corner of the black leather couch. Simon joined her at the opposite end. Darius took the matching armchair catty-corner to the sofa. How long would he have to wait for his parents to explain the reason for their visit?

"The suspense is killing you, isn't it?" Ethel sent him a knowing look.

Darius's eyes widened in surprise. Was his mother teasing him? "Yes, it is. We've been together in the same room for at least five minutes and you two haven't snapped at each other once." He straightened on the armchair. "Who are you and what have you done with my parents?"

"When we find them, we'll let you know." Ethel chuckled.

"We were embarrassed during the committee meeting Thursday." Simon's smile was crooked. "We didn't complete our assignment."

Ethel nodded. "We realized that if we didn't cooperate, we were going to continue to embarrass ourselves."

"We've been working together on entertainment ideas and the program draft since Thursday night." Simon handed the manila folder to Ethel.

Ethel offered the folder to Darius. "Here's the printout of the program. We've also e-mailed the file to you in case you want to make changes."

Darius took the folder from his mother. His parents' constant use of the pronoun *we* was disconcerting. He'd become used to their outbursts and self-centeredness. This spirit of unity was strange to him, but he was willing to get used to it.

He skimmed the draft of their program. "This looks good. Peyton and I will review it when she returns next Friday. We'll give you our feedback, then send it to the rest of the committee for their input."

"Sounds good." Simon inclined his head.

"We found a printer who'll publish the program for free." Ethel shifted on her seat. "You were right about businesses being willing to donate equipment, services, and supplies. They're probably happy for the tax deduction."

Darius shook his head at his mother's cynicism. The vast majority of these business owners were more dedicated to the community than his parents had ever been.

Three weeks out and, finally, everything was in place. All the committee had to do was print the program.

Darius closed the folder and leaned back on his chair. "We'll list on the program the businesses that have given us donations for the fund-raiser."

"I'm glad we're on the fund-raising committee." Simon exchanged a look with Ethel. "It's forced us to start talking again."

Ethel turned to Darius. "One of the things we talked about was celebrating Christmas together instead of asking you to spend it with us separately."

Darius looked from Ethel to Simon. Who were these reasonable people? He tried to mask his shock.

Simon leaned forward. "We should definitely spend Christmas together. It's a holiday for families."

Darius gave Ethel and Simon a hard look. They seemed happier and more relaxed than he'd ever seen them. Certainly they seemed friendlier toward each other than they'd ever been.

"Are you two getting back together?" He dreaded the answer.

"Well, we're—"

"No," Ethel interrupted Simon. "It'll be a cold day in hell when we reconcile. If I wanted to be married to a randy adolescent, I'd find a younger man rather than a boy in a middle-aged man's body."

"Do you think you're some great catch?" Simon scowled.

"At least I listened to our wedding vows." Ethel crossed her arms and legs.

Now he recognized his parents. But this was progress. Darius drew a deep breath, bracing himself. "We'll spend Christmas together, if that's what you want."

Ms. Helen was right. His parents needed an opportunity to work toward forgiveness. Serving on the fund-raising committee was giving them that chance. Hopefully they'd continue to work on forgiving each other.

It was as cold as the day she'd buried her husband almost two years ago. Doreen stood before Paul's final resting place, staring down at his headstone: PAUL FEVER, 1946 TO 2013, LOVING HUSBAND AND FATHER.

Her gaze lifted to a tree line in the distance. The bare branches moved in an icy breeze. Above them, gray clouds hung low and heavy in the sky.

This isn't the way our story was supposed to end, my darling.

Doreen swiped away tears with the tips of her fingers. Back in her day, they hadn't told little girls that

happily-ever-after wasn't forever. And she hadn't
been smart enough to figure it out on her own.
Even when she and Paul had opened their retirement accounts and chosen a life insurance policy,
she hadn't realized the implications of their actions.
One of them—she—would be left behind, left alone.
Stranded.

Doreen dropped her gaze to Paul's headstone
again. "I've made the best of it."

You've done better than that, Paul's smooth, rich baritone whispered in her ear, full of pride. *You've thrived.
I knew you would.*

"I'd never planned a life without you." She snuggled deeper into her sapphire-blue woolen winter
coat. "I wish you were still here to share these new
experiences with me."

Everything happens for a reason.

She'd always hated that expression. It was annoy-
ingly vague. And why did it take forever to understand the reason something happens?

"I'd already planned my future." Doreen shifted
her stance. "I was supposed to spend it with you."

*Yes, you made plans—and God had a good laugh. Take
it from me. He's still laughing.*

"Right. 'We plan, God laughs.'" Doreen sighed.
"I resented you for the longest time for leaving me.
I resented God, too."

He still loves you. We both do.

She could almost swear it was his voice in her
head, his presence beside her. She wasn't as cold
anymore.

"But then the opportunity with Books and Bakery
developed. Ean came home. And I was elected mayor.
Those things probably wouldn't have happened if

you were still alive. Sometimes I feel guilty about that."

Don't! You were right to take those opportunities. You aren't supposed to pack your life into a box and wait to die just because I did.

"I hadn't planned on falling in love again, either. But marrying Alonzo feels like giving up the last little bit of our past, leaving only the memories."

That happens. At least the memories are really good.

"Am I wrong to be in love with Alonzo?" Doreen rubbed her forehead, trying to relax the tension between her brows. "I'm not trying to replace you."

Life is for the living, Doreen. You're still living.

"If you were the one left behind, would you remarry?" She strained to hear his answer.

I don't know. Maybe I would, if I found someone who made me as happy as you made me. Wouldn't you want me to be happy, Doreen?

She scowled. "I wouldn't want you to replace me."

No one could replace you, sweetheart. But would you want me to spend the rest of my life mourning you?

She was so tempted to say yes, but that wasn't the truth. "No, I'd want you to be happy."

And I want the same for you. I like Alonzo. He was a good friend and I know he'll be a great husband for you. Don't pass up another chance to be in love and to be happy. That's what I want for you.

Doreen couldn't wipe away the tears fast enough. "Then why do I feel guilty?"

I don't know. It's silly, isn't it?

Frustration overwhelmed her. Doreen squeezed her eyes shut and fisted her hands inside her black leather gloves. "Paul, Paul, tell me what I should do."

Only you can do that, sweetheart. The decision to marry Alonzo—or not—is yours.

Doreen opened her eyes. She was no closer to knowing what Paul would want. Maybe that was the point. The question wasn't what would Paul want. What did *she* want?

Doreen's hands shook as she studied Trinity Falls Cuisine's dinner menu Wednesday night, Christmas Eve. She felt like a young girl on her first date, just like the first time she'd gone out with Alonzo.

She laid down the menu and looked across the booth at her companion. He was so handsome in his deep plum wool sweater. It was her favorite. It darkened his beautiful coffee-colored eyes. His rich, wavy, dark brown hair reflected the light from the lamp fixture above them. He must have shaved right before he left his house. The skin over his squared, café au lait jaw looked smooth and touchable. Doreen's palms tingled.

Alonzo looked up and caught her gaze. "Everything all right?"

"I'm fine." Doreen tried to read Alonzo's expression. "What made you decide to go out to dinner tonight?"

"It's Christmas Eve." Alonzo reached across the table to twine his fingers with hers. "You're cooking a big meal tomorrow. Tonight's the perfect time to pamper you."

"Thank you." Doreen pressed his hand with both of hers. Could he feel her fingers trembling?

It was also the perfect time to propose. It wasn't the day Paul had proposed, but Christmas Eve was a popular time for popping the question. Everyone knew that. A fancy restaurant on Christmas Eve? Surely Alonzo was planning to propose to her a second time. Thinking about it made her heart race. This time, when Alonzo asked her to be his wife, she would say yes.

Trinity Falls Cuisine was elegantly dressed for Christmas. A seven-foot-tall, three-foot-wide Christmas tree stood at the entrance, decorated with gold and red ornaments and pearl-white beads. Red velvet ribbons topped the mahogany wood beams that climbed the walls. Green garlands lined the rafters.

Doreen's gaze skimmed the dining area. The restaurant was filled with couples who appeared oblivious to everything but each other. She and Alonzo were lucky to have been seated so quickly. Had he called ahead for a table? That sounded like something he'd do just to make sure the evening was perfect.

Their server arrived. The young man asked for their drink orders. They both requested unsweetened iced tea.

Doreen shoved aside the question of when he would propose and set her mind to relaxing and enjoying the evening.

She sat back on the booth's bench, allowing their hands to separate. "There's only a week left to this year. It's gone by so quickly."

"You didn't think so at the time." Alonzo's twinkling eyes caressed her face.

Doreen laughed. "There were indeed times when 2014 had seemed never ending with the Sesquicentennial Celebration and the mayoral election. But we have great memories as well, times I wouldn't change for anything."

"Like luring you away from Leonard." Alonzo arched a brow. "He wasn't one of your better decisions."

"I won't argue with you over that." Doreen raised both hands in surrender.

"What are you looking forward to in 2015?"

Doreen hesitated. Was this a trick question? Was he going to propose now? "I'm nervous but excited about taking office, of course. The swearing in is just eight days away, January first."

The server returned with their iced teas, then took their orders. Doreen requested the grilled chicken breast with wild rice. Alonzo ordered the wood-fired steak and baked potato.

"I'm going to be very proud to see you sworn in." Alonzo's coffee eyes were warm with admiration.

Doreen took a long drink of her iced tea, then leaned into the table and reached for his hands. "Thank you for supporting me through all of this. I can't tell you what that means to me."

Alonzo squeezed her hand. "I believe in you, Doreen. Trinity Falls is very lucky to have you as its next mayor."

Is this when he proposes? The silence continued.

Doreen held tightly to Alonzo's hand. "What are you looking forward to in 2015?"

"Retiring." Alonzo flashed his bright white grin.

Doreen laughed. "I can't imagine you not working."

He shrugged his broad shoulders. "Retiring doesn't necessarily mean I won't be working. Trinity Falls is losing its hardest-working volunteer. I'm willing to try to fill the void. I also thought you might need help with the bakery when your mayoral responsibilities demand your attention. I can cover you there, too."

She was falling deeper in love with him. "From Jacksonville, Florida, deputy sheriff to Trinity Falls, Ohio, sheriff to bakery assistant. That's a very versatile résumé."

"Don't forget community volunteer." Alonzo shrugged again, his muscles moving smoothly under the fisherman's crewneck sweater. "There's nothing wrong with reinventing yourself."

"As long as that's what you want." She searched his beautiful brown eyes.

"I'm looking forward to it." His smile reassured her.

Their dinner arrived and conversation sailed through memories of 2014 and plans for 2015. The evening flew by, giving Doreen, and she hoped Alonzo, another wonderful memory to close the year.

But he still hadn't proposed.

Later, Doreen was distracted as Alonzo drove them to her home. The evening was ending. Was he going to ask her to marry him or not?

He parked in her driveway and helped her out of his car. Alonzo escorted her to her door. He unlocked the entrance, glanced around, then let her precede him across the threshold. She'd left a light on in her living room. Even before she'd started dating the sheriff, she'd never liked returning to a dark house.

"I'm going to get ready for bed," Alonzo announced from behind her.

"OK." Doreen spoke with her back to him.

"Is everything all right?" Alonzo paused beside her. His eyes sought hers.

"Yes." Doreen forced a smile. "I'll be up in a moment."

Well, that answered her question. She watched Alonzo mount the stairs to her bedroom. When was he going to propose again? Not tonight.

Doreen trailed her lover up the steps. Was he only going to propose once? Had she lost her window of opportunity?

CHAPTER 22

Darius waited while Peyton secured her seat belt in his black Nissan Maxima Friday evening. He'd just met her flight at the Cleveland Hopkins International Airport and had carried her suitcase back to his car parked in the airport's short-term lot.

Her copper curls bounced as she connected the safety belt. As though with a will of its own, his hand reached out to touch them.

Peyton looked up in surprise. Her eyes warmed. "Thanks again for meeting my flight."

"You're welcome again." Darius drew his hand back from her hair. His palm tingled where he'd made contact. He started the engine and reversed out of the parking spot.

Darius was relieved to have her back. They'd talked on Christmas Day and texted throughout the week. Still he'd missed her even more than he'd expected. Why? That was a question he'd been asking himself since he'd taken her to the airport last Saturday. Was it because it was Christmas, a time to spend with friends and family? Or did he feel her absence more strongly because his friends had found their soul mates?

Or had he felt lost without her because he'd finally done the impossible—fallen in love?

Peyton pulled out her wallet to pay the parking fee. "Here." She offered the dollar bills to Darius.

"I've got it." Darius paid the attendant, then merged into traffic.

"I'll pay you back." Peyton put away her money and zipped her purse. "How's my Christmas tree?"

"It's still fake."

"But you told me your Christmas was better than you'd expected."

"Yes, it was." That still surprised Darius.

"I think my little tree brought you luck."

"Maybe it did." He'd humor her. Darius checked his blind spot, then switched lanes. "Are you hungry?"

"Not yet but I will be," Peyton said on a sigh. That was understandable. It was almost six o'clock.

"I'll fix dinner at my place." Darius met her gaze. "My parents wrapped up their assignment for the fund-raising committee. We're two weeks out and everything's in place."

"That's terrific." The passenger seat rustled as Peyton settled deeper onto it. "I knew your parents would be able to work together if they just tried."

"You have more faith in them than I do." Darius tossed Peyton a look. "The ads will start running next week on the local TV news, in the *Monitor*, and on the radio. Businesses are distributing the fliers to their customers."

"It's starting to feel real." Excitement bounded in Peyton's voice.

"Yes, it is." Darius smiled. "Opal Gutierrez is doing a feature story on the event. She's going to interview Ms. Helen and the center's director."

"Terrific." Peyton snapped her fingers. "Should we give Opal the basic information: committee member names, the evening's agenda, list of business donors?"

"I gave her that information and told her to call one of us if she has any other questions."

For the rest of the one-hour drive from the airport back to Trinity Falls, Darius and Peyton talked about her family visit, the looming end to her university break, and the football games. Peyton wanted details on his parents, the same, their mutual friends, all well, and his take on the football games, great matchups.

Darius pulled into his assigned space in his apartment's parking lot. He popped the trunk, then climbed out of the car to collect Peyton's heavy suitcase. "Did you pack your textbooks?"

"Yes."

Darius stopped halfway across his parking lot to stare at Peyton in shock. "I was joking."

"I wasn't." She gestured toward the suitcase. "I have to write up my lesson plans for next semester."

Darius continued toward his apartment building. "It's a good thing your suitcase has wheels."

"Yes, that helped."

Darius broke their companionable silence with a question that had troubled him all week. "Did your parents try to talk you into returning to New York?"

"The subject came up." Peyton's expression clouded. "But I told them I'd made my decision."

"And they accepted that?" Darius followed Peyton up the stairs to his second-floor apartment.

"Not yet." She shrugged. "They're not used to me having an opinion that's different from theirs."

Outside of his apartment, Darius unlocked his door and let Peyton in first. He stood her suitcase near the entrance to his living room and turned to her.

"If this is what you want—being part of this small-town community, teaching at the local university—don't let them change your mind." He searched her eyes as he made his plea. Now that he'd found his heart, he didn't want it leaving without him.

"They won't." Her voice erased the ache of his days and nights without her.

"Then welcome home." Darius closed the gap between them and lowered his head to properly welcome her back to Trinity Falls and his arms.

The kiss was soft, slow, tentative at first. Then Peyton wrapped her arms around his neck. The hunger shot through him like a bullet. Darius pulled her small, slender body against him. She trembled in his arms. He held her even tighter.

Darius released her, stepping back to help her shed her coat, then his. "I missed you."

Peyton took his arm and drew him toward his bedroom. "Show me."

Sunday afternoon, Darius refused to think about returning to work Monday morning. He loved his job with the *Monitor*, but this had been one of the best weekends he'd ever had. He was sprawled on his black leather sofa with Peyton as they watched the college football bowl games, a right of the Christmas season.

Darius scowled as Peyton leaped to cheer the defensive player who'd just forced his team's interception. "Why are you rooting for Oregon? Before today, you didn't even know their coach's name."

"You're rooting for Ohio State." Peyton gestured toward his forty-eight-inch flat-screen television.

"We're in Ohio."

"But we can't both root for the same team. Where's the fun in that?"

Darius's doorbell rang. He stood to answer it. "The loser should have to cook dinner."

"I'd like spaghetti with a small, tossed salad."

Darius' smile faded as he checked his peephole. "It's Ginny Carp."

"I wonder what she wants." Peyton sounded as irritated as Darius felt.

He was tempted to ignore their uninvited guest and return to Peyton and the bowl game. But he suspected Ginny wouldn't go away. He opened the door, angling his body to block Peyton from view.

Ginny wasn't alone. A tall, well-dressed businessman in a black overcoat stood behind her. Darius nodded to the stranger. The other man didn't acknowledge him.

Darius turned his attention to his ex-girlfriend-turned-stalker. "Hello, Ginny."

Her chin-length, dark brown hair was wind tossed. Skinny red cotton pants showed under her quilted winter coat. Her smile didn't reach her eyes. "Hi, Darius. Is Peyton around?"

"Why are you asking?" His gut told him he wouldn't like the answer to his question.

"Oh, I'm not asking for myself." Ginny gestured toward the stranger behind her. "I'm asking for my new best friend, Bruce Grave."

Behind him, Peyton gasped. The sound was barely audible. But even with his back to her, Darius was in tune with her every movement.

His spine stiffened. He lifted his gaze to the stranger. "Who are you?"

"I'm Peyton's fiancé." His voice was taunting. His dark eyes gleamed with contempt.

Darius's gut had been right. Dammit. His world was shifting around him. The heart he was still getting used to pounded in his chest as though looking for a way out. He turned to Peyton.

"You have a visitor." His voice sounded strange in his ears. He stepped away from the door, inviting Peyton to join them.

She came forward with stiff, jerky steps as though she wasn't certain she wanted to move. She stopped beside him and pulled the door wider. Peyton ignored Ginny's smug expression and addressed only the man who'd called himself her fiancé. "What are you doing here?"

"I should be the one asking you that." The stranger's voice was pitch-perfect outrage.

What the hell is going on? Darius fisted his hands, anxious to find out.

In her peripheral vision, Peyton noticed Ginny standing back as though inviting her to take center stage. Her shock wore off as her muscles warmed beneath her temper.

"You have no right to ask me anything." Peyton

turned to Darius. She saw the hurt, confusion, and anger in his midnight eyes. It broke her heart. "He's not my fiancé."

"Then who is he?" Darius's words were cold.

Bruce looked to Darius. "Has she told you about me?"

"Why should I even mention you to him?" Peyton answered before Darius could. "You have nothing to do with us, so what are you doing here?"

"I came to talk some sense into you." Bruce gave Darius a scathing look. "I hadn't realized you'd shacked up with a local."

Peyton sensed Darius's anger stirring. Bruce's comment pricked her temper, too. "There's nothing you can say that I want to hear, so please leave."

Peyton shrugged deeper into her black-and-silver TFU sweatshirt. The cold wind had penetrated the material. Her toes were curled, seeking warmth inside her slippers. But there was no way she was letting Ginny or Bruce into Darius's apartment.

"Our engagement isn't over." Bruce pushed his hands into the pockets of his black cashmere winter coat. "I can overlook your infidelity."

"Our engagement *is* over because I *can't* overlook yours." Peyton arched a brow. "How's Leila?"

"She's fine." Bruce met and held her gaze. "She sends her best."

"How nice of her." Peyton crossed her arms. "Does she still give good head?"

"I wouldn't know." Bruce's fair skin darkened under a blush. "I don't understand why you're jealous of Leila. You have no reason to be."

Peyton settled her hands on her hips. "She's welcome to you."

"Why are you saying this?" Bruce pulled his hands from his pockets and spread his arms. "From the moment I met you, I've been faithful to you. I'm still in love with you, Peyton. I want you to be my wife."

Peyton wanted to spit. Bruce was playing to his audience. She was too afraid to look at Darius. Was he buying this? "You never loved me, Bruce. You were in love with the idea of marrying a partner's daughter just to further your career."

Ginny sighed, long and audibly. "Oh, give him another chance. The guy's in love with you. And you're perfect for each other. You're both rich New Yorkers, unlike us dumb, dirt-poor locals." She sent a glare in Bruce's direction.

Peyton turned to Ginny. "I know you were hoping that introducing Bruce as my fiancé would come between Darius and me. But Bruce and I are never getting married. I returned his ring. And since Darius has a restraining order against you, I don't see the two of you getting together, either."

Ginny gestured toward Darius. "I don't know, girlfriend. Darius doesn't look like he'll give you the happily-ever-after you're hoping for."

Peyton glanced at Darius. His features were dark with anger. "Darius?"

He spoke over her. "Ginny, you shouldn't be here. Take your guest and leave."

Ginny's jaw dropped. "But—"

Darius's voice hardened. "Take your guest and leave. Please."

Ginny sighed. "Come on, Bruce."

"Not without my fiancée." Bruce stood his ground.

Darius straightened to his full height, which was several inches above the other man. He lowered his voice. "The lady said she's not your fiancée, so there's nothing and no one for you here."

Peyton grew increasingly nervous as the two men squared off.

Finally, Bruce blinked. "I'll leave but only because Peyton Harris is hardly worth fighting over. You'll soon come to realize that for yourself."

The words stung as Bruce had intended them to. Peyton stepped back into the apartment, wishing she could sink into the floor.

Darius's growled response stopped her lowering thoughts. "You're too self-absorbed to see the worth of the woman you've lost. That's your fault."

This is what it felt like to have someone in her corner, someone who respected and valued her. Peyton blinked back tears.

Bruce shoved past Ginny and disappeared down the landing. Peyton heard his footfalls on the metal staircase leading to the apartment building's parking lot. Good riddance.

Ginny looked from Darius to Peyton. Peyton couldn't read the other woman's expression. That added to her unease.

"What are you doing, Darius?" Ginny searched his face. "You don't care about her. You don't care about anyone. You're just like your father."

Peyton glared at Darius' stalker. She stepped closer to take Ginny to task. But Darius's cold words stopped her.

"Leave, Ginny, or I'll call the sheriff's office. You don't want your name to appear in another police report, do you?"

Ginny split her glare between the two of them before disappearing from Peyton's view. Darius closed and locked his front door. His movements were controlled. What was he thinking? What was he feeling? Peyton wished she could read his mind.

"Thank you for defending me to Bruce." Her voice was tentative. "No one's ever done that for me before."

"You lied to me." Darius spoke with his back to her. His voice was taut, stilted.

Peyton shivered in the sudden cold. "No, I didn't."

Darius turned to face her, crossing his arms over his chest. "You didn't tell me you were engaged. That's lying by omission."

"Bruce and I aren't engaged anymore. I've explained that."

"When did you end your engagement?"

"Before Thanksgiving break."

"A month ago." Darius straightened from his front door and paced past her. "So you were engaged when you moved to Trinity Falls. I never saw a ring on your finger."

Peyton tracked Darius with her gaze. He was agitated, but she didn't know what to say to appease him. "I knew I wasn't going to marry Bruce. That's why I didn't wear his ring when I moved here."

"That doesn't make sense." Darius rubbed his eyes with his thumb and two fingers. "If you knew you weren't going to marry him, why did you accept his ring?"

Peyton wrapped her arms around her waist. She was more chilled now than when she'd stood before the open front door. "Because I wanted to please my parents."

Darius spun to face her. "You're kidding." He looked at her as though he didn't know her.

Peyton blushed, realizing just how foolish she sounded. She was a university professor. She'd earned a doctorate degree. She was a thirty-year-old professional. But she'd gotten engaged to a man she couldn't trust just to please her parents.

She wandered farther into the living room and sank onto Darius's armchair. "My father wanted me to marry Bruce because he doesn't think I'm capable of taking care of myself. My mother wanted my father to arrange the relationship because she doesn't think I can attract a man like Bruce on my own."

"What do you mean by 'a man like Bruce'?"

Peyton's shrug was restless and impatient. "Handsome and successful."

"What does Bruce do for a living?"

"He's a financial analyst with my father's brokerage firm. He's on the partnership track."

"Your father's a financial analyst?"

"Yes."

"What does your mother do?"

"She volunteers on boards and committees. She's planned a lot of very successful fund-raisers for museums, hospitals, and libraries."

"That's how you learned to organize fund-raisers."

"Yes."

Darius dropped his arms. "So your parents are rich and well connected. They probably wouldn't approve of you having a relationship with a small-town newspaper reporter."

"No, they probably wouldn't."

"Do they know about me?"

"No, they don't."

"Why not?" His question was cold, robotic.

Peyton hesitated. "I just haven't told them yet."

"Because you're ashamed of me?"

"No, that's not why." She was appalled at the suggestion.

"Then what are we doing here?"

"What?" Peyton stood to face him.

"You didn't tell me about your engagement. You didn't tell your parents about me." Darius paced the living room, stopping when he reached the entrance to his kitchen. "How many other secrets are you keeping?"

Peyton reared back as though he'd struck her. "I'm not keeping secrets."

"Oh, that's right. You're just not telling me anything." Darius crossed back to his front window.

Peyton's temper sparked. "I'm not a liar. I'm not marrying Bruce and I'm not returning to New York."

"And our relationship is *not* going anywhere, is it? Because you're also *not* telling your parents about me."

"I don't have to explain our relationship to my parents. It's *our* relationship."

Darius dragged a hand over his close-cut hair. "You're not the woman I thought you were."

Those words cut the deepest. "What do you mean?"

Darius faced her. "You ran to Trinity Falls to get away from your parents because you were too afraid to tell them to stop meddling in your life. What will you do if they disapprove of our relationship, move to Kalamazoo?"

Why was he saying these things? "You're not being fair."

"You're not the only one with parent issues, Peyton." He repeated her words. "I can't be in a relationship with someone who lies, including lying by omission. I can't live with someone who keeps secrets."

"Darius, our relationship isn't any of their business. I make my own decisions now."

"You ran away from your parents and your fiancé rather than standing up to them." Darius crossed to his coat closet. "What if we had a disagreement? Would you discuss the problem with me or run away?"

"I would discuss it with you." Her voice shook with outrage.

"I wish I could be sure of that." Darius pulled open his closet and yanked out his coat.

"Where are you going?" Peyton's panic spiked.

"I can't be in a relationship where there's no trust."

Peyton was desperate. "Darius, I broke up with Bruce before you and I became serious. My engagement didn't have anything to do with you."

He stared at her for several silent moments. "That's where we disagree." Darius crossed to his front door. "When I return, I want you out of my apartment."

He left without looking back, closing the door softly behind him.

Peyton stared at the door in shock and dismay. What had just happened? Tears started slowly, then flooded down her cheeks. How had she made such a mess of this? And how could she possibly fix it?

CHAPTER 23

"This will be a New Year's Day you'll always remember." Alonzo locked his front door and escorted Doreen into his family room after midnight.

Doreen was wound up. She wasn't the least bit tired, even though she hadn't slept much on New Year's Eve and had gotten up at the butt crack of dawn New Year's Day. Her day officially had started at nine o'clock in the morning with her inauguration, the culmination of a goal she hadn't known she'd had. Then there was the meeting with her new staff and luncheon with the town council members.

New Year's Day had ended with the mayor's inaugural ball. She and Alonzo had stayed until after 11:00 p.m., dancing and mingling with their guests, including Ean, Megan, Jackson, Audra, Darius, Ms. Helen, Peyton, and Vaughn. Members of the Trinity Falls Town Center Business Owners Association and the town council also were there.

"It's been a memorable day." Doreen tracked Alonzo's

movements as he settled beside her on his sofa. He was so handsome in his black suit and silver tie.

"Was it what you'd hoped for?"

"It was better because you were there, sharing it with me." Doreen lifted his arm and wrapped it around her shoulder. She snuggled against his side, breathing in his scent, soap and shaving cream.

Alonzo's chuckle sounded in Doreen's ear. "I enjoyed your company, too. But it's nearly midnight. You should get to bed. You have another long day ahead of you."

"In a minute." Doreen sat up. She took Alonzo's left hand in both of hers. "There's something I want to ask you first."

His coffee-colored eyes searched hers. "What is it?"

"Alonzo." She cleared her throat. "Alonzo, you proposed to me more than a month ago—"

Alonzo interrupted her with a self-deprecating smile. "Thirty-five days ago, but who's counting?"

Doreen's chuckle wobbled with nerves. "Yes, well, I wasn't ready then. But I'm ready now." She found and held his gaze. "I'm in love with you, Alonzo Lopez. Paul will always be the love of my past. But you're my present and my future. Will you marry me?"

Alonzo was silent for so long. Should she repeat her question?

"Your hands are shaking." His statement wasn't either of the responses she'd anticipated.

Doreen looked down at her hands wrapped around his. The trembling was spreading up her arms. "I'm nervous."

Alonzo tightened his hold on her hand. "Could you excuse me?"

Doreen blinked. "What?"

"I'll be right back. Don't go anywhere." He released her hand and rose from the sofa.

"But—"

"I won't be long." He walked away.

"Where are you going?" She followed him with her gaze.

"Just upstairs. I'll be right back. Wait for me." His voice trailed behind him as he left the living room and hurried up the steps.

Was he kidding? Doreen watched him disappear upstairs. She was no longer shaking with nerves. She was numb with shock and outrage. At least when he'd proposed to her—*thirty-five days ago*— she'd acknowledged his request. She'd responded to it. It wasn't the reply he'd hoped for, but at least she'd answered him. On the other hand, when she'd proposed, he'd walked out.

She stood from the sofa and paced the living room. Dozens of questions raced across her mind. Where was he? What was he doing? When was he coming back? Why was it taking so long? Why did he have to do . . . whatever he was doing . . . *now*?

Doreen peeked toward the staircase again. She could hear him moving around up there. She went back to pacing.

Maybe she shouldn't have blurted out her proposal. Maybe this wasn't the right time for it. After all, today had already been a very busy day for both of them. Alonzo had accompanied her to the inauguration and the luncheon as well as the inaugural ball. He was probably tired. That's what it was. She'd chosen the wrong day to spring her proposal on him. She should have waited for the weekend.

Doreen turned toward the staircase. She stilled when she found Alonzo walking toward her. "You're probably tired. We can talk about this in the morning or over the weekend."

"No." He took her hand and led her back to the sofa. "I'd rather talk about it now." He gestured for her to sit.

Doreen studied him as she lowered herself onto the brown cushions. She took in his neatly combed hair and his recently smoothed jaw. "Did you go upstairs to freshen up?"

Alonzo blushed. "Don't worry about that." He tugged on his right pant leg before going down on one knee.

Doreen's jaw dropped. "What are you doing?"

"Doreen, I understand that you're a modern woman." His voice was unsteady. "That's one of the many things I love about you. And your proposal was beautiful. I'll treasure it always."

"I know it's the wrong time. I should have waited."

"No, this is the right time." Alonzo took her hand. "It's just that I've always dreamed of this moment happening in a different way."

He reached into his pocket and pulled out a ring box. He opened the box, displaying the two-carat Monarch diamond ring inside.

Doreen covered her mouth with her hand. "Oh my word, Alonzo."

He held her teary gaze. "Doreen, I've loved you forever. Will you do me the honor of being my wife?"

Tears trailed down her cheeks. "Yes, yes, Alonzo. I'll marry you."

Alonzo blinked rapidly as he took the ring from

the box and slipped it onto the third finger of her left hand. He helped her to her feet.

"You've made me the happiest man on the planet." Alonzo wiped the tears from her face.

"And I'm the happiest woman." Doreen rose on her toes and pressed her lips to his.

"How much longer will I have to wait for you to tell me what's on your mind?" Ms. Helen set down her teacup and pinned Darius with her sharp, dark eyes Friday evening. They were sitting at the older woman's kitchen table.

"I'm fine, Ms. Helen." Darius made the effort to sound normal.

"Now that's a lie." The elderly lady narrowed her eyes. "You've been here ten minutes and haven't made one smart-aleck remark."

"I'm kind of tired after Doreen's inauguration yesterday."

"And the big news she and Alonzo shared with us this afternoon."

Darius found a smile. "Yes."

Doreen and Alonzo had glowed. He couldn't be happier for them. Alonzo had privately thanked him for his advice. If only Darius could get his own love life in order.

"You're also drinking my tea." She nodded toward his half-empty cup.

"You offered it to me."

"Since when do you drink Earl Grey?"

"I thought it tasted funny." Darius frowned at the beverage.

Ms. Helen snorted. "It tastes the way it always

does. You're the one acting funny. Have you and Peyton argued?"

"What makes you think that?"

"The fact that the two of you stayed on different ends of the room during Doreen's inaugural ball." Ms. Helen's tone was dry.

Well, dammit, had he become his parents? He didn't want to air his private life in public, even in subtle ways like avoiding each other.

"We've broken up." His fist clenched around the teacup.

Ms. Helen's eyes widened in dismay. "Why?"

"She has a fiancé."

"No, she doesn't. I asked her about that right after she moved to town."

Darius gave a wry smile. "She doesn't have one now, but she was with him until Thanksgiving. I've met him."

"He's in Trinity Falls?"

"He was almost a week ago, on December twenty-seventh. He flew in from New York to convince her to go back with him."

"Since she was at Doreen's ball yesterday, I take it the reconciliation wasn't successful." Ms. Helen seemed confused. "So if they're not together anymore, what's the problem?"

"The problem is she lied to me. She never mentioned she'd been engaged."

"Maybe she didn't think it was important."

Darius stared, wide-eyed, at his lifelong friend. "How could the fact that she'd agreed to spend the rest of her life with someone not be important?"

"She must have been intending to break their engagement for a while," Ms. Helen said pensively.

"Then why hadn't she ended it before she left New York?"

Ms. Helen shrugged. "That's something you'll have to ask Peyton."

Darius nudged aside his half-empty cup of tea. "And why didn't she tell me her parents were wealthy?"

"Why would that make a difference to you?"

Darius gave Ms. Helen a dry look. "Her ex-fiancé works for her father's financial investment company. I somehow don't think her parents would be thrilled for her to marry a small-town newspaper reporter."

Ms. Helen's eyes widened with pleased surprise. "Marry?"

Darius rubbed his eyes. "She makes me feel things I didn't think I could feel. With her, I thought I could have a normal life."

"And you're going to let a little thing like a broken engagement come between you?" Ms. Helen tsked her disappointment.

"Dishonesty isn't a little thing."

"No, it isn't." Ms. Helen sipped more of her tea as she eyed Darius. "Lies, mistrust, and suspicion are what destroyed your parents' marriage and you had to pay for it."

Darius tensed. Walking away from Peyton was the single hardest thing he'd ever had to do, but he'd learned from his parents' mistake. "You can't have a relationship without trust."

"Well said." Ms. Helen rested her skinny forearms on the table and leaned forward. "But why would Peyton lie about her engagement?"

Darius' shrug was restless. "To her, it didn't exist."

Peyton's words played like a loop in his mind.

*I knew I wasn't going to marry him. That's why I didn't
wear his ring when I moved here.*

"She came to Trinity Falls because she was looking
for a place where she could fit in." Ms. Helen took
another sip of her tea. "And that's what she found
here. She attended town council meetings, a high
school football game. She even cochaired the fund-
raising committee with you."

An image of Peyton as Catwoman lingered in
Darius's memory. "She went to Books and Bakery's
Halloween and Christmas celebrations."

"Those aren't the actions of a person intent on
misleading others." Ms. Helen sat back on her chair.
"She told you what she was doing. She was looking
for a community. She wanted to start over."

"But you can't start over by running away from
the past. You have to face it."

"And she did." Ms. Helen spread her arms. "She
ended her engagement and told her parents she
had a new address. It's up to you whether you believe her. She wasn't trying to mislead you when she
came to Trinity Falls."

Darius was silent as he considered Ms. Helen's
words. "You have a point." Or was he just looking for
a reason to give his relationship with Peyton another
chance? Was he falling into the same trap his parents had ended up in?

"From the minute I met her, I knew she was the
one for you. That's why I asked for everyone's help
getting the two of you together."

Darius stared at her. "You were the mastermind
behind the matchmaking?"

"Of course." His mentor continued. "I think Peyton deserves another chance."

"It could be another chance to lie to me."

Ms. Helen shook her head. "I don't understand you, Darius. You were afraid you couldn't fall in love. Now you're afraid to be in love. Which do you fear less?"

I will not cry. I will not cry.

Peyton pulled into the Trinity Falls University's faculty lot Saturday afternoon. The past three hours at the Guiding Light Community Center had been unspeakably difficult. She and the other seven members of the fund-raising committee—Simon, Ethel, CeCe, Stan, Vaughn, Olivia, and Darius—as well as several center volunteers had spent the morning decorating the center's community room for tonight's fund-raiser.

It had been hard enough being near Darius after not seeing or hearing from him the past two weeks. The curious looks from the other committee members had made it worse.

Peyton climbed out of her car and started across campus toward her office building. She needed additional textbooks to complete her spring semester course assignments. In the distance, she noticed the sunshine dancing across Wishing Lake. The magical image seemed to call to her. Peyton made a detour for the water. The campus was almost eerily empty and quiet during these final days of Christmas break. Classes didn't officially resume until

Monday, although some students had already returned to their dorms.

Peyton paused beside the lake. The trees that surrounded it were naked and cold. Even they appeared anxious for the warmth of spring. She stared into the water. A faint smile curved her lips. Wishing Lake. She'd seen students tossing coins into the water, especially during finals week. Desperate times indeed called for desperate measures. Peyton rummaged in her coat pocket for loose change. What would she wish for?

Her smile faded. If she believed in such things, she wouldn't wish for Bruce to change or for Darius to trust her. Those would be wasted wishes. Instead, she'd ask for whatever it took to heal her broken heart. Peyton pulled the change from her pocket. She held a nickel and three pennies . . . eight cents for a wish. Why not? She tossed the coins into the lake, watching them break the surface. What would it take to heal her broken heart?

An hour later, Peyton fumbled her way out of her Volkswagen GTI at her apartment complex, then activated the car's alarm. She slid her purse onto her shoulder and gathered her textbooks before turning toward her building. Peyton spotted Virginia Carp waiting for her beside the nearby lamppost.

"I told you he'd break your heart." Ginny offered the greeting as soon as Peyton was within earshot.

"Everything was going well until you decided to meddle." Peyton had the strongest urge to smack Ginny, but violence wasn't the answer. She tightened her grip on her books as she walked past her annoying neighbor instead.

"If everything was going so well, my bringing your

fiancé over to Darius's apartment wouldn't have made a difference. But I've heard you two broke up." Ginny's words danced with glee.

"My *ex*-fiancé. And Darius still hasn't come to see you." Peyton kept walking. "That restraining order Darius took out against you is never going away."

Ginny hurried to keep pace with her. "Maybe not. But you don't have him, either."

Peyton didn't respond. What could she say? Darius was lost to her as well. Mercifully, Ginny claimed that victory and allowed Peyton to walk away.

She'd made a mistake by thinking she could start fresh in Trinity Falls. It had never occurred to her that her past would follow and get in the way of her future. How shortsighted. She would have explained all of that to Darius if he'd returned any of her three messages. She was beginning to feel like Ginny the Stalker.

Peyton adjusted her purse strap and shifted the books in her hand as she mounted the ornate black metal staircase to her apartment. She had only a few hours before she needed to return to the community center for tonight's event. Not enough time to prepare for a repeat of Darius's emotional distance.

Her cell phone started ringing as soon as Peyton let herself into her apartment and locked her door. She dug it from her purse as she walked into her bedroom. The display screen identified her parents' home number. Peyton set the phone and her textbooks on her nightstand. She wasn't up to a conversation with them now. Maybe later. Peyton stripped down to her underwear, set her alarm to go off in one hour, then curled up under the blankets for a nap.

Minutes later, a persistent ringing woke her. Grumbling, Peyton blinked open her eyes and grabbed her cell phone from her nightstand. It was her parents' number again.

"Hello?" Peyton turned off her alarm as she accepted their call.

"Peyton, it's Mom." Her mother's voice sounded uncertain.

"And Dad." Her father must be speaking from another extension.

"Is something wrong?" She sat up in her bed, setting a pillow between her back and the headboard.

"We called to apologize." Irene's explanation startled Peyton.

She tightened her grip on her cell phone. "Apologize? For what?"

Peyton's eyes searched her bedroom as she tried to settle her mind. She avoided her reflection in the mirror across the room. She was certain she looked a mess. Shadows sketched along her beige walls as the winter afternoon lengthened.

"You were right about Bruce." Her mother's voice was low with regret. "He was having an affair with Leila."

"I know." They'd woken her up to tell her this? But of course they hadn't known she'd been sleeping.

"Why didn't you tell us?" Carlson asked.

Peyton wanted to laugh. "I did and you didn't believe me, remember?" She didn't wait for their answer. "What finally convinced you?"

Carlson's sigh traveled down the phone line. "When Leila found out you'd broken the engagement, she insisted Bruce marry her. He refused. According to Leila, he was determined to make you marry him."

Had she heard her father correctly? "You spoke with Leila?"

"I asked her whether there was any truth to the rumors of a personal relationship between her and Bruce."

"Then you *did* believe me." The revelation eased a tension she hadn't realized was there.

"We should have listened to you right away," Carlson said. "But I didn't want to believe I could be so blind to something that was right under my nose. I'd worked side by side with Bruce for years—long days, long weeks. How could I not have seen he was a fake and a cheat?"

"But you were quite passionate when you accused him of infidelity. We're sorry we doubted you, Peyton."

Am I dreaming? "What did you tell Bruce?"

"I fired him." Anger echoed in Carlson's voice. "He violated company policy by having a sexual relationship with a member of his staff. Not only does it show poor judgment, but it also leaves the brokerage vulnerable to a lawsuit."

The news took Peyton's breath away. "You did the right thing, Dad."

"Thank you for making me face the situation." Carlson sounded angry and embarrassed.

Irene broke the brief silence. "So, now that the situation with Bruce has been handled, you can come home."

"Mom, I am home." Peyton braced herself for this next confrontation.

Irene chuckled. "Peyton, Trinity Falls, Ohio, can't be your home. You're a New Yorker."

"I'm building a life for myself here. I have a job,

friends, I'm involved in the community. In fact, I'm cohosting a fund-raiser tonight."

"You are?" Irene sounded pleased and surprised. "Tell me about it."

Carlson broke into their conversation. "Before you two get started, I'll say good night. Baby girl, think about coming home, OK?"

Peyton swallowed the lump in her throat. She knew that was something she couldn't do. Regardless of whether she and Darius reconciled, she could never return to her life before Trinity Falls. "Have a good evening, Dad."

The *click* on the line signaled her father had hung up.

"So what is he like?" Irene asked.

"Pardon me?"

"When you came home for Thanksgiving, there was a glow about you. You were more assertive, more outspoken than you've ever been." Irene chuckled. "I hardly recognized you. But I liked what I saw."

"Thanks, Mom." Her mother's words warmed her.

"I'll miss having you near me, Peyton. Are you happy?"

"I am." For the most part.

"Good, I'm glad. That's what your father and I have always wanted. It's what we've prayed for. I look forward to meeting your young man."

Darius wasn't her young man anymore. Peyton needed to change the subject. "It's getting late, Mom. I need to get dressed for the fund-raiser."

"Of course. Good luck. Call me tomorrow to tell me all about it."

After making promises and exchanging well-wishes, Peyton ended the call with her mother. She took a moment to let her thoughts settle. What would her parents think of Darius? He didn't have a high-powered, well-paying career like Bruce. However, there was more honor in his breath than Bruce had in his body. But why should she care what her parents thought of Darius, especially since Darius no longer wanted any part of her?

A pulse pounded in Darius's temple as Peyton danced with Vaughn—again—during the Guiding Light Community Center's fund-raiser Saturday night. Pink's "Don't Let Me Get Me" filled the center's activity room, drawing most of the nearly three hundred guests to their feet. Darius was aware of only one couple on the makeshift dance floor. The rest of the dimly lit room, with its festive silver-and-black streamers and buffet tables, faded into the background.

His jaw clenched as the little professor shook her hips and moved her shoulders in front of the good-looking band director with the questionable goatee. They looked good together. Peyton's little black dress wrapped her like an embrace and bared quite a bit of her legs for a January evening in the Midwest.

Darius gritted his teeth. How many more times were they going to dance with each other? Peyton had partnered with several other single men, too, including Foster Gooden, who was old enough to be her father.

Jackson joined Darius at the edge of the dance floor. "It was smart to host the fund-raiser the Saturday before TFU's spring semester started. Lots of faculty, staff, and students here interacting with the rest of the community." The Harmony Cabins resort owner paused. "Jealous?"

Darius cut his friend a look before shifting his attention back to the dance floor. He sipped the lemonade in his white paper cup. His right hand shook with the urge to crush the container in his fist.

Jackson gestured toward the dancers with his own paper cup. "Instead of glaring at Vaughn, why don't you ask Peyton to dance?"

"Where's Audra?" Darius kept his eyes on Peyton's sexy little figure.

Quincy materialized on Darius's other side. "Changing the subject isn't going to resolve your problem."

Darius turned to Quincy but paused in surprise. Ean and Alonzo also had joined them. The four friends stood in a line with Darius at the edge of the dance floor. What was this, an intervention?

Darius returned his attention to Peyton. "I don't have a problem."

Ean sipped his drink. "If you're standing with friends while your woman is dancing with another man, you have a problem."

Alonzo leaned forward to capture Darius's attention with Ean and Quincy between them. The sheriff raised his voice to be heard above Pink's music. "You're good at giving advice. Now take some of your own. Whatever happened between you and Peyton, you can work it out."

Quincy nodded. "You don't have an advanced degree, but you're smart enough to know she's the best thing that's ever happened to you."

Jackson patted Darius's back. "Imagine your life without her."

Darius's blood ran cold at Jackson's words. Ms.

Helen's voice sounded in his ears. *You were afraid you couldn't fall in love. Now you're afraid to be in love. Which do you fear less?"*

Pink's song came to an end, blending into Bruno Mars's "Locked Out of Heaven." Darius saw a young man—one of Peyton's students?—making his way to her. Enough was enough.

"Here." Darius handed his paper cup to Quincy, then fought his way through the crowded dance floor to Peyton. The student had gotten there before him. Darius gripped the young man's shoulder and spoke into his ear. "Not tonight, pal."

The student had the decency to leave with a smile.

Ignoring Vaughn completely, Darius reached out for Peyton's hand and drew her away. In the middle of the crowded space, packed with moving, shaking, bouncing bodies, Darius just stared at Peyton, still holding her hand. Her caramel eyes were guarded.

Now what?

"Locked Out of Heaven" came to an abrupt end mid-lyric to be replaced by Ne-Yo's "Because of You." Peyton frowned, looking in the direction of Wesley Hayes, the event's disc jockey. Darius doubted she could see the high school senior, but from Darius's vantage point, he had a line of sight to the young man, surrounded by Audra, Megan, Ramona, Doreen, and Ms. Helen. Well, he couldn't fault their choice of song. As the lyrics said, Peyton had become his addiction.

He held her eyes. Darius offered Peyton his free hand. "May I?" She hesitated and his heart stopped. "Please?"

Peyton took his hand and stepped closer. Darius rested her right hand on his shoulder and released her other hand to place both of his palms on her waist. He began moving with her in a small space on the packed floor. Her scent—talcum powder and lily of the valley—filled his head. Darius bit back a groan. Her body was warm and soft against him. He'd missed her so badly the past two weeks. Darius drew her closer.

"I don't want to dance with you." Peyton's words, barely audible above the music, stopped Darius in his tracks. "I'd rather talk."

He stepped back and looked down into the heart-shaped face that had haunted his dreams. He searched her bright eyes and noted the confident angle of her pointed chin. Darius took her hand. He led her past the dancers and into the hall. It wasn't the most private of locations for the discussion Peyton apparently wanted, but it would have to do.

Peyton drew her hand free of his. "You wouldn't return any of my calls. Now you want to hold me in your arms like nothing happened?"

Darius brought them to a stop near the rear exit to the parking lot. "I'm sorry. I should have returned your calls, but I didn't know what to say."

"You didn't have to say anything." Peyton spread her arms. "I just wanted you to listen."

Darius shook his head. "You don't have to explain or apologize—"

"I know."

Darius's words stumbled to a stop. "What?"

"While I waited, hoping you would call, I realized this wasn't about my parents or my engagement. It's about you and me, and whether you trust me."

"I was surprised." He was a reporter. Still he struggled to find the words to tell his own story.

"I understand that. But I wasn't keeping secrets.

I wasn't lying by omission." Peyton drew a deep breath. "I came to Trinity Falls to find myself and I'd hoped to do that with you."

"Peyton—" Darius stepped forward.

Peyton stepped back. "But I agree that we can't have a relationship without trust."

Darius's lips parted in surprise as she hurried from him. His muscles were frozen in shock. He forced them to move, rushing after her. There was a roaring in his ears. His heart had returned to gallop in his chest. Darius couldn't breathe.

He caught her mere steps from the entrance to the center's activity room. He turned her toward him, shackling her forearms with his hands. Darius drew Peyton with him as he backed into the first door he came to.

"What are you doing?" Peyton tried to pull free of his grasp.

"You think I don't trust you?"

"This is a restroom." She continued to struggle against him.

"If I didn't trust you, I couldn't have let my guard down with you."

"It's the women's restroom."

"If I didn't trust you, I wouldn't have fallen in love with you."

Peyton shivered, then stilled in his hands. "You love me?"

Darius sighed but didn't let her go. "Are you sure you have an advanced degree?"

"What?"

"Of course I love you." Darius caressed her forearms, trailing his hands down the slim muscles. He felt her tremble beneath his touch. But she didn't draw away. His pulse picked up speed. "I've loved you since the first day we met, when you frog-marched me out of your office."

"You're never going to let me forget that, are you?"

"No." He stepped closer. "Do you think I give a dozen yellow roses to everyone who refuses to let me interview them?"

"I started to fall in love with you the day we were locked in the archives." Peyton's laughter was watery around the edges. "You claimed someone had locked us in deliberately. You sounded so paranoid."

"But I was right."

The sound of a toilet flushing interrupted them.

CeCe walked out of a stall and strode to a sink to wash her hands. "I was never here. You can spin this story any way you'd like."

Darius watched her dry her hands before she approached them. He straightened his posture, ignoring the heat that climbed from his neck into his face. "I'm sorry for intruding on your privacy."

"Don't be. It was very entertaining." CeCe paused beside them, smiling. "I'm happy for you both." Then she was gone.

"I'm sorry." Darius looked around as his surroundings registered with him. "I never thought I'd be in a bathroom the first time I declared my love."

"That makes two of us." Peyton threw her arms around his neck. Her honey-and-chocolate-cream features glowed. "In a bathroom or a five-star hotel, it doesn't matter. Your words were all I could have wished for."

"You're all I've ever wanted and more than I've dreamed of." Darius pulled her into his arms. This Tin Man had finally found his heart and he'd never let her go.

⌒⌒ CHAPTER 1 ⌒⌒

Audra Lane strode with manufactured confidence to the vacation rental cabins' main desk and faced the man she thought was the registration clerk. She curled her bare toes against the warm polished wood flooring and took a deep breath.

"You're probably wondering why I'm wearing this trash bag."

"Yes."

That was it. That single syllable delivered without inflection or emotion in a soft, bluesy baritone.

Audra's swagger stalled. She tugged her right earlobe.

Maybe that was his way. His manner wasn't unwelcoming. It was just spare. He'd been the same when she'd checked into the rental cabins in Where-the-Heck-Am-I, Ohio, less than an hour earlier.

In fact, the entire registration area was just as spartan as the clerk. Despite the large picture windows, the room seemed dark and cheerless in the middle of this bright summer morning. There weren't chairs inviting guests to relax or corner tables with engaging information about the nearby town. It didn't even offer a coffee station. Nothing about the room said, *Welcome! We're glad you're here.* There were only bare oak walls, bare oak floors, and a tight-lipped clerk.

What kind of vacation spot is this?

Audra pushed her questions about the room's lack of ambience to the back of her mind and addressed her primary concern.

She wiped her sweaty palms on her black plastic makeshift minidress. "I'd left some of my toiletries in my rental car. I thought I could just step into the attached garage to get them, but the door shut behind me. Luckily, I found a box of trash bags on a shelf."

She stopped. Her face flamed. If he hadn't suspected before, he now knew beyond a doubt that she was butt naked under this bag.

Oh. My. God.

She'd ripped a large hole on the bottom and smaller ones on either side of the bag for a crude little black dress, which on her five-seven frame was *very* little.

Audra gave him a hard look, but his almond-shaped onyx eyes remained steady on hers. He didn't offer even a flicker of reaction. His eyes were really quite striking, and the only part of his face she could make out. When he'd checked her into the rental, she'd been too tired after her flight from California to notice his deep sienna features were half hidden by a thick, unkempt beard. His dark brown hair was twisted into tattered, uneven braids.

They hung above broad shoulders clothed in a short-sleeved, dark blue T-shirt. But his eyes . . . they were so dark, so direct, and so wounded. A poet's eyes.

How could the cabins' owner allow his staff to come to work looking so disheveled, especially an employee who worked the front desk? Did the clerk think he looked intimidating? Well, she'd been born and raised in Los Angeles. He'd have to try harder.

Without a word, the clerk turned and unlocked the cabinet on the wall behind him. He chose a key from a multitude of options and pulled a document from the credenza.

"Sign this." He handed the paper to her.

The form stated she acknowledged receipt of her cabin's spare key and would return it promptly. Audra signed it with relief. "Thank you."

"You're welcome." He gave her the key.

A smile spread across her mouth and chased away her discomfort. Audra closed her hand around the key and raised her gaze to his. "I don't know your name."

"Jack."

"Hi, Jack. I'm Au . . . Penny. Penny Lane." When he didn't respond, she continued . "Thanks again for the spare key. I'll bring it right back."

"No rush."

"Thank you." Audra turned on her bare heels and hurried from the main cabin. That had been easy—relatively speaking. At times, she'd even forgotten she was wearing a garbage bag and nothing else. It helped that Jack hadn't looked at her with mockery or scorn. He'd been very professional. Bless him!

* * *

Jackson Sansbury waited until his guest disappeared behind the closed front door. Only then did he release the grin he'd been struggling against. It had taken every ounce of control not to burst into laughter as she'd marched toward him, the trash-bag dress rustling with her every step.

He shook his head. She'd been wearing a garbage bag! Oh, to have seen the look on her face when the breezeway door had shut behind her—while she'd been naked in the garage. Jack gripped the registration desk and surrendered to a few rusty chuckles. They felt good. It had been a long time since he'd found anything funny.

He wiped his eyes with his fingers, then lifted the replacement key form. A few extra chuckles escaped. She'd signed this document, as well as the registration, *Penny Lane.* Jack shook his head again. Did she really expect him to believe her parents had named her after a Beatles song?

Jack lifted his gaze to the front door. She'd given a Los Angeles address when she'd registered. Who was she? And why would someone from Los Angeles spend a month at a cabin in Trinity Falls, Ohio, by herself under a fake name?

"Benita, when you told me you'd made a reservation for me at a vacation rental cabin, I thought you meant one with other *people*," Audra grumbled into her cellular phone to her business manager, Benita Hawkins.

Although still tired from the red-eye flight from

California to Ohio, she felt much more human after she'd showered and dressed.

"There aren't any people there?" Benita sounded vaguely intrigued.

"The only things here are trees, a lake, and a taciturn registration clerk." Audra's lips tightened. Her manager wasn't taking her irritation seriously.

"Hmmm. Even better."

Audra glared at her phone before returning it to her ear. She could picture the other woman seated behind her cluttered desk, reviewing e-mails and mail while humoring her. "What do you mean, 'even better'?"

"I told you that you needed a change to get over your writer's block. You're having trouble coming up with new songs because you're in a rut. You see the same people. Go to the same places. There's nothing new or exciting in your life."

That was harsh.

Audra stared out the window at the tree line. She'd noticed right away that none of the windows had curtains. The lack of privacy increased the cabin's creepiness factor.

A modest lawn lay like an amnesty zone between her and a lush spread of evergreen and poplar trees, which circled the cabin like a military strike force. In the distance, she could see sunlight bouncing in the lake like shards of glass on the water. The area was isolated. Audra didn't do isolated. She'd texted her parents after she'd checked into the cabin to let them know she'd arrived safely. Maybe she should have waited.

"This place is like Mayberry's version of the Bates

Motel." She turned from the window. "How is this supposed to cure my insomnia?"

"Writing will cure your insomnia."

"Have you been to these cabins?"

"No. When I was growing up in Trinity Falls, Harmony Cabins went into bankruptcy and was abandoned. They've only recently been renovated."

"I'm coming home." But first she'd take a nap. The red-eye flight was catching up with her. She wasn't safe to drive back to the airport.

The cabin itself was lovely. The great room's walls, floors, and ceiling were made of gleaming honey wood. The granite stone fireplace dominated the room. But a large flat-screen, cable-ready television reassured her she'd have something to do at night. The comfortable furnishings that were missing from the main cabin were scattered around this room, an overstuffed sofa and fat fabric chairs. The dark décor was decidedly masculine. That would explain the lack of curtains at the windows. Men probably didn't think about details like that.

"You promised me you'd give it thirty days, Audra." The clicking of Benita's computer keyboard sounded just under her words. "I sent the rental a nonrefundable check for the full amount of your stay in advance."

Audra frowned. Benita's check had allowed her to register as Penny Lane. "It was your check, but my money. If I want to cancel this anti-vacation vacation, I will."

They both recognized the empty threat. The cost of a monthlong stay at a rental cabin was too much to waste.

Benita's exasperated sigh traveled twenty-four

hundred miles and three time zones through the cell phone. "You owe the record producer three hit songs in four weeks. How are they coming?"

Audra ground her teeth. Her deadline was August 4, twenty-five days from today. Benita knew very well she hadn't made any progress on the project. "How can you believe this place is the solution? You've never even been here."

"Do you really think I'd send you someplace that wasn't safe? I have family in Trinity Falls. If there were serial killers there, I'd know."

Audra tugged her right earlobe. She was angry because she was scared, and scared because she was outside her comfort zone. "I don't want to be here. It's not what I'm used to."

"That's why you *need* to be there. And this is the best time. Trinity Falls is celebrating its sesquicentennial. The town's hosting its Founders Day Celebration on August ninth. I'll be there."

"One hundred fifty years. That's impressive."

Benita chuckled. "I'll see you in a month."

Audra stared at her cell phone. Her manager had ended their call. "I guess that means I'm staying." She shoved her cell phone into the front pocket of her tan jeans shorts and turned back to the window. "In that case, I'll need curtains."

The chimes above the main cabin's front door sang. With three keystrokes, Jack locked his laptop and pushed away from his desk. The cabins had had more activity today than they'd ever had.

Jack hesitated behind the registration desk. It wasn't a surprise to see the chair of the Trinity Falls

Sesquicentennial Steering Committee had returned. Doreen Fever was a determined woman. "Afternoon, Doreen." He knew why she was there. She wanted every citizen to be involved in the festivities surrounding the town's 150th birthday. The problem was, Jack wasn't a joiner.

"I'm still amazed by how much you've accomplished with the rentals in so little time." Doreen gazed around the reception area.

"Thank you."

Doreen was the sole candidate for mayor of Trinity Falls. She also was the artist behind the bakery operation of Books & Bakery, and the mother of Jackson's former schoolmate, though she looked too young to have an only child who was just two years younger than he was. Her cocoa skin was smooth and radiant. Her short, curly hair was dark brown. And her warm brown eyes were full of sympathy. Jack didn't want anyone's sympathy. Not even someone as genuine and caring as Doreen.

"I hear you have a lodger." Doreen folded her hands on the counter between them.

How did the residents of Trinity Falls learn everyone else's business so fast? His guest hadn't even been here a full day. "Not by choice."

Confusion flickered across Doreen's features before she masked it with a polite nod. "A young woman."

"I noticed."

"I'm glad to see the cabins' renovations are going well and that you're taking in customers."

"Thank you."

Doreen gave him a knowing smile. "The elementary school was grateful for your generous donation. I take it that was the check from your guest? Are you sure you don't need that money to reinvest in the repairs?"

"The school needs the money more. I appreciate your stopping by, Doreen." He turned to leave.

"Jack, you know why I'm here." Doreen sounded exasperated.

Good. He could handle exasperation. Pity pissed him off.

He faced her again. "You know my answer."

"The town will be one-hundred-and-fifty-years old on August ninth. That will be a momentous occasion, and everyone wants you to be a part of it."

Jack shook his head. "You don't need me."

"Yes, we do." Doreen's tone was filled with dogged determination. "This sesquicentennial is a chance for Trinity Falls to raise its profile in the county and across the state. You, of all people, must have a role in the Founders Day Celebration."

"That's not necessary."

"Yes, it is." Doreen leaned into the desk. "This event, if done well, will bring in extra revenue."

"I know about the town's budget concerns. I have an online subscription to *The Trinity Falls Monitor*." Reading the paper online saved Jack from having to go into town or deal with a newspaper delivery person.

Doreen continued as though Jack hadn't spoken. "If we host a large celebration with high-profile guests, we'll attract more people. These tourists will stay in our hotels, eat in our restaurants, and buy our souvenirs."

"Great. Good luck with that." He checked his

watch for emphasis. It was almost two o'clock in the afternoon. "Anything else?"

She softened her voice. "I know that you're still grieving Zoey's death."

"Don't." The air drained from the room.

"I can't imagine how devastated you must feel at the loss of your daughter."

"Doreen." He choked out her name.

"We understand you need time to grieve. But, Jack, it's been almost two years. It's not healthy to close yourself off from human contact. People care about you. We can help you."

"Can you bring her back?" The words were harsh, rough, and raw.

Doreen looked stricken. "I can no more bring back your daughter than I can resurrect my late husband."

Paul Fever had died from cancer more than a year ago. He'd been sixty-seven. In contrast, leukemia had cut his daughter's life tragically short.

Jack struggled to reel in his emotions. "People grieve in different ways."

Pity reappeared in Doreen's warm brown eyes. "I went through the same feelings. But, Jack, at some point, you have to rejoin society."

"Not today." Some days, he feared he'd never be ready.

Caring about people hurt. He'd loved his ex-wife and his daughter. He never again wanted to experience the pain losing them had caused. If anything, the experience had taught him that it was better not to let people get too close.

* * *

The persistent ringing shattered Audra's dream. She blinked her eyes open. Had she fallen asleep?

Her gaze dropped to the song stanzas scribbled across the notebook on her lap. Was it the red-eye flight or her lyrics that had lulled her to sleep?

She stretched forward to grab her cell phone. "Hello?"

"Did we wake you?" Her mother asked after a pause.

Audra heard the surprise in the question. "It was a long trip." She refused to believe her writing had put her to sleep. "Is everything OK?"

Ellen Prince Lane sighed. "That's what we're calling to find out. We thought you were going to call us when you arrived at the resort."

"I sent you a text when I landed." Audra scrubbed a hand across her eyes, wiping away the last remnants of fatigue.

"A text is not a phone call." Ellen spoke with exaggerated patience. "How do we know that someone didn't kidnap you and send that text to delay our reporting you missing?"

Audra rolled her eyes. Her mother read too many true-crime novels. Her father wouldn't have suspected foul play was behind a text from her.

"I'm sorry, Mom. I didn't mean to worry you."

"This whole idea worries me." Her mother made fretting noises. "Why couldn't you have stayed in Redondo Beach to write your songs? Why did you have to go to some resort in Ohio?"

Audra wanted to laugh. No one would mistake Harmony Cabins for a resort. But this probably wasn't a good time to tell her mother that.

"We discussed this, Mom. Benita thought a change

of scenery would cure my writer's block." And even though she had her doubts, Audra didn't want to add to her parents' worries.

Ellen tsked. "How long will you be gone?"

They'd discussed that, too. "About a month."

"You've never been away from home that long."

"I know, Mom."

"You don't even know anything about that resort."

"Benita's friend owns the cabins. I'm sure I'll be comfortable here."

"How will you eat?"

"There's a town nearby. I'll pick up some groceries in the morning."

"What do they eat there?"

Audra closed her eyes and prayed for patience. "I'm in Ohio, Mom. It's not a foreign country. I'm sure I'll find something familiar in the town's grocery store."

Ellen sniffed. "There's no need to take that tone."

"I'm sorry."

"Your father's very worried about you, Audra."

Yet her mother was the one on the phone. "Tell Dad I'll be fine. The cabin is clean and safe. There are locks on all the doors and windows. I'll be home before you know it." She hoped.

Audra looked toward the windows beside the front door. She needed curtains. She didn't like the idea of the windows being uncovered, especially at night. She'd feel too exposed. She checked her wristwatch. It wasn't quite three in the afternoon. It wouldn't be dark until closer to nine at night. She had a few hours to figure something out, like hanging sheets over the windows for tonight.

Her mother's abrupt sigh interrupted her planning. "Your father wants to talk with you. Maybe he can get you to see reason."

Audra rubbed her eyes with her thumb and two fingers. This experiment was hard enough without her mother's overprotectiveness.

"My Grammy-winning daughter!" Randall Lane boomed his greeting into the telephone. He'd been calling her that since she'd been presented with the Song of the Year Grammy Award in February. Before that, she'd been his Grammy-*nominated* daughter.

Audra settled back on the overstuffed plaid sofa. "Hi, Daddy."

"Will you be home in time for my birthday?"

She frowned. Her father's birthday was in October. It was only July. "Of course."

"That's all that matters."

"Randall!" Ellen's screech crossed state lines. "Give me back that phone!"

"Your mother wants to speak with you again. Have a nice time in Ohio, baby."

Her mother was as breathless as though she'd chased her father across the room. "Aren't there coyotes and bears in Ohio? And mountain lions?"

Audra's heart stopped with her mother's questions. She was a West Coast city woman in the wilds of the Midwest. Talk about being a fish out of water.

She swallowed to loosen the wad of fear lodged in her throat. "They don't come near the cabins."

"How do you know?"

"I just do," she lied. "I'll be fine."

"I think you should come home, Audra. What does Benita know about writer's block? She's your business manager, not a writer. I'm your mother. I know what you need. You need rest."

Her mother had a point. Audra hadn't had a full night's sleep ever since she'd taken the Grammy home.

She stood and paced past the front windows. "Benita may be right. Maybe I need to get completely out of my comfort zone to jump-start my writing."

Ellen sniffed again. "Well, I disagree. And so does Wendell."

Audra stilled at the mention of her treacherous ex-boyfriend. They'd broken up three months ago. Her mother knew that. "What does he have to do with anything?"

"He's been trying to get in touch with you. He wants your forgiveness."

That made up her mind. She was definitely staying at Harmony Cabins for at least a month. "Please don't tell Wendell where I am. Even if I forgive him, we're never getting back together."

"What has he done? You never told me why you broke up."

Shame was a bitter taste in her throat. "Wendell used me. I'm not giving him or anyone else the chance to do that again."